The July snowfall and the bright edge of panic that swept the city lent a macabre, carnival atmosphere to the night.

Predators emerged, smiling, pulses quickened by screams that filled the night, blood hot as they sensed the impotence of the police in the gridlocked city. Smoke and flames rose from cars that had been torched for the simple thrill of watching them burn. The swirling snow muted gunshots, cries of rage and terror, shouted curses.

Behind locked doors, people stared out their windows at the fearsome beast of the city . . .

BLACK SUN

ROBERT LEININGER

AVON BOOKS ⬡ NEW YORK

BLACK SUN is an original publication of Avon Books. This work has never before appeared in book form. This work is a novel. Any similarity to actual persons or events is purely coincidental.

AVON BOOKS
A division of
The Hearst Corporation
1350 Avenue of the Americas
New York, New York 10019

Copyright © 1991 by Robert Leininger
Published by arrangement with the author
Library of Congress Catalog Card Number: 91-91797
ISBN: 0-380-76012-6

First Avon Books Printing: September 1991

AVON TRADEMARK REG. U.S. PAT. OFF. AND IN OTHER COUNTRIES, MARCA REGISTRADA, HECHO EN U.S.A.

Printed in the U.S.A.

RA 10 9 8 7 6 5 4 3 2 1

For my brother,
Sandy,
who would have loved it

Many thanks to my agent and friend, Marcia Amsterdam, for her enthusiasm and sage professional advice.

And to Gordon Harris of Reno, Nevada, a commercial pilot and FAA certified "repair station," who gave generously of his valuable time while supplying me with technical assistance in the matter of lighter-than-air craft.

And to my wonderful family—the Gearys, the Wards, and, in particular, the Beebes—who helped me to pursue a life-long dream.

Gabriel:
    And swift beyond where knowledge ranges,
    Earth's splendour whirls in circling flight;
    A paradise of brightness changes
    To awful shuddering depths of night.

Johann Wolfgang von Goethe, *Faust*

CHAPTER 1 ————————————————

THE GIRL STARED at Tyler across a distance of thirty feet. In the murky air of Red's Outpost, her silky black hair caught the backwash of lighting that came from the stage where Tyler played guitar.

She'd been watching him for half an hour, perhaps longer. He turned away, trying to put her out of his mind.

It looked as if Red's was going to get through the night without an official visit by the Flagstaff police. Not bad, but not unheard-of for midweek either. Wednesday was Tyler's last night until Monday rolled around again. Thursday through Saturday, Red's Outpost featured Joe Pepperdine's Fierce Wind Country Band, and then the cops were a regular attraction out at Red's, almost part of the act.

Some said that the sun acting up this summer was stirring up the same crazies who couldn't help howling when the moon was full. And, indeed, fights had broken out the previous two nights at Red's. A bottle, spewing beer as it whirled across the room, had taken out the Budweiser sign behind the bar on Monday as a pair of Cro-Magnon truckers had sought to resolve their differences with grunts and knuckles. To the dismay of the remaining patrons (who loved a good fight), Hank and Al, Red's large, nimble-footed bouncers, had brought it to an end before it was fairly under way. The following night, a "territorial dispute'' erupted over a buxom blonde in stretch pants near the entrance and carried out into the parking lot. Blood and beer, not much damage.

Friday night at Red's would be gladiatorial. Tyler was content to be on the second-string team with Sonny Sills and the Sun Devils. He'd played with the band during the past two summers, not for the money, which he didn't need, but simply to be part of the music. When Carol had packed up and split, it had helped.

The girl was still staring at him.

Right at him, with cool, unwavering eyes. She was incredible; so nearly a paradigm of beauty (and so much like Carol) that Tyler had only to glance at her to hear a chuckle of nervous laughter in a far-off corner of his mind.

Her mouth was sensuous, skin pale, hair dark and luxuriant, worn long—a work so transcendent and rare that it seemed to glow. She sat on a stool, legs crossed, back to the bar, facing him across a smoke-filled space at the edge of a bull pen that held six pinball machines. She wore jeans, but the vanilla blouse was too sheer, too stylish, too *city,* for a western dive in the Arizona highlands.

Tyler hit chords on the guitar, backup for the lead man, Sonny Sills, as they worked their way through a Johnny Horton tune, ''Down the River Road,'' gazing out over the crowd.

Tyler swayed to the music of the Sun Devils, immersed in it. Not many in Red's knew that Tyler was an astrophysicist, a professor at Northern Arizona University. At thirty-seven, he was the oldest member of the band. Graceful, lean, dark, an inch under six feet tall— frequently a target for sad, bleary women who sought romance in bars, who gave him knowing winks, trying to connect with something that existed only in their imaginations. The Carol-clone with her sights on him had none of their desperation in her eyes, but the harpoon was in her hand and she was working herself up for the throw.

God only knew why. Tyler no longer tried to figure out why people did what they did. Carol had cured him of that. Carol and Dewey.

The girl at the bar might have been Carol's twin, or at

least a close sister. Tyler found it disconcerting. He was over her, past all the pain and confusion of her leaving, and here she was, back again: elegant, slender, leggy, compact; yet full too, in that special way. Her eyes were intent. Her lips held a smile that could mean anything, including the possibility his fly was open.

He missed a chord, damaging "My Heart Skips a Beat," and picked it up again smoothly, looking away from the beauty at the bar who had, he estimated, already rejected several dozen propositions of various kinds. She had her sights sets on him and that seemed to be that.

Tyler wasn't pleased. His eyes swept the room, seeking another focus for his thoughts. He glanced at the Coors clock behind the bar: 1:29 A.M. His eyes burned. Din and chaos numbed his senses. An itchy, unsatisfied feeling came over him, the same restlessness and spiritual malaise he'd been battling on and off for months now, only stronger.

Perhaps it *was* the sun, getting to him too.

Whatever it was, the girl in the Macy's blouse intrigued him less than she annoyed him, and that was a bad sign.

The Devils launched into "Louisiana Man," followed by "Orange Blossom Special" (Sonny putting aside his guitar and picking up an electric fiddle for the occasion, from which he drew mournful, aching train sounds and hot ticking notes—Sonny was the true musician of the group). Then they cooled things down with a slow one: "Please Help Me I'm Fallin' "—giving newfound lovers a chance to solidify plans, exchange phone numbers.

The cleansing rhythms washed through Tyler and he played without thought, singing background with Evan Wilson (on synthesizer keyboard) behind the not-so-bad voice of Sonny Sills. Tyler's own voice wasn't all that great; but then, he reasoned philosophically, neither was Cash's. Of course, Cash had *presence*.

The song ended. Sonny announced last call at the bar for the evening and gave the band a plug for next Monday. Tyler glanced surreptitiously toward the bar as he swung the guitar strap over his head. The girl was gone.

"Broke off a chord back there, Tyler," Sonny said.

Sonny was just a kid; twenty-six, but wise, loaded with talent.

Tyler managed a smile. "C-minor got boring. Thought I'd see how it sounded with my foot."

"Lady rattled you, huh?"

"You saw her?"

"I'm not blind, Professor. Anyone you know?"

"Nope." He placed his guitar in its case, snapped the lid shut.

"Groupies," Sonny said with a sigh, flicking switches on the amplifiers, extinguishing their evil red eyes. "Looking for excitement where there ain't none."

"Thanks a lot." Tyler eased a sheepherder's coat on over the fringed, sequined shirt.

Sonny gave him an amused grin. "Nothing personal. It's just that life is empty repetition; only the music is real."

"Words to ponder."

"Fill me in on Monday, Tyler. Better yet, introduce me, tell her what a nice, uncomplicated guy I am."

"We might do that right now."

Sonny stared at him a moment. "I heard exercise can screw up the hormones. You might lay off the jogging a week or two, see if that helps." He unplugged microphone cables. "Hell, maybe next year we'll make Nashville. See you, man."

"Yeah."

Tyler said his good-nights to the others before stepping from the darkened stage. The floor was sticky with spilled beer, covered with a patina of cigarette butts and ash, cherry stems and pocket lint. Red's was still packed, but there was an edge of sadness in the air, a noticeable drift of humanity toward the door. Without the social glue of music to keep things together, the structure of the evening was beginning to unravel. Phil "Red" O'Connell was still doing a brisk business behind the bar in last-minute drinks, but the timbre of the place had gone hollow; voices fell flat in the murky air.

"Buy a lady a drink?"

He turned. It was the Macy's girl, giving him the same

half-formed, cryptic smile she'd been giving him all evening. She was a younger version of Carol, mid to late twenties, with nearly imperceptible laugh lines at the corners of her eyes.

He shrugged. "Why not? Beer? Wine? Coke?"

She draped a natural suede jacket over the back of a chair at a table. "Beer's fine."

Tyler raised a hand, catching Red's eye. He rested his guitar against a vacant spot at the bar, and dug in a pocket for his wallet. Red waved aside Tyler's money with a shake of his head. Tyler thanked him, placed the foam-flecked glass on the table in front of the girl, and walked away.

"Hey. Hey! Wait a min—"

But he was gone, her protests lost in the rowdy press of people near the front door.

He emerged in the cold desert night. His breath clouded, unusual for mid-July, illuminated by the headlights of pickup trucks that swept the hard-packed earth of the parking lot.

He walked toward the side lot, wondering at what he'd done. It was late, he told himself; he was tired, there was that sociology professor, Rita Kaufer, he'd taken to dinner at Mamma Luisa's the weekend before last, but what it all really came down to was that this unknown girl was too smooth and competent and arrogant, wielding her beauty like a scythe. And she looked too damned much like Carol. Tyler wasn't in the mood to go through any of *that* again.

So why the twinge of pleasure, Tyler? he asked himself. You want to take a closer look at that?

He didn't. He reached his pickup truck, sitting alone beneath a grove of ponderosa pine bordering an empty field.

He tossed his guitar on the front seat and got behind the wheel, cracked the window to let out stale air. A girl laughed drunkenly in the night; tires squealed on the asphalt of Railhead Avenue, accompanied by deep-throated racing horsepower, a quick shift of gears.

The Carol-clone came across the gravelly lot as he started the engine.

"What's your *prob*lem, fella?" Her eyes flashed in the thin light, hair askew across her forehead.

He rolled the window down further. "No problem. You got your beer, I'm going home."

She glared at him. "Are you always this goddamned insensitive?"

"It's a genetic thing," he said wearily. He put the truck in reverse and looked back over his shoulder.

"Look, I'm sorry if I stared at you in there, came on too strong, made you feel uncomfortable or any—"

"That's not it."

"All I wanted was to talk a minute—"

He edged the truck backward into the lot. She stumbled along beside it over the uneven ground. "It's late," he said. "Maybe some other time." The Chevy lurched forward.

"Hey! I didn't mean to . . . *Jerk!*"

He watched her in the rearview mirror, standing there with hands on her hips as he bounced over the rutted lot, stopped a moment, turned left on Railhead.

Jerk. Resonant, all-American idiom. Simple, effective—accurate nine times out of ten. This was not your finest performance, Tyler, he chastened himself. Not by a long shot.

But then, the girl had been lying for him. She'd moved on him like a hunter stalking game, and in a flash of discovery, he'd found himself in the mood to throw a wrench into the gears of casual love. He wasn't up for the bar games and artifice of an unknown woman who'd taken a fancy to him for reasons he would probably never know, like a girl admiring a stuffed panda at a county fair. She seemed the type who was used to getting her way. Sultry wench, ethereally beautiful, icy cold inside. He'd been burned by beauty once. Over the years it got flaky, like paint.

Buy a girl a drink? And then they'd briefly discuss the problems the sun was experiencing, and he would tell her how it was to play guitar in the band, and she would tell him how her ex-husband was (also) a jerk, and then they'd go and thrash awhile in his sheets or hers, and the next morning she would be cool, remote, faintly mocking.

"Hey, it's been real," and she would leave, taking another tiny piece of him with her, leave him staring moodily at the walls, listening to the even greater silence of his house.

He frowned at all the thundering, useless dialogue going on inside his head. The girl had rattled him, fair enough? To analyze it to death was pointless. His recent date with Rita was reason enough to reject the after-midnight advances of an unknown girl in Red's bar. If nothing else, he was an honorable son of a bitch, even if he'd only been out with Rita that one time, hadn't kissed her good night, wasn't at all sure he wanted to.

He grimaced. Honorable? He was merely drifting, had been ever since Carol had packed up and left. He doubted there was room in the closet-clutter of his life for Rita, much less a dark-eyed groupie, no matter how lovely she was.

One of the more notable mistakes he'd made in life was setting aside common sense to marry Carol. They'd never been meant for one another, but her beauty had blinded him, kept him prisoner, eventually scarred him. How many nights had he escaped out back to his private observatory to watch the stars wheel across the sky, to feel the Model T of the universe rattle-bang its way into the future, spewing time into the past, accumulating entropy on its way to inevitable heat death?

A gulf of sorts had always existed between Carol and him, growing wider as whatever sexual tension they'd once shared expended itself like a beam of light shot into the depths of the sea. His fault, her fault, no one's fault, and then, incredibly, they were shaking hands and Carol was gone, though, as she'd said, they would remain friends forever.

That was two years ago last May. Back then he'd learned that love and beauty had characteristics in common with the weather. Now Carol was living in Southern California (Redondo Beach) with a graphic artist who lifted weights and shelled walnuts with his teeth, who compensated for a height of five seven with a bulk of two hundred pounds and a simian, chesty posture popularized by Arnold Schwarzenegger. Dewey Figge, so maybe he was compensating for the name as well.

Tyler grimaced. Christened Maurice Hayden Tyler, he was in no position to cast stones at Dewey Figge.

He drove eastward past tall stands of pine on U.S. 66 to the junction of Interstate 40, and out to Winona, where a small secondary road headed toward Leupp on the Navajo Indian Reservation. Ten minutes out of Winona, he turned left on a dirt road, winding five miles through a canyon in the foothills of the mountains bordering the western edge of the reservation.

His house stood at the end of the road. Its remoteness had always been a sore point between Carol and him. She was a people person, a city girl attuned in some unfathomable and probably neurotic way to the hydrocarbon bustle and roar of the planet. He preferred the solitude, the quiet emptiness at the eastern edge of the San Francisco Mountains. In addition, the high, clear air greatly aided his solar observations. In Southern California, with its smog and wall-to-wall people, he would wither and die.

The truck bucked over a final ridge, darkened by a thickness of pinyon pine and ponderosa pine, emerging into a panorama of stars, with the constellations of Hercules, Lyra, and Cygnus scattered brightly across the sky.

He was home; the girl in the bar almost, but not entirely, forgotten.

CHAPTER 2 ————————

TYLER GLANCED UP, saw the dark-suited man sitting in the last row of the lecture hall in the physical sciences building, and thought again of the girl last night at Red's. He wondered if he was getting paranoid, or if the sun was bringing them out.

He paused, about to begin his lecture, trying to place the man. He couldn't. The fellow was wide, dark, swarthy, solid around the neck and shoulders. Glasses with thick black rims looked out of place on his face and his black hair was cropped close to his skull. Like the girl the night before, he was wearing a half smile, which was probably the reason Tyler had associated the two.

A clock on the wall read 10:02.

Tyler concentrated on the twenty-odd assembled students of the summer session of Astronomy 180, gathered near the front of a theater with a capacity of 140. "As some of you may have noticed," he said, the cavernous room lending a hollow resonance to his voice, "the sun has been very much in the news of late."

A few smiles appeared.

That's what he's here for, Tyler thought with sudden insight. The sun, something about the sun.

"Some of the reporting has been reasoned and informative," Tyler went on, "but there's been a lot of media hype too, so I've decided to alter the usual order of topics and focus our attention on the sun.''

He shuffled a stack of papers on the lectern and launched directly into the morning's lecture.

"The sun," he said, "is a hot ball of gas, some eight hundred sixty-five thousand miles in diameter, approximately ninety-three million miles from Earth. Its mass is approximately two billion billion billion metric tons—that's a two followed by twenty-seven zeros.''

The man at the back of the room sat as still as a Buddha of oiled teak, smiling, light glinting off his glasses.

"Its surface temperature is roughly fifty-eight hundred degrees Kelvin, although, as we shall see, this is subject to interpretation and depends on the method used to make the measurement.

"The sun rotates, from left to right as we view it. At the equator, a single revolution takes 25.1 days; at the poles it takes somewhat longer. This disparity in rotational velocity is known as differential rotation.

"Internally, the sun is composed of several layers, or shells.'' On the board he drew a number of concentric circles, labeling each: the core, the convective layer, photosphere, chromosphere, corona, lecturing as he went, listening to the reassuring scratch of pen on paper as facts found their way into notebooks. Synthesis of this knowledge into actual understanding was something that might or might not come later.

He punched at them in this manner for several minutes, imparting naked facts which they absorbed like photons, popping them temporarily into elevated quantum states of knowledge—perhaps enough that some of them would begin to spot irregularities in the oftimes inaccurate reporting of the sun that Tyler had observed since the magnetic anomaly of May had erupted into the largest sunspot group ever recorded.

"The energy received from the sun just beyond the Earth's atmosphere is known as the solar parameter," he went on. "The outward energy flow at one astronomical unit, or ninety-three million miles, is 1.36 kilowatts per square meter. This translates to a total power output of 3.83 times ten to the twenty-sixth power watts. That is:''

383,000,000,000,000,000,000,000,000 watts.

He liked to write this staggering number out, if for no other reason than to gaze out at the students and pick out the brighter ones from the crowd. Those who'd taken the course out of interest, not just to gather what they hoped would be a few easy science credits, tended to linger on the number, absorbing it, slightly boggled. Those without promise accepted zeros with bland equanimity. No real understanding would come in their lifetimes. The man in the dark suit—dark, *rumpled* suit, Tyler amended—grinned at him, shaking his head.

Perhaps the theoretical paper Tyler'd sent to Dr. Malcolm Cooke at the McMath-Hulbert Observatory in Michigan two years ago had finally surfaced, Tyler decided. They wanted to talk with him after all this time, now that the sun was acting up.

Nettled, he recalled Dr. Cooke's reply to his paper, a note so short it was like a slap in the face: *''Paper received. Read with interest.''* Nothing after that; not a peep.

Well, it'd been a mistake anyway. Premature. Tyler hadn't bothered to follow up on it, accepting for the time being Cooke's tacit evaluation of his work, or at least his capacity to hold a grudge. There was nothing more to be done with it until the latest of his computer simulations was finally completed, and that wouldn't be for another half year.

Now this. An emissary from Cooke, or possibly from the National Science Foundation. However, the man looked like neither; he had more the appearance of an ex-tackle for the NFL or a Colosseum guard in an old Victor Mature spectacular.

Having completed an overview of the sun, Tyler began a discussion of the theory of radiation at a level commensurate with a beginning physics course. He spoke of wavelength and frequency, the speed of light, basic black body theory, Wien's law and Planck curves, and then the hour was up and the room dissolved swiftly in predictable patterns of dispersal. A few students came to the front to ask questions, one of the parts of teaching Tyler liked best, going one-on-one with the more promising of his pupils.

"Dr. Tyler," a sallow youth with sandy-colored straight hair asked, "does, uh, the material in the core also follow Wien's law?"

Jeffrey Wright, one of the thinkers of the class. Tyler informed him that radiation in the core was indeed carried out primarily by X-rays, radiation on the order of two angstroms.

A chunky, large-breasted girl in jeans and a T-shirt with an emblem of Coca-Cola on the front asked him to explain again the relationship between wave velocity, frequency, and wavelength. He did, telling her that when all was said and done it was easier to think in terms of wavelength in many regions of the spectrum. The visible spectrum extended from roughly 3900 angstroms in the violet to 7000 angstroms in the red.

She went away, chewing her lower lip uncertainly.

"Interesting lecture, Doc," said the man in the dark suit. He'd come up front and stood to one side as Tyler fielded the questions. He stuck out a thick, roughened hand. In his late forties, Tyler guessed. A whitish puckered scar creased his forehead near the left eyebrow. His nose had been broken at least once, maybe more.

Tyler took the proffered hand gingerly. The man was six one, 260 pounds. Overweight but still powerful. Confident. His eyes hinted at a familiarity with physical confrontation. "Have we met before?" Tyler asked.

"That's not likely."

An awkward moment passed. The last of the students left the lecture hall. As Tyler began to erase the blackboard, an uneasy feeling came over him. "Can I do something for you?" he prompted.

"I hope so. The name's Blackburn, Harold Blackburn."

Tyler dusted chalk from his hands. "Perhaps we should go up to my office, Mr. Blackburn."

"That won't be necessary." Blackburn stood with his

legs widespread, stolidly cleaning a nail on his left hand with the thumbnail of his right.

"I've got things to do," Tyler said, annoyed. "If you'd just come to the point—"

"Really something, this business about the sun, isn't it?" Blackburn interrupted in a lazy, distant sort of way.

"It's a bit unusual, if that's what you mean."

"Looks bad, don't it?"

"Oh, I doubt there's any cause for alarm, Mr. Blackburn."

Blackburn's smile was empty. "I'm not alarmed, Doc. I'm not even interested."

Tyler frowned. "Then what—"

"I'm just here to deliver a message."

A sudden chill seemed to come over the room. "A message?"

Blackburn leaned forward aggressively, shifting his weight to his toes. "Right now would be a bad time for a guy who was supposed to know what he was talking about to go shooting his mouth off to television or the papers about the sun. If I was you, I'd avoid that kind of thing."

For an instant the room seemed to dim. A coolness filled Tyler's belly and he heard a faint ringing in his ears.

Blackburn regarded him placidly. "Folks might panic. We wouldn't want that, would we?"

"I don't know what the hell you're talking about."

"I'm talking about public safety. I'm talking about not getting folks upset, making waves."

Tyler stared at him. "That's insane."

Blackburn shrugged, continuing his vacant smile.

"How in the name of Christ am I supposed to make waves?" Tyler demanded.

"A paper was sent to some bigshot of some big observatory a couple years back," Blackburn said, his voice suddenly cold, his smile chilly. "Pretty wild stuff, unsubstantiated, scary. If that paper was made known just now, a lotta folks could misunderstand, take it wrong, know what I mean? And right now, a guy looking to make a big name for himself using the public's fear as a crutch might be tempted to get his face on TV or his name in the papers by claiming to know a bunch of scary nonsense. It's possible, but a deal like that wouldn't be in the public interest, what d'you think?''

"Who—" The word caught in Tyler's throat. "Who the hell sent you?''

"Let's just say I represent the interests of the country," Blackburn replied, running a finger absently along the chalk tray of the blackboard.

"Which country, Russia?''

Blackburn grinned. "Hey, that's pretty good, Doc.'' His voice grew confidential, his eyes bored into Tyler's. "This's upsetting, I know. Probably makes you want to lash out. Just in case you're thinking of doing anything dumb, though, I want you to know there's that King's College thing. You make waves and all that'd probably get dragged up again, make you out to be a loser, a real nut case. It'd work, too.''

Tyler shut his eyes, saw bright, flaring spots, opened them again. "Who are you?''

"John Q. Public, that's me,'' Blackburn said cheerfully. "Look, you got a good thing going here, Doc. A million two, give or take, so you sure don't need the money. Job must be real satisfying . . . Don't blow it, huh? So far you've done just fine. All I am is insurance—nice to have if there's a fire, but not something anyone really wants to use, understand?''

Tyler's face felt hot. He clenched his fists. "I think you'd better get the hell out of here.''

Blackburn remained where he was, arms folded across the front of his untidy suit. "First we need to come to an understanding.''

Tyler felt numbed. This couldn't be happening . . . *couldn't* be!

"Look,'' he said, "not that it's any goddamned business of yours, but I've got no intention of going public with that paper.''

"Glad to hear it.''

"That's all you'll get from me, Blackburn; now get out or I'll call the police.''

"Sounds like we're almost there, Doc.''

"Huh?"

"An understanding. We've just about got that." Blackburn stepped closer. His arm whipped out and he took hold of Tyler's left arm above the elbow, clamping down with powerful fingers. Pain shot through Tyler like an electrical shock.

Without thinking, he swung his right. Blackburn intercepted it with the ease of long practice. He pressed himself closer and Tyler could feel Blackburn's weight, his strength, the personal, humid cloud he carried with him that smelled of cheap after-shave, locker-room sweat, onions, and, strangely, chocolate.

"I don't much care for this strong-arm stuff," Blackburn said quietly. "Makes me feel I didn't do it right the first time, didn't say quite the right thing. Makes me feel as if I didn't get *through*. But we've got that understanding now, don't we?"

Tyler's eyes glazed in pain. Blackburn melted softly out of focus.

"Don't we?" Blackburn asked in a voice so low that Tyler could barely catch the words. "We've got that little thing?" The pressure of his grip increased fractionally.

"Yes."

Blackburn released Tyler's arm, smiling. "See, that's all it takes. Nothin' to it."

Tyler rubbed his arm. He backed away a few steps, his heart pounding. Through clenched teeth he said, "You've been given a fool's assignment, Blackburn. Just so you know, if I catch you snooping around out where I live, I'll shoot you on sight, without warning."

For an instant something flickered in Blackburn's eyes, then his grin broadened. "Gunfight at the OK Corral, huh, Doc? Well, that's all right. Just part of the understanding. Hell, you don't have to like me, I never said that. Just don't go scaring folks, that's all. That way you and me'll get along just fine. The biggest mistake you could ever make is underestimating me."

Tyler glared at Blackburn, outraged. The man outweighed him by ninety pounds, and the entire scene had the infuriating flavor of a fifth-grade playground confrontation.

"If anyone approaches you," Blackburn said, eyes boring into Tyler's, "like the newspapers for instance, some junior reporter out rummaging, give them something reassuring, huh? Don't do anything that'd make us both sorry."

"Who sent you?" Tyler's voice trembled with fury.

"We never had this chat," Blackburn said. He strolled up the aisle and out the door.

Tyler stood there a moment, then his entire body began to shudder. "Goddamn," he swore softly. "Goddamn, god*damn!*"

In that instant, he realized he could kill.

CRAZY. The whole thing was absolutely insane.

He thought about calling the police, then decided he had nothing of substance to tell them. He hadn't really been hurt and there'd been no witnesses. It'd be his word against Blackburn's, and Blackburn had crawled back under his rock.

Officer, this big guy came in and threatened me, told me to keep my mouth shut about the sun.

Ludicrous. It wasn't a story he wanted to trot past the Flagstaff police.

Who was behind Blackburn? The question came seething up out of his anger as he grabbed lecture notes off the lectern and stalked off toward the door. The real villains were the ones behind Blackburn, like smoke.

He climbed the stairs at the west end of the building and unlocked the door to his second-floor office. The crowded, cluttered room greeted him in musty silence. He slammed his notes down on the desk.

The observatory Blackburn had referred to was McMath-Hulbert, of course. The bigshot was Dr. Cooke. Blackburn had mentioned the King's College fiasco. Even hinted at Tyler's financial status. Blackburn had come prepared, all right; had all the facts right at his fingertips. Tyler paced the small office, tingling.

King's College, London. Yes, even though it had been

ten years, they could probably discredit him with that. His being an associate professor of physics at Northern Arizona University would mean less than nothing if someone with high-powered media connections made an even half-hearted effort to drag his name through the mud. If he went to the papers or TV, he could be made to sound like a raving lunatic, a nut case, just as Blackburn had said.

But who *were* they? He tried to think. They had the paper he'd sent to Dr. Cooke. That meant Cooke had read it, remembered it, made contact with someone or a group that had become alarmed by the possibility that Tyler might go public, create a panic.

Tyler dismissed a number of organizations immediately: the American Institute of Physics, various astronomical societies, the National Science Foundation. They wouldn't want a panic to sweep the nation; but then, such a possibility wouldn't be their concern, either. In any event, none of them would have sent Blackburn. No, it was someone or something with a bigger stake in public tranquillity than any of those, and that meant some arm of the federal government. The obvious tie-in with Cooke was grant money, and money meant power, and there were so many incestuous little groups wielding power in Washington that a Cyber 205 computer couldn't keep track of them all.

So they, the FBI or CIA or Secret Service or whatever, had been contacted and had dispatched a gorilla to keep Tyler in line. The concept was so fantastic it drew a shaky laugh from Tyler. The sound was hollow in the quiet of the room.

The idiots, the misguided, damned idiots. He hadn't the slightest intention of charging off to the press waving his paper, not even now, he realized, after Blackburn's visit. It would serve no purpose and, after all, how sure was he himself of his results?

Well, reasonably, he admitted, especially after the second computer simulation had gone unstable just like the first; but what were the odds that the sun had chosen to undergo a Tyler's Cycle at this precise moment in history—a monumental hiccup, so to speak? Astronomical. Even more to the point, suppose his hypothesis had merit; suppose further that a Tyler's Cycle was imminent (a possibility he'd only recently considered himself)—in the few days or weeks that remained before the cusp was reached, what could be done? The public's mood was currently one of cautious interest that bordered on anxiety and, occasionally, fear. How much would it take to tip the susceptible fringe over the edge into actual panic?

Not much.

Already there were signs.

He thought about Blackburn, the graceless, battered face, somehow more threatening for its placid—or possibly psychotic—smiles. Who would send that kind of a man? *Who?*

He leaned back in his chair and stared out the window. A bird sang in the cottonwood outside. He thought about Blackburn, about what he'd do if he actually caught him lurking out at his place.

Probably not much, now that he'd cooled down some. Phone the police maybe. Gun battles weren't his style.

He laughed emptily, sighed, and gazed off into space, lost in thought.

CHAPTER 3 ———————————

"SOUP'S ON. Say, what's wrong, Tyler? You look like a man with an aspirin snagged in his craw."

Tyler looked up and found Jack Anderson's head poked in his door. He managed a feeble grin. "Entrée."

"That's better." Jack bounced into the room. He was a year younger than Tyler, thin, wiry, a demon on the tennis courts. His beard had traces of red in it, curly and dense, but short—suggesting to Tyler more a tenacious species of mold than hair.

"Time for the most stochastic meal of the day," Jack announced. "Student Union, or do you want to risk health and possibly the lives of your unborn children at one of the local ptomaine parlors?" He studied a wall chart of the electromagnetic spectrum, squinting into the far ultraviolet.

"Whatever."

Jack turned his head. "You're slipping back into it." His face grew serious. "Really, is something wrong?"

"No." Tyler attempted a smile. "Well, I'm not sure."

"We all have problems we don't understand, my friend. I have a dog that pisses in my slippers . . . when I'm not wearing them, of course. You figure it out."

Tyler gave a thin laugh.

Jack's forehead wrinkled. "You want to talk, I'm here."

Tyler heaved himself out of his chair. "No, at least not yet. I need time to think. Let's eat."

ANGELO'S PIZZA SAT within walking distance of the university in the midst of a residential neighborhood, surrounded by half a dozen aging cottonwoods. Virulent pinkish red walls of disintegrating stucco, Spanish tile. A Budweiser sign glowed in one window; Michelob in another. Sun-baked weeds filled an area adjoining the parking lot.

The interior was dark, the air chilled. They ordered a medium Angelo's Special and took a table near the center of the nearly deserted room. A television on a nearby wall was running a soap opera.

Jack described himself as a "classical, good-old-boy physicist," unlike Tyler who was an astrophysicist, which was, in Jack's opinion, an impure hybrid. Jack dealt with the real world, or so he claimed: velocity, acceleration, forces, mass and gravitation and energy. Contrary to his claims as a Newtonian purist, however, Jack was a highly qualified particle physicist, up to his elbows in Heisenberg's uncertainty, quarks, and probability distributions.

Waiting for the pizza to arrive, Jack said, "Val's been asking about you lately, boy. Wondering if maybe her cooking finally drove you off."

"Sorry. I've been busy."

Jack gave him a close look. "The Egyptians worshiped ol' *Amon-Ra.* Could happen to an astrophysicist too, I suppose—stare at the sun too long, cook relatively important parts of the brain. What you need is a gal to keep your circuits humming, and I don't just mean a pleasant expenditure of energy at regular intervals either. They plot, buddy, they scheme—keep you from diving too deeply into yourself. You've gotten kinda stale lately."

"Sorry."

"There. Case in point. That wasn't exactly a blistering response."

"I suppose not."

Jack sighed. "Come on out to the house . . . say, Friday—no, better make it Saturday, around eight. Bring someone, a girl. You do know a girl, don't you?''

Tyler thought a moment, then said, "Rita."

"Rita who? Anyone I know?"

Tyler hesitated. The confrontation with Harold Blackburn seemed to have somehow disconnected him from the world. His arm still throbbed where Blackburn had gripped it. He stared blankly into space.

Jack shook his head. "Jesus."

"Kaufer," Tyler said suddenly. "Rita Kaufer. Sociology professor."

"Great. Bring her. We'll talk norms and groups. Better yet, we'll talk wine and hot tubs."

"I'll see what she says."

"You do that."

They made small talk until the pizza arrived, and then abandoned all conversation for the next few minutes. Angelo's pizza was said to be the best in Flagstaff.

The television switched to a talk program, "This Day," a half-hour weekday show hosted by the silver-haired and often brackish Finley Osborne. Tyler looked up, straight into the smiling face of Dr. Malcolm Cooke, Osborne's guest for the day. He stopped in midbite to stare.

"As I live and breathe," Jack said mildly. "If it isn't America's favorite, Pollyanna-style solar pundit."

"In the flesh," Tyler observed.

And flesh there was, Cooke's triple chin all but hiding the knot of his tie, his specially tailored blazer lying bloated across his midsection, sausagelike fingers laced together in his ample lap. He was balding, a few gray strands of hair swept laterally across his otherwise naked dome; ears tilted comically outward, almost as if by conscious effort; a putty nose. Hard to believe, Tyler thought, that thirty years ago the man had won a Nobel prize in astrophysics.

"I think I want to hear this," Tyler said, remembering the hint Blackburn had made at Cooke's involvement in the decision to keep Tyler silenced. Cooke, of all people. Well, there was a certain bizarre kind of logic to it at that.

"Science for the masses?"

Tyler shrugged.

Jack settled back in his chair with pursed lips.

". . . of the McMath-Hulbert Observatory at Lake Angelus, near Pontiac, Michigan. We're happy to welcome you here with us today, Dr. Cooke."

Cooke gave a single nod, smiled.

They passed through a chatty preamble, and then Cooke summarized what had already happened with the sun; in case, Tyler imagined, someone had just come out of a lengthy coma or only recently returned from a solo trek across Antarctica.

Cooke announced that the sunspot group was just now beginning its third passage around the sun.

"Isn't it unusual for a spot, as you say, *group*, to stay around so long?" Finley Osborne inquired, eyes bright, leaning forward slightly.

"Not at all," Cooke returned. "The large group of 1959 persisted for five revolutions of the sun. That is, roughly five months. A spot of the present size might very well be with us until, oh, at least September, possibly October." He gave Osborne a faintly patronizing smile.

"The spot is still growing?"

"Apparently. It's still a little early to tell, of course. The main group is just now making its appearance again at the eastern limb of the sun, the eastern *edge*, that is— but, yes, the leading spot has grown somewhat in size since the first of the month."

"Somewhat? Could you be more specific?"

"Well,"—Cooke spread his hands expressively—"at the time the sun's rotation took the main group beyond the western limb two weeks ago, its combined area was in the neighborhood of thirteen billion square miles. The returning spot has grown in size to slightly over twenty billion square miles."

Tyler gaped. A shudder ran through him. He hadn't had a chance to view the sun from his private observatory that morning, and he hadn't seen the reemergence of the spots.

"Twenty *billion* square miles," Osborne interjected. "I cannot imagine an area so vast. Perhaps you could put that in some sort of perspective for us, Doctor."

"Of course. The surface area of the Earth is some two hundred million square miles. Twenty billion is a hundred times that."

"So this, this *thing* on the sun, this deformity, is now a hundred times larger than the entire area of the Earth?"

"Magnetic storm, Mr. Osborne. Not a thing, not a deformity, as you call it. A sunspot is a region of solar material a couple thousand degrees centigrade cooler than the surrounding surface." Cooke's smile had taken on a somewhat plastic appearance.

"Nothing of this magnitude has ever happened before," Finley said. A statement this time, not a question.

"Not in recent times, not of this precise magnitude, no," Cooke replied. "But within an order of magnitude, yes. This is hardly an inconceivable occurrence."

"An order of magnitude? Could you recast that into plain English for us simple folk, Doctor?"

"Certainly." Cooke's rotund joviality slid visibly back into place. "A single order of magnitude is simply a factor of ten. Two orders of magnitude is a factor of ten times ten, or one hundred."

"Had enough yet?" Jack asked Tyler.

Tyler held up a hand. "Not yet."

"The great sunspot group of April 1947," Cooke went on, "covered an area of roughly eight billion square miles"—*seven* billion, Tyler corrected churlishly—"so you see, we are well within an order of magnitude of that spot with the present one. One must retain an awareness of relative sizes, Mr. Osborne. The total surface area of the sun is something over two *trillion* square miles, so the present spot, although large when we think of it in terms of human scale, still comprises not quite one percent of the sun's surface."

"The sun's magnetic field is at an all-time high, isn't that so?" Osborne asked, pressing from a different direction, eyebrows working.

"I understand the temperature of Baltimore exceeded the all-time high for the date three weeks ago," Cooke chuckled.

"Good point," Jack said, nodding.

Tyler gave him a look.

"The universe thrives on change," Cooke expanded. "And when you have change, and number scales to measure changes, you naturally have highs and lows, some of which are at times bound to exceed the highest or lowest previously observed. Such is the nature of observation."

"Still . . ."

"The present *general* magnetic field of the sun, if such a thing exists, what with the way the lines get tangled around each other, is roughly eleven gauss," Cooke said. "That's the strength of a fair toy magnet. Magnetic storms, sunspots, have not infrequently been recorded at levels of three thousand gauss and more, and the fields of neutron stars are at billions of gauss."

"Speaking of the magnetic fields of the spots themselves, isn't this one quite out of the ordinary?"

"What's ordinary?" Cooke countered. "There are few standards on the changing surface of the sun . . . Or perhaps it is better said that conditions are forever in a state of flux, change, turbulence. For dozens of years now we have observed flares and prominences, cycles of activity and relative quiet, enormous variability in the strength of magnetic fields. The field of the large spot currently stands at sixteen thousand gauss,"—Tyler exhaled air slowly at this pronouncement, so blandly delivered—"a hefty field, yes, but not an entirely unexpected one in view of the size of the group with which it is associated.

"The fact is, Mr. Osborne, this is a wonderful time for solar astronomers. Solar spectroscopers are having the time of their lives. Everyone is busy."

EVERYONE IS BUSY. The words, and the doughy mass of Cooke's white, fleshy face, accompanied Tyler as he and Jack went outside into the blinding light of midday. Cooke's implication, of course, was that this business with the sun was a good thing, a wonderful opportunity for astronomers. Tyler was by no means convinced.

The two physicists had got up and left when stock film clips had come on, narrated by Dr. Cooke in the easy, folksy manner that the public had come to know so well in recent weeks: solar prominences, the sunspot group of two weeks ago, time-lapse photography in hydrogen-alpha light.

"You're quiet," Jack said as they hiked downhill in the shade of leafy elms, past frame houses, cinder-block apartments and whitewashed churches, children on bicycles. Jack walked with his hands clasped behind his back, bent forward at the waist as if pushing into a stiff breeze.

"What do you think?" Tyler asked.

Jack sensed Tyler's mood, and answered cautiously: "About what?"

"Back there. Cooke's talk."

"He kept it simple. Removed the bones before dishing it up. What was to see? Just the usual pulp."

"Scientists have things under control?"

Jack paused. "If I were Suzie Housewife or the mayor of Bumwater, Texas, I would be reassured."

Tyler sighed. "So would I."

"But you're not."

"The sun has a mild general magnetic field," Tyler said, "as well as intense local fields. The general field normally runs about one gauss. Eleven gauss is a rather frightening increase, but you wouldn't get that from Cooke. And his comparison of the sun's field with that of a neutron star was simply preposterous. Cooke was blowing a lot of smoke."

"That business about orders of magnitude, you mean, the temperature of Baltimore?"

"That. Toy magnets. Everything. It was subtly done. Cooke managed to sidestep every issue Osborne threw at him."

"As I probably would have done," Jack replied reasonably. "Osborne was looking for trouble, trying to boost the show's ratings. Look, as a physicist with only a little more than a layman's knowledge of the sun, most of what Cooke said sounded fairly reasonable to me. Allowing, of course, for the inevitable predigestion of arcanum so it all comes out the nipple. You know how it works . . . Middle America does not want differential equations mixed into its pabulum."

Tyler grinned. "I guess not."

They drew near the businesslike rectangular buildings of the university and stood for a moment at the corner of Dupont Avenue and Knowles Drive.

"The sunspot is big," Jack said. "It's visible. It's a hot item right now, pun probably intended. You think there's more to it than that?"

Tyler shrugged. "I don't know. Maybe not."

"Neither does anyone else, buddy. But right now everyone's got their money riding on old Sol."

TYLER HAD NEVER DISCUSSED his theory about the sun with Jack, if indeed his ideas could be called theory. Not by anyone's definition but his own, he admitted to himself, and that was only a matter of convenience. It was still in the conjecture stage, the what-if stage, or at least not far beyond that. A fledgling hypothesis at best.

He'd jumped the gun two years ago in sending that paper (which was actually little more than a letter) to Dr. Malcolm Cooke. But Cooke had been more than just one of his professors at MIT: he'd personally guided Tyler through to his doctorate.

A Nobel laureate as a doctoral adviser! Such honors were reserved for only a chosen few.

During those golden years, Tyler's education and career merged with an effortlessness that seemed almost magical. His future stretched before him, preordained. A hierarchy existed among students as well as professors, a pecking order of sorts, and Tyler had been the one who wore the golden halo, destined for greatness. The halo had come down with a resounding crash at King's College two years after Tyler had earned his doctorate. By then he was Cooke's assistant and a junior professor at MIT.

As a student he might have survived the King's College disaster, but as a professor engaged in postdoctoral research at so prestigious an institution, there was no chance. He'd risen high enough to ensure that the fall, when it came, would shatter his career like the finest crystal.

Jack was aware that Tyler was engaged in research, but he hadn't questioned him about it and Tyler hadn't offered any information. The void sat comfortably between them, a point of professional courtesy. Tyler would fill Jack in when Tyler was ready. Until then, there was that reluctance to divulge information that bordered on mysticism. A discovery was something to spring upon the world, not dole out piecemeal like canapés at a faculty gathering. Northern Arizona University wasn't a big-name college, and research wasn't the lifeblood of the professor that it was at the big eastern colleges or at Caltech, Stanford, or Berkeley. Classes were smaller at NAU, professors more accessible to students, the pace slower. Even so, certain conventions applied, and Jack had earned his doctorate at Berkeley where he'd absorbed the musty, fretful lessons of academe. If Tyler wanted to talk, Jack would lend an ear, but he wouldn't pry.

The two men entered the physical sciences building and stopped at the department office to check for mail and messages.

Nora Klemowicz looked up as they came in, a tidy woman in her early forties. She had short hair and wore a perpetually serious expression, as if there was little about the business of physics or its administration to provoke a smile. Consequently, Jack was forever trying to do just that.

"Picture it, Nora," he said, leaning over her desk. "You, Tyler here, a hot tub, strawberry daiquiris, soft music."

She gave him a serene look. "Aren't you a bit old for this sort of thing, Mr. Anderson?"

"Jack, remember?"

She dismissed him by turning to Tyler, who was sorting through the debris in his cubbyhole. "You had a visitor. From *Parsec* magazine, perhaps forty minutes ago. A Ms. Gail Dionne. Said she'd call again at one-thirty at your office."

"She pretty?" Jack asked.

Nora gazed at him. "Compared to what?"

Tyler laughed. Nora was able to hold her own with Jack in spite of her quiet, reserved manner. He glanced at his watch: 1:22.

Parsec magazine was a pop-science monthly, serious to a point, geared for readers with an interest in science but no working knowledge of mathematics and therefore no real access to the subtleties of the universe. It steered away from the biological sciences and medicine, concentrating on physics, astronomy, and selected topics in chemistry. Black holes and the big bang theory were perennial favorites. Its readers received soft knowledge of the Planck wall, event horizons, and supernovas. *Parsec* had survived where others had gone under because its writing was clear and fresh, augmented by imaginative diagrams and photos in vivid color.

Tyler and Jack headed for the stairs.

"Almost had her that time," Jack said softly.

Tyler was thinking again of Blackburn. "Who?"

"Who else? The Stone Maiden . . . Nora. Almost fissured that granite countenance with a smile."

"She's married. Not exactly a maiden."

"It's all in the mind," Jack replied. "All in the mind."

TYLER SPOTTED her from his window. Long, lean legs sheathed in a businesslike brown skirt, nice calves, high heels, white blouse, glossy black hair bouncing perkily as she walked. She carried a briefcase in one hand.

The girl last night in the bar.

He knew suddenly that this was Gail Dionne of *Parsec* magazine, who had looked out of place in the smoky roar of Red's Outpost, who had stared at him so intently and then asked him to buy a girl a drink. A feeling of anger welled up in him. He'd been one kind of plaything to her last night, or so he'd been led to believe, and another kind this afternoon.

The girl *tock*ed her way along the concrete walk. The importunate sound of her heels came through the two-inch gap he'd left between the window and sill. Suddenly the tone of the message she'd left with Nora had a pushy ring to it: *I'll be there at one-thirty.*

"Yes, but I won't," Tyler said to himself, watching Gail Dionne disappear from sight as she entered the building.

He grabbed a few things from his desk and left the room,

locking the door behind him. In the corridor, he stopped to listen. The wooden *thock* of heels came from the west staircase, and Tyler went quickly toward the stairs at the east end of the building. He went down silently, feeling sly, feeling more than a little foolish besides, avoiding this strange, deceptive, lovely woman again.

He reached the ground floor and glanced down the hallway that ran the length of the building. Guilt nibbled at him in spite of all the rationalizations.

But no, *Ms.* Dionne deserved this. The subterfuge in the bar last night was her idea, and it had been distinctly unprofessional.

He stuck his head in the department office. Nora looked up. "Oh, Mr. Tyler. Ms. Dionne—"

"Is upstairs," Tyler finished. "If she returns, tell her I've left for the day."

She stared at him a moment. "You sound a great deal like Mr. Anderson. I don't believe that's a good thing."

He smiled. "It'll pass."

AT THE NEW STAR CINEMA COMPLEX on Lone Tree Road, south of the freeway, Tyler phoned Rita. She wasn't home, so he tried her university number.

"Rita."

"Yeah, Tyler here."

"Oh yes . . . Tyler." She had trouble calling him Tyler, but respected his wish not to be called Maurice or Morie or any of several other names he thoroughly disliked.

He made his pitch, surprised when she accepted readily on such short notice. He arranged to pick her up at her place at seven-thirty Saturday evening.

"How should I dress?" she asked.

"Dress?"

She sighed. "Casual, an evening gown, cutoffs, what's this supposed to be?"

"Oh. Casual, I guess."

"Let's hope."

Tyler hung up. The threads of his life seemed to dangle. The girl from *Parsec* had cut him adrift. He faced the marquee, suddenly realizing he hadn't seen a movie in years. He bought a ticket for *The Mercury Probe,* the only show scheduled to begin in the next half hour. He bought a tub of popcorn and sat in darkness for the requisite two hours, paying almost no attention to the movie, which seemed inane.

Before him, all he could see was the pale, perfect face of Gail Dionne, and, beyond that, the battered visage of Harold Blackburn.

The world had turned comic on him, but he found it difficult to see anything very funny about it.

CHAPTER 4 ────────────────

HAROLD BLACKBURN SAT in his car, an aging Chrysler with shredded seat cushions and worn carpets, forty-some thousand miles on an odometer that had already made the clubhouse turn once, staring at the theater complex with its space-age dome and plastic facade. He meshed his fingers and cracked his knuckles, yawned conspicuously.

Good thing Flagstaff was so high up, just about seven thousand feet. The air was balmy. Not quite cool, but nice. With the windows down, Harry was just comfortable, just able to enjoy the dozy warmth that caressed his thick, tanned arm on the door frame, making the hair sparkle. Not like inland L.A. this time of year, the dry heat baking the land, turning the smog a hot, brassy color.

Harry took a deep breath, admiring the pine tang of the air. No, this was a good deal. Good to get out of the blast furnace of Southern California, particularly on a nice, cushy assignment: keep tabs on Maurice Tyler, physicist; see that he didn't use this weird deal with the sun to make a big name for himself.

It didn't seem constitutional, but that concerned Harry about as much as the local politics of Tibet; and besides, Cy Hollander explained it all reasonably well. You didn't yell ''fire'' in a crowded theater, Cyril told him, patiently, a bit nervously, too, hands folded in front of him on the big walnut desk at his home in the hills of Glendale.

Which made sense to Harold Blackburn. Just look outside his second-floor office window overlooking Hollywood Boulevard at the crowded toilet of the street, all fumes and hustle and noise. Could be a crowded theater, sure—Harry could imagine that. Get people worked up, panicked, and what would be the difference? Lives might be lost like at some goddamn English soccer stadium, folks caught in a big rush to get out of the city—not that Harry gave a damn about people. There were too many of them to get upset over a few of them checking out, but he understood the concept and he understood that others might get worked up over it.

However you looked at it, it was worth two hundred bucks a day, the money coming out of some backroom slush fund of the FBI. Cy hadn't said anything about that, but Harry knew. This one wasn't going through payroll or accounting.

He unwrapped a Hershey bar and dropped the wrapper behind the seat into the rear of the car, chewing thoughtfully as he stared at the professor's three-quarter-ton Chevy.

From what Cy had told him, Harry had expected an anemic, bookish sort of fellow, not some tanned athletic type with a backbone. Not bad on the guitar, either. Good-looking kid too, Harry thought in a random sort of way, remembering the way that chick had come on to the professor at Red's Outpost the other night. Then the doc had surprised him, walked out on the fräulein, leaving her there with hands on outraged hips in the parking lot. That had got a smile from Harry, but he'd wondered about the professor for a while, turning down prime goods like that.

Could mean the doc had a limp wrist, but Harry didn't think so. The doc had been married once and the wife was the one who'd filed for divorce.

Anyway, Harry had seen Tyler's eyes in the lecture room. The doc wasn't the pansy sort, nor was he one of those pasty-faced android types that gather in universities like dust balls beneath a bed. Cy hadn't been entirely square with Harry about that, but then, maybe Cy hadn't known much about Tyler either.

Cy had told him that the orders (and the dossier) had come from above. How far above, Harry didn't ask. That would've bent a few unspoken rules, and besides, Harry was reasonably certain he didn't want to know.

It was enough that Cy had given Harry the pitch from his home and not at his office in the Federal Building. That made it unofficial, and neither he nor Cy had mentioned that little fact, not that they needed to. Harry knew how it was, how the world went around. Cy was an old friend— or if not a friend, at least the two of them understood each other and had reached an accommodation that was workable, almost comfortable. Cy had said his piece and then shoved the dossier across the desk toward him with no further comment, along with an envelope of bills, payment for the first two weeks.

Absently, Blackburn licked chocolate from his fingers. Again he yawned, blinking his eyes in the mellow warmth. In the past few hours he had slowly been coming to a decision, and now it prompted him to action. He got out of the car and stood in the parking lot with its scattering of cars. Overhead was blue sky, a soft yellow sun.

Tyler wasn't going to be the easy mark Cy Hollander had said he'd be. He had a tough streak in him. Harry grinned, remembering the swing the doc had taken at him.

The rural microbeam telephone setup that linked the doc's house with the line that ran out to the Navajo settlement at Leupp had been a cinch to intercept, it wasn't even bugging, hardly. But the doc had a phone in his office and the world was full of pay phones. Harry had watched helplessly as Tyler made a call from the booth that stood between the theater and the variety store next to it. The call had been short, but it had thrown the problem into sharp relief, and Harry was concerned. It wasn't so much the phones, really. An army of guys tracking Tyler wouldn't be able to keep him from calling someone if he wanted to, not without tying him to a chair and watching him, and Harry could do that all by himself if it came to that. No, what bothered Harry was that tiny gleam of rebellion he'd seen in the doc's eyes just before he left him there in the lecture hall. The doc couldn't be given a clear message and then be trusted to fly on automatic pilot, this dreamy little side trip to the movies notwithstanding.

That crack about taking Blackburn out if he caught him on his property was a case in point. Even though Harry had told the doc it was all part of the understanding between them, it wasn't really part of *Harry's* understanding at all. But some guys were like that. You had to keep them on a tighter leash than most.

Harry sighed, and the sigh became another yawn. He'd been up late last night after installing the telephone intercept—downing beers at Red's where he'd begun his first real surveillance of Tyler, trying to get a feel for the man. Then sleeping in that pinyon grove off Tyler's dirt road, hidden in shadow, waiting for the doc to come out and start the new day. Getting a feel for the country—or giving the country a feel for him, Harry thought, grinning, remembering how Tyler had come by just as Harry was taking a leak against a tree, fifty yards off the road. Harry had given him a minute and then followed in the weary Chrysler, taken in the doc's lecture, given him the spiel afterward.

Hard to tell what the doc was thinking now. It wouldn't hurt to have some backup on this one. At least for a while. Have to see how serious Cy was about this deal.

He crossed the lot, patted the hood of Tyler's truck as he went by, and stopped at the same phone Tyler had used. He fed a quarter into the slot, dialed the long-distance number, fed in more quarters until the computer-operator was satisfied and the phone on the other end was ringing.

Cyril Hollander wasn't pleased to hear from the private investigator, but, Harry reflected, the old FBI man was reasonably cool about it too.

"I delivered the message. The doc wasn't thrilled," Harry said.

"I'll phone you tonight," Hollander said curtly. "Where're you staying?"

"Tell you what, rather than go through all that, how

about I just tell you what I need. Save some time that way. What I need is some help down here.''

"What've you got in mind?" Cautiously.

"A guy I know."

"Who?"

Harry closed his eyes and pressed his forehead against the building's cool stone wall. "You want a name?"

"Ah, no."

"What I need is for you to just say yes so I can phone the guy, get this thing rolling."

"Okay, yes."

"And authorize the necessary funding."

A pause.

Harry said, "You should see the place down here, Cy. You should see the guy. Doesn't want to play ball. Alone, I'm not sure I can—"

"Do what's needed."

"I'll get back to you." Harry hung up.

He glanced at Tyler's truck out in the lot, grunted in satisfaction, and wandered into the variety store where he bought half a dozen assorted candy bars, handing the scrawny high school girl at the checkout a twenty.

"Give me five bucks in quarters, honey."

'Gee, I don't—'

"My wife's sick. Up in Oregon. I got to call home."

Like taking candy from a baby, he thought, outside again. He plunked quarters in the phone while consuming a Baby Ruth, finally getting through to Gordon Tate.

"Gordy. Harry."

"You owe me forty bucks, Harry. You calling to pay up?"

"Better. I've got work for you."

"I got work already."

"Sure. That why you answered the phone like a piranha going for a wounded duck?"

"It's phone work I'm doing, trying to track this guy down. I got this phone practically stuck in my ear."

"Cut the crap, Gordy. I need you here in Flagstaff."

"Ari*zona?*"

Harry looked around. "Last I heard."

"Christ. What're you doing out there?"

"Offering one-twenty a day, no expenses. Easy job, probably run a couple of weeks. You leave L.A. today, soon, fly into Pulliam Municipal, and you get paid for today."

"How can I find you?"

Harry told him to check into the West End Motel, wait for him there.

"West End Motel? Where's that from the airport, Harry?"

Harry hung up on him.

Tyler's truck was still there, sitting in the sleepy mid-afternoon glare of sun. Hard to imagine dark spots on that little bright disk up there; hard to imagine getting all excited about them either. People were nuts. He went into an ice cream parlor on the other side of the variety store from the theater, took a seat next to the windows facing the parking lot, and slowly ate a pair of hot fudge sundaes.

CHAPTER 5 ————————————————

GAIL DIONNE WAS breathing hard, maintaining a fast pace in spite of the unaccustomed altitude. In the Boston suburb where she lived, she often pinned her hair back when she ran (she did not *jog!*), but now it bounced around her shoulders in the cool early evening air, continually renewing her sense of femininity when little else about the strenuous activity could be seen as feminine, partly the fault of society's prejudice, and partly the mundane fact of salty sweat.

Horses sweat, men perspire, ladies glisten; wasn't that how it went? Close enough, and if so, then she was a mare on the track—not terribly flattering, but she wasn't out there to gather whistles or turn heads. That came later, she thought with satisfaction, but the real benefit, the reason she was in jogging shoes and running clothes come hell or high water, in Boston or Flagstaff or Brashears, Arkansas, five days a week, was the sense of being master of her fate, of being *capable*.

Her breath came in steady puffs, drawing in the rarified air as she circled the oval track at the northeastern edge of the university.

There was nothing ladylike about the way she ran. No dainty shuffle this, but a quick, determined stride that ate up ground at a fierce pace. Her legs were long and feminine; pale, but hard with well-used muscle. Her jogging shorts were made of filmy black nylon. She wore a loose-fitting red top of the same material; beneath that, a bra with the give of cast iron, fashioned with what sometimes felt like all the ergonomic sophistication of a sixteenth-century hand-me-down.

It was unnatural, some said, that Gail's weight had not strayed four pounds above or below her norm in the past five years. Well, this was the reason why. She was five six and weighed 120 pounds; definitely not skinny, but she wasn't packing around anything that wasn't useful, either. In September she would be thirty years old.

Sweat stung her eyes as she approached the end of her run on the twelfth lap, three miles, and as she crossed the imaginary line bisecting the stadium seats, she pushed a button on the chronograph on her wrist.

She slowed to a fast walk to cool down, getting her wind back quickly. Orange light from the fiery sky settled on her heated skin, lighting her. She felt good, as she always did after a hard run—the obligation to self diligently carried out. She glanced at the watch on her wrist: 19:49, nearly a full minute slower than her New England best, but she rarely got the opportunity to run at such a high elevation. She was competitive, even against herself.

Two laps later, filled with a fuzzy, mellow inner peace, she walked to her rented car and drove away.

SHE SLIPPED into a buoyant warmth of bubbles and steamy hot water. On a chair beside the tub was a telephone and a gun.

She'd rejected a few motels that had showers only, and, because it had a tub, taken a room at the Idle Hour Motel on Santa Fe Avenue. The water caressed her legs and flooded the flat of her stomach as she lowered herself in, taking care to keep her hands dry. She blew an iridescent foam of bubbles away from her face. A few drops of Shalimar bath oil turned the water silky.

"Oh God," she sighed in contentment, then frowned at the awkward way her hands were positioned, like something in a grade-B movie rising from its coffin. Business first, girl, she admonished herself, then pleasure.

She sat up and set the gun aside, a snub-nose Charter Arms .38 revolver that was not a toy, and which she never treated as a toy. She was licensed to carry the weapon in the state of Massachusetts. Two years earlier, a prowler had broken into her house. He'd held a gun on her when she went downstairs, vacillating uncertainly before fleeing out the front door, leaving Gail weak-kneed and pale, but unharmed, suddenly aware of her vulnerability. The next day she'd marched down to City Hall and demanded to see this official and that, tracing out the circular and oft-times frustrating route that led toward the legal possession of a handgun. She talked to an assistant DA, went through the mandatory training, filled out the papers, paid the fees, and in the process gained a respect for the weapon she might not otherwise have gotten.

Over two thousand rounds had gone through the re-volver in the time she'd owned it, until it felt as comfort-able in her hand as her hair dryer or a telephone receiver, the kick of the weapon just another part of the sequence of aim and fire, aim and fire, until she was deadly with the gun, but safe too.

She was aware that her strange affinity for the sixteen-ounce weapon was part of her need to be in charge, the independence she had manufactured for herself. The op-posite side of that tarnished coin was the woman who wilted at danger, who gave off shrill, ineffectual shrieks and couldn't run half a mile without fluttering to the ground in a faint.

You do what you have to do, she thought. It was im-portant to acknowledge the dangers of an imperfect world.

She took the receiver off the hook and dialed the num-ber she'd committed to memory. A heated feeling spread through her as she realized she was naked, soaking in warm water, listening to the ringing of his phone. *His* phone. In spite of the impropriety of the situation, or per-haps because of it, she felt her belly flutter.

God! Not for him!

* * *

TYLER JOGGED straight up the side of Angel Canyon, a steep climb of almost one thousand feet, before falling into the easy, almost slalomlike traverses that let him back down the canyon face without bone-jarring thuds. At the top of the ridge he saw the final wink of the sun as it passed below the rim of the world, sending diffuse rays of orange light into the alligator juniper that clung to the dry earth.

Down again, descending through murky green shadows of Douglas fir and ponderosa pine; north, south, north again, feet sending up puffs of dust as he passed funnel lily and blackbrush, losing altitude. The Little Colorado was a thin silver trail to the east, winding through mesa flats on Navajo land, south of Wupatki National Monument. Beyond, the desert lay flat and serene, its canyons and arroyos ironed flat by distance.

It was almost dark when Tyler came out of the sloping foothills, the black side of Angel Canyon blotting out the western sky, a yellow half-moon overhead. Here, the world of nature seemed utterly removed from the world of man. In the hills there were no Blackburns, no pursuing science writers, no sounds but the rhythms that had gone on for ten thousand years.

Movement caught his eye and he looked upward, saw a red line of ruler-straight cloud trace itself across the sky. He frowned at this intrusion, streaking across the spreading dark of night, and went inside.

He showered quickly and came out with the towel wrapped around his waist. The dark mat of hair on his chest was still damp as he went into the kitchen to pour himself a glass of orange juice, listening to the familiar silence of the house.

The phone rang just as he opened the refrigerator.

He got few calls out here. A premonition seized him, and he was suddenly certain it was the girl, Gail Dionne. Certain enough to risk a little subterfuge. He lifted the receiver on the fourth ring.

"This is Tyler. I'm not home right now, but at the beep"—he began to look about frantically—"leave a message and I'll get back to you." He held the phone next to a glass and tapped it with a fork.

ding

Not a very convincing beep, he thought wryly.

"Dr. Tyler, this is Gail Dionne from *Parsec* magazine. I'm sorry we missed each other at the university today, and I'm . . . I. . . . There wasn't any answering machine at your house when I phoned earlier this afternoon."

He grimaced, caught.

"Oh, that's cute," she said icily.

"Perhaps," he replied. "However my standing in the art of deception is strictly amateur."

"So you *are* there. What do you mean . . . deception?"

" 'Buy a girl a drink?' That line ring a bell?"

"Oh, for heaven's sake. Look, I'm sorry about that, really I am, but—"

"Good night, Ms. Dionne."

He hung up gently.

"DAMN," she cried. *"Damn* it!"

She dialed again, but there was no response. She replaced the receiver and sat there, fuming. "Well, girl," she informed herself, "you have well and truly screwed things up this time."

Somehow the ploy that had served her well in the past had come unglued at Red's Outpost when the gorgeous man had turned down bait that red-blooded men everywhere were supposed to strain cords in their necks to look at; at least that was the way it was supposed to work.

What had gone wrong?

She lifted a limber leg to the vertical and examined its smooth curves critically, the shapely layered depth of muscle in the thigh, the slender, functional ankle. She returned her leg to the water and glanced down the tiered front of herself—full, rounded breasts giving way to the hardness of her stomach, the result of a hundred sit-ups twice a day, *every* day.

Well, the man was clearly out of his mind, that was all. She leaned back and let the warm, sudsy water wash over her, disturbed by the familiar bittersweet ache that swept through her, like a particularly stupid form of flu—a syrupy feeling coursing through her veins, seeking . . . seeking . . . something . . .

Contact. Closeness. A way past this featureless, antiseptic wall that separated her from the world.

Her thoughts spiraled into the familiar misty gulf. Was it so much, she wondered, to ask for these few things of life, or (let us be honest) a man: commitment, stability, caring, gentleness, sensuality, freedom? Oh, but double-edged swords, each and every one, and who had the skill and the perceptiveness to juggle them all and keep them sharp without one day finding all the lovely dreams impaled on one or more of them?

Tony, poor disturbed Tony, who had married her for her looks and ignored the rest, and then wandered away looking for more, always more, leaving her with a daughter two years old.

Her mother had warned her that Tony was a loser before she married him, but the advice had been delivered in too overbearing a manner, as it always was, and Gail had rebelled, as she always did, battling to find her own space within the walls of mother-love, mother-smothering. And it had indeed been a mistake, but then, that was how one truly learned, wasn't it? Not by absorbing words of wisdom, but by experiencing the pain of failure—that was how life hammered its lessons home.

Four years ago Tony had drifted away, leaving her alone with Nikki. It'd taken Gail several months to realize it was for the best. Then there'd been John, the tough guy, equally disturbed, who had in some absurd way thought he could control her and make her passive and compliant with violence, and failed utterly and quickly, thank God.

Then Eric, and that was the hardest of all to make sense of because there'd been nothing specifically wrong with Eric; it was just that there was no spark between them . . . helium and argon, endlessly circling one another, unable to penetrate their own stable shells. When Eric shrugged and pecked her cheek and walked away with a suitcase in one hand and a tennis racket in the other, he failed only to remove the vacuum they had shared. Even

Nikki, then just four, seemed to sense that not much had changed, that the quality of the new silence was little different from that of the old.

Yet there was a difference. In a way Gail didn't quite understand, Eric took with him all hope, at least for a while. He was pleasant, he was intelligent, he was neat and clean and even ambitious, all the things a girl could want, and still it hadn't worked. What was left after a failure like that?

She'd slid into a mild depression that had partly lifted when she threw herself into her work—everything but time for Nikki, and the kitchen sink—since she couldn't be a wife and friend and lover. She avoided the trap her high school friend and college roommate at Penn State, Dinnie, had tumbled into: that of an endless succession of immature, semialcoholic boyfriends, sinking slowly into a state of hopelessness and cynicism in the search for Mr. Right.

Floating in the now-lukewarm water of the tub, Gail accepted that Mr. Right would come ambling along when the time was right. But God!—how she missed the vagrant fool right now, wherever and whoever he was; wishing he could take her in his arms and hold her, comfort her, take her to bed. By taking charge, being capable and tough, she'd managed to fill most of the voids in her life; but there were voids she couldn't fill alone, that toughness and capability couldn't touch.

She flipped the drain lever with a toe and stood up, rinsed in the shower and washed her hair, then stood in front of a mirror while she spread lotion over her entire body, a ritual she'd performed for years. Long ago she'd taken heed of warnings of the damage caused by the sun's rays, and now she permitted herself but five hours of intentional exposure a year, in ten sessions lasting but half an hour each, spread over the summer; a fussy yet somehow easy arrangement, and the results had definitely been worth it. Her skin was the color of pale gold, soft as proverbial cream. The daily applications of lotion prevented the mild color from fading quickly. She was no California sun bunny, but her skin was silkier than that of most girls a decade younger than herself.

She slipped on a robe and phoned her older sister, Nan, in Encino, at the southern edge of the San Fernando Valley.

"I didn't phone too late, did I?" Gail asked.

"Oh, no, no," Nan said. "Dan's in the kitchen right now, fixing something or other, and I—"

For several seconds Gail tuned out, imagining the frenetic gesturing that must be accompanying this rather dull and inevitable accounting. She loved Nan, but it was difficult to accept the way Nan had become so scatterbrained after moving out to the West Coast. Perhaps Southern California's freeway system had gotten to her, or the pressure-cooker life-style.

Nan and Dan; the rhyming of their names was something of a joke in the family. Gail wouldn't have given two cents for the marriage five or six years ago, but somehow Nance and Dan Kinder had made it work, even if it was a less-than-perfect union. Little Dan was almost nine now, and Lila was six, the same age as Nikki.

"—and Nikki is still up, watching the tube. Well, we both were, some detective show that seems—"

"How is she?" It was Nikki's first real trip away from Boston.

"Nikki? She's perfect, a little angel. Can't seem to get enough of the ocean. Yesterday after you left I took the kids all the way over to the beach at Topanga—"

"Don't let her get too much sun."

"She wore that number thirty sunblock you left, and the sun hat. Well, if she ends up with skin as great as yours I suppose all the hoo-ha will be worth it."

"Can I talk to her?"

"Of course. Hold on."

A moment later the familiar little voice sounded in Gail's ear. "Hello?"—less a greeting than a question.

"Hello, darling, this is Mommy."

"*Mommy!* We went to the *zoo* today and got hot dogs and popcorn and ice cream and Little Dan threw up."

"Oh, how fun."

"Well, *that* wasn't. When are you coming back?"

"I guess it's going to be a while longer, darling."

"How *much* longer?"

"At least a few days. This is going to be a tough one."

"He's being a stinker?"

Gail laughed. How quickly they picked up their parents' language, threw it back at you. "Yes, honey, he's being a bit of a stinker."

"They have a dog here. His name is Charlie."

"Yes, I know." In time, she said her good-byes to Nikki and Nan, and hung up. She did her hair, then turned out the lights and lay on the bed in darkness, eyes open, listening to the murmur of a television in a neighboring room.

Tomorrow, *Dr.* Tyler, she thought. Tomorrow you *will* talk to me!

AT 9:42 P.M., United flight 318 from Los Angeles landed at Flagstaff with twenty-six passengers on board. Gordon Tate, a tall man with sloping, narrow shoulders, a heavy mustache, a watchful, wary expression on his face, entered the terminal. He lit a cigarette and drew smoke deeply into his lungs. In the fifteen minutes before his luggage arrived at the carousel, he downed two beers at the lounge.

Outside, he found a taxi. "West End Motel," he said, and settled back for the ride.

CHAPTER 6 ─────────────

By EIGHT-FIFTEEN Friday morning, the sun had risen high above the dry Sierrita Mountains in the southern Arizona desert. Fifty miles west of Tucson at the edge of the Papago Indian Reservation, the domes and towers of Kitt Peak National Observatory lay sprawled over the mountain site. Amid them stood the McMath solar telescope, the largest such instrument in the world.

The massive water-jacketed housing of the visible portion of the telescope rose a hundred feet in the air, glaring white in the sunlight. The mirrors of the telescope's optical system formed a huge primary image of the sun nearly a meter in diameter in the high-ceilinged observation room, a short distance below ground level.

With the aid of his staff, Dr. James Carleson had completed the standard morning photographic series. A number of eight-by-ten photographs were taped to a wall below pictures of the previous morning's sun. Photos, now a month old, were also on display for comparison.

In the center of the room, at the large, round observation table behind Director Carleson, Marcel Vergucht was examining the direct visual image of the sun, wielding a pair of rubber-tipped dividers. His hair was dark, worn long. Dark glasses covered his eyes. An exchange scientist from Belgium, Marcel had completed his doctoral studies three years earlier at the university in Antwerp. A third man, Dr. Raymond Abbott, was tinkering with the photographic equipment, and the summer doctoral student from UCLA, Linda Moell, stood at a table, gazing down at a Hewlett-Packard strip chart recorder.

With pursed lips, Dr. Carleson viewed the new pictures. He stood stoop-shouldered, his hair white, long at the temples where it sprang out around the frames of his glasses. His face was gaunt, cheeks hollow.

The rotation of the sun had brought the trailing spot into view, and the lead spot had grown more distinct on the eastern limb. An incredible spot, the physicist thought in wondering silence, covering a huge fraction of the solar disk. Its area was almost thirty-three billion square miles, an appreciable increase over the day before, although some of that was due to the appearance of the trailing spot. Almost invariably, sunspots came in pairs, and this one was no exception. The sun was in the declining stages of its eleven-year cycle, theoretically down from the peak that had occurred five years ago.

So much for theory, or at least historical observation. This storm would throw all the charts into disarray; and maybe a few theories as well, Carleson thought with a thin smile. It would give solar astronomers something to tabulate, chart, and ponder for years once the activity tapered off. Even more surprising was the location of the spot, something Dr. Cooke had entirely disregarded in his talk on "This Day" with Finley Osborne. The spot had appeared at the unheard-of latitude of forty-nine degrees, at a time when the spot cycle was usually converging on the equator.

Forty degrees off the main track! Unbelievable! Dr. Carleson had no idea what to make of it.

The spot was cooler than most, too—some 2,360 degrees centigrade below the normal temperature of the photosphere, depressed 750 kilometers below the surface. Dr. Chang-sun Chang, in the adjoining magnetograph tower to the east, had phoned only minutes earlier to inform him that a magnetogram of the field surrounding the spot showed it was now at 20,750 gauss. Suddenly everything about the sun was being measured by excesses, by numbers that had strayed far beyond all previous limits.

"Dr. Carleson?"

He turned. Linda Moell, the grad student, was standing behind him. As usual, her eyes were downcast and slightly clouded, as if she were observing gravy stains on his tie and wondering what, if anything, she should say about them. In spite of his efforts to get her to just relax and enjoy her summer, she continued to regard him with nervous awe. Her not-quite-pretty face was flushed a pale rose color, left open and defenseless by straight brown hair cropped an inch or so too short.

"Yes?" he inquired.

"I . . . I think you sh-should see this, D-Doctor."

She stuttered when she got excited, which was nearly every time she spoke to him. Earlier that morning he had turned her loose on the spectrobolometer, just to give her a feel for the instrument. The SBM measured radiation intensity throughout a designated spectrum, in this case, the visible spectrum of the sun.

She led him to the corner of the observation room. With its tangle of cables and equipment, it seemed to fit no aesthetic sense, all angles and awkward projections. Still, there was a certain beauty in function, Dr. Carleson supposed. He saw it, therefore it existed—a comfortably egocentric position. The strip recorder was still moving, nearing the end of its run.

She indicated the peak of the power spectrum. "It's sh-shifted," she said. "The whole p-plot is skewed to the right from the one you showed me. Ten angstroms. I know it's not a lot, b-but . . ."

Cooling! The thought skittered through Carleson's head. Impossible!

"What's the source?" he asked sharply, staring at the plot. "Are you using the sun's center, away from the activity?"

"Of course." She gave him a reproachful look.

"You calibrated the instrument properly?"

"I d-did it like you showed me. The reference lines were all okay." Defensiveness gave her face a sullen cast.

"Okay. Look, I'd like to see a simple total flux reading, solar disk only. Can you do that for me?"

"Of course."

"Thank you."

He walked quickly to the computer console and sat down, typing rapidly. The direct-access link to OSO-15, the Orbiting Solar Observatory that had been placed in orbit two years ago, had been installed since early spring. OSO-15 did the usual housekeeping observations, sending streams of data into electronic storage at the facility at Pasadena where it was stored on disk for ninety days before being offloaded to tape. He requested an update on the current solar parameter, the energy received from the sun just beyond the Earth's atmosphere, and its value each day at the same time for the past week. In a matter of seconds, the console's screen filled with the information requested:

DATE/TIME	ENERGY—kW/M**2
7/12:1623Z	1.359
7/13:1625Z	1.359
7/14:1622Z	1.359
7/15:1623Z	1.358
7/16:1623Z	1.358
7/17:1622Z	1.357
7/18:1625Z	1.354

A minute later, the current reading flashed on the console's screen:

7/19:1623Z	1.347

He stared at the screen, feeling a chill blossom in the pit of his stomach. Such a fluctuation simply wasn't possible—not over so short a period of time. Not in a year! He picked up a calculator and punched buttons, then read the result. If OSO-15's readings were correct, the sun's energy had dropped by almost 0.9 percent in only five days.

He got up suddenly and went over to where Linda was struggling to calibrate the primary bolometer.

"Trouble?" he asked, trying to keep his voice steady.

"I took a r-reading. It was off, down eight-tenths of a percent. I'm recalibrating it. It's probably nothing b-but atmospherics."

Eight-tenths of a percent. A remarkably close fit with the OSO-15 data.

My God, he thought, crossing the room. At that moment the gray phone at the main console rang. He snatched it up.

"Carleson."

"Dr. Carleson, Dr. Massey at Mount Climax. I'm calling to verify a solar spectral energy-density shift of—"

"The peak intensity has moved a bit toward the red."

"Ah, yes, you've got it too, then?"

"Couldn't miss it. Total spectrum power is down almost a full percentage point."

Massey paused. "My God, are you sure? We didn't pick that up. Too busy with the details."

"I checked it out with OSO in Pasadena."

"I was just about to phone McMath-Hulbert with this, but it appears that you're a step or two ahead of us. Do you want to claim it instead?"

"I don't care. You take it." Massey, Carleson reflected, was a stickler for protocol.

"I don't want to step on anyo—" Massey's comment disappeared under a sudden roar of static, white noise pounding like surf. Dr. Carleson held the receiver away from his ear, then brought it back slowly.

"Dr. Massey?"

A thin ghost-wail wavered in the noise. Dr. Carleson hung up, shrugging. If Massey had more to say, he would have to call back on a clear line.

McMath-Hulbert—which meant Dr. Malcolm Cooke. Like a good soldier, Massey was following orders. Well, Carleson thought, another few minutes and he would have done the same. Cooke was a bureaucrat; he had divorced himself from a direct involvement in science years ago and moved into the political arena. He was the one who carried the astrophysical banner high in Washington these days, and that's where most of the money came from. Years ago Cooke had outmaneuvered them all, Carleson admitted with reluctant admiration, and now Cooke's pudgy fingers took the pulse at all their throats: Kitt Peak, Mount Wilson, Mount Climax, Sacramento Peak, Big Bear Observatory. A remarkable coup.

"Dr. Carleson, a look, please."

Carleson's thoughts were interrupted this time by Marcel Verguacht, his Flemish accent more pronounced than usual in his excitement, calling to him from where he stood at the primary image at the center table.

"A flare," Marcel said, pointing. "Very big."

Dr. Carleson donned a pair of viewing glasses. The sun's image was just beginning to lose its quality in the morning heat, the surface granulation beginning to blur. What he saw was unlike anything he had seen before. A brilliant eruption south of the sun's equator was apparent. Marcel was using the calcium K-line filter, and the hot plasma reached out toward Earth like a twisted blue claw from the chromospheric network.

The flare was much larger than the X-15 flare of March 1989. X-19 at least, Dr. Carleson thought with awe, perhaps as big as X-21. And if you could see it, it was already upon you. The noise that had torn apart his conversation with Dr. Massey suddenly made sense. Protons traveling at near light speed were crashing into the Earth's magnetosphere—spiraling down through the Van Allen belts, causing even greater disruptions in the Earth's magnetic field.

There was much to be done. Dr. Carleson got to it, consciously aware that he was by no means dashing to pick up the phone to call Marty Holt of the *Arizona Daily Sun* in Flagstaff, or any of the affiliate television stations in Phoenix or Tucson that had been breathing down his neck of late. Nor, he knew, would Massey be talking to reporters in Colorado.

Orders were orders.

* * *

CLOUDS COVERED THE SUN, turning the sky over British Columbia a uniform, troubled gray. Robert Witherell looked up at the ridge line. Somehow it had gotten turned around in his mind. This was supposed to have been an easy four-day outing, but he felt it slipping away from him. Scott, his younger brother, looked out over the valley at snow-covered peaks ten or twelve miles in the distance. The trees around them obscured much of the immediate features of the terrain.

"I still think this way's east," Robert said, not feeling or sounding very confident.

"Doesn't feel right."

"Which way, then?" He felt angry, frustrated. He was twenty-one, two years older than Scott, more experienced, and here he was, fighting to control a surge of panic, a weakness in his knees. They were attempting what should have been a simple backpacking trip, a due-east crossing from 70 Mile House on Highway 97 to Bonaparte Lake, and from there to Chinook Cove on Highway 5. The trouble was, the lake should have been in the valley to their right, and it wasn't.

"I . . . don't know," Scott replied.

"Big help."

Robert consulted his compass again. Carefully he set the instrument for the amount of variation between magnetic north and true north. The needle wandered, hesitated, pointed reluctantly. East seemed to lay at an angle over the ridge they had been following.

"We'll climb it to the top and follow it," he said. "Probably see the goddamn lake from up there anyway. We must've gotten too far south somehow."

"Still doesn't feel right," Scott muttered to himself.

They worked their way up the rocky granite slope, angling toward the northwest and, twelve miles away, the western edge of Green Lake, almost at a right angle to the direction that would have taken them to Bonaparte Lake. It was July, but the air had a noticeable autumn chill to it.

CHAPTER 7 ——————————

TYLER SAW Harold Blackburn outside the physical sciences building, but, Tyler noted with annoyance, not before Blackburn had spotted him. Blackburn stood in the shade of an elm on the north lawn, leaning comfortably against its gnarled trunk. He gave Tyler a tiny salute and a grin as Tyler passed by, just twenty feet away. Tyler looked right through him and kept walking.

That was all. Just a wave and a grin . . . keeping contact, letting Tyler know he was around. Inside the building, Tyler was tempted to phone the university police. He would have Blackburn removed, tell the police . . . what?

His sails sagged as the wind fluttered out of them. Nothing had changed. He had nothing of substance to tell anyone. His story would sound no more believable today than yesterday. He might have enough clout to have Blackburn escorted off the campus, but then Blackburn would probably turn up elsewhere, angry, and Tyler didn't want to keep glancing over his shoulder any more than he already was. Better to let Blackburn play his strange little game for the time being. At least Tyler knew where he was.

The lecture hall filled quickly in the last minutes before ten o'clock. At ten, Tyler picked up where he'd left off the day before. Emission and absorption of radiation, Boltzmann's constant, the kinetic energy of a gas expressed as a function of its absolute temperature—and then a door swung open in back of the room and Gail Dionne came in, took a seat in the upper tier against the rear wall, the same seat Blackburn had taken the day before.

Dionne and Blackburn, shadowy bodies that seemed to be in the same orbit, only narrowly missing one another.

Tyler stumbled over a few words and then coughed awkwardly. He rambled a bit as he went over number densities of air molecules in the Earth's atmosphere and gas particles on the surface of the sun. Gail Dionne's presence had a considerably greater effect on him than Blackburn's had. His face warmed as the previous night's foolishness on the telephone with the reporter from *Parsec* flitted through his mind.

He turned toward the blackboard and wrote out a set of simplified equations, feeling a sense of composure return as he worked through the equilibrium state of gas pressure and gravitation that existed at each point within the sun. The hour dragged however, and Tyler felt the woman's eyes on him every minute, remembering the way she had watched him at Red's Outpost, the way she'd approached him, not as a journalist but as a . . . a whatever, one of Red's lonely happy-hour ladies.

He dismissed the class early and then spent a few minutes answering the inevitable after-class questions, noting that Gail Dionne remained seated in the back of the room. When the last student was gone, Tyler began to gather up his notes.

He glanced up. "You're everywhere."

"Like air," she said agreeably, rising.

She wore a businesslike white blouse with a high collar and a gray plaid skirt that came to just above midcalf, belted at the narrow waist. She was lovely. Like Carol, she was not a classical beauty. Her mouth was too wide; her eyebrows a shade too prominent. The combination made her face more interesting, however, without detracting in the slightest from her looks.

"Maybe I should get a court order of some kind," he said mildly.

"That won't be necessary, Dr. Tyler." She gave him a wonderful smile. Her eyes were a deep blue, direct.

He held the door open for her as they went out into the hallway. "Please follow me, Ms. Dionne."

"Gail."

He took the lead, letting her trail along behind as he walked purposefully to the department office, opened the door, and ushered her inside.

Behind the desk, Nora Klemowicz beamed at them. "Oh, good, I see you two have finally—"

Tyler broke in: "Please make an appointment for Ms. Dionne to see me, Nora."

Nora gaped at him, eyes darting to Gail and back to him. "But she's . . . I mean . . ."

"An appointment?" Gail said, confused.

"For next Monday."

"Monday!" Gail exclaimed.

"Tuesday morning, actually," Tyler said to Nora, who was now looking visibly upset. "Shall we say, one-forty-five in the morning. That's when I get off work at Red's."

Abruptly, Nora laughed. Her expression, however, was one of utter perplexity.

Gail's eyes flashed. "If this is your idea of a joke, Dr. Tyler, I assure you—"

"You get your way quite often, don't you?" he asked, facing her.

"I, uh . . . *what?*"

"One-forty-five at Red's Outpost, Tuesday morning, Nora. Until then, my schedule is too full to permit me to meet with anyone." He moved toward the door.

Gail stamped a foot furiously. "Look here, Dr. Tyler—"

"It was your idea for us to meet at that time and place, Ms. Dionne," he said firmly. "Now live with it."

LIVE WITH IT.

Gail slammed the door of her Avis rental, an underpowered boxy damn thing, pale yellow, built somewhere in the heartland of America.

Damn Dr. Tyler! Dr. Maurice Hayden Tyler, the arrogant son of a bitch.

Suddenly she laughed, a shrill burst of sound that ended abruptly. Tuesday morning! . . . Which would then become Tuesday afternoon at the very least, since Tyler would certainly have no intention of granting her an interview at such an ungodly hour. This was simply his way of punishing her for what was proving to be a very costly mistake.

"Well," she said softly, staring up at the physics building, "we will see about *that*, Dr. Tyler!"

CHAPTER 8

"IN THE FUTURE, at least for the duration of the, ah, crisis," Dr. Malcolm Cooke said, oblivious to the bombast in his voice, "I must recommend that that man, that impossible media *clown,* Finley Osborne, be granted no interviews with any responsible member of the astrophysical community." He sensed impatience in the group, but continued to press the point anyway: "I warned him to tread softly before the show was taped, but the man is fundamentally argumentative, quite intractable."

"Yes, yes," soothed the chairman of the Subcommittee, Dr. Charles Hooper, director of the editorial advisory board of the prestigious *Journal of Social Issues.* "However, it would seem that that sort of thing must be left in your hands, Dr. Cooke. There's very little the Subcommittee can do to muster unity or . . . censorship, shall we say, in that area." He seemed uncomfortable with this line of thinking.

They called themselves the Subcommittee: this ad hoc gathering of four senior members of the president's National Advisory Commission on Civil Disorders, appointed by the chairman of the commission, E. Lamont Greene, when the first rustle of unease began to stir the general population. Chairman Hooper, composed of jowls and black-rimmed spectacles; Allister Kiefman, the lean, gray-haired attorney from New York; Dr. Ernest Golden, the portly Harvard professor—a specialist in mob psychology; quiet, sour-faced Judd Ingram.

The four members of the Subcommittee and Dr. Cooke, the group's science adviser, were seated around a polished oak table on the second floor of the tree-shaded courthouse in Arlington, Virginia, overlooking the Potomac River with its barges and sailboats. Through an open window, a distant, continuous susurration of traffic noise wafted into the room, carried on a pleasant but unseasonably cool springlike breeze.

"It was only a comment," Cooke said irascibly, quite unlike the man he was on television.

Judd Ingram suppressed a desire to simply get up and walk out. At seventy, Ingram was the oldest member of the Subcommittee—a former FBI deputy director who had for a number of years directed that agency's elite counterterrorist division. In Ingram's opinion, the Subcommittee was an impotent group of old men, charged with studying a situation that would undoubtedly resolve itself in time without their help. They would give their recommendations to the larger parent organization—another superannuated, impotent fraternity, which would in turn submit fainthearted, impractical suggestions to the White House staff and the president's Cabinet.

It was, Ingram understood, the nature of bureaucracy to discuss, to recommend, to bluster and pose and ultimately do nothing—expensively. Well, Judd Ingram had done something, and if it wasn't entirely legal and proper, it was *something,* and may God *damn* the fat asses who would in all probability censure him for it if they learned of it, who sat around whining and blowing wind, lamenting their semiofficial status and uncertain influence.

At the last meeting of the Subcommittee, three names had come to light, Dr. Cooke supplying each: Dr. Michael Bennett, a Mr. Saverio Spallino, and Dr. Maurice Tyler. The first two were what Ingram, in the parlance of his earlier profession, regarded as "soft targets," easily persuaded (or dissuaded), wielding but small clubs.

Tyler, however, was another matter.

Cooke had stressed Tyler, the cockamamie paper the Arizona astrophysicist had sent to him, the fact that if Tyler went public with it the uneducated masses might lap it up, particularly if this unwarranted alarm continued to spread throughout the United States and the rest of the world, creating just the sort of mindless havoc the Subcommittee had been impaneled to study, and, if possible, prevent.

So they had wrung their hands and included in the report of last week the possibility that a charismatic or scientific figure might rise up and lead the public, knowingly or unknowingly, into hysteria. At that time the Subcommittee had determined that a scientific figure could do the most harm at this point. After all, religious leaders seemed most able to sway followers on matters of moral principle or religious interpretation, not science (at least not since the days of Galileo), although, as Hooper had pointed out, pseudoscience and pseudoreligion was rampant in the world nowadays, and who could figure any of that?

In keeping with the collective do-nothing, wait-and-see attitude of the Subcommittee, no specific recommendations had been made. Judd Ingram had taken action, however, as he had so often in the past. He had shut Tyler down. When you had a problem, you did something about it . . . none of this namby-pamby crybaby shit. Ingram had called due a few old debts with Cy Hollander in Los Angeles and dumped everything in Cy's lap—after all, Ingram was a chief (or former chief), not one of the world's Indians. And even though the glory days were over, he was, by God, a chief who could still get a job done, not some inert, fat-assed, buck-passing bureaucrat.

Now, almost as if Ingram's thoughts about Tyler had been stripped and laid bare, the Harvard expert in mob psychology, Dr. Ernest Golden, said, "What I'd like to know, Dr. Cooke, is how this increased activity with the sun fits in with the paper of Dr. Tyler's we discussed last week."

Ernest Golden was in his mid-forties, the only one among them who had not yet passed the sixty mark. His dark, close-set eyes were piercing—the dominant feature of his face in spite of a large, beaklike nose. His formerly jet black hair had thinned and grayed considerably.

Malcolm Cooke inspected a blunt fingernail. "Dr. Tyler's paper was the usual concoction of buzzwords and pseudoscience that too often appeals to the uninitiated, and, unfortunately, to a disturbing number of scientists who should know better as well. I had hoped that we'd gone over the problem of Tyler and the others in sufficient detail at the meeting last week."

"What do you mean, 'appeals'?" Golden pressed. "How does a pseudoscientific paper, as you call it, 'appeal' to members of the scientific community?"

"The sun is a complex object," Cooke replied, tenting his fingers. "A gigantic ball of plasma—heated ionic material—continuously variable in pressure and temperature, capable of a stable, sustained thermonuclear reaction. In spite of all the research and rhetoric, gentlemen, few aspects of the sun's makeup and activity are completely or even adequately understood. The magnetohydrodynamic behavior of—"

"Ah, magneto*what?*" Dr. Hooper interrupted, aghast.

"Magnetohydrodynamic." Dr. Cooke shrugged apologetically. "A term referring to the behavior of conducting fluids in the presence of electric and magnetic fields. The sun is composed of just such a fluid, an ionic soup, steeped in a complex and highly variable magnetic field. Tyler's model is only that, a model, not a formal theory . . . a model not of the sun per se, I might add, but of a proposed state of solar turbulence. While the words may have a superficial appeal, his theory is way out in right field, the mathematics tenuous, the conclusions quite insupportable."

"In your opinion," Dr. Golden said.

Cooke's eyes narrowed. "In my opinion, yes."

"Ah, I believe that is more than sufficient for our purposes," Dr. Hooper said hastily, attempting to divert the conversation toward a more congenial track. "The state of the sun is not precisely the concern of this committee now, is it? Although I must admit, there *is* a connection that we—"

"What I'm driving at," the psychologist persisted, "is that other scientists might credit Tyler's paper?" He gave Cooke a searching look.

"They might, yes, but few would care to align themselves with Tyler at this point. Remember what I told you about Tyler's debacle at King's College, ten years ago last June."

"Yes, of course," Golden said, his eyes bright. "But what I'd like to know is . . . could Dr. Tyler be *right?*"

Cooke stared at him a moment, then his face opened in a smile. He chuckled. "At some level we are all children, are we not, Doctor? What you really want to know, and are afraid to ask, is whether or not you should dig in, run to the root cellar and hide. Well, by all means do so if it makes you feel secure. You hardly need my blessing for that."

Dr. Golden's mouth dropped open. "My God, you truly are an insufferable, arrogant bastard."

"At times I wonder just how far our technological culture has removed us from the primitives who worshiped the sun and all the visible objects of the night sky," Cooke said serenely, distributing his great bulk more comfortably in his chair. "Deep down, we all sense our relative insignificance in the vastness of the universe, do we not? A great comet, a bolt of lightning, a few spots on the sun. Then the savage in us is set loose, particularly in those whose veneer of civilization is thinnest." He gave a small, mocking laugh.

Golden's face grew dangerously apoplectic. A shocked silence fell over the room.

Finally Charles Hooper cleared his throat and said, "Perhaps it would behoove us to take a short recess, gentlemen."

Dr. Golden stood abruptly and left the room. Cooke sat back and gazed out the window at the river, blinking frequently and smiling to himself. Allister Kiefman, who had bunkered himself in his chair and kept out of the line of fire, drifted quietly out the door.

Judd Ingram struck a match and lit a cigarette, wishing he were back in the FBI again. He exhaled smoke, coughed. He and Dr. Cooke quite pointedly did not look at one another.

THIRTY-TWO THOUSAND FEET above the western edge of Pennsylvania, the sky was a weighty blue. Dr. Cooke sat with his eyes closed. The flight from the nation's capital to Detroit would take roughly two hours. He hadn't expected the Tyler thing to come up again; as a result, he'd lit into Ernest Golden with more vigor than was strictly defensible. Still, there was something about the man that rubbed Cooke the wrong way, no doubt about it. A great many people rubbed Cooke the wrong way.

Tyler. Cooke had sensed that Tyler could be a problem; he'd therefore consented to a private interview with Judd Ingram across the Potomac at Ingram's two-story frame house in Hillcrest Heights after that first meeting of the Subcommittee. Ingram had quizzed him on Tyler and Bennett and Spallino, but Cooke had intuitively soft-pedaled the latter two and steered Ingram toward Tyler. The ex-FBI man had dropped several hints that something could be done to ensure the cooperative silence of these men. Cooke had not pressed him about it, didn't really want to know anything at all about that sort of thing, but he had told Ingram everything he knew about Tyler, which was a considerable amount.

That damned paper—why hadn't he taken the time to look it over more carefully; and why, oh why, had he ever brought it to the attention of the Subcommittee?

Because, he thought . . .

Because he had read the conclusions of Tyler's paper and laughed outright, passed it along to his assistant at McMath-Hulbert, Dr. Glen Dietrich, without bothering to plow through the body of it himself.

Because he, Cooke, was the expert, and the Subcommittee had wondered what, in Cooke's opinion, was the prevailing attitude of the scientific community concerning the sun, whether any trouble could be expected from that direction. Cooke had thought immediately of Tyler and that damn fool letter he'd sent, not a paper really, without thinking it through all the way to this bitter conclusion.

Because at King's College, in the process of destroying himself, Tyler had also managed to take a bite out of Cooke's professional hide and make him out as something of a fool as well, and for that, Cooke would never forgive the man. Never.

Now the members of the Subcommittee and the board of directors of the North American League of Astrophysicists wanted to know if the paper had validity, and all Cooke knew was that the conclusion had been preposterous, just as this incredible ongoing outburst on the sun's surface was preposterous. One seemed to augment the other, conspiring in some arcane fashion to damage Cooke's career.

He hadn't read Tyler's paper. Dietrich had only skimmed it, not really absorbed it, and now the paper was gone, lost. Events and timing had turned against Cooke. Seeking to sling some spiteful mud at Tyler, he had assured those few people who had learned of the existence of Tyler's paper that it was nothing but the sheerest poppycock, but as the activity of the sun intensified, questions were being raised.

Right from the start he should have admitted he hadn't actually read the paper, absorbed its contents, exposed its fundamental errors; but that position had seemed as untenable then as now. He couldn't step forward at this late date and admit he'd condemned a man on the basis of prejudice rather than fact. Tyler's underlying assumptions were faulty, Cooke had told his limited audience, his conclusions erroneous, almost quackish. And, he pointed out, it'd been two years and Tyler still hadn't published. Draw your own conclusions.

So far, Cooke's word and reputation had sustained him, but the private dam he'd constructed was weakening and would soon burst. The board of directors of NALA (of which Dr. Cooke was a senior member) was all but ready to contact Tyler on its own, against all Cooke's exhortations to the contrary.

Perhaps, Cooke thought, it was time to change tactics, to relent a little in Tyler's favor to relieve some of the pressure. After all, Tyler's conclusions *were* outrageous.

At this point it might very well benefit Cooke to turn the rope over to Tyler with sufficient slack to permit him to hang himself.

The thought had a certain appeal. The more Cooke thought about it, the better he liked it. He would appear reasonable, fair, tolerant. Tyler would ruin himself . . . again.

He remembered Judd Ingram's words: *Perhaps Tyler will be enjoined to act in a judicious manner.* Cold and aloofly confident, with the cut-crystal desk lamp deepening the wrinkled, pouchy sockets of his eyes, Ingram had betrayed nothing by this statement, either by inflection or facial expression.

What had Cooke gotten himself into, he wondered now, by accepting a private audience with Judd Ingram? In that moment in the man's study, Ingram had seemed barely sane, lost in a netherworld that no longer existed. Could he actually accomplish what he had so deviously implied? Had he already taken action of some kind? And if so, how would it affect the new tack Cooke was about to take regarding Tyler?

Delicate forces were at work, some of them poorly understood, nibbling at the structure of his life: the sun, Tyler and his ridiculous paper, Ingram, the mood of NALA. The problem was how to find that narrow path that would optimize the outcome for himself, or at least limit the damage.

He popped an antacid tablet in his mouth. It was a tricky business he'd gotten himself into. Tricky.

CHAPTER 9 ─────────────

THE PHONE BEGAN to ring as Tyler crawled out of the musty hole that led into the shelter. It shrilled ten times and then fell silent, while Tyler stared at it, drinking a glass of water. Very likely Gail Dionne, he thought, but there was a chance it was Jack or even Rita. The call's timing—Saturday morning, ten o'clock exactly—might have been journalistic reflex. Or, he thought with a sigh, the mark of a compulsive physicist or sociologist. Perhaps Rita had changed her mind about dinner that evening.

He called Jack first.

"Buddy, your timing is absolutely impeccable," Jack said, out of breath.

Tyler grinned. "Kids out playing somewhere?"

"What do you want, Tyler?"

"I got a call a few minutes ago. I gather it wasn't you."

"Wait, I'll ask. Val's right here. Nope. Wasn't either of us, my intrusive friend."

"I should've known. You aren't the compulsive type, are you?"

"Hah?"

"We still on for tonight?"

"We are if you'll kindly hang the hell up."

Tyler hung up. Then, on a hunch, he dialed Rita's number at the university instead of her home.

"Hello?"

"Rita, this's Tyler. Did you phone a few minutes ago?"

"No."

"Oh, I've been getting crank calls lately. The phone rang and I didn't answer. Then I thought it might've been you."

"I make relatively few crank calls, Tyler."

But for the odd lack of humor in her voice, it wouldn't have been a bad comeback. "Of course not," he said.

"Maybe you should get an answering machine. That usually discourages them."

"Why didn't I think of that?"

"I'm up to my eyebrows in essay papers. Could we continue this discussion later, maybe tonight?"

"See you at seven-thirty."

He set the receiver back in its cradle, shaking his head. Maybe the call *had* come from Gail Dionne. For a few unguarded seconds the thought was curiously pleasant.

TSELAA.

Tyler's Folly. He called it that sometimes, this ultimate personal survival shelter—particularly when he was in the mood to poke fun at himself. Otherwise he called it *Tselaa*, the old Navajo word meaning refuge, still in a faintly mocking tone, although only to himself. He'd never told anyone about it; which, he reflected, had as much to do with keeping his foolishness to himself as keeping the shelter a secret.

A monument to paranoia or temporary insanity or whatever dark emotion had taken hold of him two summers ago when Carol left. He had built it himself, alone; operated the bulldozer that had gouged the earth, used the cutting torch, nestled the huge culvert pipe on its bed of sand, welded it all together, buried it. Therapy for a mere thirty-five thousand dollars initial construction cost. Three months of backbreaking labor from sunup to sundown to finish the rough work. It had filled his life, left him without time to brood.

Nothing was visible now but a low, sculpted hillock of blackbrush and juniper in the backyard, growths of deer grass and muhly, indistinguishable from the rest of the terrain.

Tyler lowered himself through a hole in the kitchen floor over which the refrigerator had stood, into a circular shaft that led down ten feet through the concrete slab of the house to an intersecting tunnel, four feet in diameter, that sloped downward into the earth.

He wrestled a canister of wheat along in the confined space, crouching as he inched backward down the wooden catwalk. Sixty-watt bulbs lit the way, strung on an extension cord that passed through loops welded to the curved ceiling.

Tselaa, Tyler's Folly: a cylindrical chamber thirty-two feet underground, twelve feet in diameter, twenty-eight feet long; crammed with food, clothing, bedding, rifles and ammunition, rope, tools, seeds, countless other sundries.

He'd designed it to get two people through the expected nuclear winter an exchange with the Soviets would bring, so he could emerge half-mad and pallid in the nuclear spring to face whatever remained. To observe, as a scientist, the ultimate result of applied science. He had noted this same fascination in others of his kind—the desire to at least glimpse the Other Side, to witness the first days or weeks or even years of the second great barbarism of mankind. Collectively, in its modern social and political institutions, the human race had all the survival instincts of skin cancer.

And, if superpower restraint prevailed indefinitely, at least he had his Folly, his secret monument to science, to Carol, to upheaval and disintegration in his personal life.

He emerged in the main room and stood up, looking around the subterranean cavity with that mixed feeling of satisfaction, awe, and ill-defined horror the sight always gave him.

It was a cramped, utilitarian space, cold and lonely and desolate. He tried to imagine himself cooped up here with Rita for a year, and failed. He tried to envision several other unlikely possibilities and failed at them as well.

Year-round, the temperature inside *Tselaa* was a chilly

fifty-one degrees, varying less than half a degree between summer and winter. In the event of nuclear winter, fallout shelters built in the fifties would be but tombs for their inhabitants. The so-called survivalists who took to the hills would freeze, fingers clutching the stocks of their guns. *Tselaa*, on the other hand, had been buried deep enough to take advantage of the heat and insulative power of the earth. Twenty feet below the surface, an eighteen-hundred-gallon tank of propane held enough fuel to run the stove and oven and keep the living space comfortable for at least a year, even if the above-ground temperature should fall to a hundred below zero.

He checked the batteries of a flashlight held by its clip to a wall, depressed by the dense silence of the shelter, the musty cold. Lifting the cap off the well, he lowered the specially designed bucket until he felt it touch water sixty-five feet below. He cranked it up, swung it free of the shaft, and tipped some water into a cup, dumping the rest back down the pipe. The water was cool; minerally, but good.

He recapped the well and took a final look around. Now that *Tselaa* was completely stocked, he visited it only a few times each year, mostly to rotate certain foodstuffs and check for water leakage. So far, there'd never been any.

Back in the kitchen he unplugged the extension cord and dropped it back down the hole. He lowered the heavy slab of reinforced concrete into place and unscrewed and removed its handles. He applied a claylike mixture to the perimeter crack and to the final half inch of the small handle holes, after first protecting the sunken threads with a plastic sleeve. The compound, when dry, would blend invisibly with the surrounding concrete. In a rectangular niche in this 120-pound slab was a small steel cashbox, containing sixty-five hundred dollars in twenties, fifties, and hundreds. Anyone who stumbled on the break in the flooring above would logically assume the box and its contents were what was being hidden, not a secret opening that led beneath the house.

A James Bondian arrangement, if ever there was one.

It resonated with a part of his psyche he'd never examined deeply. A part of him that was childlike and sly and had delighted in building magnificent, secluded "forts" in grade school.

His phone began to ring again, but he ignored it. After a dozen rings it quit. She was persistent, he had to give her that.

The plywood plug went on next, fitting snugly into its recess, conforming to the rest of the subflooring. A slab of linoleum followed, slipping almost seamlessly into place. On top of this, he shoved the refrigerator back against the wall. He stood back and inspected his work, pleased as always with the result. It might not fool professionals whose job it was to sniff out such hidey-holes, but he was willing to bet that few others would stumble upon it, particularly if they had no reason to suspect that such a hole existed.

Now that magnetic storms of unprecedented magnitude were wracking the sun, he wasn't sure his former justification for building the shelter, nuclear war, wasn't about to be superceded by one of the single most unlikely events to ever occur in the cosmos.

WHAT ARE YOU DOING HERE, GIRL?

The question repeated itself at frequent intervals in Gail's head. From her vantage point partway up the slope of Angel Canyon, she had a clear view of Tyler's house or ranch or whatever he chose to call it.

Spying on the pretty man, the reply came unbidden. She shivered in the chill air beneath a stand of pines.

She hadn't seen much of the man, however, but she was becoming familiar with his house. It was large and rambling, built of natural, indigenous rock and cedar, with a pitched roof of brown Spanish tile. Inside would be at least three bedrooms, maybe four. She tried to imagine the layout. A satellite TV dish stood in the yard out back, a short distance from the white, domed observatory.

Earlier, she'd caught glimpses of Tyler as he carried stubby cylindrical objects from the barn or garage into the house. That was all.

Back in town, when she learned that Tyler lived alone way out in the sticks, the idea of reconnaissance had seemed appropriate, even reasonable, appealing to that shadowy part of her personality that delighted in pretending to be someone or something she was not—as she had done with others in the past with such striking success. Tyler, though, had been her most notable and frustrating failure to date. The jerk.

Others had accepted her style as quirky but fun, harmless. Her smile disarmed them. But not Tyler. He hadn't given her a chance—that Gila monster sense of humor of his.

Now she wasn't so sure this idea of scouting Tyler's domicile was all that terrific, but what else could she do? She had to complete the interview by Monday morning at the latest. Her flight out of Los Angeles with Nikki was at 6:10, Monday evening. She could probably catch a later flight, but that wouldn't solve her primary problem. *Parsec*'s senior editor, Chris Stampfli, wanted the article on his desk no later than eight o'clock Wednesday morning. If she worked on it all day Tuesday and Tuesday evening, she could meet that deadline, but not if Tyler persisted in continuing his miserable little game.

The entire next issue of *Parsec* was to be devoted to the sun, and Tyler, whether he appreciated it or not, was meant to be a part of it, possibly a big part, although Gail was beginning to wonder. Chris had heard that Dr. Tyler at Northern Arizona University had come up with an unusual theory concerning the sun. No details, however, since Chris's source, having heard only a rumor of a rumor, had been unable to supply anything more than that. Gail would have to pry it out of Tyler from scratch, if there was anything to pry. Chris had handed her the assignment because her record was the best of anyone on *Parsec*'s staff at unearthing this kind of thing.

Until now. Tyler, the detestable creep, was going to grant her an interview no earlier than Tuesday, and nothing would sway him from it. She'd seen it in his eyes.

But, she thought with a determined smile, Tyler didn't know the first thing about Gail Dionne.

She scanned the house again with a pair of 8×40 secondhand Zeiss binoculars—garage, observatory; no movement inside or out for the last half hour. Chevy truck parked out front.

She'd bought the binoculars that morning at a pawnshop, aided by a chubby clerk who probably got as much exercise in a decade as she got in a week. He'd stared at her the whole time, a vacuous expression on his face as the higher functions shut down—what questionable higher functions he might have possessed. The response had been repeated so often over the years by so many men that she'd become immune to it, amused and resigned. She was studied avidly wherever she went, memorized, packed away into whatever organic storage bins stored such images—bits and pieces of her strewn across the continent, fading away slowly in numerous male heads like the interplanetary sprinkling of ice crystals from a passing comet.

A shaft of sunlight fell on her shoulders. She shivered at the sudden touch of warmth.

She was going to get that interview with Tyler if she had to tie him to a chair and feed him scopolamine until he choked on it. Well, maybe not, but one way or another she was going to have to jolt him out of the mind-set he was in. Once she'd derailed his ridiculous response to her (that she'd unintentionally brought about), maybe she could humble herself to him, apologize for what she'd done, talk to him like a real person. Get the damned interview.

The problem was how to give him that jolt.

"No one answers," said Dr. Joan Lockwood. She hung up.

The delegation was looking slightly more fierce than Dr. Cooke had anticipated; five members of the board of directors of NALA in all their finery—tweed and broad ties, Italian shoes, silk, gray hair.

"Someone has *got* to go out there and talk to Dr. Tyler," said the spokesman for the group, Dr. Raymond Goehring—in Cooke's opinion, a most unfortunate surname.

The sun's total flux output had slipped from 99.1 percent of normal yesterday morning, to 98.5 percent—a drop of over one-half of one percent in just twenty-four hours. Incredible. So far the public hadn't gotten wind of it, but already that morning the president's science adviser had been on the phone, and nothing was going to prevent hundreds of amateur astronomers from reporting to every local paper and TV station in the country that the spot had grown even larger. Forty-one billion square miles now—an enormous blot and still spreading. The delegation had come steaming in with fire in their eyes, demanding that Tyler be contacted immediately, that his theory about the sun be reviewed.

Dr. Malcolm Cooke had proven surprisingly amenable to the suggestion, even to the point of suggesting that Dr. Tyler be phoned right away, from his own office. But the phones had gone unanswered in Arizona, both at the university and at Tyler's residence.

"Someone's got to go—" Goehring began again.

"Yes, of course," Cooke responded.

"We thought it should be *you,*" Goehring said, eyes bright in his thin, cadaverous face.

Cooke looked startled. "Me?"

"You were his doctoral adviser at MIT—"

"Years ago, yes."

"He sent his paper to you." Goehring's tone was almost reproachful.

Cooke leaned forward in his chair and placed his forearms on the desk. "I have commitments, obligations. I can't go traipsing around the country right now. Tomorrow afternoon I'm scheduled to appear on 'The Hershel Andrews Show,' which, I shouldn't need to remind you, is a syndicated—"

"Your assistant, Dr. Dietrich, can take your place."

"—and two days after that, I'm appearing on the 'Tonight Show'—"

"In Southern California, Burbank."

Cooke blinked. "Yes."

"Then you'll be near Flagstaff. A short hop by plane. The trips can be combined. Really, it only makes sense . . ."

They wore him down quickly. It seemed to Cooke that Tyler, even in his absence, was suddenly holding all the cards, and it occurred to Cooke that it might actually be to his advantage to be the first to contact Tyler—to disarm his former student, in more ways than one.

He swept his most sincere smile over the group. "Perhaps you're right. I will go and have a chat with Dr. Tyler."

Flagstaff. It sounded like a million miles away.

CHAPTER 10 ─────────

"Oh, you get used to it," Valerie Anderson said in response to Rita Kaufer's question. "Physicists are a lot like children, I've found. Always ready to play. Mathematicians too. You've got to know when to listen, and when to tune out."

"They look so . . . so involved," Rita said, looking out over the counter that separated the kitchen area from the spacious dining room. Through floor-to-ceiling windows she could see the redwood deck outside that ran the full length of the rear of the house, high on the hillside north of the city. On the deck, Jack and Tyler were gesticulating in silence at the sky. Flagstaff twinkled below, and mountains rose darkly in the distance. The last vestige of the sunset was a purple, Zane Grey haze across the horizon.

"They *always* look involved," Val replied. "They're probably talking about women."

"I don't think so." Rita was dressed in a yellow sleeveless cotton print dress with a modest neckline. Her hair was short, blond, cut in a functional, easy-to-care-for style that emphasized the gauntness of her face, and which, in turn, drew undue attention to the spareness of her figure. She was five five and weighed 103 pounds. Thirty-four years old, intense, just short of being pretty. Glasses with huge violet-tinted lenses gave her a starved, owlish appearance.

She looked around with an inward wistful feeling at Val's home, neat but lived-in, bordering on elegant without being fussy or contrived. Jack was warm and funny, and seemed to be genuinely in love with Val. Their two children, Shannon and Jimmy, were well behaved, already packed off to bed.

Rita lived in a three-room apartment without a view, a place where neighbors fought and young, greasy, *frightening* kids raced car engines in the parking lot, raising blue, smelly clouds of exhaust. Day and night around her, toilets flushed and garbage disposals growled in the walls. Her only companions were tropical fish in a big forty-gallon tank: Rasboras, Glass Fish, Barbs, Tetras. Life had stagnated in this condition six years ago. She felt a kind of desperate, inexpressible longing for something more, for someone, possibly Tyler.

"It's cold out tonight," she said. "Like fall."

"Want to toss the salad?" Val asked.

"Okay."

"EVEN WITHOUT CORRECTING for surface curvature," Tyler said, "a planimeter reading of the spots shows they cover a region of at least forty billion square miles." They came inside, out of the unseasonably chilly air. Tyler handed Jack the pictures he had taken of the sun through a hydrogen-alpha filter that afternoon in his observatory. He'd developed the film himself in the adjoining darkroom.

Jack frowned at the pictures. "Yeah. But what does it *mean?* I mean, these are nice, impressive even—better than the stuff they print in the newspapers, but all this is still out of my bailiwick."

"These spots are at least five times larger than anything previously recorded."

"And one day a nearby star will supernova and we'll get a light show more impressive than anything seen before. But I repeat, what does it *mean?* You got some inside information on this, Tyler? Why do I get the feeling there's music playing, but you're too shy to ask me to dance?''

Val walked into the room, trailing Rita. ''That's enough shop for a while, guys. The coals are hot, the wine chilled, the women hungry. Let's get the steaks on, huh?''

''All she does is nag,'' Jack said mournfully.

Val smiled at him. ''It's a lousy job, dearest, but someone's got to do it.''

GORDY PUT his binoculars down. ''He's still in there. I saw him and that other guy, Anderson.''

Harold Blackburn said nothing. He bit off another square of chocolate.

''They could be talking about anything in there,'' Gordy persisted. ''Anything.''

''Maybe you oughta bust the door down, find out.''

''Ha ha,'' Gordy said. ''Very funny.''

THE COLLECT CALL went through quickly.

''Nan?''

''Gail, where *are* you? I thought you'd be back by now.''

''So did I.''

''You didn't get the interview?''

''Not yet. I'm still working on it.''

''Are we going to have time to visit?'' Nan asked plaintively. ''You promised.''

''I know. Dr. Tyler is being difficult. I messed up good on my first approach and he wants to put me off until Tuesday.''

''*Tues*day! But you—''

''I know. Listen, I'm going to do something, well, unusual, even for me. Shake him up a little.''

''Oh God, Gail, don't go getting in trouble.''

''What makes you think—''

''Hey, this is Nan, remember? We went through the hell years together. I know you. I know what you're capable of. I saw those pictures you took of Bill . . . Bill whatever his name was.''

''Wittmer. That was almost fifteen years ago.''

''So—what's changed?''

Gail sighed.

"You always had your own rules," Nan went on in a lamenting tone. "Always doing things your own way, sneaking in in the early hours of the morning. Getting me to fib for you."

"That's ancient history. I just want you to know I'll be a day or two late getting back to Los Angeles."

"Don't do anything dumb, okay?"

"If I thought this was really dangerous I wouldn't do it, all right? I'm sorry I brought it up. I've got to get this interview, tomorrow, and that means I've got some demolition work to do." She grinned wickedly.

"Demo*lition* work? I don't *believe* you," Nan cried in exasperation. "Sometimes you're so impulsive I want to grab you and give you a good shake. You can't keep on like this."

"I know. Gypsy in the woodpile. Is Nikki there? I want to talk to her."

She looked around Tyler's huge darkened kitchen as she talked to Nan and then Nikki. Moonlight illuminated the backyard and threw a dim glow into the house. In every corner she felt him, Tyler, lurking, disapproving. The little .38 lay on the counter beside the phone. Her fingers trembled.

THE SALAD AND STEAKS WERE GONE, the wine consumed, the plates cleared to the kitchen. Bartender Jack had made Rita a Havana cocktail—pineapple juice, lemon, and rum—surprising her, delivering it with a flourish that made her flush with embarrassment and pleasure. Val had artfully steered the conversation in the direction of Rita's expertise, trying to draw her out, and the flow of words had twisted and turned until it had arrived here, in controversy, in conflict with Tyler.

Worse, she couldn't back down, couldn't move away from the hard line she was wielding defensively, like a club. She felt as if she were two people: the soft Rita watching in horror as the hard Rita grew increasingly brittle and out of control. At issue was whether sociology was or was not a "true" science.

"Some of the world's finest minds," Rita said in a tremulous voice, "capable of dealing with ideas of great abstraction, have been drawn to the field of sociology."

"I don't doubt that, but it hardly qualifies sociology as a science," Tyler said in a calm, objective manner that only infuriated her further.

"Because its concepts aren't easily quantifiable?" she retorted angrily. "Reducible to holy numbers?"

Tyler smiled. "Perhaps. And perhaps because its concepts aren't quantifiable even in a philosophical sense."

"Philo*soph*ical? What does *that* mean?" She pushed her glasses up on her nose with an angry gesture, aware that Jack and Val were silent and uncomfortable, that Val seemed unable to come to her rescue.

Rita wanted this to end. She couldn't back down. How had she gotten caught up in this? Did she *really* believe sociology was a science, and not just a discipline? Why was she such a miserable priggish klutz around men? And if she *knew* she was being an MPK, why couldn't she just *quit?*

Tyler shrugged. "The gravitational constant is known to only three or four decimal places, yet it undoubtedly has a much more precise value that could, philosophically speaking, be expressed to many more decimal points."

"Spoken like a true physicist," Rita said acidly, utterly dismayed at her tone of voice.

Tyler's eyes narrowed. "The problem with sociology as a science is that it doesn't allow one to predict events or determine the consequences of existing situations with any certainty. In its own jargon, which certainly doesn't qualify it as a science, it describes what has happened or conditions that now exist, but it fails to provide reliable models of future behavior."

"I don't think—"

"Suppose truck drivers and railroad workers went on strike, disrupting the normal flow of food supplies to a large city. Using norms and group dynamics and mass hysteria and whatever else, could you make reliable predictions on the various effects on society when supermarket shelves were being radically thinned out?"

"That's a poor sort of example."

"It's a poor science that sidesteps real-life problems."

"The question is too complex, Tyler. No one could give it a definitive answer."

"My point exactly. Sociology and related fields are still too imprecise to supply predictive answers to major real-world problems."

Rita's face was white, rigid. "I haven't heard anything on the news for the past few days but this stupid thing with the sun," she said piercingly. "As a physicist, what's your in-depth answer to *that* major real-world problem?"

Val stood up suddenly. "Uh, would anyone care for some chocolate mint ice cream? Tyler? Rita?"

"YOU BLEW IT, buddy. What was that all about, anyway? Coming at her with the long knives."

"I don't know," Tyler said, slumped in a chair. Jack and Tyler were in the living room, seated on opposite sides of a coffee table. The women were gone, off in some other part of the house where Val was trying to help Rita regain her composure. Too late, Tyler had seen tears in Rita's eyes. He felt wretched, guilty, yet somehow betrayed by the evening's troubling turn.

"I don't think the lady is going to invite you in for a nightcap or anything else when you take her home," Jack replied.

"I wasn't looking for a nightcap or anything else."

"Bad attitude. Maybe you need a week or two off. Maybe a couple of months."

Tyler leaned forward suddenly. "You once asked if I had an inside track on what's going on with the sun."

Interest gleamed in Jack's eyes. "Do you?"

"I don't know."

"But not definitely no."

"Something like that."

"Okay, what gives?"

"Nothing I want to get into deeply right now."

"Then what're we talking about here?"

"You remember that cave you and Val and I found partway up that ridge by Trinity Mountain a few summers ago?''

"North of Seligman on Interstate Forty. Sure."

"The mouth of that cave wasn't much over two feet across," Tyler said.

"Yep. Lucky we stumbled across it." Jack sipped his bourbon. "Looked like we might've been the first ever to find it, except maybe Indians."

"It went back pretty far."

"We could've seen more if we'd had a flashlight along," Jack agreed, adopting Tyler's rhythm.

"What I'm about to suggest might not be such a good idea. What I mean is, the merit of this particular idea is something you and Val will have to decide for yourselves."

"Weasel words?"

Tyler shrugged. "For whatever they're worth."

"Okay."

"What I would do real soon, tomorrow, is go there with a lantern and look around, check it out. If it looks suitable, I'd be inclined to stock it with food and water, fuel, guns; warm, durable clothing. I'd think in terms of how to survive a cold spell. Real cold. And I'd take a close look at that entrance, figure out some way to keep out cold air."

"How cold?"

"I've got no idea. In round numbers, let's say a hundred below, give or take forty."

Jack's face paled. He gazed into Tyler's eyes for a long moment. "Jesus, you're serious," he said finally.

"It's what I'd do."

"What you'd do would cost a lot of money."

"It'd have to be something a person thought was worth doing. He might very well be throwing money away."

"How much food?"

"Say four months, minimum. More if possible."

Jack stared out at the colorful constellation of the town, bright against the black of night. "This inside knowledge of yours . . . who else has it?"

"The infamous Dr. Cooke. Probably a few others." He

was tempted for a moment to tell Jack about Harold Blackburn.

"How sure are you of this?"

"Hard to say. After today, maybe fifty, sixty percent."

Jack stared into the amber of his drink. "Once this cold spell ends—if it happens—what sort of a world do you come back to?"

Carefully, Tyler said, "A person would have to think a project like this through, be sure it's something he really wanted to do."

Val and Rita came into the room. "It's early yet, guys," Val said. "How about some pinochle. Boys against girls."

CHAPTER 11 ——————————

TYLER HALTED his truck and extinguished the lights. The headlights that had followed him out of town most of the way from Rita's place glided smoothly past the turnoff to his ranch and continued on toward the Navajo town of Leupp. If it was Blackburn, he was being cagey.

Tyler put the pickup in gear and got moving again. It was almost one o'clock in the morning. The girls had whipped the guys soundly in pinochle, twice—Val subdued but competent, Rita out for blood. Tyler's blood. Jack had been right about Rita. She hadn't invited Tyler in for a nightcap, not that he would have accepted if she had. Conversation en route to her apartment had been limited to neutral, semiarticulate gruntings about the weather.

Autumnal temperatures across the country in mid-July, huge sunspots. News commentators were making the connection, but scientists were resoundingly pooh-poohing the idea. The public was vacillating in its collective opinion, pushed one way by increasingly sensationalistic journalism on one hand, pulled back by the soothing voices of scientific reason on the other, Dr. Malcolm Cooke's paramount among them.

But was it really a Tyler's cycle, or just a huge sunspot? Did a Tyler's cycle even exist, except in flawed theory? Had he done Jack a favor by suggesting that he and Val take refuge in a cave, for God's sake? Had Rita gotten in the final word with that quip about physicists and the sun? It was too late in the evening to worry about any of it now.

The house appeared ahead, dark, moon-silvered. He drove into the separate, barnlike garage and parked, got out, went into the house after only a brief glance up at the faded band of the Milky Way. The house was cold. He'd rebelled at the thought of firing up the heater in the summer, but if this got any worse he'd be forced to relent. He went down the hall to his bedroom, snapped on the light, saw the lump in his bed.

For a moment he stood there, stunned.

Carol.

Uh-uh.

Blackburn!

No. Absolutely not.

He moved quickly, opened a dresser drawer that held his shirts. He took out the .357 Magnum, thumbed back the hammer, aimed the weapon.

"Hey!" he yelled.

His eyes widened as the lump stirred, the blankets moved, and Gail Dionne looked out at him sleepily, eyes blinking.

"What time is it?" she asked.

"What . . . ? *What the hell are you doing?"*

"You don't have to yell."

"Get out of my bed!"

She propped herself up on her elbows. "Are you always so surly at . . . at . . ." She stared at the clock on the night table. "Quarter past one? My God, do you often drag in this late?"

He lowered the gun slowly. "Jesus H. Christ. Of all the crazy goddamned stunts. Are you out of your mind?"

"Is that a rhetorical question?"

"Do you think this is funny, Ms. Dionne?"

"It might be, if you'd only laugh."

Her hair was tousled, framing her pale, pretty face. Lips sensuous, eyes a vibrant blue, almost violet, regarding him with a kind of humorous curiosity. The blanket was pulled up almost to her chin.

He set the gun carefully on the dresser top. "How the hell did you get in?"

"The back door was open."

"No it wasn't. I remember locking up before I left this evening."

"Why bother? That no-name, discount hardware store junk was the easiest thing I've picked in years." She smiled.

"You picked my lock?"

"That thing resembles a lock like a canoe resembles the battleship *Missouri.*"

"Goddamn, you picked my lock. I don't believe it." He began to pace.

"Would you rather I'd used a crowbar?"

"And you're in my bed."

"Yes, it's not very comfortable, is it? Too soft." She sat up. The blankets tumbled down to reveal green and black flannel pajamas complete with a collar, buttons, pockets. "I thought about using the bed in the guest room, but then it occurred to me I might miss you if I did that. You're a difficult man to pin down, Dr. Tyler."

"I think maybe I'd better phone the sheriff."

"That's not the most popular response to finding a girl in your bed."

He stared at her, face blank. "In ugly pajamas."

"Aha! A sense of humor emerges. I was hoping it would." She wrapped her arms around her legs and put her chin on her knees.

"Counting on it, looks like."

"I suppose."

"You seem to think breaking and entering is a joke, Ms. Dionne. It's not."

"Gail. And no, I don't think it's a joke. It took me hours to fall asleep. A few times I almost got up and left."

He moved restlessly around the room. "Why didn't you?"

"I had to apologize—"

"*This* is your idea of an apology?"

She looked down at the bed around her. "No, but at

least I've got your attention, so here goes and I'd appreciate it if you'd let me say the whole thing in one piece. I'm sorry I tried to meet you in such a devious way at that bar, Red's Whatever. I enjoyed your singing, though. Really. But it was a lousy idea and I'm sorry it bothered you.'' She took a deep breath. ''I'm sorry for what I said in the parking lot too. I didn't mean it. And I'm sorry if I disrupted your lecture Friday morning, but by then I was getting desperate. I'm sorry for all the trouble I've caused you, really I am. I'd like us to start over again, as friends if possible.''

''In my bed?''

''Oh . . . I'm sorry about this too.''

He sighed, ran his fingers through his hair. ''I guess I haven't been very civil.''

''No, don't apologize. You wouldn't have done what you did if it hadn't been for me.''

''An explanation then. You . . . well, you look a lot like my ex-wife.'' He went to the closet and pulled out a picture in a small wooden frame. ''Carol.''

She stared at it. ''Oh my.''

'' 'Oh my' is right. When you showed up that night . . .''

''Just my luck. She looks more like me than I do.''

He smiled. ''I was tired.''

''It was late.''

They both laughed, and suddenly Gail blushed. Tyler put his gun back in the drawer.

''You took quite a chance,'' he said. ''What if I'd reacted violently? I could have, you know.''

She reached under the pillow and pulled out the snub-nosed .38, leaned over the side of the bed, put it in her purse.

''Jesus,'' he said.

''I'm a nut,'' she said, ''not an idiot. There's a difference.''

''Someday we'll have to debate that.''

''About that interview, Dr. Tyler . . .''

''Tyler. Everyone calls me Tyler.''

''Not Maurice, or Morie or Morris?''

"Not if you're hoping for any cooperation from me. Only my mother ever called me Morie."

"Okay, Tyler it is. I don't want you to confuse me with your mother too."

"This interview must be important to you."

She dug into her purse and opened a wallet, held a picture out to him. "I have responsibilities."

"Your daughter?"

She nodded. "Nichole. Nikki. She's six."

"Cute. Looks just like you. By the way, how does your husband feel about the tactics you use when interviewees get troublesome?"

"Ex-husband. He lost the right to worry about me about the time he started running around with girl number ten after we were married. We're divorced."

"Guy's out of his goddamn mind."

"Thanks. So now I've got this great little kid to worry about—the only thing Tony ever did right in his life—and if I don't get this piece on the editor's desk in Boston by Wednesday morning, I'm dead."

"And the physicist was being a jerk."

"Just intransigent and impossible. I've rescinded jerk."

He sat on the edge of an easy chair. "This stunt you pulled at Red's. You do it often?"

"Variations on the theme. Coffee houses, restaurants, bowling alleys. Even supermarkets. Bars, I haven't done much. You're my first singer."

"And it works?" He slumped back, adrenaline finally wearing off.

"Until now," she said. "I get them talking—"

"To the pretty lady."

She smiled. "Thank you. If people, men, respond to their illusions, it helps."

"I wouldn't exactly call you an illusion, but go on."

"Well, I get them talking, I listen, learn, and after a short while, usually no more than ten or fifteen minutes, I let on who I am and go on to a more formal interview, either then or later."

"And no one minds?"

"I had one minor glitch, before you. But for the most part it works well enough that my articles have a sort of special feeling to them that comes out. A kind of glow. I make people come alive on paper. I'm good at what I do and I make a decent living. I'm raising my daughter with no help from anyone." Her eyes were bright.

He glanced down purposefully at the bed. "And this little stunt . . ." He looked up again.

"Is a first, believe me. A last-ditch effort to get you to hear me out, maybe change your mind about me. And just in case you have any idea this was meant as an offering—" She threw aside the covers and stood up. The pajamas had sleeves to the wrist, bottoms that reached her ankles. "Sexy?" she asked.

"You buy that at Frederick's?"

"There's more." She tugged down one side of the pajama bottoms and exposed dark blue slacks, belted at the waist.

"Everything but a Russian greatcoat."

"Damn right."

"Looks warm," he said noncommittally.

"Fortunately, you keep the house fairly cool."

"Not my fault. The sun's anemic."

She cocked her head. "Tell me more, Tyler."

"You'll get your interview. Tomorrow. Right now it's late and I'm beat. I assume you've got a room back in Flagstaff, and a way to get there?"

"My car is half a mile up the road, parked under some trees. It's dark. I'm tired too, and it's over twenty miles to town. Be nice, Tyler, let me use the guest room."

He waved a hand toward the hall. "It's yours."

She picked up her purse. She brushed his cheek softly with her fingers as she went through the door. "You're a sweetheart; not much of a lecher, though."

"I'm too tired to be much of a lech."

"And I look a lot like your ex-wife."

He smiled. "But you're not, thank God, so that doesn't matter anymore."

* * *

SHE LAY BACK in bed, thinking. She wore only panties and the top half of her flannel pajamas, which came to just above midthigh. The room was cool, the house quiet.

Tyler was asleep, maybe thirty feet away. The male beast, resting, gaining strength. Somehow the thought, the *image,* was pleasing. Her heartbeat thickened. What was he wearing? Perhaps he slept in the nude, as she normally did. She imagined him lying there beside her, sleeping, dreaming, starlight falling across his shoulders. With that thought in mind, she drifted off to asleep.

"SONOFABITCH," Harold Blackburn growled. Stars blazed in the trees overhead. A rock dug into his spine through the sleeping bag. He scooted over awkwardly, irritated by the steady, untroubled sound of snoring that came from Gordy's bag, half a dozen feet away. It was cold outside. Too cold for this Boy Scout crap.

Something scuttled through the underbrush in the blackness where the slope of the ridge began to rise. Blackburn's hand settled on his big .45 automatic. He lay there tensely for a few minutes and then relaxed. He pushed a button on his watch and read the illuminated numerals: 3:22.

Was the girl still in there with Tyler, or had she left before he got home? Gail Dionne. She'd given her name to the operator when she phoned her sister in L.A.—said she was going to interview Dr. Tyler, said she was going to do some demolition work on him. Well, the doc had been home for over two hours, long enough for her to demolish him but good.

Dionne. Same girl who'd phoned the doc two nights ago, the one the doc had hung up on. The one in the bar the night before that. Interesting.

Blackburn ran her unexpected phone call through his mind again. He and Gordy had checked the tap, seen the red flashing light that meant something had been recorded, listened in amazement to the girl who'd used the doc's phone while he was out partying.

So, assume she was still there—her and the doc wrapped around each other like a pair of eels. Harry and Gordy could go in and roust them now or in the morning, but Blackburn thought the doc might've meant what he'd said about trying to put holes in Blackburn if he caught him on his property. It was the doc's turf. Besides, the doc might just play it smart and not grant the girl her interview. No sense making waves. Not yet anyway. Better to intercept Gail Dionne on her way out, see what she took with her, decide what to do about the situation then.

One thing was sure, she wasn't coming out again at least till morning. Blackburn closed his eyes and rolled over. His hand pressed into a soft, creamy substance—a stray, heated square of milk chocolate.

"Shit," he said, then licked his fingers.

CHAPTER 12 ─────────

"YOU GOING to sleep forever?"

"Mfff. Huh?"

He lifted his head. Gail was standing in the doorway to his bedroom, dressed in the same blue slacks she'd had on the night before, a straw-colored, long-sleeved blouse, and tennis shoes. Her hair was combed, spilling around her shoulders.

"Is this your rendition of the bachelor life?" she asked. "Drag in late, sleep late?"

"What time is it?"

"Almost ten-thirty, sleepyhead."

His head dropped back on the pillow. "I was kept up late by circumstances beyond my control. It still doesn't feel entirely real to me."

"How do you want your eggs?"

"Huh?"

"Are you always this sharp in the morning?"

"How would I know?"

"Okay, one more time. How do you want your eggs?"

"Over easy, bacon not quite crisp."

"Over easy. That means heated a lot on one side and only a little on the other, right?"

He lifted his head and peered at her with one eye. "Maybe I should do the cooking."

"Take a chance, fella." She made no move to leave.

He swung his legs to the floor. The sheets pooled around his waist and over his thighs. She took in his chest and his lean, well-muscled shoulders in silence.

He said, "Give me a few minutes before you start throwing food on the griddle. I need a shower."

"So do I." She gave him an uncomfortably direct look, an indecipherable smile.

He paused before replying, then said carefully, "The way you said that is most interesting, Ms. Dionne. It makes the physicist wonder what the lady would do or say if he invited her to get mutually wet. You see, he is by no means as honorable or principled as he may have appeared to be in the wee, tired hours of the morning."

"The lady would find such an invitation most awkward. To tell the truth, she might be tempted, and she's not sure the resulting confusion would allow her to conduct a professional, coherent interview."

"Are we going to talk like this all day?" he asked.

"God, I hope not."

"Good. There's a shower in the bathroom down the hall. It's all yours."

"Guess that's just as well. Is there a spare towel I can use?"

SHE PRESSED her face into the spray, felt warmth flood over her breasts, down the flat of her belly, down her legs. Sexual energy made her feel light-headed, almost giddy. God, what had all *that* been about?—the lady this, the physicist that, invitations and temptations. What she wanted was just to feel his arms around her, feel his chest pressing firmly against hers, trapping her against the tiled wall where there could be no retreat, no escape, have him kiss her mouth and throat, run his hands gently over her soapy breasts. Simple, bittersweet animal heat. How long had it been? Eighteen months? Almost two years?

"Oh God," she breathed into the steamy air.

TYLER HAD DONNED old khaki slacks and a flannel shirt. He watched Gail move about in his enormous pine-paneled kitchen, stacking dishes in the big double sink, cleaning the table. She had insisted—telling him it was his food so the least she could do was cook and then wash up. Her movements were economical, supple and easy, full of an athletic grace that fascinated him. She had smooth, creamy skin, almost unreal. She was glowing, alive, chatty in a pleasant way, unafflicted with the usual depressed miasma he'd almost come to believe was normal for women her age. He found he was glad to have her there, this strange, animated girl who picked locks and kept a .38 revolver under her pillow—loaded, no doubt.

Outside, the air was cold, the sky blue and bright. A large black bird hopped up on the concrete patio outside the dining room and regarded its own reflection in the window intently with yellow eyes, head cocked.

"Tell me who you are, Tyler," Gail said, slipping into a chair opposite him at the dining table.

"Am I being interviewed now, ma'am?"

"Sort of. I'd like to know who you are."

"Well, I'm thirty-seven, divorced, parents both deceased, a sister and brother-in-law living in Winnemucca, Nevada—"

"What was the name of your first dog?" Her elbows were on the table, face cupped in her hands, watching him.

"Uh, Dino. Just a mutt, but he liked to howl. Dad named him. God, that was a long time ago."

Slowly she drew him down into himself, into the dim tunnels of past, of memory; into proms, his first drink, his first drunk, his first kiss, first love, first car. He told her the names of his best friends at Griffin High School in Springfield, Illinois. His favorite classes had been, predictably, math and science. He'd been interested in the sun since about age fourteen. At ten or eleven he'd shoplifted a screwdriver from a hardware store, and the experience had so profoundly disturbed him, even though he hadn't been caught, that he'd never had the urge to steal again. His undergraduate degree had been earned at Ohio State, his doctorate from MIT, magna cum laude.

"We lived within ten miles of each other for a while," she said.

"While I was getting my graduate degree, you were chewing gum in high school."

Her eyes held his. "Albert's theory of relativity states that age differences tend to lose significance over time."

"I don't think that's exactly how it goes," he said, smiling. "So tell me about Gail Dionne."

He thought she'd resist, claiming this was his interview, not hers, but she complied with a willingness that surprised him. A sister, Nan; a brother, Warren; a mother who domineered by smothering, caring for them out of a need to control; a father who was often absent. Big frame house in Needham on the outskirts of Boston. She'd run away from home twice; once as far as the bus station in Boston at the age of fourteen; all the way to Richmond, Virginia, when she was sixteen. A year at Wellesley before demanding and crying her way to Penn State where she earned two degrees, in physics and journalism.

"Physics. I'm impressed."

"My mother wasn't. She wasn't ecstatic with journalism, either. Or Penn State. She wanted me to major in Tea and Etiquette and How to Marry Rich. She's something of a snob, I'm afraid."

"So with physics and journalism behind you, you ended up at *Parsec*."

"It seemed the natural thing to do. They liked me, liked my background, gave me a shot at it. It's working out."

"You don't have the usual Boston twang."

"Both my parents came from Minnesota. Not everyone from Boston sounds like they came from outer space."

"And you're still living in Beantown."

Her blue eyes pierced him. "Still close to Mother, isn't that what you mean?"

His eyebrows lifted. "No. Just an observation. Just trying to get to know the lady."

"Let's not start that again."

"Okay."

"To answer your question, I own my own house in Reading, twenty miles from mother. Tony's family lived in Reading, so we bought there, which was fine with me. Now Tony's gone, the house remains. It's home. Mom visits once a month or so, and I usually leave Nikki with her when I travel. At times it's a struggle, but I've found I'm stronger than she is. Need is a weakness in one's personal armor; when I got older I found that she needs me more than I need her. I'm not gloating, I'm just stating fact."

He noted the edge that had crept into her voice. "You're tough."

"You're damn right I am!" Her eyes blazed.

"And defensive as all hell."

She stared at him and then laughed suddenly. "That too." She looked at the coffee mug in her hands. Her face grew softer. "The scars we carry around from our battles for independence," she said, shaking her head. "All those ridiculous bloodied years."

Was it an interview, or a budding friendship? Tyler wondered. Or possibly a budding relationship. It was nearly one in the afternoon, and all she'd gotten from him was background information. And he from her. First-date, second-date, getting-to-know-you stuff. He didn't want it to end.

"Let's swap divorces," she said. "Tell me about Carol, I'll tell you about Tony."

He did. She did. He felt drawn to her, an uncomfortable feeling of need, of *wanting*. Carol was flighty, Tony was shallow; two of a kind, each in their own way. Carol was with Dewey Figge and the odds were Tony didn't have the slightest idea who he was with. Tyler and Gail had learned from their mistakes. Undercurrents of tension swept through their conversation, filled with an unbearable, unspoken longing.

"When does the real interview begin?" he asked.

"This is it."

"Do you usually go into this much background?"

"Never before." Her eyes dropped to her hands. She took a deep breath. "Maybe you'd better give me the nickel tour of the ranch or observatory or whatever you call this backwater castle."

"I figured you'd done that before I got home."

"I found the kitchen and the bedroom and the bathroom, but I didn't open drawers or snoop around or anything."

"You drew a strict line at breaking and entering."

"Right. I have scruples. And I noticed you have a computer running in the study or den—"

"Library."

"—or library, just what I was about to say. A new row of utterly meaningless numbers appears on the screen every few minutes. And the hard drive spins up. The computer was still running this morning. Are you going to tell me about that or is it a secret?"

"Maybe later."

He loaned her a sweater, which bagged around her, slipped on a light jacket himself, and led her outside to the observatory. The temperature was in the mid-fifties, a light breeze blowing. The sunlight was a mellow golden color.

"July in Arizona," she said, shivering. "You think it's really the sun?"

"Maybe, maybe not."

"How absolutely, incredibly scientific."

He grinned at her and produced a key, opened a door to the octagonal building.

"What every well-rounded solar astronomer should have," she said, walking into the room. "His own private observatory." She stopped, stared. "My God," she whispered, "what a beautiful instrument!"

A massive telescope dominated the center of the dimly lighted room, supported at both ends on an equatorial mounting. Stray light reflected off its lines and angles, limning its functional structure.

He stood beside her. "Sixteen-inch f/twelve primary mirror. Convex hyperbolic secondary mirror. At the moment it's configured as a coudé system. I completed it six years ago."

"You built it yourself?" she asked incredulously.

"It took over two years."

She touched the steel support structure reverently. "It's wonderful. These things have a beauty all their own, don't they?"

"They do indeed."

"You use it for solar observations?"

"Primarily, yes. The instrument is registered with the American Astronomical Society," he said with a hint of pride. "You're in the Tyler Observatory."

She wanted to photograph it, and the observatory, and Tyler. He was surprised to learn she had a camera with her. She went back to the house and returned with it.

"Parsec thrives on pictures," she said. "Hold still." She took his picture, then spent another five minutes on the observatory and the telescope, changing filters often.

He threw a switch on a panel mounted on a wall. Overhead, the roof rumbled, a crack appeared, and light spilled through. When the slit was about four feet wide, the rumbling stopped. The dome rotated and the sun appeared in the slit, now just beyond its peak elevation of the day.

She snapped more pictures, sunlight producing dark, dramatic shadows in the instrument's geometric framework.

"Can we look at the sun now?" she asked. "Through the telescope, I mean. I'd love to. I was at Palomar once, but they were taking a time photograph that was taking hours. All I did was ask questions and get in the way."

He smiled. "Of course."

"Is it dangerous? I mean, I know you can't just stare at the sun, and through a telescope . . ."

Tyler pulled a flat glass plate from a recess in the instrument. It was a deep blue, almost black.

"A Lyot interference filter," he said. "At the K Fraunhofer line at 3933 angstroms." He slipped it back in place.

"Calcium."

"Very good," he answered, pleased. "This particular filter has a bandpass of about a tenth of an angstrom, so very little light passes through. In addition, the secondary mirror is only partially aluminized. The amount of light that reaches the eye is low enough that a viewing shield is needed to block out ambient light. That answer your question?"

"Rather completely."

He selected an eyepiece and swung the telescope around, ducked his head under the hood and centered the image before turning the job of tracking over to the built-in microcomputer. He was quiet a long time, staring.

"Tyler . . ."

He pulled his head out of the hood. His face was white. "The spot's grown," he said. "And a number of smaller spots, almost pores, have popped up in the southern hemisphere. Here, have a look."

She sat in the viewing chair and pulled the black canvas hood over her head. He heard her gasp at the sight. The sun filled most of the field, a ghostly blue-violet silent seething ball of gas in the K-line filter, its surface covered with the distinctive "fishnet" pattern of emission at the K Fraunhofer line.

"At the, uh, left-hand edge of the sun—the eastern limb, as solar astromomers call it—the leading spot has moved to a position almost midway to center," he said.

"It's monstrous," came the muffled response.

"It's insane," he said quietly.

Her head came out of the hood. "Huh?"

"Nothing. Look at the brightness around the dark spots. Those are flares. Huge."

She went back to the telescope again. "I see them."

"I'll bet the neutron count at ground level here on Earth is skyrocketing," he mused.

"Is that bad, dangerous?"

"Not generally. But it's an indicator of solar activity—flares, ejected plasma."

"It's . . . it's fantastic," she breathed.

"Without actually taking a planimeter reading, I'd guess the main group of spots encompasses at least ninety billion square miles now," he said. "About fifteen percent or so of the apparent visible disk."

She gazed up at him again. "What's going on? Is the sun dying or what?"

"The sun's not dying."

"Then what?"

He saw fear in her eyes. "I don't . . . I'm not sure."

"Tell me about that theory of yours."

His eyes narrowed. "What theory?"

"I heard you came up with an unusual theory about the sun a couple years back that might be relevant now. No one seems to have any record of it, though—at least no one is talking about it, except in rumors."

A dawning light grew on his face. "So *that's* why you're here, talking to me instead of one of the really big guns in the business. That damned paper."

"The sun is news right now, Tyler. Anything having to do with the sun is news."

He took a step backward. "My God, I think I just woke up."

Her eyes flashed. She stood up suddenly and faced him, hands on hips. "And I think you just fell asleep," she said angrily. "I came out here to interview Dr. Tyler of Northern Arizona University, that's *all*. I do that kind of thing for a living, in case you didn't know. I found the man surprisingly attractive but obdurate, rather grim and inflexible for a few days, and then . . . then, after I got to know him better, I found to my surprise I like the unpredictable son of a bitch. Don't ruin things."

"You mean the interview?"

Tears glistened suddenly in her eyes. "Sure, that's right, the interview."

A faint roaring sound filled his ears. "Ruin *what?*"

She turned away. "Whatever you think, Tyler. Whatever the hell you think."

Quietly he said, "I've only known you a few hours . . ."

"No one's asking you to marry me or even hustle me into bed. I just . . . dammit, how come this is getting so messed up?"

"It's rather worse than you think. It's true—there is a theory."

She dried her eyes with the back of her hand. "Terrific. Why's that worse?"

"Because if the theory's right, it can't be printed, not right now. And if it's wrong, it's unprintable, period. Your story's down a rat hole."

She stared at him. "Dammit, Tyler."

CHAPTER 13 —————————

"TELL ME about this theory of yours," she said. They walked back to the house, Tyler leading the way.

"I'd call it more conjecture than theory."

"Conjecture away then."

"What's the point? It can't be published." They went inside. Tyler banged the door shut.

"Why not? What's the big deal?" She circled him, keeping him face-to-face with her. "Why can't we decide together what is or isn't publishable?"

"Your position is predetermined, that's why."

"Try me."

He began to move about the kitchen, building a fresh pot of coffee. "For the sake of argument, let's assume this trouble with the sun—whether or not it really *is* trouble— gets a lot of people spooked, perhaps even bordering on panic." He gave her a serious look. "Such an assumption might not be far from wrong in the near future if things continue as they are. Already there are signs. Then your story, my supposed theory, comes out in the next issue of *Parsec* or is leaked even sooner by someone on your staff. It might be enough to send a lot of people over the edge."

"That sounds pretty farfetched. In a nutshell—what does your theory say?"

"It's not for publication," he replied stubbornly. He

thought suddenly of Blackburn. Screw Harold Blackburn, this was Tyler's personal decision, not Blackburn's or whoever was behind him.

"For me then. Just me."

He gave her a stern look. "I'll hold you to that."

"Fine," she said curtly.

"In a nutshell—if the theory is right, and I'm not yet entirely convinced myself that it is—the sun may be in the beginning stages of a convulsive period of instability in which all but five or ten percent of its energy will be lost for a while. Things might get cold here on Earth, real cold."

She swallowed. "Would you excuse me, please? I've got to use the bathroom."

SHE SLIPPED a microcassette into the recorder and ran the microphone lead inside her clothing to the rear connection of the button mike on her shirt. Before leaving, she pushed the record button. "Tape one," she said softly. "July twenty-first. Dr. Tyler's residence."

Tyler was sipping coffee, standing by the sink and staring into space when she came into the kitchen.

"It's crazy," she said.

"I know."

"The sun is a stable entity," she said reasonably. "It's been shining for five billion years and it's expected to shine for about five billion more." She poured a cup of coffee and plopped down at the dining table.

He sat opposite her. "The sun may look simple," he said, "but that's just an illusion. It has flares, prominences, spots, spicules. It even rings like a bell. The surface is granulated with convection cells larger than the state of Arizona moving up and down at speeds of several kilometers per second. It's an incredible, churning, roiling sea of ions and tangled, stretched magnetic fields."

"Okay, so it's kinda messy. It's not going *out!*"

"I didn't say it was. If my theory is correct, however, it's going to, well . . . blink."

"Blink?" She frowned. "I know stars seem to twinkle, I even know why, but they don't blink."

"I don't expect you to believe it. I'm not even sure I want you to."

"Oh, great. What's that mean?"

He ran his fingers through his hair. "There's no story in this for you."

"Okay, there's no story," she fumed. "The sun is fizzling out and Dr. Tyler is going to sit on his information, thumbing his nose at the world."

"I sent a preliminary paper to Dr. Malcolm Cooke. If anyone is sitting on my theory, he is."

She leaned forward earnestly. "Maybe he is. Don't you think you still have some responsibility to get this out even if he is? Don't you think the public has a right to know, to prepare?"

"Prepare how?" he shot at her angrily. "Can you imagine a city like New York preparing—as you say—for a disaster of this magnitude? Millions of people competing for limited food and fuel supplies, fleeing the city in panic. Where do you think they'd go? What would they do?"

"Why should they go anywhere?"

"Human nature. Instinct and common sense tells us that as individuals we have a better chance to survive chaos if we aren't packed together like BBs. Cities are entirely artificial creations, hopelessly dependent on outside support for their existence. Remove that support, and they'd die. And they wouldn't die quietly."

She frowned at him. "Others would handle evacuation, if it came to that. It's not your problem."

"It damn well would be my problem if my theory turned out to be *in*correct, Ms. Dionne."

"Thank you for that, Dr. Tyler. What about the thousands of lives that might be saved if your theory *is* correct?"

"You haven't heard it yet."

"I said *if!*"

He closed his eyes and sighed wearily. "I've been over this a hundred times already. I'm not qualified to play God. I don't want the job." He paused, and then went on dejectedly. "Thousands might be saved if the theory proves out, but even more could lose their lives for no reason if it doesn't. It's a nightmare.'' He gazed at her. ''Do you believe any of this?''

''In what? Your theory? Like you said, I haven't heard it yet. At this point I'm by no means convinced.''

''At least you're honest.''

''In case you hadn't noticed, you're not exactly a pillar of faith yourself. By the way, how long does a . . . a sun blink last?''

''That depends on how you define it in terms of total flux levels.''

''Oh, for heaven's sake, rough it out. An hour? A year? A century?''

''As little as three weeks, maybe as long as two or three months. The phenomenon is related to that of sunspots, a bit more complex, however.''

For a long moment she stared at him. ''If you're right . . . how cold would it get?''

''Now *there's* a complicated problem for you.''

''Interstellar black body radiation,'' she said in a precise voice. ''Initial conditions reasonably well known.''

''I keep forgetting. You're one of us.''

''Haven't you at least taken a stab at it?''

''Anyone who lives in the desert knows the air temperature can drop sixty degrees overnight due to outward radiation if there are no clouds and the air is dry.''

''That's as far as you've taken it?''

He sighed. ''In the absence of clouds, both land and water could be handled in a relatively simple manner, straight black body radiation, like you said. But you have oceans and atmosphere, unknown currents in each with unknown mass and energy transport going on, probable fog and clouding which would further reduce dwindling energy input due to reflection, heat contained in the outer skin of the Earth itself, huge amounts of rain and snow when temperatures all over the world drop and wring out the atmosphere. Then, without clouds, more plunging temperatures, a sun supplying five or ten percent of its usual energy. A real SWAG—'' He lifted an eyebrow at her.

''Scientific wild-ass guess,'' she responded. ''Go on.''

"—would put the Earth's temperate zones in three or four weeks at a hundred to a hundred and forty below zero, Fahrenheit. Tropics at sixty to eighty below zero, poles as much as two hundred below."

"Jesus."

"Right. Let's hope it doesn't happen."

"My God, no one could go outside. Crops would be totally ruined. Ports would freeze."

He smiled grimly. "From the standpoint of survival the magnitude of the disaster would be beyond imagining. Look at just a tiny part of it—the heating of houses. The national power grid would fail, of course; but suppose it *didn't*, and temperatures fell to a hundred below. A typical residential heating system operating at full capacity is capable of maintaining an inside temperature roughly a hundred degrees above that of the outside. Even with fully functioning furnaces, houses might not get above zero degrees Fahrenheit. Without heat, of course, they would go to a hundred below. So, with or without power, houses would be uninhabitable."

"That's a frightening scenario."

He said nothing.

"Not a very believable one, though." She gave him a direct, skeptical look.

"Fine." He smiled at her.

"Dammit, don't play games. Temperatures would plummet if the sun were to, as you say, blink. But you haven't given the slightest reason why it might do so."

He shrugged.

"I deal in facts," she said. Her eyes bored into his. "Theories with sound scientific bases, conjecture in the scientific community that appears to be gaining support. *Parsec* readers aren't idiots."

"Good—that probably means you have job security."

"I'm going to *strangle* you. This isn't getting us anywhere. Why don't you explain your theory to me, just me. Convince me there *is* a theory and we'll hash out our differences about publication afterward."

"And if I say no in spite of your best efforts to change

my mind?—because I will say no, and you *will* try, I know.''

"Then it's no. Period. No story.''

"That doesn't sound like the Gail Dionne I've been listening to for the past few hours.''

"We haven't plumbed moral depths yet. Off the record means off the record. As a journalist, I have a code of ethics.''

"That's what I'm afraid of.''

"Tyler—''

He stood abruptly. "Come on.'' He picked up his mug and marched out of the dining room into the huge, underfurnished living room with its oak and brass, heavy beams, high ceiling, and rock fireplace, and from there to the library at the north end of the house.

Two thousand volumes in floor-to-ceiling shelves filled two walls. Textbooks, tomes of esoteric technical subjects, atlases, home improvement volumes, mathematics, history, rows of popular novels. The room had a dark and cozy feel to it, womblike. It reeked mustily of knowledge, comfortably self-important in the manner of all libraries.

A computer sat on a table against one wall—an Ardax-II, a powerful thirty-two-bit personal minicomputer. Its cooling fan made an airy droning sound in the dim, windowless room.

Tyler switched on the indirect, overhead lighting. On the wall above the computer were several framed pictures: Tyler, in his teens, wearing a baseball outfit; Tyler smiling, standing in the basket of a hot-air balloon; Tyler in a small group photograph, arms around an older man and woman.

"Your parents?'' Gail asked.

"Uh-huh.''

She leaned closer. "You look a lot like your mother.''

"So I've been told.''

Gail looked around. "Nice computer, nice house, fantastic telescope. How does the university professor manage all this . . . or is the question in hopelessly bad taste?''

He smiled. "It's not exactly a state secret. I came into an inheritance at just the right time to take advantage of the great bull market of the eighties.'' He shrugged. ''I was still in school. I didn't have time to deal with it personally. An investment counselor, a good friend of my father's and a hell of a sharp lady, turned a hundred and eighty thousand dollars into almost seven hundred thousand after taxes in about eight years. Some of that came in the mini-crash of eighty-seven. I had twenty thousand in put options working that Monday.''

''Nice.'' The word came out rather more wistfully than she intended.

''I've added to it since then.''

''So the professor thing is just a hobby?''

He gave her a sharp look. ''The professor thing is work I happen to love. Turning money into more money is the hobby, and, for me, not a very interesting one, I might add.''

''Sorry. That wasn't the most astute quickie observation I've ever made.''

The center of the room was taken up by a rectangular mahogany table almost eight feet long, four feet wide, with four matching chairs upholstered in natural suede. Tyler flicked a switch and several overhead spotlights cast a useful glow over the table.

He turned to her. ''There's something you ought to know. I'm not the only one who thinks the story shouldn't come out. I've been approached by . . . well, by someone with orders to make sure I don't go public for now, if you can believe that. He's got a lot of Neanderthal in him, and I imagine he'd take a dim view of my talking with you like this.''

She looked at him in wonderment.

''I know how that sounds,'' he began. ''But I swear—''

''Just a minute.'' She silenced him with a hand. She went to her room and fumbled in her overnight bag. A new microcassette went into the tape machine. ''Tape two,'' she said in a low voice. Back in the library, she handed him a photograph.

''This the Neanderthal?''

Harold Blackburn was staring at something off the picture to the left, a half smile frozen on his face.

Tyler sucked his breath in sharply. "Where did you get this?"

"Last Friday, before your morning lecture. The man seemed inordinately interested in you, so I took his picture."

"You followed me?"

She smiled. "Call me irresponsible."

"Impossible maybe."

"Tell me about the bouncer," she said, indicating the man in the picture.

"Harold Blackburn—at least that's the name he gave me." He told her what had happened after Thursday's class.

"Censorship," she said, excited. "That amounts to prior censorship. Unofficial, of course, but we can't let them get away with it."

"We? You offering to scare Blackburn off for me, or suggesting we shoot him and bury his remains in the south forty?"

"We have a court system in this country."

"Great. His word against mine, absolutely nothing else. You think many judges would get worked up over that?"

She bit her lip.

"The crazy part," Tyler went on, "is I agree with them, whoever the hell *they* are. Not with their methods, but with their concerns."

Her mouth tightened. "So the ape wins, then?" She tapped Blackburn's nose.

"The ape is just the tip of an iceberg. I'm not going to let him or the rest of the iceberg influence me one way or the other. I'm going to act as if he doesn't exist. Now, are you interested in hearing my theory or not?"

"I am. I'm not about to forget Harold Blackburn, though." She took back the picture covetously and wrote his name on the back with a pen.

"Suit yourself." He sat at the table, indicating for her to take a chair. "What do you know of the Spörer and Maunder minimums?"

She blinked. "Not a thing."

Tyler smiled. "I would've been surprised if you did. In one way or another, sunspots have been recorded for centuries. A period of reduced sunspot activity, called the

Spörer minimum, took place in the fifteenth century. The Maunder minimum came later, in the seventeenth century, documented by a great many sources. Together, these minimums seem to have been responsible for what is known as the Little Ice Age, in which the average temperature of the northern hemisphere was reduced by about one degree centigrade.''

"One degree constitutes an ice age?''

"The world's climate is a delicate thing,'' he said. "That slight reduction in temperature went on for many decades, and rivers and seas that had previously been clear froze over in winter. The Baltic Sea, the Thames in London, glaciation in the Alps. The why of it is still a mystery, but broad dips and swells in the weather appear related to sunspot activity.''

"The major ice ages,'' she said, sipping tepid coffee and making a face at it.

He nodded. "Possibly. In fact, that's what I was looking for when I first began to study mechanisms that might produce a long-term reduction in the sun's output. A drop of only one percent over a long period of time would be enough to cause a bitter ice age. The Little Ice Age was probably caused by a solar deficit somewhat less than that, and it didn't go on for thousands of years, either.''

A mantel clock in the other room struck two o'clock.

"We're still a long way from what you described, Tyler,'' Gail said impatiently.

"What do you know about catastrophe theory?'' he asked.

She frowned. "Is that a serious question?''

He rose, took a book off a shelf and handed it to her: *Catastrophe Theory for Scientists and Engineers*. She flipped through the pages briefly, noting the sprinkling of matrices, partial derivatives, and oddball integrals.

"Okay, so catastrophe theory exists. What is it?''

"Briefly, it seeks to determine the properties of systems of equations of great complexity. Poincaré was a pioneer in the field, as were Lyapunov, Smale, Whitney, Andronev.''

"Household names, every one,'' she said dryly.

He gave her an amused look. "I combined catastrophe theory with what is sometimes known as the dynamo theory, which seeks to show how a conducting gas flowing in a magnetic field can set up currents that maintain the field in spite of its natural tendency to die out. In short, dynamo theory is an explanation of how a magnetohydrodynamic perturbation might tend to propagate itself.''

"Instability," she said, ignoring the five-dollar words.

"Precisely. J. Larmor pioneered the theory. It was then taken up by Elsasser in the nineteen forties and Parker in the following two decades.''

"And after that, M. Tyler."

He bowed politely, smiling. "The problem is devilishly complex. To simplify the model, I made the assumption that the sun's core and radiative zone create and release energy in a stable, unvarying manner.''

"Sorry, I'm a semiphysicist, not an astronomer. Cores and radiative zones don't mean much to me.''

"The core of the sun is its nuclear furnace, a sphere of very dense gas at a high enough temperature and pressure to sustain nuclear-burning—energy production. Around the core is the radiative zone, a dense gas which does not move about freely. In both the core and the radiative zone there are no significant currents, no convection cells. Energy moves almost exclusively by means of radiation, taking millions of years to randomly 'walk' through the sun's material to the convection layer, where turbulence and great rivers of ionic gas dominate in the transport of energy to the surface.

"Because it takes so long for radiation to reach the convective layer, about ten million years, I made the assumption that something in the convective layer must be responsible for any short-term radical fluctuations in solar output—fluctuations measured in units of several hundred thousand years or less. The convective layer is roughly two hundred thousand kilometers deep, a heaving ocean of plasma, electric currents, and knotted, stretched magnetic fields.

"I sought to re-create this region of the sun in terms of an unusual statistical model, using magnetohydrodynamics, turbulent flow, heat and pressure gradients, electric and magnetic fields, energy balances—using catastrophe theory.''

"It sounds impossibly complicated.''

"It is. That is to say, no one could hope to solve the

resulting nonlinear systems of equations that spring from all these interrelated factors.''

''But Hal over there might,'' she said, indicating the computer.

He grinned. ''Yes, Hal, as you call him, might. In fact, Hal has . . . is.''

''Is? I thought you sent Dr. Cooke some sort of a paper a couple of years ago.''

''I did. 'Hal' is currently working on the most recent version of the statistical-numerical model.''

''How many have there been?'' she asked, looking into his eyes, her face pale and pretty and distracting under the soft lighting.

''Four major ones, each a bit more inclusive and refined than the last. I sent the results of the second simulation to Dr. Cooke—prematurely, it would seem. It's a tendency I've got, but I'm learning.''

''And the upshot of all this was?''

Tyler took a black three-ring binder from the bookshelf and opened it, turned to a page flagged in red.

''This was the first unstable solution,'' he said. ''It represents almost a week of computer time on the Ardax.''

''Hal.''

He smiled. ''Hal.''

She gazed at a graph of solar flux versus time. The plot showed power holding steady, then sagging, diving almost vertically to a fraction of its normal level before climbing steeply again, terminating in a series of mild oscillations.

''It took me months to even consider the possibility that the computer simulation might represent a real phenomenon, an actual possibility. In that time, I went over assumptions and program logic with a fine-tooth comb; but, as you can see, the result repeats itself remarkably well in succeeding runs.''

Gail flipped through pages of graphs, all similar, with only the slightest of variations between them.

''What you see is a modification of the dynamo theory in action,'' Tyler said. ''The sun's output is driven down to less than ten percent of its normal value for a flicker of geologic time by energies that feed upon themselves. A point of criticality is reached and energy flow is driven back up. It's known, formally, as a cusp catastrophe.''

She was quiet for a long moment, then she said, "If energy flow from the core isn't interrupted, where does it go?"

"Smart girl. The answer isn't easy to pull out of the program results, but I have reason to believe that much of the energy is going into the creation of enormous magnetic fields, as much as eighty percent. The rest may be going into an expansion of the solar volume.''

"The sun's getting larger?" she said incredulously.

"Not measurably." He folded his hands on the table before him. "Before nuclear reactions were understood or even thought of, scientists sought to explain the sun's energy in a multitude of ways. Infalling meteorites was one. Another hypothesis was that the sun was contracting, and the energy resulting from that contraction was responsible for the sun's output. Calculations by Lord Kelvin and von Helmholtz showed that a shrinkage of just twenty meters a year in the solar diameter would generate sufficient energy for the sun to shine at its present rate for something over forty million years.

"Later, the geological record indicated that the sun must have been shining for several billions of years, so the theory was abandoned. Still, it can be shown that if the sun's output were channeled into nothing but an *expansion* of its own diameter, it would grow at a rate of only about two meters per month. Such an increase couldn't possibly be detected in anything less than a hundred years.''

She got up and began to pace. "So what you're saying is, energy production goes on, but energy doesn't get out?"

"That's right. For a short time the convective layer of the sun acts as an insulator, powered by the sun itself.''

Staring at the rows of books before her, she said, "It all sounds like Stephen King, not Stephen Hawking.''

He chuckled.

She whirled on him. "It scares the hell out of me. You don't *sound* lunatic.''

"But the theory does.''

"I don't know. It's way out of my league. This is postdoctoral stuff you've been at for years. I've forgotten much of what I learned to get my undergraduate degree. The words sound plausible in a vague way, but when you get around to stating conclusions it all sounds so unlikely.''

''Not very publishable, huh?''

''Don't start that with me again, buster.''

He smiled at her.

''Darn coffee,'' Gail said. ''I'll be right back.''

WHILE SHE WAS GONE, Tyler phoned Jack's home, wondering if his friend was going to take his advice of the previous night. The call was taken by an answering machine.

''Gone spelunking,'' said Val's recorded voice. ''Leave your name and number and we'll get back to you.''

Tyler grinned. He left a short message and hung up with a damned-if-you-do-damned-if-you-don't feeling in his chest.

''TAPE THREE,'' Gail said, before leaving the bathroom.

In the library, Tyler was sitting with his eyes closed.

''Penny for your thoughts.''

He turned, looked at her. ''You know what the temperature of a sunspot is?''

''I've waited all my life for someone to ask me that,'' she said, taking a seat beside him.

''Want to quit talking about the sun, then?''

''No way, Professor. Continue.''

He showed her the hydrogen-alpha photographs of the sun he'd shown Jack the night before. ''The dark inner spot here is called the umbra. The somewhat lighter region surrounding it, still darker than the photosphere, is called the penumbra.''

''Darker because they're cooler.''

''Right. In fact, the umbra is about two thousand degrees centigrade cooler. That such a temperature differential can exist on the sun in such a turbulent environment for such a long time, as much as four or five months, is remarkable. It shows that an incredibly effective refrigeration or insulating process is going on.''

''Lending support to your hypothesis.''

''Perhaps. Anyway, the phenomenon of sunspots is

enormously complex. It's certain that a lot of energy is going into huge magnetic fields, since sunspots are associated with fields several thousand times stronger than the sun's general field.''

She gazed searchingly into his eyes. ''You know, I don't want to believe any of this.''

''Do you, though?''

''I . . . don't know. If stars blink, how come no one's ever seen it happen before?'' A challenging look filled her eyes.

He stood and snapped off the lights. ''Let's continue this in the observatory. I want to photograph today's sun.''

She went outside with him.

Tyler opened the door to the observatory and ushered her inside. ''To understand how stars might blink unobserved, you have to know something of the probable frequency and nature of what's happening. Several fairly unlikely conditions have to occur simultaneously in order to initiate the process, which, by the way, I call a Tyler's cycle.''

''How very pompous of you, sir.'' She flashed him a smile as the dome rumbled open.

''Yes, quite,'' he said in his best British accent, setting up the instrument to allow her to view the direct image while he readied the camera. ''Four primary factors seem operative, internal conditions existing within the sun or star, and when the odds of the occurrence of each are multiplied, the odds of a cycle occurring in any given year in a star are roughly one in a billion.''

''One in a billion . . .''

''It could be as little as a hundred million or as great as ten billion. I only use the geometric mean as a matter of convenience.''

''One 'blink' every billion years?''

He nodded. ''If we take the time of reduced luminosity as one month, then throughout the galaxy one star in roughly twelve billion is actively undergoing a cycle. With a hundred billion stars in the galaxy, of which less than twenty billion are of the proper type, no more than one or two will be in the midst of a cycle at any given moment.''

''Needle in a haystack.''

''Worse. Of the twenty stars each year that blink, and I

sometimes think the actual number may be less than half that, many will be on the opposite side of the galaxy, too remote to have ever been cataloged, others obscured by clouds of galactic dust.''

''Not much chance of spotting one, huh?''

''Not much. It's very much the opposite of trying to find a supernova explosion. A supernova draws attention to itself with violence, but how do you find a star that simply goes dim and then returns to normal brilliance? It's not surprising that none of them have ever been caught in the act.''

''Except our own, lucky us.''

''Maybe.''

''Maybe?''

''You keep forgetting. There might be no such thing as a Tyler's cycle.''

She peered into the eyepiece. ''Wouldn't your theory make a big splash in the scientific world?'' Her voice was muffled by the viewing hood.

''Not very.'' He pried open a film canister. ''There's a big difference between proof and hypothesis, between feeling something strongly in one's heart and proving it beyond all reasonable doubt. To be accepted, this thing will need a scrutiny by the scientific community that could easily last decades. I practically stumbled over it. I'm just one person.''

''And Hal.''

''And Hal, faithful electronic companion.'' He held the camera, ready to attach it to the eyepiece mounting. ''How's Shamash doing now?''

She withdrew her head. ''The big spot is still huge, and I think those little spots we saw earlier are bigger now.''

''Let's have a look.''

He sat, adjusted the eyepiece. ''My God,'' he said, almost too low for her to hear.

CHAPTER 14 —————

"My God," breathed Dr. James Carleson.

"I was thinking this too," replied the Belgian scientist, Marcel Vergucht. He sat with his elbows on the Kitt Peak observation table, staring at the image of the sun.

The pores that had been discovered earlier that morning in the southern hemisphere had erupted into spots that were spreading at a fantastic rate, already 70,000 by 120,000 kilometers, an area of over three billion square miles.

For the first time since the sun had started acting up, Dr. Carleson felt a twinge of panic. His knees felt trembly. The sun hung over the western sky, a yellow-orange ball even though sunset was still a few hours away. Solar flux levels had fallen to 96 percent of normal as recorded by OSO-15, implying an average surface temperature of 5,740 degrees Kelvin, sixty degrees low.

Dr. Carleson was weary. Both Linda Moell and Dr. Raymond Abbott had grown increasingly skittish as the day wore on. The outside temperature at Kitt Peak was fifty-one degrees, down over thirty degrees from the average at that time of year.

"Photograph the new spots at five-minute intervals," he told Marcel. "Extreme close-ups. Give Ray something to do."

"Yes, Doctor," Marcel said quietly.

James Carleson phoned across to the magnetograph tower and spoke with Dr. Chang-sun Chang.

"Chang, Jim . . . How does the field look in the primary spot group?"

Chang-sun answered in a suppressed Korean accent. "It is up to 28,850 gauss, Jim. Nice calcium flaring in the corona, have you seen?"

"We have. Look, Chang, I want a full-disk magnetogram and a detailed partial of the new group."

"Can do," Chang said, and Dr. Carleson could almost see him bowing. "Is that all?"

"Yes, for now."

He rang off. 28,850 gauss. Good Lord. He tried not to think of the energy contained in such a field.

THE SACRAMENTO PEAK OBSERVATORY in New Mexico, east of Alamogordo, was originally designed to study solar flares. As time passed, its scope broadened to that of a general solar observatory, yet it retained its place as one of the premier laboratories for flare research in the world.

Its director, Dr. Avery Charles, was crouched over the viewing table with his assistant, Dr. Richard Zadra, when the big flare of July 21 erupted. Viewed in retrospect, the Kitt Peak magnetogram showed the emergence of the magnetic field of over 44,000 gauss near the sun's equator, aimed almost directly at the Earth as though it were a gun. The field was broad and twisted, covering a wide area, reversed in polarity from Hale's Law, a sure sign of trouble. It showed up suddenly, associated with nothing more prominent than a meandering dark filament that lay upon the solar surface like a root that had broken through forest sod.

Charles and Zadra were examining the smaller, newer spots as the sun lowered in the sky, the heliostat rotated westward to direct the sun's rays into the instrument. A subdued bustle of activity filled the observation room.

Both men crowded forward as the flare suddenly appeared in bloodred hydrogen-alpha light on the table, expanding within minutes to an enormous twisted blot.

Lights flickered in the room, went out momentarily, caught again, and then went out entirely. Emergency lighting came on.

"Photographs!" Dr. Charles cried. In seconds, film was being exposed as the flare blossomed. The local time was 6:34 in the afternoon.

In orbit, OSO-15 recorded a huge burst of X rays at 1.78 angstroms from twenty-five-times ionized coronal iron at temperatures exceeding one hundred million degrees. The data was down-linked just twelve seconds before OSO-15 went off the air permanently. At Sydney, Australia, the receivers of the big radio telescope saturated with a great burst of Type-III radio emission at 11:34 in the morning, while the Mount Norikura solar observatory on the Japanese island of Honshu recorded the flare at 10:34 A.M. and continued its observations throughout the day.

The energy of the flare was a hundred billion billion megajoules, the equivalent of twenty-five billion hydrogen bombs, each with a yield of one megaton. A tiny wanderer in the path of a high-speed cloud of protons and alpha particles, the Earth was severely bombarded. Auroral displays on that and succeeding nights were like none that had ever been seen before.

HAROLD BLACKBURN PACED in the growing shadows under a stand of ponderosa pine where he and Gordy had maintained a vigil on Tyler's road since early morning, three miles from the house. At three that afternoon, Gordy had made a run into Winona for provisions: cold, soggy hamburgers and fries, beer, pretzels, chocolate bars.

One of the old tunes, "I Heard It Through the Grapevine," by Marvin Gaye, was playing on a radio that sat on a rock when a burst of static drowned out the music. White noise spewed from the speakers. Blackburn grabbed the radio and shook it.

"Piece of Japanese junk," he growled.

"Probably made in Korea or Taiwan, Harry," Gordy said, his eyes on the road to the north. "Maybe Singapore."

"Slant-eye shit, then."

He changed stations, found nothing, slammed the radio back down. "Shit," he said. He looked off toward Tyler's house, hidden by the rolling terrain. "What the hell's going on over there, anyway?" As he fingered the grip of the .45 in its shoulder holster, the music returned, filled with solar grit.

AT PULLIAM MUNICIPAL AIRPORT, Dr. Malcolm Cooke labored down the ramp to the terminal floor with his coat in hand. The exertion caused a sheen of sweat to pop out on his brow. Before proceeding to the baggage claim area, he went into the bar and ordered a plain Coca-Cola. The bartender gave him a sidelong look as he made change.

Dr. Cooke collected his bags and found a taxi standing in the freakish orange light of dusk. He directed its driver to take him to Hotel Weatherford on North Leroux Street. He checked in and then debated the wisdom of phoning Dr. Maurice Tyler right away, finally deciding the distasteful task would keep until morning.

He ate a late dinner at the hotel's restaurant—roast duckling, asparagus, baked potato, half a liter of claret—and sat in his room going over notes of the points he wished to make during the Tuesday taping of the "Tonight Show." As he read, his thick, parted lips moved slightly, his breath rasped sibilantly in the quiet of the room, glasses perched on the end of his florid nose, cheeks puffed and pink.

Not until the following morning would he hear news about the flare.

THE DIM RED LIGHTS in the darkroom went out, leaving Tyler and Gail in total blackness. Chemical smells filled the room, the pungent odor of acetic acid.

"Very clever, Professor," she said.

"What?"

"Get a girl alone and helpless in your darkroom and then arrange for the lights to go out."

"Alone, yes; helpless, by no stretch of the imagination."

She heard him groping in the dark, and suddenly a portable lantern illuminated the room in the dimmest imaginable amber glow. He continued his agitation of the bleach-fixer.

Electrical power was reestablished and red lights came on again just as a timer made a mechanical burring sound. Tyler lifted the picture from the bath of fixer and plunged it into the final fresh-water rinse. He snapped on the white lights.

"Done," he said. He rinsed the picture awhile longer and then clipped it with the others to a line that ran overhead.

"This one's nice," Gail said, indicating a blue-violet shot of the entire sun.

"It's yours. I've got the negative."

"Thank you. After all the trouble you gave me, I think I deserve it."

"All the trouble I gave *you?*"

"I've never worked so hard for an interview in my life."

He dumped fixer and developer down the drain. "I think we better have that talk about publication now."

"Forget it."

He gave her a sharp look. "Hey, you promised—"

She touched his arm. "I've had time to think it over, what you said about panic, people fleeing the cities. You're right. Now's not the time for it."

"Not spoken like a true reporter," he said suspiciously.

"Wrong. What I've heard today has been very persuasive, Professor. This thing with the sun was beginning to worry even *me,* and your little spiel hasn't helped things one damn bit." She walked to the edge of the confined space, spun, and faced him. "If temperatures are going to drop as low as you think they might, then almost nothing anyone does in the next few days or weeks will do any good. And if you're wrong, the story could cause bedlam the likes of which Orson Welles never dreamed."

"So—you're learning to play God, too."

"Don't rub my nose in it," she said, annoyed. "I didn't have all the facts before, now I do."

"Sorry. So, you believe this theory of mine? Such as it is."

"No," she said, too quickly. "Yes . . . Oh, I don't know."

"That's a nice mix."

She gave him a troubled look. "I guess I believe, but I don't want to. I have an awfully nifty little daughter in Los Angeles right now who needs me, who has to grow up and experience the world, date boys, go to proms, get married, have kids of her own—"

He saw a wink of moisture in her eyes as she turned away. An uneasy feeling stole over him, a flash of terrible comprehension. Until now, the contemplated disaster had been scientific surrealism to him; theory, not fact. An intellectual exercise, not unlike Einstein imagining a nuclear chain reaction, a fission bomb, and thinking: *Hey, that might just work!*

He hadn't comprehended the suffering a Tyler's cycle would create, the degree of misery and death. His mind had circled the image of a frozen world, frozen cities, failing to understand what it all would mean. The scale had been too vast, the focus too broad. Now, suddenly, he saw Gail frozen, limbs rigid, lips pulled back in a crusty grimace as her eyes stared milkily out at sheets of driving snow.

He closed his eyes and stifled a shudder, seeing, at last, beyond the wonder and extraordinary improbability of it all to the horror of what would happen if his theory proved to be true.

"Are you hungry?" he asked gently.

"Starved."

"Let me take you out to dinner. Someplace nice, with dim lighting, fantastic food, and formal, obsequious waiters."

"This is so sudden, sir." She smiled, trying to break her own somber mood.

"I found you in my bed, remember."

"That's right, you did. But I've got a six-twenty flight to L.A. tomorrow morning—and worries I didn't have a couple hours ago. I'm really not up for restaurants and all that.''

"I understand," he said softly, trying not to sound overly disappointed.

"I could whip up something here, though. You have food, I have incredible culinary skills.''

"Hardly sounds fair. You made breakfast." He pushed open the door and switched off the lights.

The darkroom was a low cinder-block addition to the observatory, with a door in the north wall of the dome. They came out into the high, shadowy room where the telescope stood in majestic silence.

"Come on," Gail said. "It'd give me another chance to impress you with my domesticity.''

He shook his head morosely. "Women's lib has been set back a decade.''

"If you believe that, meet me on the firing range some day. Rapid fire, thirty feet." Her eyes sparkled.

"No, thank you. My kitchen is your kitchen.''

They crossed to the house on a flagstone path. Gail began sorting through Tyler's kitchen, opening cabinet doors as he sat on a barstool at the counter, watching.

"Your interview is a shambles," he said.

She opened the refrigerator and began assessing its contents. "Not really. There's no theory, no blockbuster story—that's what I'll tell my editor, Chris Stampfli—but there's a nice article about a super little solar observatory way out in the Arizona desert, operated by a sincere and rather hopelessly proper university professor whose first, last, and only apparent love is the sun.''

"Proper!" He laughed.

Her eyes held his. "Depressingly so.''

"Good God," he said carefully, "if you only knew what I've been thinking the past few hours.''

"Tell me.''

He smiled. "Not a chance.''

She turned back to the refrigerator. "Perhaps maddeningly discreet is a better way to put it. Where do you keep the butter?''

"Try the cheese bin.''

"Figures."

In the living room, the clock struck six. Tyler turned on the kitchen television. "News," he said.

"Got to keep up on those current events," she said over her shoulder.

White noise filled the screen. He locked the dish on a different satellite and was rewarded with a picture of questionable quality, a war movie. A few channel changes brought in a news program, filled with hash.

"Sun's really playing hell with it," Tyler said. On the screen, a man in a white lab coat was talking rapidly, gesturing with his hands. Tyler recognized Dr. Wesley Potter of the Mount Wilson Observatory.

". . . first correlation of solar phenomena and conditions here on Earth was in September 1859, when the English amateur astronomer R. C. Carrington actually witnessed a solar flare much like the one that occurred, well"—he glanced at his watch—"just about thirty minutes ago. Of course, Carrington's flare was probably no larger than the great flare of, ah, August 7, 1972—nothing like the present doozy, which, of course, is still in progress."

The camera jostled, tilted a bit, focused obliquely on what Tyler recognized as the observation table at the solar tower telescope at Mount Wilson. The sun was a deep burgundy red. A bright twisted region was near its equator, the earlier spots dark and prominent.

A newsman's voice came on. "The flare, which, ah, showed up a few minutes after five-thirty Pacific time—Pacific *day*light time—disrupted communications and caused power outages across the country. This is it here, right, Doctor?"

"That's correct," Dr. Potter said, off-camera. "Here at the Wilson solar telescope we form a sixteen-inch image."

"My God, which way is *up* on that thing?" the reporter wailed.

Gail came to Tyler's side. "Poor slob is on live. Scooping the world in style. Look, they're using a hydrogen-alpha filter."

"Very good," Tyler said.

"I'm a quick study. Can we see any of this on your telescope?"

He shook his head. "Not now. The sun is below the ridge this time of day."

"Too bad." Her hand rested on his shoulder and seemed to burn there. A pleasant tingle went through him.

Someone at the Mount Wilson observatory said, "Hey, watch where you point that light! Jeez, he ruined *that* photograph, I'd say."

"Sorry," the reporter gasped in dismay. "Bring it over this way, Fred. Can't we go ambient?"

The camera swung, found Dr. Potter's thin, handsome, suntanned face again. In a more steady voice, the reporter said, "Looks pretty bad, doesn't it, Doctor?"—holding the microphone out with a freckly hand.

"Bad?" Potter seemed genuinely surprised. "Heavens no. Oh, we'll have trouble with radio and television for a while, like we have been. These power outages won't continue for long. For anyone who has never seen the aurora borealis, however, tonight will be the opportunity of a lifetime. The show should be top-notch above the fortieth parallel wherever the sky is clear."

"Aurora borealis," the commentator repeated, interested. "The northern lights. Could you explain exactly what causes them, Doctor?"

Tyler changed the channel, passing through a fuzzy baseball game and a sitcom before finding another news program.

"—in Denver, Colorado," a young, pretty newswoman was saying, "where"—she looked around and smiled at the lawn and trees around her—"the temperature at two in the afternoon is a chilly fifty degrees, thirty-five degrees below normal for the date." The camera followed along as she took a few steps toward a young man with long, wind-sprung hair, standing nervously beside a ratty jumble of scientific equipment.

"Edgar Collins is a senior engineering student at the University of Denver," she said with practiced ease. "Edgar, what can you tell us about this apparatus?"

Edgar Collins grinned and spoke hurriedly into the microphone. "Well," he began pointing, "this is an Eppley pyrheliometer; thermocouples in the back, here, wired to a digital voltmeter—"

"What does it all *do*, Edgar?" she broke in smoothly.

"Uh, well, it measures the intensity of radiation from the sun. You see, there's a black plate over here that—"

"And what have you found with all this?"

He lowered his eyes. "Well, it sort of looks like the, uh, sun's energy is dropping off. I mean, just a couple of days ago it was pretty much normal, but now it's four or five percent low, at least as near as I can tell. I've corrected for atmospheric absorption and all that and it's going down, I'm sure of it." He looked up. The camera caught a gleam in his eyes.

"Why do you suppose that is, Edgar?"

"Well, the spots on the sun, I guess. The sun's, I dunno, fritzing out or something, losing power."

She smiled, thanked the boy, and returned control to the studio.

An anchorwoman of coast-to-coast renown gazed into the camera and said, "At twenty minutes past noon today in Charleston, South Carolina, a man shot his wife and two children to death and then turned the gun on himself." Her face remained serious but untroubled. "The man, Jason Lee Lansford Jr., has undergone treatment at various state hospitals in the past eight years. He was unemployed and, acquaintances say, depressed about his inability to find work. In a note found in the Lansfords' apartment, Lansford expressed fears that the sun was, in his words, 'going to explode and blast the Earth with fire and I ain't going to have my wife and kids go through all that.' " A wry smile flickered across her face.

"A search in British Columbia has been mounted for two brothers, Robert and Scott Witherell, who did not show up as planned at the town of Chinook Cove Saturday afternoon. The two were on a four-day outing, hiking alone in the Canadian wilderness. Nighttime temperatures in the mountainous region north of Kamloops have been reported in the low teens as the unseasonable cold spell gripping the northern hemisphere continues."

A short clip followed, in which a CalTech professor of physics, Dr. Stephen Bell, captain of a large, cluttered desk, expounded on the effects of solar flares and charged particles entering the Earth's magnetic field.

"During periods of solar activity, such as we're experiencing now," he said in a precise and fatherly voice, "the impact on the magnetic field of the Earth can be considerable. The horizontal component becomes unstable and compasses can become quite unreliable. Hikers would be advised at this time to navigate in the wilderness by means other than a compass—the stars, for instance. In addition, large electrical currents can be induced in long runs of conducting wire, and components in power stations can be burnt out or relays tripped, causing temporary blackouts."

The camera returned to the studio newswoman.

"The miniexodus from New York City continues. For the third day, the twenty-four-hour bridge and tunnel tallies have shown significantly more vehicles outbound from Manhattan than inbound. The deficit, recorded at midnight on Saturday, July twentieth, was 48,870 private vehicles, up from Friday's total of 33,250. City transportation officials pointed out that much of this is the usual weekend junketeering, and the trend will probably reverse itself on Sunday and Monday; however, overall traffic volume is clearly up from that of the previous weekend, and many motels, hotels, and rental cabins in upstate New York are operating at almost full capacity, many of them rented out for as long as two months."

Tyler switched the television off.

"My God," Gail said. "Already they're beginning to go off the deep end."

"I'm not surprised. This is just the fringe of society, the unstable ones and maybe a few with intelligence and imagination. If the greater mass of society begins to panic, what we've seen so far will be nothing."

She took her hand from his shoulder. "I doubt that all this news coverage is helping things any."

"You're probably right. But that's how it's always been. Anything to sell cars and cornflakes."

* * *

SHE PUT TOGETHER a spinach salad with bottled dressing, halibut steaks with tartar sauce and lemon wedges, green beans, a small fruit salad for dessert. The sun went down and the light left the sky and, except for a yellow three-quarter moon overhead, the land grew dark.

It was nine-thirty when Gail gathered up her belongings and stuffed them into her travel bag.

"Got everything?" Tyler asked. "Pictures, pajamas, camera, gun?"

"I think so," she said with a thin smile.

"I'll drive you to your car."

He draped a jacket over her shoulders for the walk out to his truck. He started the engine and soon they were bumping along the rutted road in an uneasy, expectant silence. Gail stared out the side window.

"Here," she said, after they'd gone about half a mile. He pulled to a stop.

They got out. Her car was nowhere in sight. He switched on a flashlight and she led him into the trees, into darkness. Ahead, the yellow beam glinted off chrome.

She opened the driver's door, swung her bag across to the passenger's seat, then turned to face him.

"It's been a memorable twenty-four hours, Professor."

"Says the lady."

The light reflected off the ground, throwing her face in shadow. He snapped it off.

"Says the lady," she repeated quietly.

Clumsily he found her hands in the darkness. They were damp, cool.

"I hope I'm wrong," he said. "About the sun."

"Me too."

His hands tightened on hers. "Go get Nikki and come back. Don't go to Boston."

She was quiet for a few seconds, not even breathing. Then he felt her head shake. When she spoke again, her voice was soft and sad. "I've got a story to turn in, but the offer was . . . nice, very nice."

"I'd like to insist."

"And I'd like to accept, but I can't let this thing run my life. I've got to keep on like I always have."

An emptiness settled inside him. "The offer stands regardless. Anytime."

She pulled her hands free and reached up, found his face. She gave him a gentle, nibbling kiss. "You're a nice man once the walls are breached, fella. The world could use a few more like you. If I happen to be in the neighborhood someday and give you a call, you'll remember me?"

"Most definitely." He wanted to say more but his mouth felt numb.

"Good." She pulled away. "No long good-byes, huh?" She got into the car, started the engine, backed out, waved, and drove away.

He took a step forward and then watched the tiny red taillights until they disappeared into the night. With a soulful, wretched sigh, he climbed into his truck and went back to the big, empty house.

CHAPTER 15 ———————————

"LIGHTS COMING," Gordy called out.

Harold Blackburn popped the last of a Hershey bar in his mouth. He went to the edge of the road, loosened the .45 in its holster, and settled into a crouch behind a thick stand of juniper bordering the road where they'd decided to make the stop, three miles from Tyler's house, two miles from the road out to Leupp. In the distance, the lights of a car came winding down off a low ridge, flickering through the trees.

GAIL DIONNE FELT a thickness around her heart, a heaviness that bordered on pain. Tyler, Nikki, deadlines at an office in downtown Boston, evil black spots erupting on the sun. It all added up to too many choices, too many dire consequences, too narrow a gap to negotiate safely at the usual speed and no way to slow it all down. How easily her well-regimented world had been turned upside-down! An aching need came over her to feel Nikki in her arms again, to know her child was safe.

A dinged and rusted Chrysler loomed unexpectedly in her headlights, blue, slanted across the road. Juniper on one side, an unnavigable rocky downslope on the other. A man was behind the wheel, head back, eyes closed.

Gail slammed on her brakes and looked out at the tableau uncertainly. As she reached into her purse and withdrew the .38, the passenger-side window exploded in a shower of glass and a man thrust an enormous gun into the breach. She dropped her weapon on the floor almost without thinking.

"Mrs. Dionne," he said, "I am an agent of the federal government. Turn off the engine, please, *now.*"

The man in the Chrysler got out, approached on her side.

She turned the key and the engine stopped. "It's *Miss* Dionne, Mr. Blackburn." She nudged her gun beneath the seat with a foot. "And you're a federal agent like I'm the Queen Mother."

He grinned, stuffing his gun back in its holster. "Call me Harry." He reached in and grabbed the travel bag off the front seat, and her purse. "Hand over the keys."

She did. The door on the driver's side opened and a tall man with a mustache stood there, holding it for her.

"So, Harry, you have an accomplice," Gail said.

"An assistant. Miss Dionne, meet Gordy. Gordy, Miss Dionne. Or can we call you Gail?"

"Whatever," she said tiredly.

Blackburn chuckled. "Get out of the car. We'll go chat in my office. Yours is drafty."

In the Chrysler, Gordy sat behind the wheel, Gail between the two men in the front seat, crowded on either side by their thighs and shoulders. Gordy flicked the dome light on.

Blackburn scanned her appraisingly. "You're too scrawny to hide much of anything on you, so let's see what you got in the bag here before I search you."

"You put your hands on me and you'll know you've been in a fight," she said calmly.

He grinned at her. "I expect you mean that sincerely, and I suppose if I was maybe eighty pounds lighter and didn't know what the hell I was doing you might inflict a small amount of damage at that. But the plain truth is I could turn you black and blue and never get scratch one on me, so why don't you and me just be friends, huh?"

"How do you know my name?"

His eyes glinted. "That's my little secret."

He unzipped the bag and pulled out clothing, wadding each piece carefully, feeling for hard spots and listening for the crinkle of paper. He held up her bra, dropped it without comment on the floor along with the rest of her things.

He pulled out a camera. "Now we get to the interesting stuff."

"Careful with that," she said.

Harry opened the back of the camera, extracted the film cartridge and tucked it in his pocket. "That careful enough for you?" In the bag he found two more rolls and pocketed them as well. "If the doc told you about me, he probably also told you what my job is." He reached into the bag again.

"Terrorism, illegal search and seizure, bad breath."

Harry let out a bray of laughter. "Got a sense of humor, doesn't she, Gordy? See, right now old Sol's acting up and it wouldn't do for the professor to go and—"

"Tyler told me. It stinks."

"I guess you could see it like that. Someone with more public spirit might see it as a kind of service, though. Well, what've we got here?" He held up her miniature tape recorder. "Tapes, too," he said, unzipping a small leather pouch. "Let's have a listen, why don't we?"

He put in a tape and pressed the play button. A dry hiss came from the machine.

"You have to rewind it," Gail said with icy sarcasm.

"Thanks, sugar. I would've gotten around to that pretty quick by myself."

"You're a bloody genius, Harry," she said as he rewound it partway.

". . . was looking for when I first began to study mechanisms that might produce a long-term reduction in the sun's output." Tyler's voice was pitched high, made slightly anemic by electronics. "A drop of only one percent over a long period of time would be enough to cause a bitter ice age."

Harry turned it off. "See, that's the kind of thing that might scare the hell out of a lot of folks right now."

"You're the kind of thing that would scare the hell out of a lot of folks."

"Got some mouth on her, doesn't she, Gordy?" He leaned over and grinned at his companion. "Okay, what else we got here?" He pulled out a manila envelope and shook its contents out on his lap.

"Picture of the sun. Very nice." He flipped to the next one and stopped, stunned.

Gail felt suddenly warm.

In Harry's hands was a picture of himself. He turned it over. *Harold Blackburn* was printed on the back in Gail's neat script.

"Friday," Harry said slowly. "A little before ten in the morning. University parking lot."

"The man has a mind like a steel trap," Gail said.

"What I think I'll do," Harry said, "is just take all this stuff with me, look it over later." He dumped everything back in the travel bag, except her clothing.

"Add armed robbery to your list of accomplishments."

He smiled. "Nothing personal, Miss Dionne."

"Wrong. This is about as personal as it gets. If I ever get the chance, I'll cause you a lot of grief. That goes for you too, Gordy Whatever-your-name-is."

"Funny," Blackburn mused. "The doc said pretty much the same thing." His right hand whipped across his body and took her by the throat, closed on softness. He forced her head back until the cords in her neck stood out and the bones popped. In a quiet voice he said, "I'm gonna make a guess and figure you and the doc are pretty good friends by now, so listen up. The doc told you some things he wasn't supposed to. I'd take it real personal if they reached the papers or television—likewise if you went charging off to the police about any of this, making waves. The doc could get seriously hurt if any of that was to happen, am I coming through?" He eased the pressure on her throat.

She managed a hoarse reply. "Yes."

"Great. Maybe we got us an understanding then." He took his hand away.

Gail drew a ragged breath. "Tyler didn't know I was taping our talk."

Harry looked at her. "Little bitty recorder. You wired yourself, huh?"

"That's right."

Harry's eyes grew bright, opaque. He opened the car door and stepped out. He pulled her out and crammed her clothing into her arms. "The doc was warned not to talk to reporters about the sun," he said in a low, ominous voice. "So, okay, he needs a little reminding, no big deal."

"If you do anything to hurt Dr. Tyler, I'll see that you end up in prison, I swear it."

"Spunky. Looks like I was right about you and the doc, so I guess I can count on you to be reasonable, right?" He tossed her bag on the front seat of the Chrysler, slammed the door shut. He walked to her rental car and popped the hood, worked in darkness for a moment before emerging with something in his hand.

He said, "Road's two miles that way. Pretty girl like you shouldn't have any trouble flagging down the first car to come along." He held up the object he'd removed from the car. "In town, tell 'em what you need is a—"

"Rotor for the distributor."

He beamed at her. "Correct. And don't worry yourself none about the doc. I'm not going to hurt him one bit. I'm just going to joggle his memory about our earlier discussion, that's all. You want to help him out, keep your mouth shut."

He climbed behind the wheel of the Chrysler. He backed the car up, then edged around Gail's car and sped off in the direction of Tyler's house.

Gail stood in the bright beams of her own car and watched Harry's wreck move away, the clothing still in her arms. Fear for Tyler spilled through her. For an instant she felt overwhelmed, numbed.

"Dammit, *no!*" she cried suddenly. She flung the clothing aside and ran to the car, found her gun under the seat. In the silvery moonlight, she began to run back in the direction of Tyler's house.

* * *

WITHOUT GAIL, the house was too large, too quiet, too cold—a hollow, half-familiar place filled with the ghosts she'd left behind: her smile, her laughter, the warm woman-scent of her that seemed to linger in the air. She had slept a few hours in his bed, and she was there too, stretching languidly, extending her limbs and joints to their fullest before contracting with a purposeful, challenging look in her eyes. He caught himself drifting from room to room, trying to catch hold of her again, and suddenly he laughed, an empty sound that brought him up short in the darkened library where numbers glowed on Hal's newly christened face.

Messages of doom?

He went out to the observatory, into the darkroom, where he stacked trays and wiped down the sink and mopped the floor, dissipating nervous energy in tasks that required minimal concentration.

In the observatory he turned on the sputtery radio with its mixture of music and solar static and began sweeping the floor. She was there too, running her delicate, pale fingers over the steel frame of the telescope, unaware of his awareness of her. He was no longer offended that she'd picked the lock on his back door and come into his house, crept into his bed with a certain animal wariness to wait for him. He would sweep the floor and go back to the house and she'd be back in his bed again, all mischievous eyes and elfin smile—

"Nice place you got here, Doc."

Tyler almost dropped the broom. In the doorway, twenty feet away, Harold Blackburn stood like a marble obelisk in crumpled clothing, an interested look on his face as he took in the surroundings. He stepped a few paces inside.

Tyler picked up a length of steel pipe that lay on a work-table. "I told you what I'd do if I ever caught you out here, Blackburn."

Harold Blackburn folded his coat back and casually drew his gun. He drew back the slide, took aim at the radio on the workbench behind Tyler, and squeezed off a quick, thunderous round. The dome of the observatory shook.

The sound of the blast took several seconds to die away, and the radio spun away to the floor, silenced. Tyler stood frozen with the pipe in his hands.

"Put it down," Blackburn said. His gun was centered on Tyler's chest.

The pipe clattered to the floor. At the door, another man appeared, taller than Blackburn, with nervous eyes and a large mustache. He set a travel bag down at his feet.

Tyler took an involuntary step forward. "That's Gail's. What've you—"

"Relax, Doc. She's fine," Blackburn said. He took the rotor from his pocket, held it up, tossed it back to the man in the doorway. "Why don't you grind that up some, Gordy, now that the doc's had a look at it. See, Doc," he said, moving closer, "Miss Dionne's a strong girl. Probably take her only thirty or forty minutes to reach the main road." He kicked the length of pipe against a far wall and then stuck his gun back in its holster.

He looked around the observatory with an appreciative expression on his face. "You've been a bad boy," he said abruptly. Behind him, Gordy stomped the rotor to powder beneath his shoes.

Tyler's voice trembled. "If you laid so much as a finger on Gail, I swear to Christ, Blackburn, I'll hunt you down."

Blackburn sighed. "So much melodrama. I think it's television that does it. The lady's fine. It's you and me that's got a problem. See, we had an understanding a few days back"—he drew his gun silently and nudged open the darkroom door with his foot. He scanned the room swiftly and then put the gun away again. "An understanding, at least so I thought. Now it looks as if we had us a *mis*understanding. Play the tape, Gordy."

Gordy punched a button on a tiny black recorder.

". . . shows that an incredibly effective refrigeration or insulating process is going on," Tyler's voice said.

"Lending support to your hypothesis," replied Gail.

"Perhaps. Anyway, the phenomenon of sunspots is enormously complex. It's certain that a lot of energy is going into huge magnetic fields, since—"

Blackburn held up a hand and Gordy stopped the tape. "Recognize the voices?" Blackburn asked.

Tyler's face was ashen.

Blackburn regarded him solemnly. "She told us you didn't know about it."

Tyler said nothing. He sat in the chair by the telescope, slumped, his head bowed.

Blackburn circled the massive instrument. "Guy's always the last to know, isn't that right, Gordy?"

"Looks that way."

Blackburn ran a hand along a tubular crossbar. "Puts me in an awkward position, though."

Tyler looked up. "She said she wasn't going to use it. There wasn't going to be any story. It was just talk between friends, that's all."

"Je-sus, Gordy. Ain't love a blind old thing?"

Gordy stood at the entrance, arms folded across his chest, enjoying himself. "Sure is," he said.

Tyler made a sour face. "For God's sake, Blackburn, will you at least shut up your dummy over there?"

Blackburn pulled his gun, aimed, and squeezed the trigger. The sixteen-inch mirror of the telescope exploded into chunks as the bullet whistled down through the open framework and ricocheted back up into the dome.

"My God!" Tyler screamed. *"What have you done!"*

Blackburn's gun held unflinchingly on Tyler's chest. "Just getting your attention, Doc. We're going to arrive at a new understanding."

Tyler ran to the viewing platform and peered down through the struts at the mirror. A sick feeling came over him. The mirror lay in three large pieces at the base of the tube, with smaller fragments scattered around. Crystalline dust.

Tyler's hands began to tremble.

"Two years work. Two *years,* you shit-for-brains Neanderthal son of a bitch!" He whirled on Blackburn.

Blackburn put away his gun and regarded Tyler placidly. "Maybe you'd like to punch me out, huh, Doc? Make you feel better?"

The two men were about ten feet apart. Tyler felt a red haze come over his eyes. His chest felt swollen.

A strange wooden knocking sound came from the doorway and Gordy crumpled to his knees and fell facedown on the concrete. Gail appeared in the opening. She held her .38 in one hand, a short length of two-by-four in the other.

Blackburn's hand dropped to the gun under his coat.

"Easy, Harry," Gail said. She let the hunk of wood fall to the floor. She gripped the gun competently in both hands, holding it with utter steadiness on his thick belly. "The gun's cocked and I'm a bit nervous right now even though I've qualified several times on police ranges. The gun is loaded with Glaser rounds. I take it you've heard of Glasers."

Blackburn's swarthy face paled.

"Prefragmented bullets. Tear up everything inside. Get your hand out of your coat before we see how well they work."

Gingerly Harry pulled his hand clear. "You're making one hell of a big mistake, girl," he said.

Tyler stood frozen, watching Gail.

"And you're making me nervous," she replied. She glanced down at the man at her feet and then walked swiftly across the room to within eight feet of Blackburn. "Turn around, hands on your head. No sudden moves. I won't risk anything to save your worthless hide, buster. Now walk, straight ahead."

Harry moved cautiously forward.

"Hands flat on the wall," Gail said. "Walk your feet back—farther . . . farther, come on, you know how it goes."

Harry was stretched, trembling with effort. "Christ," he groaned. Sweat popped out on his forehead.

She put the barrel of the gun behind his ear. "I've got about a pound of pressure on the trigger. It won't take much more. Don't twitch or anything, okay?" She reached under his jacket, withdrew his gun, and stepped back.

"Okay, turn around and sit, right where you are." She uncocked her gun and handed Harry's weapon to Tyler.

He crouched beside Blackburn and put the gun to the man's temple. His hand trembled. "I've got ninety pounds of glass I'd like to feed you with a spoon."

Blackburn's eyes flickered. He licked his lips.

"C'mon, Tyler," Gail said. "Why don't you check out Gordy No-name there, see if he's got a gun too, maybe a wallet."

Tyler gave a low snarl and then went to the fallen man, rolled him over, found the nine-millimeter automatic in its shoulder holster. He took out Gordy's wallet, then grabbed him by the wrists and dragged him across the floor to a spot several feet from Blackburn.

"California driver's license for a Gordon Tate," he said. "Address in Glendora. Where's that?" he asked Blackburn.

"Couple miles east of Pasadena," Blackburn growled.

"Your turn, Harry," Gail said. She cocked the gun and aimed it at his chest. "Let's see how slowly you can produce a wallet."

As Blackburn's hands went to his right rear pocket, Gordon Tate stirred, groaned, tried to lift his head. "Easy," Gail cautioned Harry. "Don't get distracted."

"Careful with that thing," Harry said in an airless voice. He slipped his wallet out, tossed it a few feet toward her.

She uncocked the gun before picking up the wallet. "Harold Brice McGill," she read without surprise. "West Hollywood. Do you lie about your age too?"

He closed his eyes and leaned his head back against the wall.

"Our friend Gordy here is a private investigator," Tyler announced, holding up a card.

"Harold McGill too," Gail said. She looked at Tyler. "By the way, it's nice to see you again."

He gave her an accusing look. "You taped our talk."

"Habit," she replied. "I'm sorry. By the end of the day I knew I wasn't going to use those tapes. Can we talk about it later?"

"Count on it."

Gordy sat up uncertainly and looked around. "Harry?"

he said. He felt the knot at the back of his head, then touched a bloody patch on his cheek. "Jesus." He looked up at Gail with pained eyes. "You hit me?"

She nodded. "My pleasure."

Harry gave her an odd look. "We haven't been gone more than twenty-five minutes from where we left you. Three miles. What'd you do, fly?"

She smiled at him. "That's *my* little secret."

Harry said, "You just bought yourself a load of trouble. Both of you."

"PI's are a nickel a truckload," Tyler said.

"Hired by people with more influence than you ever dreamed in your worst nightmares, buddy."

"And who might they be?" Gail asked.

"You're a riot, sugar."

Gordy's eyes went back and forth between Tyler and Gail. He was rapidly collecting himself again. Cold air poured in the open door.

"What'd you hit me with?" he asked.

"Piece of two-by-four," Gail said happily. "A story you can tell your grandchildren with pride. Okay, get up, both of you, and strip."

Harry's eyes bulged. "Hah?"

"Strip. Take off your clothes," she said.

"Very funny," Harry growled.

"You heard her," Tyler said. He waved the gun. "Get up. Get out of those things." He gave Gail a questioning look and her eyes sparkled at him in return.

Harry folded his arms across his chest. "No way, Doc. You've got the guns, but I don't think either of you're ready to commit murder to pull some dumb stunt." He stared at them and leaned back obstinately.

Tyler retrieved the length of pipe McGill had kicked across the room. He stood in front of Harry and said in a deadly calm voice, "You destroyed a mirror that took over a thousand hours to grind, polish, and figure. It was a part of my life. So I'll tell you what, you ignore the lady the next time she tells you to do something and we'll see if I've got what it takes to break bones with this pipe: shins, forearms, wrists. I think I can, but I'm not certain. I know

I'm real angry, so the next time she tells you to do something will be a big moment for both of us.''

He held the pipe in a baseball grip. "See if he's changed his mind," he said over his shoulder to Gail.

"Strip," she said.

Harry got up slowly and took off his coat.

"You too," Gail said to Gordy, and he stood and shrugged out of his jacket.

Coats, shirts, shoes, pants, undershirts, socks. McGill and Tate stood in undershorts and goose bumps.

"Everything," Gail said.

"Jesus, miss," Harry said.

Tyler stepped closer and swung the pipe at Harry's legs. Harry danced backward. The pipe grazed his shin before smashing into a wooden leg of the workbench. Tyler drew it back for another swing.

"Okay," Harry shrieked. He jammed his thumbs under the elastic band of his shorts and stripped them down around his ankles and kicked them free. A trickle of blood ran down his leg. His breath came in short gasps and his hands hovered in front of his groin. Gordy's undershorts quickly followed.

Gail smiled at McGill, eying him critically. "It'd help if you jogged," she said. "Now, we go out to your car and the two of you drive away."

"Without our stuff?" Harry asked incredulously.

"You're so perceptive," she said. "Let's go. Not through the house. Around the south end." She wiggled the gun. "Single file, Gordy first." As they moved away, Gail reached down and lifted a set of keys from Harry's pocket.

Over the coarse ground they went, Harry and Gordy moving as if they were stepping on live coals. They made little grunts of pain, whistles of indrawn breath, hisses and sighs and bleats. Tyler and Gail walked behind them, Gail with the .38, Tyler with the pipe and the .45. At the front of the house, Tyler ran ahead and turned on the porch light. The two men stood shivering in the cold with breath pluming from their mouths. Gail searched the Chrysler for weapons, clothing, blankets, rags. Tyler held Harry's .45

on them as Gail pulled almost everything out of the trunk, including the jack and the spare tire.

"Pile in," she said finally.

Teeth beginning to chatter, Harry got behind the wheel. "Keys," he said.

"This one makes it go, right?" She held up a key and smiled sweetly at him.

Harry glowered, nodded.

She took it off the ring. Before she gave it to him, she said, "It would be amusing if you thought about using the car as a weapon. The two of us shooting at the two of you. I'd be going for your tires, and if I flattened any you'd have to walk out. It'd get cold, your feet might get awful sore, and I wonder if anyone would stop and pick you up, dressed like that." She tossed him the key. "Bon voyage."

"Next time, lady, I'll kill you." A psychotic light shone in his eyes.

"There won't be a next time, Mr. McGill."

"We'll see, bitch." He started the engine, dropped it in gear, and the rear tires kicked up dust as he circled the yard and roared off down the dark and bumpy road.

CHAPTER 16 ───────────────

GAIL LAUGHED.

Tyler stared at her. "What's so funny?"

"I've always wanted to do that," she said, giggling.

"What? See Harry in the buff?"

She made a face at him. "No, dear. Play Jane Wayne. Win a round against the bad guys." Her eyes danced.

"Fess up. You found Harry exciting."

"He's grotesque."

"Your victory might not last," Tyler said. "Harry knew about the paper I'd sent to Dr. Cooke. He knew a lot of other things he had no business knowing, too. Whoever's behind him has connections."

"What do you suggest?"

He turned and headed toward the house. "I think we ought to get out of here, now."

"I think you're right," she said, galloping to catch up. "Maybe we should call the police first."

He gave her a sidelong look. "That might not be the best idea you've had all evening."

She grimaced. "I see your point. Connections, right?"

"Right."

In the kitchen, he ran his fingers through his hair. "They smashed the distributor rotor of your car."

"Which is three miles up the road anyway. I'll call Avis tomorrow, tell them it broke down."

"How *did* you get here so fast?" he asked. "Three miles at night?"

She held out a leg. "These're useful, fella, not just shapely."

"Shapely too? I never got a look."

"You didn't try hard enough. Maybe some other time. I've got a flight to catch in the morning, remember? Let's get moving."

He shook his head. "If Black . . . If *McGill* has the kind of clout he says he has, the airport might be watched. You want to risk it?"

A desperate, comprehending look came into her eyes. "I've *got* to get back to Los Angeles!"

He gazed at her a moment. "I'll drive you."

"You . . . what? You don't have to do that."

"I probably shouldn't stick around here. Besides, it's something I'd like to do."

Her dark blue eyes settled on his face. "Why?"

"I . . . I'd like to, that's all. I want to spend more time with you, meet your daughter."

"Those are pretty good reasons," she said softly.

"Then it's settled?"

"I don't know. If you say."

"I do." He began pulling the refrigerator away from the wall.

She stared. "Perfect time to rearrange the kitchen."

"Each of us has our eccentricities."

"Yours have a special potency."

She watched over his shoulder as he pulled up the strip of linoleum and then pried up the plywood with a screwdriver.

"The professor is full of surprises," she said when she saw the cashbox in its niche.

He opened it, drew out a wad of bills that made her gasp, counted out five thousand, and put the rest back in the box. "Mad money," he said with a grin. He was tempted to tell her about the tunnel hidden beneath the concrete, about *Tselaa,* but the memory of his voice on tape stopped him. He replaced the box, the plywood, the linoleum, and shoved the refrigerator back into place against the wall.

He got the .357 Magnum, found a coat for himself, a jacket for Gail that billowed on her, grabbed the truck keys, and they went outside to the garage. The double doors were flung wide, the truck in darkness inside. When the dome light came on, Tyler saw the open hood above the engine compartment.

"Oh, Christ," he said.

He snapped on overhead lights and looked into the greasy tangle of wires and rubber hoses surrounding the engine block. The distributor cap was missing, along with the rotor.

"Harry's favorite trick," Gail said in a flat, defeated voice.

They found the rotor crushed in a vise, the cap carefully smashed in a dirty blanket lying on some bricks.

"Well, that's that," Tyler said.

"We could walk out to the main road, thumb a ride."

He shook his head. "Too risky. It'd take an hour to get out there. We might end up flagging down one of theirs."

"Okay, you suggest something."

He turned off the light and they stumbled out of the garage into the lesser darkness of night. Overhead, pale bands of red and greenish light shimmered against the stars.

"An aurora," he said in wonder.

"I've seen them a couple times before. In the country, outside Boston."

"Me too, but this is Arizona."

"It's very pretty, Tyler. Now, what're we going to *do?*"

He gazed toward the north. "We go out there."

She stared. "Where?"

"The desert."

"You're not serious."

"I am." He started back toward the house. She caught his arm and spun him around.

"Out *there?*" she said. *"Why?"*

"I have friends who can help us."

"Friends? Like who?"

"Sam Hatathli for one. He's a Navajo. If we can get to Sam, we've got a good chance of making it to Los Angeles."

She gazed doubtfully at the darkness. "How far is it?"

"Twenty, maybe twenty-five miles."

"Oh, that isn't so bad." She sounded relieved.

"Not yet, anyway."

He continued on toward the house. She followed closely on his heels, shivering in the cold.

In a walk-in closet, he located a bright orange backpack and other camping equipment. He handed her a pair of two-quart canteens.

"Here, rinse and fill."

She hurried off. He felt the heavy press of time as he went through drawers and closets, picking out clothing for them: fresh jeans, wool shirts, socks. He came across two olive green army blankets and tossed them on his bed with the rest of the things.

She came back with the canteens. "Now food," he said. "Canned stuff we won't have to cook. Maybe some bread. We won't need much. Two days, tops."

She left without a word.

He frowned at the only sleeping bag available: polyester with cotton lining, nearly ten years old. It and the blankets would have to do. He packed nylon rope and a first aid kit in the pack. Water-purification tablets, Swiss army knife, large plastic garbage bags, a few utensils from the kitchen where Gail had all the cupboard doors open and was sorting through the possibilities.

"What about the stuff in the observatory?" she asked. "My bag, Harry's and Gordy's clothing?"

"And your tapes?" he remarked coolly.

She put her hands on her hips and squared off on him. "A few days prior to making those tapes, I was given a tremendous amount of trouble by the eminent Dr. Tyler."

"Oh, Lord," he said.

"I started with minimal knowledge of the man, and upon hearing an encapsulation of his so-called theory I had no faith whatsoever that it'd cause millions to flee in panic. After hearing him out, however, I felt like running for cover myself. Suddenly it didn't seem like such a good idea, racing off with a sizzling scoop in my fist. I'm sorry about the tapes, okay? They weren't going to be used for anything.''

He looked into her eyes. ''Okay.''

''No more hassles or comments?''

''Not about tapes.''

''Great. Shall we check out the observatory?''

In Harry's pockets they found three Hershey bars, two dimes, a pair of nail clippers, and a key to room seventeen of the West End Motel. They found $564 in his wallet, nothing else of interest. They left the money where it was. Just touching it made Tyler feel itchy, unclean. Gordy's pockets held a pocketknife, another motel key, a lighter, cigarettes, assorted change. His wallet contained twenty-one dollars.

They left it all in a wad by the door. Gail gathered up her things and put them in the travel bag. The tape recorder was cracked, evidently from Gordy's fall when he was clubbed. Back in the house, Tyler stuffed the travel bag up into the attic through a hole in the hall ceiling. Into the backpack went the film, the picture Tyler had given Gail, and the one she'd taken of Harold Blackburn/McGill.

They quickly loaded food into the backpack. Tyler tied the sleeping bag to the harness.

''That's it for two days?'' she asked, staring skeptically at the arrangement.

''We won't have crepe suzettes in the morning, if that's what you mean.''

''No, looks like we'll end up with tuna. Even so . . .''

''It's enough.''

He went into the bedroom and thrust some clothing into her arms. ''Put this on. You can't go dressed like that.''

''Bet it fits just super,'' she said.

He kicked off his shoes and looked at her. ''Turn around or leave the room.'' He started unbuttoning his shirt.

She smiled and turned her back to him. ''Says the prude.'' She began unbuttoning her blouse.

His stomach felt fluttery. "Shameless," he intoned in a thick voice.

"We're in a hurry, aren't we?" Her blouse came off, revealing a slender, well-formed back, no bra, a delicate ripple of muscle beneath the smooth, honey-colored skin. Without turning, she reached behind her and snagged the T-shirt he'd given her. It dropped shapelessly around her.

He shucked off his slacks and stepped quickly into heavy denim jeans. The slide and whisper of clothing filled the room, and a minute later she faced him, a helpless, lop-sided grin on her face as she held the slack waistband of the pants out with a thumb. Across the hips, the fit was almost right; the length was wrong by inches.

"Perfect," she said. "I'll take a dozen."

He found a length of nylon cord, which she threaded through the belt loops and knotted in front of her. Safety pins held up her cuffs.

"I guess tennis shoes'll have to do," he said, frowning at her feet. He handed her a western hat.

"I have to look like a cowboy?" she asked.

"Cowgirl. Definitely cow*girl.*"

"Cowgirl then."

"It's customary."

"Oh. Well, I wouldn't want to offend anyone."

"And it helps keep the head warm. You'd be surprised."

Almost as an afterthought, Tyler went into the library and retrieved a pair of matching green cloth-bound notebooks with the legends M-1 and M-2 printed on their spines, and put them in the pack.

"What're those?" she asked.

"The two most important volumes of my work. If I could take it all, I would. These are critical, however."

He shrugged on his coat and hoisted the pack to his back. The .357 was in a holster at his waist. The two army blankets had been tied in rolls, and Gail had them strapped around her waist, riding across her rump. Tyler handed her a canteen.

He checked his watch: 11:25.

"I see we have only one sleeping bag, Professor."

"And a couple of blankets."

"It's going to be an interesting hike," she answered with a thoughtful lilt in her voice.

IN MOON-SILVERED DARKNESS, the sky lit by the shimmering band of the aurora, they climbed a low rise to the north and then walked an uneven game trail through trees, around a black knob of earth until they reached the long, downward-sloping crest of a ridge. As they lost altitude, the trees began to thin. Gail could see a dark expanse of land before them, mountains looming in the far, shadowy distance.

She wore two baggy flannel shirts and a jacket over the T-shirt. Still, a sense of coldness surrounded her, almost like pressure. The chill breeze made her eyes water, her cheeks burn. She was thankful for the hat. She sensed more than saw the mist of vapor that came from her mouth. In a pocket of the jacket was her gun.

Tyler was a dark moving mass ahead of her, the silhouette of his pack rising above his head.

Tyler: miscreant and good guy—genius, recluse guitar player, probable millionaire, professor . . . outcast. The day before she'd flown out West, she'd unearthed the King's College fiasco and established Tyler as a possible dud.

He was slender for thirty-seven, but not skinny. His shadowy jaw would almost certainly turn to Carborundum overnight. He was capable of both rage and tenderness, and she sensed that of the two, the show of rage would bother him more because the tenderness came from a more real place within him, and this pleased her. She'd found an old rock, and unearthed diamond glints beneath its gritty surface.

So now what, girl? After so many harmless millennia the sun is suddenly a rogue elephant in the sky, and Nikki is far away in Los Angeles, and an editor is drumming his fingers on a desk in Boston, and that is how food gets on the table and the mortgage gets paid—by satisfying that drumming. It's a jigsaw puzzle with too many pieces, so which of them do you throw away? What picture do you want to complete?

Her feet suddenly slid out from under her on the pebbly slope. She landed on the padding of the blankets with a jolt that bounced her to her feet with a surprising effortlessness.

"You okay?" Tyler's voice came floating back.

"Wonderful."

She dusted herself off. The aurora had grown stronger, now misty green tapestry blowing in the breeze of night up in the ionosphere. Her feet were cold. Her nearest bra was lying somewhere on Tyler's bumpy private road. She missed it. There was an annoying amount of swaying and bouncing going on underneath Tyler's borrowed shirts.

Tyler turned due east off the ridge and they headed down a hard, scrabbling slope of loose gravel and tricky hardpan. Tyler took her hand.

She stared. "Down this?"

"Trust me."

"Oh, I trust you. You didn't even peek back there in the bedroom, did you?"

"I saw your back. That count?"

"Hardly."

She skidded, felt herself falling, and for an instant he took her weight. The strength in his arms was reassuring. He pulled her upright and they stood there, swaying in darkness, somewhere on the edge of the world.

"Do you know how to fall on a hill?" he asked.

"I'll get the hang of it."

He chuckled. "If you're ever thrown from a moving car, tuck and roll; it might save you broken bones. On a mountainside, however, you splay out as quickly as possible to try to keep from building up speed."

"All my life I've waited for someone to tell me that."

He didn't move. She was aware of him standing close, and she sensed a subtle change in the air between them. A melting feeling came over her, making her legs go soft.

"Tyler?" she asked.

His face was suddenly close, and then his lips were on hers, just for an instant—a strangely gentle insistence that ended quickly. As he pulled away, she touched his cheek.

In a husky voice she said, "There could come a time when I might want a lot more of that, sir."

He was quiet, then he said, "We've come about three miles. Not far enough. We'd better keep moving."

"Darned difficult to pitch a tent on this cliff anyway."

"Wouldn't be easy."

He kept her hand as they sidestepped down the slope, facing each other, groping with their feet for purchase on the face of the rocky talus. After fifteen minutes they reached a knobby trail only a little less treacherous than the hillside itself, and Tyler led the way downward to the southeast.

"I thought we wanted to go north."

"Patience."

In time, they reached the base of the slope. The trail flattened out and disappeared. They turned northward again, over ground composed of gentle dips and swells. To her left was the darkness of the mountain they'd just descended.

The bitter wind cut her face, and she bent her head low, using the brim of the hat as a shield. Her legs felt chilled as frosty jets of air shot up around her ankles. They hiked along for an hour, stumbling over unseen projections of rock, scraping past the tough fingers of sagebrush, until Gail saw a deeper darkness to their right. She caught up to Tyler.

"What's that?"

"The canyon of the Little Colorado."

"Looks deep," she said nervously.

"Couple hundred feet. We'll go down in the morning. We have to cross the river."

"Wonderful."

"We'll make camp a little farther on. You tired?"

"Don't be silly."

Half an hour later, a dark line appeared ahead. They went down into a dry wash, partially sheltered from the wind. In a flat, sandy place, in the lee of several waist-high boulders, they unrolled the sleeping bag and spread the blankets.

"Who gets what?" she asked dully.

"Sleeping bag for you, blankets for me."

"I won't argue."

She pulled off her shoes and wormed her way into the bag. The ground dug into her hip and she squirmed, then rolled over on her stomach and fell asleep thinking about how crummy a bed the earth made.

THE DIGITAL CLOCK in the Chrysler was one of the few things that hadn't needed repairs or replacing during the years that Harry McGill had owned the car. As they passed Gail Dionne's car, the numerals showed 10:46 and the speedometer read forty-eight miles an hour. The car bucked and heaved dangerously over the road.

"Jesus, Harry, take it easy!" Gordon Tate cried.

"Shut up!"

"We got no spare tire."

"Shut up!" The car slewed sideways around a turn, raising a red cloud of dust in the taillights, straightened, bounded up a rocky slope. A rock hammered the suspension, ringing the car like a bell. "Goddamn," McGill intoned. "Goddamn, goddamn, *goddamn!* Goddamn bitch. Gonna fix that whore."

The Leupp-Winona road came up fast, and Harry took the turn with enough speed to kick up gravel from the far shoulder of the road before roaring off at a hundred miles an hour toward Winona, his big, hairy knuckles white on the steering wheel. A sticky film of sweat had already formed between his naked skin and the impervious plastic cushions of the seat. A spring dug into his right buttock.

Eleven miles to Winona, another thirteen to the eastern edge of Flagstaff; Harry did the whole thing in just nineteen minutes. He slowed to seventy on the interstate through town and squealed the tires exiting on the cloverleaf that arced off toward the West End Motel, just off Milton Road.

"Now what?" Gordy asked, rubbing the knot on the back of his head. The car jerked to a stop in front of the units of the south wing.

"Now we get dressed!" Harry thundered. He slammed

open the door and stalked off toward the motel, his rump pale and surprisingly small beneath the barrel torso.

"We got no keys," Gordy's thin voice trailed after him. "Jesus, Harry!"

A young couple stopped dead and watched open-mouthed as Harry Brice McGill rounded a redwood planter filled with hearty juniper. He half trotted down the concrete walk toward unit seventeen, keeping no secrets from the world. He hit the door with his foot and it flew open with an explosive, jamb-shattering crash. It swung shut again as he went straight to his suitcase. Gordy came rushing in, panting.

"I got no key," he said in a high voice.

"Kick your own door in," Harry barked. He pulled on undershorts and faced Tate. "Christ, get that covered up, huh? And move it. We're rolling in two minutes."

Gordy grabbed the spread off Harry's bed and went outside. A few seconds later, three hammering blows rattled the windows of Harry's room. By then, Harry had on trousers and was pulling on socks.

If anything, the trip out was even faster than the trip in. Harry drove in compressed silence, eyes fixed on the road, mouth grim. Wisely, Gordy said nothing.

Forty yards from the turnoff to Tyler's ranch, Harry drove the Chrysler onto the shoulder and parked, lights off.

"Little over fifty minutes," he said. "Could they've made it out on foot in the dark in fifty minutes?"

"I doubt it," Gordy said judiciously.

"Me too." Harry pulled a snub-nose .38 out of his pocket and swung open the cylinder, snapped it shut, gave it a spin. He always carried a spare gun in his suitcase. This was the first time he'd ever needed it.

"Glasers, the bitch uses," Harry snarled. "If they don't come out by dawn, we go in, give her a chance to match shots with a pro."

CHAPTER 17 ————————

COLD AWAKENED HER. She was shivering uncontrollably and her legs felt achy, her feet numbed. She'd drawn herself into a ball while asleep, but it hadn't helped much. All around her the night sighed, breathing hungrily. The temperature had dropped another ten degrees, maybe more. She was suddenly aware that the situation had become dangerous.

"Tyler," she called softly. Overhead, the aurora blazed, now a pastel rainbow of dancing, shimmering color. Tyler was a dark lump beside her.

"T-Tyler!"

"What?"

"I'm f-freezing."

He stirred. "Do you want a blanket?"

"Oh sure, and wake up next to a corpse. Get in here, will you?"

"Huh?"

She sat up and stripped off her jacket. "This is no time to be dumb or prudish or anything else. It's goddamn cold out here. I'm stripping down to panties and I want you to do the same and get the hell in here. Put the blankets on top of us. Where'd you get this anemic bag, anyway?"

"K-Mart, I think."

"Figures. It's like it was designed to repel insects, not

cold." She removed her jeans and shoved them to the bottom of the bag. She heard him move, felt the weight of the blankets land on top of her. She began working her shirts off, hearing the sound of him removing his clothes.

"Christ," he muttered, and then he was shoving his legs down beside her, inching his way into the confines of the bag. After a minute of awkward labor, he settled, facing her, and she put her arms around him.

"God, you're like ice!"

"B-blankets were t-thinner than I thought." His body began to shake.

"Macho man. You trying to kill yourself out there?"

"Just b-being respectful."

"Practically the working definition of a jerk."

"Thank you."

"You deserve it."

She held him close, realizing guiltily that he'd been much colder than she had been. He trembled. His fingers were like chips of ice against her hip.

Slowly, as they warmed, she grew more and more aware of him, his firm chest pressing against her in rhythm to their breathing, the heated, humid bubble of air that lay between their bellies, the casual entanglement of their legs. The emptiness of the past two years was suddenly close, bumping sullenly against her consciousness, the long, restless nights bitter and meaningless.

"Dammit, Tyler . . . ." she breathed into the darkness.

"Now what?" His voice came muffled against her throat, the air moist and warm and filled with this close new scent of him.

She felt a tiny bit faint. A pulse throbbed in her neck. A dampness had formed where their thighs touched. She stirred against him.

"It's warmer," she said, hardly trusting her voice. Her fingertips brushed the lean washboard of his ribs.

"So I've noticed."

She pressed her lips gently against his, listening to a thin humming in her ears that came from so deep within her, it seemed to have no identifiable source. She pressed herself against him, felt a pressure against her prepuce, and felt him respond in that secret way she'd missed for all those empty months.

"Tyler—"

His voice was whispery, hoarse. "Sorry."

"For what?"

"For getting . . . uh, carried away."

"Like I'm really making it easy for you, huh?" she said softly.

His arousal gave her a buttery feeling of satisfaction. A man she'd known less than twenty-four hours! She felt herself blush. All that nonsense at Red's Outpost and the days spent tracking Tyler down didn't count. She hadn't really begun to know him until just the other morning, barely enough time to scratch the surface, and here she was, in as compromising a position as one could imagine, feeling that soft, flowery, wrenching feeling of need spill through her.

She let her breath out in a hitching sigh. "The things a man will do to get a lady in the sack," she said.

"The bag."

"Okay then, the bag."

His hand traversed the swell of her hip carefully, caressing the firm, smooth muscle of her thigh. "What do you do?" he whispered, "Play soccer?"

She shivered under his touch.

"I'm a wide receiver for the Patriots . . . and if you don't stop that pretty soon, we're going to end up making utter damn fools of ourselves in this ridiculous little bag."

Suddenly everything came loose inside—a water main of emotions bursting, flooding, and to her horror, she began to cry, and the crying became sloppy, snuffling, half-hysterical laughter that finally ended in a flow of quiet tears.

Alarmed, he said, "I didn't mean—"

She put a finger to his lips. "Hush. The lady is just feeling a little stressed and buggy by all the foolish yearnings of her body, combined with certain impossible contradictions of heart and mind. It's not your fault."

"Had me fooled."

"Don't ask me to explain." She sighed, sniffed, managed to rise up on an elbow above him. "I feel like a little girl who was desperately longing for an ice cream cone, and found herself suddenly dropped in an entire swimming pool of raspberry ripple. I'm drowning in you, Tyler, and I don't know hardly anything about you. You know—important things, like your mother's maiden name."

"Giordano. How about yours?"

"Ceragioli."

"Good God, we're both certifiable wops."

She laughed, almost soberly. She lowered herself on him and put her cheek against his chest. "All these histrionics . . . that's not me, really."

He was quiet, stroking her hair.

"I . . . I guess I need more than twenty-four hours," she said quietly. "Me, the big talker. Would I seem terribly balky if I wanted to know you for at least forty-eight hours, before . . . before we . . ."

"Not really."

"You'd understand? I mean, here we are. This has got to be a bit rough on you, too, sir."

For a long moment he didn't answer. "Tyler?" she said in an uneasy whisper.

His hands tightened on her. "Um?"

She crawled a few inches higher on him and melted against him. "You didn't answer the question," she breathed. "I don't want to be a problem."

"You're already a problem."

"No, really."

He sighed softly. "Now that our immediate survival seems likely, I suppose we could put on more clothing. Might help clear up this roaring sound in my ears."

"Uh-huh."

He paused. "But to be truthful, you feel too damned good. I'd like to keep holding you, even curbing impulses that probably go back ten million years. I can wait for you to feel comfortable. If it takes a month, or even a year, I'll wait."

"It couldn't possibly take a year." She kissed him. "Or even a month. But thank you."

Around them, the bitter night moaned. She looked down at his face, dimly illuminated by the aurora. The moon had gone behind the hills.

"You don't have to go all the way to Los Angeles with me," she said. "It's a sweet offer and I appreciate it, but you could stay with friends awhile, or go on back and raise some sort of a fuss about McGill."

"You're fishing."

"No, I'm not."

For a while he was quiet. "When you drove away," he said finally, "I felt more empty than I've felt in months. I want to be with you, that's all. It's not really very complicated. There's something about you . . . about us. Unless, of course, you don't feel the same—"

Again she put a finger on his lips. "I said I'm drowning in you, sir. It's not a bad thing. It does seem kind of hopeless, though, considering this business with the sun."

He shook his head. "Maybe not. I have a place we can go."

"A place?"

He described *Tselaa* to her, told her what it was designed to do.

"A nuclear winter bomb shelter," she said slowly, wonderingly. "How morbid." A vague hope filled her, and an uneasiness, similar to the feeling she got in graveyards.

"I was feeling morbid when I began the project," he said. "Suddenly I had this tremendous hole in the ground and huge lengths of pipe all around, and the fact that Carol had left me wasn't quite so terrible, so immediate. The work helped. Once I started, I just kept at it until it was done."

"A chance to survive and see what's left." She clung to him. "What kind of a world would remain if the sun goes out for a month or two?"

"I don't know."

It was strange even to think about it, she decided, holing up in a dank lair while the world above them froze. Creepy, really. Her daughter's face appeared before her. The thought of Nikki dying slowly in terrible cold was unbearable. She trembled.

"This can't be happening," she said in a barely audible whisper. "It can't be."

"Let's just take it one step at a time. First we've got to get to Sam's."

CHAPTER 18

BEYOND THE EASTERN HILLS, a deep, cobalt blue glow heralded the dawn. The Chrysler's engine idled, its heater keeping the interior of the car warm. McGill put the vehicle in gear and rolled toward the turnoff to Tyler's house. The movement woke Gordy. His hair was mussed. He wore different-colored socks, shirt untucked, and his mouth felt like a lint trap.

"Pretty dark out still," he mumbled.

"I want some cover when we move on them."

"Wish I had a gun."

Harry drove fast, but not as fast as the night before. A faint puling noise came from the right front wheel. After a while, the girl's abandoned car appeared ahead, her clothing strewn about on the road. Harry tore on by without slowing.

The house was dark, just beginning to show detail in the gray light as Harry and Gordy crept over the final hill with the lights off. Harry stopped the car and got out.

"Now we walk," he said.

"I got no gun," Gordy complained again.

"Whose fault's that?"

Harry set off at a brisk walk, darting from one place of concealment to another, his gun in hand. He shivered in the frigid air.

Twenty minutes later they had determined there was no one at the house. The front door was splintered, hanging half off its hinges from the kick Harry had given it. Tyler's truck was still in the garage. Several battering-ram blows with a four-by-four post had demolished the hasp on the observatory door, and Harry and Gordy had found their wallets and clothing inside. Both guns were there, all their papers and money. No doc, no Gail Dionne with her gun.

Back in the house, feeling better with his gun tucked in the holster under his arm, Gordy said, "They're gone."

"No shit, Perry Mason."

The two men stood in the library. A computer whispered in a corner. Harry pulled the .45 out of its holster and fired a round into the screen. A hole blossomed in the glass, cracks flared in all directions, and the numbers disappeared. A phone on the table clattered to the floor. He shot it, too. In the living room, he put a bullet through the mute gray eye of the television and another into a framed picture on one wall, a third through the slats of a rolltop desk. The acrid smell of gunpowder filled the air.

He stared around the room, his face a blank, pale madness.

Nervously Gordy said, "Where do you think they went?"

"Must've slipped by us somehow. Maybe saw the car and circled around before picking up the road to Winona. We'll check there and then we'll go on back to Flag, see if we can pick them up at the bus station or the airport."

"Why don't we just get the hell out, Harry? This whole deal's gone bad, real bad."

"Got a job to do," Harry said tonelessly. "Got a score to settle, too."

AT 8:05, Dr. Cooke, still wearing the heavy overcoat he'd worn in the taxi, strode importantly into the physics department office and said to the secretary, "I would like to see Dr. Maurice Tyler, ma'am."

She gazed up at him in shock. "Why, you're . . . you're . . ."

"Dr. Malcolm Cooke," he said with a certain degree of satisfaction.

"Omigod," Nora said faintly. "You're . . ."

"Dr. Malcolm Cooke," he repeated, his smile fading. "It's urgent that I speak with Dr. Tyler."

"He isn't in yet," she said in a tiny voice. "He won't be in until almost ten for his morning lecture."

Cooke frowned. "Perhaps you would be kind enough to call him at home for me. I'll wait."

Nora was galvanized by the imperious manner in which he delivered this command and sat down opposite her to wait for it to be carried out. She looked up Tyler's number and dialed it.

"No answer?"

"It . . . doesn't seem to be ringing. It must be off the hook or something."

He leaned forward slightly. "Try the operator, dear."

The operator had no better luck, informing her the line was indeed open.

Dr. Cooke stood, looming over Nora's desk. "If you would be so kind as to supply me with an address, I will go and seek out Dr. Tyler myself."

"I'm not sure . . . I mean, I shouldn't . . ."

"I assure you, Dr. Tyler would want you to bend whatever mundane restrictions apply. It is a matter of grave urgency."

She hesitated. She looked toward the door of the department head, Dr. Wahlburg, but he hadn't come in yet.

"I come as a representative of the United States government, ma'am," Cooke said solemnly.

That did it. She even called him another taxi. By eight-thirty, Dr. Malcolm Cooke was in the rear seat of a cab, headed eastward on Interstate 40. The taxi driver had a map to Tyler's house that Nora had xeroxed from the files.

The ride out was a silent one. The driver was a small brown man with wrinkles and a sour, withdrawn look about him, a garlicky odor. The cab turned off the narrow highway and began jouncing along a rutted road.

"Good Lord," Dr. Cooke said in dismay.

A few minutes later, they came upon a car stalled in the

middle of the road. Its hood was up, the driver's door open, the passenger window smashed in.

"Stop," commanded Dr. Cooke.

He and the driver got out. Clothing was scattered about, dusty and tire-tracked. Cooke frowned at the bra that lay at his feet. He could make no sense of the scene before him, but a feeling of foreboding began to steal through him. The day was still cold, the sun yellow against the bright blue sky.

"Let's go on," he said.

Ten minutes later they arrived at the house. The taxi stopped in the drive and Dr. Cooke got out. The morning was eerily quiet.

"Come with me," Cooke directed.

"You want me to wait, I'll wait," the driver said. "But I'm staying put right here and the meter's runnin'."

"Ten dollars," Cooke said, gritting his teeth.

The driver shrugged. "For ten dollars, you got comp'ny. You don't get along with this guy, or what? I'm not gettin' involved in nothin'."

They found the bashed-in front door, the bullet hole in the television screen, the bullet hole in the computer. The phone lay on the floor, smashed. The observatory door was splintered. A radio was inside, another bullet through it. Dr. Cooke found the shattered mirror of the telescope.

"My goodness," he said. He found it suddenly difficult to draw the rarified air into his lungs. He put a hand to his chest.

"Looks like there was a war or something out here," the cabby observed with interest.

Dr. Cooke took charge of the phone in the kitchen after the cabby had dialed the sheriff's office for him. It took several minutes to establish his credentials and work his way up the chain of command of the Coconino County's Sheriff Department to Sheriff John Gabel.

"Dr. Maurice Tyler's place?" Sheriff Gabel said. "Doesn't ring a bell, least not right off."

Dr. Cooke did his best to explain where it was, since there seemed to be no address beyond a post office box in Winona.

"Wait a minute," said Gabel. Cooke heard the man's hand clamp down over the mouthpiece. "Northeast of Winona?" Gabel asked a minute later. "Fair number of miles up a dirt road up Angel Canyon? All by itself out there?"

"That sounds more or less correct," Cooke said.

"Okay, got a deputy here knows the place. You say there's bullet holes all over, busted-in doors, an abandoned car on the road with a woman's clothing on the ground?" An intensity lay behind the surface calmness of Gabel's voice.

"That's right." Cooke outlined Tyler's sudden importance as regards the outbursts on the sun, and the sheriff told Cooke to stay where he was, they'd have someone out there on the double.

Twenty minutes later, a big county helicopter swooped down from over the ridge west of Angel Canyon and raised a dusty cloud from an open area south of Tyler's house. Sheriff Gabel and Deputy Glenn Hawkins got out, wearing heavy green jackets and sidearms, dark green hats without any curl at the brim, and trotted to the rear of Tyler's house. A while later, two county cruisers pulled up and a uniformed deputy climbed out of one car while a deputy and a pair of civilians piled out of the other.

"You touch anything?" the sheriff asked. He was a heavy, florid man with a meaty nose, wide-set pale blue eyes, a small mouth with large, tobacco-stained teeth.

"No," said Cooke.

"The phone," said the cabby. "And the busted phone in the room with all the books."

"Yes, well, those," Cooke said, annoyed.

"Sat in the chair over there too," the cabby said.

"I was feeling a little, well, dizzy," Cooke said, beginning to dislike the taxi driver. "The altitude, you know."

A forensic surveyor began taking measurements and drawing on a pad. Another man went around photographing bullet holes, the broken doors, and the mirror of the telescope.

"Twelve-thousand-dollar mirror?" asked the sheriff.

"It was handmade, I understand. But yes, twelve thousand would be a conservative estimate of its worth."

A man named Arv found traces of white dust in the hallway, and deputy Hawkins stood on a chair and shined a flashlight in the attic and discovered a travel bag. A camera was in it, and a tape recorder and microcassettes. The name Gail Dionne was on a plastic tag attached to the bag.

The sheriff nosed around, made some phone calls, listened to a few comments by his men.

The cabby departed.

"You say this Tyler is important somehow?" Sheriff Gabel asked Dr. Cooke, talking around an unlit cigar wedged in the corner of his mouth. They sat in the living room. The eye of the television with its bullet hole stared at them, lamenting in silence the strange violence that'd befallen it. The mantel clock showed twenty past ten. "Something about this weird deal with the sun?"

Cooke nodded. "A couple of years ago he sent me a paper about . . . well, I suppose it doesn't matter. The paper was unfortunately lost, and now it's possible Tyler knows something that might shed some light on what's happening. I think you ought to have some men out looking for him."

Sheriff Gabel gave him a narrow look. "That's already been taken care of. A ten-man search team will be here soon, and a couple more helicopters. From the looks of things, the two of them might've left on foot, though we still can't rule out the possibility of a kidnapping."

Cooke gave him a startled look. "The two of who?"

"Car out there on the road was rented last Wednesday to a Gail Dionne. Her name was on the travel bag in the attic, so we can assume she was here. Don't know what the bag was doing up there, though." He appeared thoughtful for a moment.

"Strands of long black hair in one of the showers and the bed in the master bedroom and one of the spares." Sheriff Gabel seemed to be talking to himself as much as to Dr. Cooke. "Rental agreement with Avis indicates that Miss Dionne is a reporter with a magazine, *Parsec*, and an editor in Boston confirms that she was here to interview Mr. Tyler, so for now we'll assume that's what she was doing.''

His eyes grew opaque for a moment. He looked down at his hands, looked up again. "How well do you know Mr. Tyler?"

Cooke shrugged. "Ten years ago, quite well. Now, not very well at all, I'm afraid. This wasn't a social call."

"Right now we've got no real proof that a crime has been committed. Bullet holes, property damage. Mr. Tyler could've done that himself, and that's no crime. Still, there's reason enough to mount a search for him—for Miss Dionne too, but it might not be proper for me to parade around what I find of his personal life."

"I understand."

"Girl's clothing in his bedroom; his things too, like they changed into some other duds, maybe dressed for cold. Then there's canned goods all over the kitchen counters, bits of nylon rope in the bedroom. Adds up to people leaving on foot, I'd guess, in a hurry but not what you'd call a panic . . . which brings us to his truck and her car. Distributor rotors missing from both, one found in that observatory place, smashed, the other in a vise in the garage. Not likely they'd do that to their own cars, or each other's cars, so it's likely the two of them had some company. After that, it gets kinda hazy. There's a pipe in the observatory maybe has a trace of blood on it. Mirror in there was probably busted with a bullet, same as the radio."

Cooke suddenly remembered the talk he'd had with Judd Ingram concerning Tyler at the former FBI man's Maryland home. A shudder passed through him.

"You just think of anything that might help out?" Sheriff Gabel asked.

"No, just cold. What about roadblocks, Sheriff?"

"I'll handle it," Gabel said. "This is my county. I know my way around it pretty well."

AT KITT PEAK, Monday morning came up cold and sallow. A chill wind blew from the northwest, tapering off by eight o'clock to a stray westerly breeze. In the observation room of the McMath solar telescope, Drs. Carleson and Vergucht stared at the sun's image on the big, circular table, awed by the terrible changes the new day had brought. The site of the previous day's gigantic flare was covered by a swarming, irregular spot some 30 billion square miles in area, and the other groups had gotten larger. About 180 billion square miles of the sun's surface had been taken over by evil-looking purple-black blisters, and more pores had recently appeared.

"This is trouble," Marcel Vergucht said. "I would like to go back to Belgium, to my family."

"I need you here," Dr. Carleson said.

"I would only like to go," Marcel replied in a quiet, resigned voice. "I will stay, of course. Maybe it would be hard to leave, I don't know. You have heard the news?"

Dr. Carleson nodded. The New England and Great Lakes regions of the United States were experiencing snow flurries. In July! Chicago had six inches, and St. Paul had over a foot. At moments, Dr. Carleson found it difficult to breathe and he had to fight an inner, suffocating fear to maintain a professional demeanor. The devils of his long-forgotten ancestors were possessing the sun. Atavistic chills ran up his spine.

OSO-15 was out, and would probably never be operational again. Solar flux readings would have to be made on-site.

Dr. Carleson bounced a laser beam off a mirror atop Keystone Peak, thirty-five miles away across the Brawley Wash. The amount of local atmospheric absorption was determined by the attenuation of the beam, and used to correct the spectrobolometer, which recorded the power spectrum of the sun.

Total power was down to 86.2 percent of normal. Average surface temperature was just 5,587 degrees Kelvin.

"It's cooling," Dr. Carleson said in a shaky voice.

Marcel Vergucht crossed himself.

CHAPTER 19 ——————————

TYLER CHECKED his watch. Twenty minutes past nine.

He lay on his back in the murky warmth of the sleeping bag. Gail was pressed against his left side, cupped in his arms, long and leggy and warm, her breath coming slow and even against his neck, an arm slung across his chest. That night his dreams had been erotic and repressed; nubile prizes held up, taken away. He'd groped in darkness for something that had eluded him nimbly, staying just beyond his grasp. Gail's breasts pressed against him, firm and warm, and his arousal was swift and inevitable. He felt the pressure of her inner thigh against his hip, the weight of her leg. This was the Ice Maiden he'd repulsed at Red's. He smiled at the thought. He allowed his hands to move down her body, past the slender waist to the abrupt flare of her hips, and from there back to her shoulders. He forced his hands to be still.

"Again," she murmured.

He said nothing, but complied with the request, feeling the wondrous smoothness of her skin beneath his fingers. He touched the elastic band of her panties, slipped his fingers an inch inside, and moved his hands around her, exploring the rich swell of her hips.

"How bold we are becoming," she said drowsily.

"Sleep well?"

"Once I had company, yes."

She stirred and yawned and then clung to him, moving her legs silkily to a new position.

"Do that again," he said, "and I refuse to be held accountable for my actions."

She looked up at him. "If something were to, well . . . happen, it'd be difficult for me to escape, I suppose?"

"Extremely."

"Screams would go unheard?"

"Out here, yes."

"It would be foolish for me to resist, then?"

"We might tear the bag if you did."

"Still, two problems remain," she said comfortably.

"And those are?"

"I'm starving and I have to pee terribly, darling. What time is it anyway?"

"Almost nine-thirty."

"So late?" She pushed herself off him.

"We didn't get to sleep until after three. But you're right, we better get a move on."

She groped around and began pulling clothing up into the light, sorting it out. The temperature was warmer than the night before, the sun providing a small amount of heat to the new day.

"This's yours," she said. "And this's mine. I think my jeans are at the bottom near our feet. Maybe you should climb out and dress first. I won't peek . . . I think," she teased.

Breakfast was canned chicken on bread and canned peaches, eaten in the lee of a low, wide boulder. There was very little movement of air. The sun warmed the side of Tyler's face; a December sun, he thought. Gail sat with her back to it, protecting her skin.

They teased each other about the night before, Gail taking the lead. He sensed a great need in her, tempered by caution and a restraint that came from a good place within her, not out of rejection of the sexual act but out of a wholesome respect for it. She could laugh at their silliness, the way she had imperiously called him to her bed and warmed him, responded to him; and then shed tears in her confusion and desire. Her eyes held him in a steady gaze that made him feel like warm pudding inside, promising without the need of words that sometime soon she would engulf him.

They gathered up the blankets and rolled the sleeping bag and tied it to the pack. They set out side by side toward the northeast, following the rim of the gorge that led down to the Little Colorado.

The grayish red river flowed northward, winding through a canyon composed of red and yellow sandstone; steep, grainy slides of layered rock. Turbulence churned the water as it passed through a bouldery gap only twelve feet wide and fell with a distant roar into a plunge pool. Across the river, the land was a banded flatness of reds and tans, yellows and purples, that rose in the distance to mountains from which the Dinnebito Wash drained. He could see the western edge of the Hopi Indian Reservation, which lay in the middle of the Navajo Reservation. Overhead, a hawk was a dark spot looping across the sky.

"Navajo land," Tyler said, pointing across the river.

"It's desolate," she replied, "but so beautiful."

"This is the southern part of the Painted Desert."

She stared. "I've heard of it. Like a fable in a storybook."

"It's real enough."

"I know. I've got some in my shoe."

They walked quickly as they spoke, moving with a sense of urgency. They passed through minor washes, over sandy ground covered with blue grama grass, mesa dropseed, saltbush, random sprawls of Indian ricegrass and shad scale. A mile ahead, the river twisted around a weathered pyramid of rock that was flat on top. The southeastern side of this mesa remnant faced the river, dropping precipitously toward the water. Tyler continued to follow the canyon rim, seeking out the almost invisible trail that would take them down the cliffs to the river.

"Can you swim?" he asked.

"Yes, of course." She hesitated and then added, "I don't have a bathing suit with me, though."

"Me neither. We'll figure something out."

"I'll bet." She looked up. "The sun looks more yellowish today, not as bright."

"I've noticed."

He found the old Navajo trail that had been in existence for over four hundred years. Over the years, with little use, it had grown treacherous, the narrow ledge of rock covered with a fine layer of sand and gravel from the unending aeolian erosion of the cliffs.

She gave the trail a doubtful look, but said nothing. He started down and she followed, clinging to his hand.

In a tight voice she said, "If I fall here, I don't think sprawling will do the slightest bit of good."

"Don't fall," he said.

"Wonderful advice."

"Plant your lead foot and don't transfer your weight until you're sure of your footing. Take your time."

"We don't have lots of time."

"For this we do. Don't look down unless you have a love of heights. Concentrate on the path."

"Indians used this?"

"They built it."

They inched down the steeply sloping trail. It rounded great protrusions of rock and wound across the sides of sheer cliffs two hundred feet high. Millions of years of history passed by as they descended, caught in narrow bands of rock. A hawk screamed overhead. The sound of the river grew louder. From time to time, the pack on Tyler's back scraped the rock wall ominously.

In time, the floor of the canyon grew closer. The cliffs loomed above them. Granules of sand sprinkled down. A breeze picked up as they neared the bottom, funneled by the rising walls. By the time they reached the bottom of the gorge and stood on a narrow, gravelly beach, Tyler felt sticky with cold sweat. A film of perspiration was on his brow.

"Now, wasn't that fun?" he asked, his breath clouding in the cold air.

She looked up. "We came down *that?*"

"You were terrific."

"I was scared numb for all but the last thirty seconds."

The beach was just four feet wide, twenty long, terminating at either end in nearly vertical walls of sandstone. The water of the Little Colorado lapped the sand at their feet. The river here was fifty feet wide, flowing with oily, swirling smoothness through the chasm at a rate of about half a foot a second.

Tyler shrugged off his pack.

"It looks cold," Gail said.

Tyler opened the pack and took out several large plastic garbage bags. He stuffed the sleeping bag in one of the bags and twisted the end, looped it back upon itself and secured it with a rubber band. "Like that," he said, "Everything we don't want to get soaked, we'll float across. Shoes, clothes, blankets. I'll worry about the food."

"And the pack?" she asked.

"It gets wet. The nylon won't absorb much, and it'll dry quickly." He gave her a wry look. "Anything you wear across, you'll either have to take off when we reach the other side, or wear wet."

For a long moment she stared silently across the water. In time, she turned to him with a half smile on her face. "Last one in's a rotten egg."

She removed her jacket, stuffed it in a plastic bag, and then began to unbutton her shirts. He started taking off his clothing.

She said, "It's a weird game, Tyler. I'm still working out the rules." She nudged off her shoes. "Boy meets girl, or vice versa, and after two days they're dodging half-naked in and out of sleeping bags and rivers. The dumb thing is, it's so preposterously necessary."

"It's a conspiracy."

"Must be."

"I could turn my back."

"Don't bother," she said in a quiet, composed voice. "We'll just play the game."

She took off her jeans, leaving only the T-shirt and panties. Clothing went into the bag. In a final reckless gesture, she pulled the T-shirt over her head, pushed it in the bag, and began securing the end.

She was lovely, stunning, well defined with sleek muscle that moved beneath the smooth skin. Moderately large-breasted with dark areolas. Strong arms, good shoulders, flawless skin of pale gold.

"It's cold out here, Professor," she said. "Hurry."

Wearing nothing but Jockey shorts himself, he secured the final bag. Inside was his clothing, food, the logbooks he had taken from the library, her film.

She was standing ankle-deep in water, putting her hair up with a rubber band. "Water could be worse, I guess."

"Not very many days ago the temperature in central Arizona was over a hundred degrees," he replied. "It hasn't had much time to cool down."

She gave him a long, appraising glance. "You look good, sir. Terrific for thirty-seven."

He hoisted the pack to one shoulder and struck a jaunty pose. "I've been stared at like that before, ma'am."

"Oh?" She raised an eyebrow.

"Few days ago. Some woman in a bar where I was playing guitar."

She smiled. "Probably a floozy, up to no good."

"That's what I thought. I gave her the brush-off."

"An excellent, farsighted decision. Now, shall we get across this river?"

The water turned out to be less than warm, but it wasn't numbingly cold either. The river bottom fell away in rocky ledges; twelve feet from shore, the water was over their heads. They struck out for the opposite side, finding it necessary to swim with considerable energy toward a point well above the place they intended to land, tugging the wallowing bags behind them. Gail took two bags while Tyler wrestled with a single bag and the pack, using a ragged sidestroke that was more a choppy, violent scissors kick than anything else.

Ahead of him, Gail stood waist-deep in water and tossed her bags onto the gravel bar. Tyler reached out his legs and made contact with the bottom. Gail took the pack from him and they climbed out, trembling.

"It wasn't all *that* warm," she said accusingly.

"Yeah, but wasn't it refreshing?"

"Uh-huh. I suppose you forgot towels?"

"Yep. Turn around, please." He stripped off his under-wear and wrung them out, put them back on. He kept his back to her as she did the same. They dressed quickly in the cold air, and Tyler buckled his gun around his waist and arranged the sleeping bag and the pack while Gail tied the blankets around her waist again. She looked up at the sheer sandstone walls of the gorge rising above them, but said nothing.

The climb up was easier than the climb down. The trail wound upriver, toward the south, passing beneath over-hangs of rock and across great slopes that fell away, end-ing in broken piles of rocky debris.

In places, the way was wide enough that they could walk two abreast, narrow enough in others that Gail was afraid her heart would stop as they inched along.

Tyler heard it first—a distant rhythmic, choppy sound over the murmur of the river, the sigh of wind.

"Hurry," he said. Twenty feet ahead, the trail widened, strewn with fallen rock. "Untie the blankets." He shoul-dered himself out of the pack.

"What is it?" She scrabbled at the knots.

"Helicopter."

He looked up and saw it, flying above the center of the gorge, following the river, coming in their direction. It was three-quarters of a mile away, approaching rapidly.

"Move slowly," Tyler commanded. "Draw yourself up into a ball and pull a blanket over you. Tuck in the edges and then keep still, pretend you're a rock."

He did as he had told her, covering both himself and the glaring orange of the backpack.

The helicopter drew closer, the snapping of its blades echoing malevolently throughout the gorge. It passed by, 150 yards from them, and roared swiftly off to the north. Within a minute, even its sound was gone.

"All clear," Tyler said.

Gail poked her head out. "Looking for us?"

Tyler shrugged. "Could be. I don't want to find out. It might be that government muscle McGill mentioned."

She stood up, frightened. "How much farther are we going?"

"Fifteen miles, give or take."

"With helicopters buzzing all around?"

"We'll keep alert. And we'll keep the blankets ready to go into our rock routine at a moment's notice."

"Pretty sneaky. Old Indian trick?"

"Nope. Old Italian trick. Used for ducking irate wives, the IRS, mothers-in-law, process servers, helicopters."

"Uh-huh. You do this often, I suppose?"

"Only now and then."

In twenty minutes they reached the rim of the gorge and began hiking northward again, looking around jumpily. Tyler had covered the brilliant pack with one of the olive blankets. His brown coat and Gail's blue-gray jacket blended into the colorful earth tones of the desert. They angled away from the river and moved across the flat of the desert, following dry, scoured depressions where water flowed during sudden thunderstorms. The helicopter went past again on the far side of the river, a silent black dot speeding southward against the sky. They stood still and watched, feeling no need this time to take cover.

Clouds began to form in the north, and the wind began to pick up. Sand eddied at their feet. Gail heard the helicopter when it returned again—behind them, this time. They slumped down where they stood and became invisible in the empty wasteland. The helicopter went by without slowing, a quarter mile east of them.

And then they were alone in the unchanging desert. The miles passed slowly beneath their feet. Gail walked beside him, and asked Tyler about his past in greater detail than she had at his house. He answered willingly, sensing that she was trying to bridge the inevitable gaps of knowledge that existed between them. As they talked, one or the other of them would suddenly turn a head, listen, stare intently at the horizon, then shrug and walk on.

They came upon the Dinnebito Wash, a steep ravine that cut across their line of march, choked with blowsand deposits. She insisted on carrying the pack awhile. He took it back after she'd carried it three or four miles. They ate bread and tuna as they hiked along, and drank from the canteens.

By late afternoon clouds filled the sky overhead, blotting out the ailing sun. The air grew colder. Occasionally one or the other of them would stumble, and for a short while they would lift their feet an inch or two higher and strides would lengthen. Her strength pleased him, the way she kept up with him without complaint.

The light was failing when the familiar stand of twisted cedar and juniper appeared ahead. The river gorge had grown deeper and more inhospitable with the miles. Sam's place was tucked in the shelter of low, gnarled trees.

Tyler pointed. "There it is."

She took his hand and walked with him, just able to make out the dark bulk of a house trailer in the dusky gray light.

CHAPTER 20 ─────────────

GAIL GAZED around as they walked through Sam Hatathli's camp. She knew little of the Navajo and less of Sam, and had no idea what to expect. She saw poorness and deprivation in the surroundings—and an unexpected tidiness. A dark-hued trailer sat beneath the dark, protective branches of gnarled, one-seed juniper trees twenty feet tall. The wind-scoured trailer was rust-spotted, battered and peeling. Its original color could have been anything from forest green to a deep aqua.

A fire pit in the center of a courtyard of packed earth was sheltered from the wind by trees. Wooden crates, lacking tops, lay on their sides and provided storage for canned food, clothing, and sundries. Recently washed shirts and denim pants hung from juniper branches, swinging eerily in the wind.

A gleam of light caught Gail's eye. Almost hidden between two bulky junipers was an aging camper shell up on blocks, the closed door facing east, away from the river. From the camper came the muffled sound of someone singing.

"Sam," Tyler called in a low voice at the door. He rapped on the aluminum shell with a knuckle.

Moments later, the door opened and a wedge of light spilled onto the ground outside.

"Yá' át' ééh," Tyler said softly.

"Yá' át' ééh, young Tyler,"* Sam replied, standing in the doorway. "Men are looking for you. This is the girl?"

The question startled Gail.

"Yes," Tyler replied simply.

"Welcome to my hogan. It is cold outside."

Tyler ushered Gail inside and shut the door.

The camper was cramped but warm, illuminated by a small Coleman lantern hanging from an overhead vent. Sam Hatathli sat opposite the door at a tiny booth wrapped around a minuscule table. To the left was a Formica counter with a sink and a stove, cabinets, a small closet. A bed was in the forward portion of the camper, cantilevered out into space. A large Mickey Mouse alarm clock stood on the counter, along with salt, a sack of flour, coffee, sugar, utensils, an expensive-looking walkie-talkie. On the table before the old Navajo was a stick with feathers on one end, a small earthen bowl of whitish yellow powder, a few colored stones.

"Interesting hogan, don't you think?" asked Sam. "My nephew gave it to me. Easy to keep warm."

He was a small, wrinkled man, with rawhide brown skin loosely attached to thin bones. His hair was iron gray, long, held close to the sides of his head by a red scarf folded into a slender band and knotted at the side. His eyes were sunken, wise and ancient, filled with resignation, understanding, and an almost startling awareness, glinting with humor. A brow of leathery wrinkles, sunken cheeks with high cheekbones, a flat face, wide nose. More teeth were missing than remained intact, and those still in place were yellowed and old. His hands were bony and gnarled. He wore faded jeans, a plaid flannel shirt, and a heavy silver belt of conchos and leather. His voice had a rough, aged timbre and was pitched high.

Tyler and Gail sat at the table, Gail's left knee touching Tyler's thigh. Tyler made introductions.

"Pretty woman," Sam observed, speaking as much to her as to Tyler. "But strong. One to take in the land with you." He looked into her eyes as if searching for something.

"Thank you," Gail said, wondering exactly what Sam meant, hoping her response was appropriate, yet feeling inexplicably comfortable in the old man's presence.

Tyler said, "You moved from the trailer."

"Almost a year ago, young Tyler."

"Too long," Tyler agreed. "People were here looking for us?"

Sam nodded. "A helicopter came. National Guard. A man in a nice suit showed me pictures of you. He wanted to know if I had seen you, but of course, I see nothing."

"How long ago?"

"Mickey said it was quarter to four." He nodded seriously toward the big windup clock with its gaudy brass bells.

"Did they say what they wanted?"

"No. But you're a scientist and Father Sun is sick. The *Bilagáana* will look to science for answers to questions of the spirit."

"*Bilagáana?*" Gail asked, stumbling over the word.

"The White Man," Sam told her, smiling.

Tyler said, "They want to keep us from telling the world of the sickness of the sun."

"The world can see for itself," Sam replied. "They do not need you to turn their eyes to the sky. The *chindi* of Father Sun grow strong. Every day the *Naayéé*, the sickness, grows stronger too."

"There's little I could tell them anyway."

"And the world does not need to hear. Still, they look for you."

"We might bring you trouble."

A light appeared in Sam's eyes. "There is nothing anyone can do to an old Indian, young Tyler."

Tyler leaned forward, his forearms planted on the table. "We have to get to Los Angeles as soon as possible, Sam. But we have no transportation."

"You want to go to a bad place," Sam said. "Too many people, too many crazies, especially now." He gave Gail a gentle smile. "I lived in Los Angeles with my first wife, Bahajibah, after the war with the Japanese. For three years I put rivets in the wings of airplanes for the Lockheed company, so I know about Los Angeles. Now it is much worse.''

"My little girl is there," Gail said.

Sam nodded. "Family should be together now. You must go. You must hurry."

"Can you help us?" Tyler asked.

"When Mickey says seven, tomorrow morning, I will tell my old friend in Gray Mountain on the talkie what you need."

"No sooner?"

"My friend listens at seven in the morning and seven in the evening. Now is too late. We will talk about what you need, young Tyler, and we will eat and drink and enjoy each other's company. That is all we can do." He paused. When he spoke again, his voice was sad. "No one listens to the old people anymore. The young do not come to visit and to learn. The old fires die."

"You have taught me much, Sam."

"Too much remains inside," Sam said, thumping his breast with a closed fist. "Too many years. But now we will eat."

"We brought food with us."

Sam stood up with a slow fluidity. "This is my hogan. I have kneel-down bread, and this." From a cupboard he produced a very large can of hash. "It is too big for me, young Tyler. I have been saving it for a special time."

"Can I help?" Gail asked. She gave Tyler a perplexed and helpless look.

"This is my hogan," Sam repeated with simple dignity. "Do you know how to play cribbage?"

The question surprised her. "Y-yes."

His old eyes took in her face, and his mouth widened in a large smile. "Perhaps we can play a game tonight. I like to play cribbage." He cleared the feathered stick, stones, and powder bowl from the table.

"Why, I'd be happy to."

Sam heated the hash on the propane stove in a large iron skillet. He put several corn husks in a large covered pot without water, and set it over a low flame on a second burner. When the food was cooked, he dished it up on chipped plates of different colors and set them before Tyler and Gail. Without a word, he slid open a window near his feet that would have opened on the rear window of a pickup truck if the camper had been in place, and brought in three cans of beer.

"Now I have a fridge," he said with quiet amusement.

Gail couldn't remember the last time she'd had a beer, but she wouldn't insult Sam Hatathli by refusing the offer. She was famished, and the hash smelled surprisingly good. She wasn't sure what to do with the corn husk on her plate.

"Kneel-down bread," Tyler told her, peeling the husk away from a moist, doughy core. "Green corn cut from the cob and ground up, salted, packed in husks, and baked."

She tasted it, found it unlike anything she'd ever eaten before. "It's good!"

Sam's eyes smiled at her.

As they ate, Tyler told Sam about the visit the previous night by Harry McGill and Gordon Tate. He described the hike they'd begun in darkness and continued the next day, told him of the helicopters they'd seen on the way to Sam's place. The old Navajo listened with solemn intensity.

"The men who came today were not these men, not McGill and Tate," Sam said when Tyler finished.

"No, but McGill could have spoken to the men who hired him, and they might have instigated a search for us."

Sam's dark eyes grew distant. "Maybe," he said. "So, you need a truck?"

"Anything that'll get us to Los Angeles and back. This isn't an easy request, I know."

"Maybe not so hard," Sam said. He stooped over.

Before Gail could object, Sam opened another can of beer and placed it before her. He gave Tyler another, then got a cribbage board and a deck of cards out of a drawer and set them on the table. His old hands shuffled the cards slowly.

"Stole-Two-Mules was a code talker during the war," Tyler said, leaning back to watch.

"Who? A what?"

"Stole-Two-Mules," Sam said with a dry chuckle. "Me." He began to deal the cards.

Gail didn't know how to respond. "I, uh . . . how did you . . . I mean, why . . ."

"When I was young, I was foolish and reckless," Sam said. "I took two mules from the army. They put me in jail for one day and made me give the mules back." He grinned at her.

"You were bad, Sam," she admonished, smiling. She fanned her cards and looked at them.

"I was a devil. I would not listen to the old people." He shrugged. "This is how we learn."

"He made up for it during the war," Tyler said. "Pacific theater."

The game went on and the story of Sam's part in the Second World War progressed in fits and starts between the rituals of pegging and the counting of points.

At the age of thirty-two, Sam had been trained as a "code talker" under the tutelage of Johnny Manuelito and John Benally at Camp Elliot in California. The code talkers spoke Navajo, a language for which there was no written form. The Japanese had proved adept at breaking American codes, and early in the Pacific war, Philip Johnston, an engineer who had grown up on the reservation, proposed that Navajo Indians be used to man critical radio circuits, speaking Navajo in coded form.

The idea was genius. Wherever they were used, the code talkers completely frustrated Japanese efforts to intercept Allied radio communications.

In September of 1942, Sam Hatathli was behind Japanese lines on the northern slope of Mount Austen on Guadalcanal, overlooking the "Bloody Ridge" perimeter the marines had set up around Henderson Field. Sam supplied information that had helped the marines turn back General Kawaguchi's attack on the base. He had been at Bonriki on Tarawa Atoll in the Gilbert Islands during the Japanese suicidal defense of the stronghold at Betio. By the time Mount Suribachi was taken on Iwo Jima on February 23, 1945, Sam was in a position of relative safety at the coastal city of Lingayen, 110 miles north of Manila on the Philippine island of Luzon, recovering from a bout of malaria. In August of that year, he returned to the United States to Barstow, California, where he and dozens of other code talkers were honorably discharged from the Marine Corps at the Marine Corps Supply Depot there.

" 'A' was for 'ant,' " Sam said. *"Woll-a-chee.* 'J' was for 'jackass'—*tkele-cho-gi.* I still remember."

Gail gave Sam a new look of respect. "You were behind enemy lines. Not many can say that."

Sam shrugged. "It was a job I could do."

The game went on. Sam pegged out, beating her by just three points. Outside, the wind gusted and made a mournful sound in the trees. Gail yawned. Mickey, she noted, said it was ten-thirty.

"Time to sleep," Sam said.

"I'm exhausted," Gail admitted.

"The trailer is open," Sam said to Tyler. "The bed is clean. It is cold, but with two, you will not be cold." He said this in the same matter-of-fact manner he might have used to describe the nesting of waterfowl.

Gail glanced at Tyler and he smiled back at her. Sam gave them a second small Coleman lantern, which Tyler pumped up and lit. They said good night to Sam and went outside. Gail felt unsteady from all the beer. She carried the lantern as Tyler hoisted the pack, and, buffeted by a bitter wind, they crossed the clearing. Shadows leapt in the trees. Gail could see no stars, no sign of the moon. Behind them, Sam's "hogan" was a pale rectangle in the darkness. They went into the trailer.

Tyler took the lantern from Gail and held it aloft. The trailer was narrow and cold. Down a hallway wide enough for only one to pass at a time, the bed was visible, covered with a Navajo blanket.

"Who gets the bed?" Tyler asked.

"Don't get coy with me, buster."

He smiled at her. "Before you get too comfortable, the toilet facilities are outside, and the only water is what we've got in our canteens."

"I wish you'd told me that before I drank two beers. And how am I supposed to brush my teeth?"

"We'll figure something out." He opened the door for her and they went outside.

Five minutes later, they were back. "He's chanting again," Gail said, shivering.

"The Navajo have literally hundreds of chants and songs. Right now, all over the reservation, thousands of them will be chanting for the sun."

"I wish them luck."

They moved to the rear of the trailer. Tyler hung the lantern from a loop of wire fixed to the ceiling over the bed. Gail undressed quickly. She felt unexpectedly self-conscious, slipping between the chill sheets in underwear and a T-shirt. Tyler got into the bed on the opposite side after turning a valve, extinguishing the lantern. It took the light a minute or so to go out, changing from white to a guttering yellow to a dull red. Just like the sun, Gail thought with sudden sadness. A visceral longing twisted inside her as her awareness of Tyler intensified.

He reached for her in the final dimness of the lantern and gave her a tender, lingering kiss before snuggling down quietly beside her.

She waited a few tense moments and then said, "Tyler?"

"Mmmmm?"

"Is that it?"

"Is what what?"

"That husbandly little peck. Is that all there is?"

"It wasn't any good?"

"It was fine, and what's the problem? I expected to be out of this T-shirt by now, after all the antics of last night and this morning."

She felt him rise up on an elbow. "The requisite forty-eight hours isn't up yet," he said.

"Don't play games with me, Tyler, please."

"No games." His voice was somber.

She sensed his mood. "What is it then?"

For a moment he was silent. "We've got something here, you know, something real that we can't ignore."

"I know." Her voice was almost a whisper.

He struggled for words. "I feel . . . I don't know,

rushed, I guess." He touched her cheek. "All this, being here with you this way . . . it makes me feel achy inside, but good. It's enough for now."

"Achy? . . . Enough?"

He sighed. "I'm not doing a very good job of explaining how I feel," he said finally. "Perhaps it's ridiculous, but I'd like to savor this moment before we move on. I've got an achy, fluttery feeling inside that a person only gets a very few times in his life. For a while I'd just like to look at you and . . . anticipate. I suppose what I'm saying is I want to possess you, all of you, and that means consuming you by degrees. You're so beautiful, it almost hurts just to look at you, and I—"

She felt a great swelling within her. She twisted to one side and straddled him on hands and knees. "God, Tyler," she said in a thin, whispery voice.

"I'm still being a jerk, aren't I?" he said.

"Very likely, but so terribly damned sincere, too, in a silly, sweet sort of way. I don't know if I want to kill you or just rape you and get your achy, blissful anticipation over with. Where does all that nasty restraint come from, anyway?"

"I have no idea."

"I don't want to be on a pedestal."

"You're not. I just need a while longer to let all this sink in."

She took his face in her hands. "Just so you'll understand . . . for months now, years, I've lived with this feeling you're so carried away with. I knew that somewhere out there in the world a guy was wandering around utterly unconscious of the fact that one day he was going to turn me inside out. He was *real* to me, Tyler, if a bit indistinct. I made him real because that's all I had, and I ached for the big oaf to touch me, to hurry up and find me, and now that he has, that *you* have, I guess I can wait a few more minutes or hours or days for you to catch the hell up—but I want you to know, sir, that I'm feeling ever so slightly volcanic."

"I'm sorry, I didn't know—"

She bent down and kissed him. "Don't apologize for

being Mr. Nice Guy. I'm not angry with you, for heaven's sake. I want you to be comfortable when the inevitable happens. I only want you to know that when the time comes, I may do you serious bodily harm."

"We'll be sure to have a resuscitator handy."

"You might just need it."

She worked the T-shirt off and grabbed his hands, lifted them to her breasts, felt the almost instantaneous hardening of her nipples. "If you're going to ache," she said softly, "do it right."

For a few minutes he explored size and shape and texture, then let his fingers trail gently over her ribcage to the flat of her stomach.

"You feel fantastic," he said. "How do you do it?"

"Is that a rhetorical question?" she asked in a dreamy voice.

"If it wasn't, how would you answer?"

She gazed at the dark shadow of him, lying half under her. "I'd tell you I work damned hard at it, every day." She leaned into his touch. "We each have our own private image of ourselves, not of how we'd *like* to look and be, but how we truly *are*. It's that self-image that molds us, no matter what we wish, or what lies we tell ourselves. I couldn't imagine being unable to run a dozen or so miles, fast, anytime I want or need to."

"All the work's been worth it. You're exquisite."

"Thank you, sir."

For a few minutes his hands explored her in silence. He kissed her lips and pulled her down beside him and was still.

"Oaf," she said to the night. "Go ahead and ache, then."

CHAPTER 21 —————

AT SIX-FORTY Tuesday morning, Tyler and Gail were back in Sam's camper, awaiting the seven-o'clock "talkie" call to Edward Theleklii in Gray Mountain. Sam was alert, appearing to have been up for hours. Both Tyler and Gail had slept as if dead after the previous day's trek, waking when a stronger than usual gust of wind shook the trailer. Gail had draped a strong, slender leg over Tyler's waist and teased him about the previous night. They got up, looking at each other with a piercing, electric intimacy as they hurried into their clothing in the frigid air.

Outside, the sky was dense with clouds. The pungent smell of coffee in Sam's camper made Tyler's nostrils flare. He poured a cup for Gail and himself, and they crowded over an old Texaco map of Arizona to discuss alternate routes out of the state.

At seven, Sam switched on the walkie-talkie and began speaking in Navajo. Edward Theleklii, Tyler explained to Gail, was an old code talker like Sam. They had both been at Tarawa and had marched together with the code talkers in the Pasadena Rose Bowl parade on New Year's Day 1975, with the Navajo Tribal Band.

A rapid stream of information passed between the two men, and after a few minutes Sam turned off the transceiver and put it back on the counter. "My friend will call back at ten," he said.

"What did you tell him?" Tyler asked. "The tribal police might've been listening."

"They would learn nothing," Sam said with sparkling eyes. "The police are all young men. Too young."

"You spoke in code?" Tyler said incredulously.

"I still remember."

Tyler shook his head. Still, it wasn't so surprising. The Navajo have prodigious memories. The language was spoken, not written; all legends and stories had been passed down from generation to generation. A Navajo felt rich by the number of songs he knew. Even today, for many, memory was their closest link with the culture and lore of the past.

They had a breakfast of plain tortillas *(náneeskaadí),* pinyon nuts, apples that Gail and Tyler had brought with them, and more coffee.

Gail was restless, worried about Nikki. She was able to listen with only half an ear as Tyler and Sam caught up on events of the past year. The conversation was sprinkled with a few Navajo words, which Sam translated for her. The slender red line of a thermometer mounted on an outside wall climbed slowly, eventually reaching only twenty-three degrees.

At ten, Sam turned on the radio. The ensuing conversation lasted only a few minutes.

"A truck is coming for you," Sam told them. "One-Boot's wife in Cow Springs has a vehicle you can use."

Fifteen minutes later, a dusty pickup truck with a cracked windshield and dented doors and fenders came rattling up the road that wound along the river. A young Indian climbed out and began unloading supplies, carrying them to Sam's camper. Tyler helped with five-gallon containers of water. The backpack went into the bed of the truck, and the Indian, who had so far said nothing to either Tyler or Gail, got behind the wheel again and waited for them.

Tyler gave Sam his logbooks to hold for him. Graciously, Gail said good-bye to Sam, holding his thin hands in hers.

His old eyes betrayed nothing as he presented her with a delicate necklace of silver and turquoise. He placed it over her head. "Bring you luck."

"It's beautiful," she replied. "I can't accept this."

"You cannot refuse."

To her amazement, he then sprinkled a small amount of the yellowish white powder over her and over Tyler, chanting in a withered yet melodious voice. He smiled. "You go now."

"Good-bye, Sam," Tyler said, holding the old Indian briefly by his thin shoulders. "Thank you, old friend."

"Hózhǫ́ǫ́gó ninániná doo," Sam replied.

They got in the truck, and the young Navajo driver circled and drove away. Gail sat in the middle, between the two men.

"What's this?" she asked, brushing powder from Tyler's hair and her own.

"A blessing," Tyler said with a grin. "For fertility."

"Oh. How nice."

THEIR DRIVER'S NAME was Timothy McCabe. McCabe was one of several names assigned to Navajo Indians at Fort Defiance in the nineteenth century when it proved too difficult to pronounce the Navajo names. McCabe had been Timothy's family name for seven generations.

The road wound along the east bank of the Little Colorado for twenty-three twisting, jarring miles, past seven or eight traditional earthen hogans and a number of trailers nestled in stands of juniper. The day was raw. A biting wind gusted out of the northwest.

In time, they reached a highway. Timothy McCabe pointed to the left. "The Navajo police have blocked the road into Cameron from the south. They are cooperating with the county police in a search for a man and a woman." He said this with typical Navajo blandness and, Gail noted, little or no accent. "The roadblock will be moved north to Cedar Ridge by two this afternoon."

He turned right and sped northward on U.S. 89, slow-

ing after not quite fifteen minutes at the junction of 89 and
U.S. 160 to Tuba City. Where the roads met, an elderly
motor home stood in a triangular patch of blackbrush and
needlegrass. Timothy McCabe pulled up next to the squat
vehicle. "You can use that," he said. "It burns oil, but it
runs good."

They thanked him and got out. A middle-aged Indian
came out of the motor home and gave Tyler and Gail a
vacuous smile as they thanked him. He would take no
money from them. "On the house," he said in halting
English, as if it were a phrase he'd heard many times before in other circumstances. He got in the truck and it
rumbled off toward Tuba City.

"It's . . . different," Gail said, looking askance at the
RV, a Winnebago at least twenty years old. It was twenty-
four feet long, a chubby, frumpy vagrant of the highways.
Red dust coated its scaly blue paint and rust-spotted
chrome. Bits of sagebrush were caught in the rear bumper.
It had a slight list to port, a chip of plastic missing from
one of its taillights, assorted scars, balding tires.

They went in through the side door, which opened on
a tiny combination living room/kitchen/dining room. Raw
wood showed through gouges in the cabinets, and the Formica counter was a mosaic of knife slashes and burn
marks. But the interior of the old motor home was clean,
as if it had been recently wiped down and scrubbed. A
short hallway led into the back, into a cramped bedroom
with a small double bed, neatly made up and covered with
the inevitable Navajo blankets.

Tyler got behind the wheel. Gail sat beside him in the
passenger's seat. The hump of the engine rose up between
them, providing a resting place for maps and drinks. The
odometer showed 13,282 miles. How many times it had
turned over, Tyler didn't care to guess. He turned the key
and the engine caught willingly enough, filling the interior
of the motor home with a lusty roar.

"Which way?" Gail shouted over the noise. She had
located a map and had it open in her lap.

"North," Tyler hollered back. He put the Winnebago
in gear and eased out onto the highway.

They passed through Cedar Ridge just before one in the afternoon with what appeared to be plenty of gas to get them to the next town up the line, Marble Canyon, on the far side of the Colorado River, just past Navajo Bridge.

At Marble Canyon, Tyler stopped at a tiny store with a single pump out front and topped off the tanks. He fed the engine a quart of oil. Gail bought food and phoned Nan and Nikki to let them know she was coming. She wore her cowboy hat low, her hair pinned up.

They munched sandwiches on the way to House Rock, unable to converse comfortably over the steady, numbing roar of the engine. They passed through House Rock and Jacob Lake in the Kaibab National Forest. Later that afternoon, on the way to Fredonia, flakes of snow began to sputter from a gunmetal sky.

CHAPTER 22 ─────────────

WHEN DR. GABRIEL SUSMAN ARRIVED on Tuesday afternoon, Dr. Malcolm Cooke was seated at Tyler's desk in the physical sciences building on the campus of Northern Arizona University. Stacks of books, computer printouts, and loose-leaf binders were on the floor, brought in from Tyler's library at Cooke's request.

The book on catastrophe theory was lying open, and Cooke was pondering this pregnant tome and a sheaf of Tyler's more promising papers, transferring his attention from one to the other like the ticking of some great, erratic timepiece. He mopped his humid brow with a linen handkerchief at frequent intervals. He hadn't worked this hard in years. All the old knowledge felt clotted and stale inside his head.

"Dr. Cooke," Nora Klemowicz said, standing deferentially at the entrance to the room.

He looked up. "Yes?"

"Dr. Susman is here."

Dr. Susman appeared at Nora's right shoulder, and for an instant the two men gazed at each other. Gabriel Susman was a midget of a man, five foot one, 114 pounds, with a dark goatee, dark little eyes sunken far back in pouchy eye sockets, a razor nose, and thin lips. He wore a dark suit with a pink shirt and carried a briefcase in one hand.

Cooke frowned at the sight of Susman's negligible form, and Susman frowned at Cooke's generous one, and then Susman bounded energetically into the room and gave Dr. Cooke's hand a vigorous, impersonal shake.

"You have need of a magnetohydrodynamicist, yes?" Susman said in a loud, resonant, appalling voice.

Nora hurried away.

"That is correct," Cooke boomed back, not about to be outdone in volume by the tiny physicist from the California Institute of Technology.

As the afternoon hours wore on, Dr. Cooke told Dr. Susman all he had learned in the past twenty-four hours about Tyler's theory concerning the sun. There were huge gaps in his knowledge. Susman was impatient and asked piercing, intelligent, imperious questions for which Cooke rarely had an answer.

It seemed that if the two men could eventually establish a smooth working rapport, it would not be in this century or the next. Still, Cooke's knowledge of magnetohydrodynamics was marginal at best, and Susman's knowledge of the sun was, in Cooke's view, contemptible. Neither had dealt with a statistical convection model interwoven with the usual magnetic field equations and hydrodynamic flow, and Tyler's model contained a dynamic loop that was most annoying. Susman, like Cooke, had but the haziest knowledge of catastrophe theory. What little knowledge they held in common served only to drive a wedge deeper between them.

At six o'clock sharp, Dr. Carl Hussbarger from the mathematics department of Stanford University arrived. Hussbarger had recently coauthored a text on catastrophe theory. He gave a single derisive snort at the volume that lay open on Tyler's desk, and replaced it with his own. He was tall and gaunt, utterly bald, prone to sneezing explosively and unexpectedly, and had red, rheumy eyes. He provided a much-needed link between Cooke and Susman; under his guidance, Tyler's formulation of the problem began to grow more comprehensible and to take on greater significance.

They listened to selected portions of the tapes Gail Dionne had made at Tyler's house, copies of which had been sent to the director of the National Science Foundation and to the president's science adviser. In the end, Hussbarger declared it too watered-down an account to be of any practical value, and they pressed onward. Cooke and Susman explained certain specifics, and Hussbarger gathered it all up into the form and method of catastrophe theory.

There were significant, annoying gaps in the work, references to documents entitled M-1 and M-2, but it quickly became apparent that Dr. Tyler's research was of the first caliber, revolutionary, marked with genius and precision and an unflagging attention to detail.

Under the circumstances, Cooke could not celebrate the fact that one of his former students would almost certainly receive a Nobel prize for his work—if a world remained to award such prizes after "Tyler's cycle" had run its course. Cooke felt snared in his own sticky web; every indication of Tyler's genius made him grit his teeth with envy, and fear of eventual exposure. The offhand and sweeping virulence with which he'd discounted Tyler's work now seemed like madness.

By midnight it was five degrees above zero outside, and dropping. In the quiet of the night, the three men worked on, while the campus physical plant labored under the strain of falling temperatures.

TYLER'S HOUSE WAS quiet now. Tuesday afternoon had seen the last of the detectives and sheriff's deputies, the last of the helicopters, the last county car in the front yard. Although there was still no direct evidence of a crime having been committed, the search for Dr. Tyler would continue. Pressure to locate him was being exerted by the National Security Council and by senior members of the National Science Foundation. Dr. Charles Hooper, chairman of a subcommittee of the President's Commission on

Civil Disorders, had also made several inquiries as to Tyler's whereabouts.

The sheriff's office was again the base of operations for the search, staffed in part by men from the FBI, a cliquish, overbearing group, in Sheriff Gabel's estimation. Roadblocks on critical arteries would remain in place until noon Wednesday, and pictures of Dr. Tyler and Gail Dionne (the latter faxed to Flagstaff late Monday afternoon) would be kept in circulation for at least a week. The two National Guard helicopters that had been used in the search on Tuesday would try again on Wednesday, joined by units from Luke and Williams air force bases outside Phoenix.

At midnight, Sheriff Gabel, who hadn't slept in over forty hours, went home to his wife after leaving instructions to be called if the slightest lead was turned up.

TUESDAY AFTERNOON, a blinding July snowstorm and temperatures of only twenty-one degrees resulted in the worst traffic snarl and wave of looting and general destruction in the history of the five boroughs of the city of New York.

It began slowly, when a car ran out of gas in the right-hand lane of the Holland Tunnel.

The driver of the car, Glenda Moor, was an ineffectual young woman, hampered in her efforts to think clearly by three hungry, squalling children from one to four years of age, and a hysterical desire to reach her parents' home in Bridgewater, New Jersey. Without thinking, she opened her door. It was immediately torn away by a slow-moving panel truck, which thumped over the twisted hunk of metal and continued on its way. Cars slowed for the obstruction, and Gus Pozzi, who'd been yelling at his wife for the past twenty minutes, plowed into the rear of the car ahead of him at about ten miles an hour—just hard enough to give them both a good jolt, stall the engine, and shower them with clothing and Gus's relatively worthless coin collection.

In the stream of cars exiting the city there was a sense of haste, an undercurrent of incipient panic as discernible and real as the lowing of a herd of cattle as the gray clouds gather and the wind rises and the far-off thunder draws near. The mass of cars moved too quickly for the conditions and too slowly to suit its individual drivers, who, like cattle, could think only in terms of movement, escape, a blundering charge out into the stormy night—no time for the brain to cease its churning and assess the situation rationally. This disparity between desire and circumstance was responsible for irrevocably plugging first the Holland Tunnel, and then every bridge and tunnel leading from the island-city.

When Gus's car slammed to a halt, blocking the second lane from the right, a two-axle U-Haul truck behind Gus swerved abruptly into the next lane to the left, sideswiping a low, red sports car. The car ran partway under the truck with a screech of metal before the driver of the truck slammed on his brakes, locking the two vehicles together. The two were then rammed by a limousine, and within half a minute, every lane of the tunnel was plugged solid.

A ragged void slowly opened ahead of the blockage. From behind came a deafening chorus of horns.

A man in a Cadillac put the front of his car against the rear of Glenda Moor's Chevy and punched the gas, driving both cars thirty feet along the tunnel before swerving left and roaring around her. Three more cars made it through the gap before it closed again with a dull *crump* of metal.

Cars came to a halt with bumpers touching, filled with drivers whose minds were clouded and dangerous with panic. Fistfights broke out. People left their cars and ran toward the retreating line of taillights. The driver of the Cadillac was dragged from his car, beaten, replaced. Gunshots rang out. Cars idled away their gasoline, pouring fumes into the air; others were abandoned.

As the tunnel plugged, its entrance ramps jammed. The streets around the entrances filled with immobile vehicles, many of which were quickly abandoned as well. Police cars were caught like bugs in amber. All the arteries clotted: the Lincoln Tunnel, Brooklyn Battery Tunnel, Brooklyn Bridge, Manhattan Bridge, Queens Midtown Tunnel, Triborough Bridge.

The Brooklyn-Queens Expressway went solid with the refuse of automobiles and vans—an asphalt snake of steel and hydrocarbon, revving engines, blaring horns, and noxious fumes. A man in a pickup truck began repeatedly ramming the little Ford sedan ahead of him, pounding it to scrap before being dragged from his truck and beaten insensible by a trio of youths. Similar concretions occurred on every major route leading north from the city, from White Plains and the Tappan Zee Bridge all the way into the Bronx and Manhattan.

As the exodus achieved critical mass, a remarkable buying spree began. Days earlier, a nervous accumulation of food had begun, a slow but steady increase in the volume of food passing through the city's checkout stands. Tuesday afternoon the wave broke, and every food outlet in the city, big and small, was stripped clean within hours in a spate of panic buying. As dusk fell and the streets grew dark, buying degenerated into violent looting and thievery.

Inevitably, radio and television played up the turmoil and made it worse. The July snowfall and the bright edge of panic that swept the city lent a macabre, carnival atmosphere to the night.

Predators emerged, pulses quickened by screams that filled the night, blood hot as they sensed the impotence of the police in the gridlocked city. Smoke and flames rose from cars that had been torched for the simple thrill of watching them burn. Swirling snow muted gunshots, cries of rage and terror, shouted curses.

Behind locked doors, people stared out their windows at the fearsome beast of the city.

Jay's Delicatessen on Hudson Street was gutted by fire that roared upward into the overlying structure. Firemen could only watch as flames reached the fourth floor, still climbing. Dozens of other fires broke out. People stood in the street and watched as an entire block between Seventy-eighth and Seventy-ninth streets went up, gouting flames and a writhing orange-black pillar of smoke. No emergency vehicles gathered below, no red flashing lights—only an unmoving knot of cars and vans caught beneath a rain of glass and bits of flaming debris.

Food had taken on new importance and value, and the city's miscreants soon found a new thrill to quicken their blood: the doors of the elderly were battered down and gray-haired men and women were terrorized, beaten, or killed, and then robbed of their small stores of food.

Retired taxi driver Erwin Schmidt was eighty-six years old and owned a huge single-action Colt .45 revolver that he hadn't fired in thirty-one years. He held it up in a thin, trembling fist, aimed at the door to his third-floor walk-up when the first shuddering blows came.

"Get out, get out!" he screamed in a shrill, terrified voice.

Dark laughter answered; the door splintered inward, pounding against the wall. The revolver boomed and the thin bones in Schmidt's wrist came apart. Rafael Galvez was thrown back into the hallway by the heavy bullet, his clavicle and scapula shattered. He lay dazed for half a minute, then staggered to his feet, lurched inside, and stomped Erwin Schmidt to death before collapsing and dying several minutes later of blood loss.

Refugees from the violence crowded the hospitals and police stations. All through the night the snow came down and the temperatures continued to fall. The tempo of violence dropped in the early hours of the morning as the brutes became sated with the game and policemen patrolled the streets in groups of three and four, dressed in riot gear and winter coats, holding shotguns and rifles at the ready.

Statistically, between three and four hundred people are expected to die each day in New York City due to normal attrition of the human race. That Tuesday, 13,447 died in violence and fire. Of these, 308 were thugs, burglars, and killers; the rest were relative innocents. Another 592 died as a result of the cold wave that gripped the city.

The following day, things got worse.

BY FOUR O'CLOCK Tuesday afternoon, the only solar observatory in the United States free of cloud cover was Sacramento Peak in New Mexico. Colorado's Mount Climax was buried in clouds extending four thousand feet below the level of the observatory; the outside temperature was minus three degrees Fahrenheit. Similar conditions held at the McMath Observatory in Michigan, at Mount Wilson and Big Bear in California, and Kitt Peak in Arizona.

So it was left to the Sacramento Peak Observatory to take the only official U.S. photos of a sunspot within a sunspot. The sunspot groups had grown to encompass much of the sun's surface. Only narrow channels of bright light remained, like the fissures in a skull lit from behind by an arc lamp. Surface temperature in these bright lanes and near the poles was only 5,260 degrees Kelvin, and in the dark umbras of the spots, the temperature had fallen to as low as 3,430 degrees. In the terrible black spot within a spot, the temperature was only 2,750 degrees. Total flux stood at 52 percent of normal.

"Fifty-two percent," breathed Dr. Avery Charles. "We are dead."

IN THE LEE of a massive outcrop of granite rock, Robert Witherell held the cooling body of his brother, Scott. Robert's mind was numb. Cold was an animal with red eyes and savage teeth burrowing into his flesh, consuming him. The sleeping bags had been rated at only thirty degrees, so they had pushed one inside the other and gotten inside after spreading a brilliant orange tarp on the ground nearby. But the clouds had brought a freezing rain, and the temperature had sunk to twenty below, and snow had fallen like a shroud over the boys and their tarp.

At six-fifty, Tuesday evening, five miles east of Lone Butte in British Columbia, Robert Witherell whispered, "I'm sorry, Scott." He died thirty-five minutes later.

THE RIGHT FRONT WHEEL BEARING of the Chrysler was shot. The car was in the weedy rear yard of T&H Garage, awaiting a new bearing from Phoenix. Three blocks away, Harry sat with his legs curled around the scuffed wood lattice of a barstool in Duke's Tavern on Highway 66, at the western edge of Flagstaff. His mood was foul. He said nothing to Gordy, who sat next to him, chain-smoking and nursing a bottle of Michelob.

Harry was drinking doubles of bourbon and water, hunched over the ringed and burned wooden bar, his shoulders gathered around his neck. An ambience of rage filled the air around him like a mist of poison gas.

"Let's go back to L.A., Harry," Gordy said. The raw spot on his cheek had scabbed over.

Harry turned a bleary, malevolent eye on him. "Go, then."

"They just closed the airport."

"Catch a bus."

"The girl's gone. What're we doing here, anyway?"

"Drinkin'."

"Jesus," Gordy breathed.

Harry grabbed him by the arm and squeezed. Gordy's face went white. "The car won't be ready till tomorrow," Harry hissed, his eyes crazed. "We'll go then. That soon enough for ya?" Saliva flashed on his teeth in the light of a Budweiser sign.

"Sh-sure, Harry."

"Then shut the hell up."

Gordy shut up. Harry had another double, then another.

They had driven past the road to Tyler's place and seen police cars crawling up and down the road, helicopters flying all over. If the county mounties couldn't find them, what could Harry hope to do? Still he hoped. He thought of Gail Dionne and he thought of himself standing naked and cold in front of her—that nasty smirk she'd had on her face as her eyes took in his private parts.

He closed his eyes and tasted blood in his mouth. His brain seemed to pulse in his skull. There was only one thing he wanted to do, and that was kill Gail Dionne. Nothing else mattered. Nothing at all.

But she was gone.

CHAPTER 23

THE WINNEBAGO HAD COME without tire chains. As a result, at five-ten that Tuesday afternoon, on the snow slicked, two-lane road between Colorado City, Arizona, and Hilldale, Utah, Tyler and Gail were turned back by highway department workers. As they backtracked over the dreary miles, Gail's face showed the strain she was under.

"They said chains are available at Fredonia," Tyler said.

"I know."

"Cheer up. We'll make it."

She gave him a wan smile and stared silently ahead at the oncoming traffic, which was light: pickup trucks and vehicles with four-wheel drive, not many passenger cars.

They reached Fredonia a few minutes after six and found Ed's Texaco at the north end of town. Ed Farrel was a lean, grizzled man with big, dirty hands. His eyes were dark beneath a sodden ball cap; ears red from the cold.

He glanced at the Winnebago's tires and said, "Run you a hundred and sixty bucks. Two hundred, installed."

Tyler nodded. "We'll take a pair. Installed."

"Cash."

Tyler pulled some bills from his wallet. "How soon?"

"Take a while—hour, maybe hour and a half. I got gas to pump." His hawk eyes gleamed in the fluorescents.

"Get us out of here in twenty minutes and I'll add another fifty."

"Everyone's in a big damn hurry," Farrel observed darkly. "But you think on it, son. They ain't no place to go, no place to hide. Same sun shines all over."

"A hundred," Tyler said.

Ed Farrel gave a grim laugh. "Maybe it's gonna turn out that money ain't worth anything at all. Who knows? Who gives a shit? Comes right down to it, it's nothing but green paper. For a hundred I'll do what I can, take it or leave it."

They left Fredonia forty-five minutes later, full of Ed's gasoline and clopping on chains that added a new rumble to the noise of the Winnebago, a nervous vibration to their passage.

The snow came down harder, and Tyler and Gail were held up several times behind snow-removal equipment. It was midnight before they reached the turnoff to St. George, Utah, and began hammering their way slowly down I-15 toward Las Vegas.

The night wore on; a dirty crust of snow covered the road. The radio was gritty with the noise of solar activity, almost drowned out by the roar of the engine, the clatter of chains. Even so, they managed to piece together the horror stories of New York City, Chicago, and Boston.

Gail switched it off. "I can't listen." Her eyes were luminous in the glow of the instrument panel.

"If we leave it on, we might hear something about Los Angeles," Tyler suggested.

She shook her head. "All we can do is what we're doing. If we learn that L.A. is gridlocked or burning or under fifty feet of water, it wouldn't keep me from trying to get to Nikki, so I don't want to hear about it. Not right now anyway."

He looked over at her and saw tears streaking her cheeks. "You ought to get some sleep."

"I couldn't."

Ahead, the road was dark and treacherous, empty but

for the lights of a diesel rig ahead. "We've got a long way to go yet," Tyler said. "Suppose I need you to drive?"

"Then I'll drive. I won't sleep for the next million years anyway."

Even so, she slept, bobbing bonelessly in the seat with the shoulder strap holding her up.

A strange gray light began to fill the sky as they rolled past the Logandale-Overton turnoff in southern Nevada. The snow had let up and it looked clear ahead. A quarter inch of broken, choppy ice covered the road. It didn't feel slick. Tyler pulled to one side and removed the chains in a paralyzing wintry breeze that numbed his face and hands.

Gail was awake when he got back inside. "Where are we?" She looked drawn and groggy.

"The last sign we passed said it was fifty-eight miles to Las Vegas."

"Oh God, it's morning already."

"We'll be in L.A. by nightfall."

She gave him a thin smile. "Sure."

IN THE MIDDLE of Las Vegas, Tyler got off the interstate at the Sahara Avenue exit. He turned left, toward the strip, and found an Arco station. Traffic was surprisingly light considering what they'd heard of New York City. It moved quickly, however, with jerky stops and starts, nervous lane changes, a reluctant obedience of traffic lights and signs.

Tyler filled the tank while Gail bought sandwiches and coffee. A yellow, sickly sun shone through scattered clouds, having little effect on the bitter cold. When Gail returned, Tyler told her to buy a map of the city and look in the phone book for sporting goods stores that carried winter clothing. She came back with a map and a few yellow pages in her hand.

"I'm too jittery to remember any of this," she said, handing him the pages. "Do we really need warmer clothing? It's warm enough in here."

"I think we'd better have it, just in case."

"Maybe we could buy it in Los Angeles."

He shook his head. "Things don't look too bad here, but L.A. might be something else again."

He looked at the map as Gail read off street names where sporting goods stores were located. They left the Arco station and found Dave's Alpine Shoppe on Oakey Boulevard. When they got there, a sign said it opened at nine o'clock, weekdays. It was seven-fifty. Lights were off, the store dark.

"They might not open today," Gail said. "Let's just go."

For two hundred miles, Tyler had been turning an idea over in his mind. Now his heart began to race as he pulled out into the street, heading uptown on Las Vegas Boulevard South.

"Do you have a driver's license with you?" he asked.

"In my pocketbook," she answered. "In the backpack. Want me to drive awhile?"

"No. Let's get married."

She stared at him. *"What?"*

"We've passed half a dozen chapels already. Twenty-four-hour service. Nondenominational. Free parking. Let's get married."

Her eyes were huge. "I . . . God . . . how *could* we?"

"For openers, we could stop at one and ask. I've heard it's easy to tie the knot in Nevada."

"You're crazy, Tyler!"

He grinned. "Maybe so, but what do you say? It'd give us something to do until the store back there opens."

A smile illuminated her face. "You're *ser*ious!"

"Of course."

"Just like that?"

"It's sudden, I know, but we don't have much time to think it over."

She laughed shakily. "It hasn't even been a week since we met. In that bar."

"Red's Outpost."

"This is insane. What am I supposed to *do*, Tyler?"

"Follow your heart, I guess. This is new for me, too."

"My heart feels like it's going to explode."

He looked over at her. "Is that a yes?"

"Why *now*, Tyler? The sun?"

"That's partly it, yes. But I feel there's something inevitable about this, don't you? So, why not now?"

"Are you faithful, Tyler? Are you sincere and kind and considerate and . . . oh God, I'm starting to rave." She leaned back in her seat and closed her eyes. "Yes," she said softly.

"Huh?"

Her eyes were shiny. "Yes, yes. The world is spinning. Hurry up and find us a minister before I pass out."

He found a chapel near Charleston Boulevard, the Chapel of the Sands, and pulled to the curb in front. They went inside and stood in muted lighting that reflected off a pale yellow ceiling, making everything in the room seem warm and old. Mullioned windows veiled by white lace curtains looked out on the street, and the scent of a dozen perfumes hung in the air.

A plump woman of fifty with a sleepy, pleasant face came yawning and smiling out of a back room when they came in. She told them they would have to obtain a marriage license first, and gave them a map showing them the most direct route to the courthouse downtown (only a mile away), and asked them if it wasn't simply amazing, this strangeness with the sun and the dreary January weather in July.

The courthouse at eight-fifteen in the morning was doing a brisk business in licenses. It took twenty minutes to reach a clerk, a black girl with a gap between her front teeth who asked rapid-fire questions in a loud monotone. She took a pair of twenty-dollar bills and made change.

Minutes later, Tyler parked the motor home across the street from the Chapel of the Sands.

Gail looked at him. "You sure you want to make an honest woman out of me?"

"Absolutely."

"You won't buy me a beer and run out, leave me stranded at the altar?"

"Not this time."

"Okay, then."

She took his arm and they dashed across the street. "My

mother would never understand," she said in a thick voice as they went inside.

The minister, Cecil J. Orum, was portly and grave, attired in a dark blue suit that fit him beautifully.

"No best man or maid of honor?" he asked, giving the room beyond them a questing glance.

"No," Tyler responded.

"No witnesses or guests," he observed. He raised an eyebrow suspiciously. "No rings either, I suppose?"

"Sorry."

Orum smiled. "Fortunately, we have a large selection of rings right here, quite reasonably priced, I might add."

He showed them a velvet tray of gold bands in five basic styles, and told them he had every conceivable size in each style, for both men and women. They decided on plain rings, plated with eighteen-carat gold.

"A marvelous choice," Orum purred in a happy baritone. "You prefer to remain dressed like that?" he asked, gazing at their clothing in evident distress. Gail still wore Tyler's jeans, knotted at the waist with nylon cord and pinned at the cuffs, a baggy flannel shirt. "I have a selection of gowns and suits that may be rented for the occasion."

"We're in a bit of a hurry," Tyler said. He ran a hand over his stubbly cheeks.

Gail gave Tyler's arm a squeeze. "He's scruffy, but he's mine."

The minister tugged on an earlobe and frowned. "Yes, well, you certainly seem old enough to know what you're doing. Shall we begin?"

The chapel itself was a room to one side of the waiting room. At the far end, a tiny altar was sheathed in red velvet and flanked by a pair of flickering electric candles. The center aisle passed between Lilliputian benches painted white and decorated with peach bows. The air in the room was thick with dreams.

The heavy woman proved to be Mrs. Cecil Orum. She did a surprisingly adequate job on the organ, whipping up an energetic wedding march that lasted some thirty seconds and left them all standing expectedly at the altar.

Minister Orum was a flexible man, experienced in his craft. He did not ask if anyone would step forward and give reason why these two should not be united in holy matrimony. He made their newly purchased rings a part of the ceremony. He gave a pleasant three-line speech in his warm baritone and then elicited the two critical words from each of them before God and witnesses (the minister and Mrs. Orum), and then pronounced them man and wife, even managing a fond, avuncular smile as they kissed.

The license was signed and witnessed and a copy given to Gail. Fees were paid. An official copy of the marriage license would be mailed to the Tylers' residence in Arizona. The Orums wished them well, and waved as Tyler and Gail ran back across the street to the motor home.

The Orums watched them pull away. Mrs. Orum tilted her head to one side quizzically and said, "Funny. She didn't *look* pregnant."

CHAPTER 24 ———————————

GAIL HELD UP her ring. "I'm a bride. I don't believe this!"

Tyler grinned as he swung the Winnebago into the parking lot outside Dave's Alpine Shoppe. "Believe it, Mrs. Tyler," he said. It was ten minutes past nine, and a dozen or so cars were already there, nearly filling the lot. The store lights were on.

"I can't go on calling you Tyler, Tyler. That's both our names now, for heaven's sake."

"It wouldn't cause any great confusion, but what would you rather call me?"

She thought about it a moment. She sighed. "Nothing, I guess. You're really not a Morie, are you?"

"Or a Morris or Moritz or Maurizio."

"I guess you're still Tyler."

"Good."

Inside the store, a middle-aged salesman told them the "adjusted" price of winter clothing was fifty percent above the sticker price.

"Sort of a reverse sale," Tyler remarked mildly.

The eyes of the salesman narrowed.

"It's called a gouge," Gail whispered in Tyler's ear, "not a reverse sale."

"Oh."

"These social gaffes of yours are sometimes embarrassing, dear."

"I'll try to do better."

"Thank you."

They bought heavy down parkas for themselves and Nikki, complete with insulated hoods. One-piece ski suits, gloves, boots, ski masks. The two warmest sleeping bags they could find. Two large packs and two roomy nylon tote bags.

"Three thousand six hundred and fifty-six fifty-two," the salesman said with a malicious grin and a note of triumph in his voice. The grin faded and he licked his lips greedily as Tyler counted out bills from a thick wad.

"Sun's got you scared, huh, mac?"

"You've got green paper," Tyler replied, remembering Ed Farrel's words. "We've got survival clothing. It's a matter of priorities, that's all."

At a supermarket, Tyler bought canned food and bagels. The pace was hectic, the selection narrowing; patrons glassy-eyed and rude. Gail remained in the locked RV with her .38 hidden but ready, guarding the newly acquired survival gear. In the store, Tyler picked up a map of California.

By ten-thirty they were back on the interstate, headed for Barstow, winding through desolate, snow-clad mountains on wide, divided lanes. Northbound traffic was heavy out of Southern California, moving swiftly. Pale light tinged the mountains an eerie mustard yellow through patchy clouds.

"You haven't slept in almost thirty hours," Gail said, half shouting over the din of the engine.

"I'm all right."

"Drive now, pay later?"

He smiled grimly. "Maybe. But we can't ease up. What happened in New York will probably happen in Los Angeles, and soon."

"So we get in and get out fast," Gail said, noting that the speedometer needle was on seventy-five and the motor home was swaying alarmingly, its engine howling.

Tyler nodded. "We try."

She turned on the radio but found nothing across the dial except scratchy noise and mumbly, unintelligible voices.

"So," she said, switching it off, "tell me what happened at King's College back . . . what was it, eleven years ago?"

He stared at her, then looked back at the road. "Really came loaded for bear, didn't you?"

"All part of the job. Now that we're married, practically on a first-name basis even, shouldn't I know these things?"

"There's not much to tell."

"The new darling of the astrophysics department at MIT is given his walking papers and ends up in Arizona after delivering a paper that bombed at King's College in London, and you say there's nothing to tell?"

"Sounds like you've got the story already."

"Bits and pieces. Nothing really juicy."

"Why do you still sound like a reporter on assignment?"

"Habit. But my curiosity is that of a wife."

He smiled at her. "Wife. I like the way that sounds." He turned back to the highway. "What happened at King's College wasn't very inspiring. And it was ten years ago in June."

She waited for him, looking at the firm jaw and tired eyes of her husband of less than two hours.

"There was once a cocky assistant professor who'd been the golden boy, riding on top of the world for a number of years, first as a graduate student and then as the bright new boy on the block."

Tyler stared straight ahead as he spoke. "He was given the opportunity to present a paper at a solar colloquium to be held at King's College a week from then. Seems there'd been a last-minute cancellation. So, being not nearly as sensible or brilliant as he thought he was, he said yes, and then found he had nothing really significant to present. He could have cancelled, *should* have cancelled, but instead got almost no sleep for a week as he whipped up something that looked slick and commendable, and rushed off in a tizzy to wow the oldsters and lock arms with them in the lounges of the Tavistock Hotel and the Elephant and Castle.''

Gail gave him a pained look. ''If this is something you'd rather not do—''

''The third person narrative—like it happened to someone else? Sorry. It happened to me. I thought I'd come to terms with it better than that.

''I sat through two presentations in the morning and then went up and delivered a paper—'A New Statistical Convective Microcell Model of the Sun.' An imposing title, *nicht wahr?*

''Dr. Karl von Hasse was in the audience, a Nobel prizewinner from Munich about fifteen years prior to that. He sat in his chair like an old field marshal, and when I was through, he took me back to an early part of the development of my thesis and pointed out that while simplifying a set of equations, I had dropped second-order terms in an expansion that couldn't logically be discounted, that were, in fact, critical.

''After von Hasse pointed it out, it was obvious, of course. I still remember the silence of the room when he finished, the way my ears seemed to roar. It was a schoolboy's mistake, unforgivable and clownish, made before some of the most influential solar physicists in the world. There was nothing clever to say, nothing I could do to save myself, and I knew it. It was like, I don't know, watching yourself in a car accident, I suppose, sliding in slow motion under the wheels of a semi.

''I walked off the dais and went outside, got stinking drunk in a little pub I couldn't find now if my life depended on it. Two weeks later, I was told my contract for the coming year wouldn't be renewed.''

Her eyes were soft, serious, understanding. Her voice was gentle. ''It must have been terrible.''

He shook his head. ''I was due for it, or something like it. Scratch the golden boy and you'd have found lead beneath the surface.''

''Nick him even deeper and you'd reach gold again.''

''Brides are so damned impressionable.''

''You still yell a lot, though. Girl climbs into your bed and you come all unglued.''

He smiled. "I'm working on that."

"The next girl that climbs into your bed, mister, you had better count on holding long and tight. I'm not going to wait around all unconsummated and deprived while you go on exploring this blissful achiness of yours."

"Pushy little wench, aren't you?"

"You haven't seen anything yet."

CLOUDS COVERED the sky like wet plaster; flakes of snow began to fall. Tyler and Gail passed through Barstow at one o'clock Wednesday afternoon. Traffic was snarly and gas lines stood three blocks long, reducing the main street to single lanes in either direction. Tension filled the air. The mood was dangerous, unstable. They left town on U.S. 58, headed west.

In Mojave, traffic was heavy and erratic. The light at the junction of Highway 14 and Highway 58 was out, swaying in the wind on snow-crusted wires. Cars and trucks thundered by, some turning onto 58, others going straight through town, in the direction of Bakersfield and the Owens Valley.

Tyler nosed the Winnebago out as far as he dared into the uncontrolled intersection. Fifteen minutes passed before a break came up. He gunned the engine and they jounced and slid across the deadly space. An oncoming car hurtled around them, horn blaring, and then they were through, moving almost due south on Highway 14.

Tyler pushed the Winnebago to its maximum safe speed on the icy highway. Traffic coming from Lancaster and Palmdale was heavy. Once they passed Palmdale, it fell off abruptly to an ominous, sporadic dribble of speeding cars.

Gail turned on the radio, her lips white. A newscaster told them that wheat and corn crops in the midwest had been blanketed by two feet of snow under blizzardlike conditions. Citrus in Florida had been all but wiped out by temperatures in the teens the previous night. A tremor ran through the professional calm of the man's voice. Tyler and Gail learned nothing useful about Los Angeles.

South of Palmdale, several miles past Tenhi Mountain, a Pontiac in the northbound lane took a curve too fast, slewed sideways on the icy road and slammed into a guardrail, rebounded back across the road, spinning lazily, and ran its rear wheels partway up a rocky slope before coming to rest. Tyler dropped his speed a little and gripped the wheel more tightly, his brow furrowed in concentration.

At the Escondido Canyon Road exit, they came upon a roadblock: two police cars facing each other across the highway, lights flashing.

A patrolmen waved them down. Tyler slowed, rolled down the window.

"Road's closed," the patrolman said. He was young. His eyes were quick and hard and he had an implacable, unfriendly mouth, thin lips. Wisps of snow clung to the brim of his hat. His sleeve patches identified him as a member of the Palmdale police department.

"Our daughter is in L.A.," Tyler said. "Encino."

"Don't matter. You can't get through. Freeways're all plugged solid right where Fourteen goes into the interstate and all the way down past Long Beach and Anaheim."

"We've *got* to get through," Gail cried.

He glanced at her. "You couldn't get into Encino with a tank, lady." To Tyler he said, "What you got to do is drive up the off ramp here, cross over the overpass, come down the other side, and move out. Hell, you're lucky you're not in that god-awful ball-up in L.A."

"My child is in there!" Hysteria filled Gail's voice.

The patrolman's eyes narrowed to slits. "Orders, lady. No one goes through. L.A.'s closed to incoming traffic."

Quietly Tyler said, "Our little girl is in there."

"So you're some kind of special case, right?" The man's voice shook with unaccountable anger. "Everybody's a goddamn special case. Move out, *now!*" A car pulled up behind them.

"We can't do that, Officer."

The patrolman's voice grew dangerous. "You're holding up traffic. I told you to move out." His hand crept toward his service revolver.

A second patrolman strolled over. He was older, heavy, in his forties. "Got a problem, Johnny?"

"Couple of suicides here."

"You can't get through," the second officer said.

"My wife and I have a child staying with a sister in Encino," Tyler replied evenly.

"Sorry. Don't know what to tell you. The entire freeway system is kaput. Where the road here joins Five, you got ten dozen major accidents, fires, cars stalled, abandoned, reports of gunfire. Nothing's getting through, and I mean nothing."

"We've got to try," Tyler said hopelessly. "We'll walk if we have to."

"You wouldn't have any choice. You couldn't drive a kid's tricycle through that god-awful mess down there."

"You have any children, officer?"

He frowned. "Three girls."

"In my position you'd just leave them? Just turn around and drive away?"

A dark, thoughtful expression came over the patrolman's face. The younger of the two said, "C'mon, Ralph."

Ralph sighed. "What you do is drive up the off ramp here. Go straight on through at the top and you'll come back down to the highway."

"Ralph—"

Ralph waved a silencing hand at the younger cop. He gave Tyler a resigned look. "If you happened to get on the highway here at, say, Agua Dulce Canyon Road—that's about three miles up ahead—then we never saw you."

"That's exactly what I did, Officer."

"Good luck, buddy. You think I'm doing you a favor, but I'm not. Keep your eyes peeled. There's been cars coming up Fourteen on the wrong side of the road. Fast, too."

Tyler drove up the off ramp and down the other side.

Tears ran down Gail's cheeks. She gave Tyler an anguished look. "I had my hand on my gun," she said. "That young one wasn't going to let us through. I was thinking about . . . about sh-shooting him. I think maybe I would have if the other one hadn't . . . hadn't . . ."

He took her hand for a moment, his heart pounding hollowly, struggling to think of something adequate to say. "We'll do what we have to do. I'm with you, you know that."

Her face was puffy. "They said Los Angeles was like New York."

"We'll get through somehow."

They passed Agua Dulce Canyon Road. Along the margins of the road they passed stragglers on foot, wrapped in blankets, wearing bulky, shapeless clothing. Gail was silent for a few miles and then she sniffed and said, "I love you, Tyler. Did I ever tell you that?"

He smiled. "Not yet."

"Well, I do."

"We'll get to Nikki, I promise."

NINE MILES from the junction of Highway 14 and Interstate 5, the first car came speeding at them in their lane. Refugees plodded along the road in greater numbers than before. The Porsche, its horn drilling a path, raced through those on foot like a bullet. As it tore past, Tyler and Gail had a fleeting glimpse of a white, panicked face behind the wheel. The car's fenders were crumpled, smeared with blood. A tire gave off a thin, blue skein of smoke. It missed them by less than four feet as it roared by, moving at seventy miles an hour.

"Christ!" Tyler exclaimed.

The next vehicle was a pickup truck, just a quarter mile behind the Porsche, followed closely by two more cars. Tyler pulled to one side and slowed but kept on moving. The first car tried to pass the truck on the left, and then the driver saw the Winnebago, pounded the brakes, and went into a slide, kicking up a spray of dirty snow.

"Watch out!" Tyler yelled. He gunned the engine and spun the wheel, but the motor home responded sluggishly.

The car plowed into the left side of the RV, glanced off, sailed across the road and off a low embankment into a rocky area between the divided lanes of the highway. The Winnebago shuddered and tilted. Its windshield popped out in one piece as the frame flexed, and the motor home spun to the left. The fourth car passed within two feet of their front bumper, fishtailed, and kept on going.

"You okay?" Tyler asked Gail.

"I-I think so. God, they must be crazy!"

"Panicked."

The RV was sideways in the road, stalled. Tyler started the engine and cranked the wheel hard to the right. When he pulled forward, the coach vibrated horribly.

Ahead, the road was clear. People on foot had given way before the speeding cars. Tyler got out and inspected the damage. The outside left rear tire was flat, the inside tire crooked on its axle.

He got back in the cab. "Looks like we go slow from here on." Wordlessly Gail handed him his gun from the pack. He buckled it around his waist and covered it with his coat.

At ten miles an hour they wobbled toward the junction of Highway 14 and the interstate. A frigid wind poured through the gap where the windshield had been. In the distance, the hills were obscured by a pall of smoke.

They came upon two smashed cars, a Ford on its side in a ditch, and a Toyota with its front end crushed, blocking the right-hand lane. A young man with a beard was in the Toyota. A man and a woman, each in their forties, were trying to rock the Ford back onto its wheels.

Tyler stopped and got out. As he drew near, he could see that the man in the Toyota was dead. The right side of his head was crushed. Bits of his skull glinted white, and he had a squashed and pulpy look, like a melon that had gone bad.

Tyler backed away from it.

"Tyler!"

He spun. Twenty feet away, the man who'd been with the woman by the other car was walking cautiously toward him. He was big and soft, with heavy features and a blunt, wide nose. He held a jack handle menacingly in one hand.

"Easy there," Tyler said.

"Me and the missus gotta get to Idaho," he said in a toneless voice. "We'll take your rig there."

Tyler pulled his gun. "Sorry."

The man hesitated. He stared at the gun and a growling sound came from deep in his throat. His eyes were red-rimmed and crazed, but his lips were quivering, as if he were about to cry.

Tyler backed toward the RV, got inside, and drove on. As they passed by, the man lunged at the motor home with a howl of frustration and rage. The jack handle slammed against the side of the vehicle, then crashed into the rear window, showering the interior of the coach with glass.

Gail twisted toward the rear, holding her gun in a combat grip. Tyler concentrated on putting distance between them and the maniac.

"It's going to be bad, isn't it?" Gail asked. She faced the front again and rested both hands in her lap, still holding the gun.

"Probably."

A look of horror was on her face. "This isn't what I expected. This is . . . madness."

"It's unorganized flight. The cop was right . . . everyone's special, looking out for number one."

She took a deep breath and let it out slowly, completely. Her eyes were still wide, but her mouth was set with a resolve that hadn't been there only minutes earlier.

When she spoke, her voice was flat. "I almost shot that one too. You're right about us doing what we have to do. I won't lose you or Nikki by being unable to . . . oh, God . . . pull the trigger at the last moment, or whatever. No more tears. I won't let you down."

"I never thought you would. From the start, you've been wonderful."

"I haven't, but thanks."

He steered the RV around two people who were walking up the middle of the road. One of them glared savagely at him. The Winnebago crossed Placerita Canyon Road on an overpass. Ahead, Tyler could see a line of perhaps three hundred people trudging up the highway toward them.

Abruptly the vibration of the RV grew worse. A grinding sound came from in back, and the left rear wheel assembly came off, wobbled to the center of the road, and fell on its side. With difficulty, Tyler guided the motor home off the highway. He switched off the engine.

"Well," he said. "That's it for this thing."

CHAPTER 25 —————————

DR. MALCOLM COOKE PINCHED the bridge of his nose between short, thick fingers. His eyes were red, sunken into tired sockets. He gave Drs. Susman and Hussbarger a defeated look and said, "Dozens of references to documents entitled M-1 and M-2, evidently the theoretical and procedural groundwork Tyler used in formulating his theory. We missed them somehow, but those works are clearly essential, gentlemen."

"What do you suggest?" said Carl Hussbarger, the Stanford mathematician. He had a wilted look, his long, lean frame bent by exhaustion, face haggard, cheeks stubbly.

"M-1 and M-2 must still be out at Tyler's place," Cooke replied listlessly. "I have a key. The sheriff entrusted it to me after the president's science adviser spoke to him." He stood slowly. "I suppose I'll have to go out again and see if the documents were somehow overlooked."

Without enthusiasm, Susman asked, "Do you want help?"

Cooke tried to shake his head, gave up, and said, "That won't be necessary. The two of you are making some progress on the MHD model; you might as well keep at it. Besides, I've been out there. I know where to look."

In truth, he'd had all of Susman and Hussbarger he could

stand for a while, especially Susman, but it would have been counterproductive to say so.

Without another word, he shuffled from the room and went downstairs. Nora Klemowicz phoned for a taxi. The time was three-forty, Wednesday afternoon.

The cab driver was a scrawny young man with wandering eyes and long, stringy hair. On the way out, he kept up a litany of small talk with few pauses.

"Somethin', this cold, huh?"

"I guess," Cooke replied, trying to put a final note in his voice that would terminate the conversation.

"Think it's really the sun, like they say?"

"Maybe."

"Airport's shut down. You hear?"

He hadn't. A tremor of fear passed through Cooke at the thought of being trapped in Flagstaff during the crisis. What if Tyler *was* right? His palms began to perspire.

"Temperature's just two degrees above zero now. Dropped all the way to four below last night. Crazy, huh?" His eyes locked on Cooke's in the rearview mirror.

Snow lay upon the land. The desert was white, desolate, serenely quiet. The road to Tyler's house was buried beneath a crusty mantle that obscured bumps—which the taxi pounded over heavily, each and every one. Dr. Cooke noted that Gail Dionne's rental car had been removed.

"Wait for me," Cooke said as he got out in front of the house.

"This your place?"

"A friend's."

"Gonna be long?"

"I'm not sure. Would you rather come inside?"

"I'll stay out here," the driver said suspiciously. He let the car's motor idle.

Cooke shrugged. He went to the front door. The air was like Michigan in winter, and Cooke's nose turned pink. Inside the house, he went to the library and began looking through the desk and the bookshelves, opening cabinets of natural oak, sorting through files. The lights flickered and went out, came back on. The house was cool even though the sheriff had ordered the electric heat left on low to keep the pipes from freezing.

Outside, the cabby turned the taxi around. He looked up at the sky. The sun was visible through a hole in the clouds, just above the trees on the ridge of Angel Canyon. A dingy shade of orange.

Scare the shit out of Sheila, he thought with a shudder. Scare the shit out of me. Sheila was a short, sallow, overweight, immature girl with perpetually dirty feet and a yellow smile who waited on tables at Cleo's Cafe, a sweaty, six-booth greasy spoon just off Highway 66 by the railroad.

He'd known her two months now, the two of them living in a run-down apartment owned by a fat old woman who leered at them and gave them knowing winks. This weirdness with the sun had Sheila spooked. Just that morning he'd caught her throwing clothing into a scabrous cardboard suitcase. She said she was going to her ma's place in Dumas, Texas, and it had taken him twenty minutes to sweet-talk her out of it. Without him right there to steady her nerves, sure as hell she'd get all worked up again, run out, leave him all alone.

He glanced at the house and honked the horn. Fat old son of a bitch. Better hurry the hell up.

Dr. Cooke heard the horn. A few minutes later, he heard it honk again, three times. He was tired. His brain was fogged and his thoughts were slow. It finally occurred to him that the driver might want to leave, and that it might not be good if he did.

He stood up, took one step, and the lights blinked out. He took a few more steps in the darkness and almost tumbled headlong over an easy chair. "Damn," he muttered. He stood teetering in the darkness, eyes adjusting slowly to the wan, diffuse light coming in through the living room windows. By the time he reached the front door, the taxi was gone. He trotted outside ponderously and stood watching as the taxi, a quarter mile away, bounded over a wooded rise and disappeared.

In the house, the phone was dead. The microwave system that connected the house phone with the unit by the main road had been powered by house current.

Dr. Cooke gazed around the cold, empty, silent house that belonged to his former student, and shivered.

CHAPTER 26 ———————————

THE WINNEBAGO HAD given up the ghost about two miles from the junction of Highway 14 and the Golden State Freeway. In the distance, clouds of smoke rose from cars and trucks stalled on the concrete ramps south of Valencia and Newhall. A ragtag collection of people trudged along Highway 14, stretching all the way back to the interchange. Those nearest the motor home were regarding it with great interest.

Tyler and Gail hurried into the back, shook bits of glass from the clothing they had picked up in Las Vegas, and donned one-piece insulated ski suits—navy blue with gray piping for Tyler; pale cranberry with a frivolous rainbow design across the front for Gail.

They grabbed the rest of their things and Tyler threw open the door. Two men and a woman came around the rear of the RV.

"You leaving her?" asked one of the men, eyes bright.

"Yes." Tyler and Gail jumped down and hurried away.

The three climbed eagerly inside. As Tyler and Gail stopped to put on parkas and help each other into the packs, the engine of the motor home started up. It pulled forward, beginning a cautious turn.

"It's missing a wheel," Gail said incredulously.

"They'll try anyhow. I would."

They each picked up a bag. Gail put her gun in a pocket; Tyler wore his in a holster around his waist, concealed by the parka, which he'd left unzipped.

"Ready?" he asked.

She nodded.

He slipped the map in a pocket. Encino lay some fourteen miles away, over low, snow-sprinkled hills to the south at the southern edge of the San Fernando Valley.

The motor home began crabbing up the slope behind them, front wheels skewed, engine racing.

Tyler and Gail followed the highway toward the huge interchange in the distance. Few of the people coming toward them were adequately clothed. Most had the empty, haggard eyes of refugees.

Tyler and Gail kept to one side of the road, hands close to their weapons. A man and a woman went by on a motorcycle, weaving around those on foot. The woman held a handgun menacingly in one hand.

They passed abandoned cars. One was on fire, burning quietly. A man in his sixties was seated on the ground by a Cadillac with his face in his hands, sobbing. Nearby was the body of a woman of about the same age, smashed and bloody. She had been hit by a speeding car, and grooves in the inch-deep layer of snow on the road indicated that she'd been dragged by her arms for some distance in the direction of the city. Most of her forehead was gone.

The man gazed up at them as they passed. "Help her," he said in a cracked, phlegmy voice. His soft, bloated face was crumpled in pain.

Tyler put a hand on the man's shoulder. "She's gone," he said gently.

The man rose with astonishing suddenness. *"Help her!"* he cried. His lips were pulled back, exposing teeth. "Help us!" He grabbed the front of Tyler's coat.

"I'm sorry, it's too—"

"Help her," the man hissed. He reached for Tyler's eyes with a hand formed into a claw. Insanity glowed darkly in his eyes.

Tyler shoved him away. He stumbled over the body of

the woman, fell, began to sob again. Gail grabbed Tyler's arm and pulled him away.

"You can't do anything." Tears filled her eyes. "All we can do is try to reach Nikki."

They passed more ruined cars as they approached the interchange, finally reaching a hopelessly wedged mass of vehicles that filled the highway from the steep verge on one side to the canyonlike ditch on the other. Several cars had gone over the edge and lay crumpled at the bottom. It was a scene out of a modern version of Dante's *Inferno*: locked bumpers, wind-whipped fires, and the pungent smell of scorched paint, vinyl, gasoline. Glass everywhere. Cars trapped, unable to move.

Shouts filled the air. Somewhere nearby, a horn went on and on, an angry, helpless sound.

Tyler took Gail's hand and they climbed an embankment, skirting the destruction below, moving toward the ramps that joined U.S. 14 with the interstate. A shot rang out. Then another. They ducked reflexively and hurried on.

The ground sloped down to the interstate. A frozen river of cars perhaps a hundred yards wide was in their path. Most were undamaged, unable to move only because those around them were similarly trapped—like grains of sand that had jammed while passing through the neck of an hourglass.

Gail put a hand to her mouth. "Look."

To the south, thousands of people were climbing over the wreckage. A chaotic, milling swarm moved through a landscape of glass and steel that extended for miles until it was lost in the smoke blowing eastward from the city. More thousands were climbing into the hills beyond. Cries of pain and rage and terror rose from the devastation.

Somewhere in the crush of cars, a motor wound up tightly as a car tried to batter its way out, like a beast caught in a pit of tar. A helicopter hammered the air overhead, working its way northward.

Tyler and Gail scrambled down a slope to the interstate and started across, climbing over bumpers and hoods of cars. A man with an empty face was on his knees between two cars, methodically hitting the slack, dead face of a woman: great, wet blows with bloody knuckles, holding her head up with one hand, fingers wrapped in her hair. He was weeping, grunting with effort.

A woman lay crumpled on the ground, nude, dead, staring sightlessly up at the sky. A few feet from her, a plump man in his fifties lay facedown with his arms at his sides. His body had been stripped and he wore only an undershirt and ludicrous green bikini briefs.

Most of the cars were empty, having been abandoned when the hopelessness of the situation became apparent. A highway patrol car with broken windows sat fire-gutted and smoldering.

Tyler helped Gail over the trunk of a car and over the crumpled hood of the one next to it. A greasy-haired young man with a bloody baseball bat stood up.

He grinned at Tyler and raised the bat over his shoulder. In a crazed, giddy voice, he said, "Good day to die, man."

Tyler pulled his gun, cocked it, aimed.

The youth, not more than twenty years old, fled. The battered remains of an elderly woman were on the ground where he'd been standing.

"You should've killed him," Gail said tonelessly. Her gun was in her hand.

"Waste of bullets," Tyler said. "If he'd made a move at us, I would have, but I've only got about twenty rounds." Not all the cartridge loops on his belt were full.

"I've got five."

"So we don't shoot vermin unless we're forced to."

"I'm scared," she said. Her face was drawn. "For Nikki, for us. How on earth are we going to get out of here?"

"I don't know. First we have to reach Nikki."

They worked their way across and climbed an embankment. Dozens of people stood near a flattened section of Cyclone fence, staring silently down at the scene. On a ridge that paralleled the freeway, thousands of people were leaving the city, many with packs or luggage, one pushing a wheelbarrow.

They began walking south, keeping well to one side of

the oncoming crowds. The sky was gray, clouds low and thick. A bitter wind scythed out of the west.

They reached a cut in the hills where Balboa Boulevard fed into the interstate. The road was solid with cars. Somewhere south of them, in the direction of Granada Hills, a battle was raging. The crack and boom of guns echoed up the canyon.

Dense combers of smoke rolled out of the valley.

Moving warily, Tyler and Gail crossed Balboa Boulevard and climbed into the hills overlooking Upper Van Norman Reservoir. Vehicles with four-wheel drive tore through the hills, seeking a way out of the city. Balboa Boulevard to the west and the Golden State Freeway to the north had effectively cut off all hope of escape. Motorcycles buzzed over the land, like angry, wheeled insects.

People had gathered at the shoreline of the reservoir and the banks of the Los Angeles Aqueduct. Hundreds lay huddled on the ground, wrapped in blankets, perhaps dead of exposure.

"It's crazy," Gail said softly.

"Inevitable, though," Tyler said as they hurried on, moving downhill into the San Fernando Valley.

She glanced at him. "That sounds so . . ."

"Uncaring?"

"I don't know. I suppose."

He gave her a weary look. "It's not that. I care . . . a lot. But suffering of this magnitude can overwhelm you if you don't distance yourself from it somehow—particularly if there's nothing you can do about it. We can't allow ourselves to fall apart now. It's somehow easier to see all this as part of an overall pattern."

"The way generals see things," she responded woodenly. "As campaigns and objectives, not as people dying."

"I take it you don't care much for generals."

"Anyone who is capable of viewing war as an abstraction scares me. I don't see Nikki as part of an overall pattern."

His face looked suddenly older, lined and drawn. "Neither do I."

"You need sleep," she said, concerned.

"Maybe, after we reach Nikki."

They kept the reservoir to their left, moving behind houses on Woodley Avenue that ringed the Knollwood Country Club. The Van Norman storm water control basin passed behind them and they came out on Rinaldi Street. Already their packs and nylon bags felt leaden, pulling them down.

Rinaldi was choked with driverless cars, some aimed east, others west. Screams and curses filled the air; the sound of breaking glass and, in the distance, splintering wood. Fences had been battered down, building fronts torn up by cars that had sought to escape by racing along the sidewalks.

People moved like ants along the street, bundled against the cold, hauling possessions over the hulks of cars. A woman with gray hair held a dead cat in her arms, calling for someone named George in a plaintive, empty voice.

Tyler checked the glove compartments of cars, looking for a street map of Los Angeles. Finding one, he and Gail oriented themselves and planned a route through the valley toward Nan's house in Encino.

They crossed Rinaldi and went down Woodley Avenue. An apartment building was ablaze, radiating heat. Woodley was less crowded with cars, and they made better time, weaving in and out of people and abandoned vehicles.

A boy of fourteen sauntered by, grinning nervously, lugging a small color television set. A neighborhood market had been stripped of food, then hammered with rocks. As Tyler and Gail passed by, an explosive sound of breaking glass came from inside, accompanied by dark laughter.

They had to clamber over more cars and trucks to cross Devonshire. Down the street, a gas station was burning, throwing off a heavy black spire of smoke.

A youth in his twenties stepped out of a doorway. "Nice coats, dudes."

Tyler's hand found the grip of his gun.

"What you got in the packs, man?" The kid wore an army jacket, jeans, a knit cap. In his hands was a golf club with a bloody head. He grinned at them. His breath plumed white in the cold air. Black, stubbly beard covered his cheeks, and his pupils were dilated.

"Nothing that would interest you," Tyler said. He pulled the .357 and aimed it somewhere around the boy's feet.

"I'm interested in lotsa things." He licked his lips. "Got any food?"

Gail raised her gun. "Get lost."

He backed away, his smile becoming a jaded, crafty look as he circled slowly, watching them. Tyler and Gail hurried onward. Twenty yards behind them, the young man followed.

"Where are the police?" Gail asked breathlessly.

"Jammed up," Tyler said. "Outnumbered. Protecting their own. This is a big, uncontrolled riot."

The sky began to dim. By Tyler's watch, it was forty minutes past eight. "Be dark in a while," he observed.

They moved as quickly as they could through the debris, watching for danger. Smoke poured out windows of the VA hospital to their left. They crossed Plummer Street and then Nordhoff. The homicidal kid in the army jacket kept pace with them. Glass crunched under their feet as they passed a pickup truck with four flat tires.

Tyler spotted the second youth. Shouts and hand signals passed across Woodley Avenue. A kid in a black jacket trotted ahead of them, met by a third youth dressed in khaki, wearing a red headband and carrying a rifle.

"Let's go back," Tyler said. "Get your gun ready."

They backtracked suddenly, catching the kid with the golf club by surprise. Shouts came from behind. The youth stood his ground nervously, clutching the club in both hands. Tyler raised his gun, cocked it, aimed it at the kid's chest.

"Drop it," he said. "Now!"

The kid leered at him. "You drop those packs and maybe me and my buddies'll—"

Tyler leaped forward and caught the youth in the groin with a foot. He slammed the barrel of his gun against the back of the kid's head, and the kid sprawled on the ground. Tyler and Gail ran, ducking around a corner and jogging west on the car-strewn sidewalk of Nordhoff Street. They passed a number of bodies as they ran, one a young girl no more than seven or eight years old.

A lone policeman in full gear came diagonally across the

street toward them, carrying a shotgun. His face was a stoney mask. He passed behind them, and Gail looked back just as the shotgun swung down, boomed, and the kid in khaki slammed against the side of a van and went down, rifle flying.

"Tyler—" Gail said breathlessly.

He pulled her onward. "Street justice. That one's on his own, a maverick, maybe more dangerous than the kids. Nothing we can do."

A tangle of stalled vehicles on Balboa Boulevard slowed them. They crossed forty yards of useless machinery, and hurried one block west to Louise Avenue, where they turned south again. Louise was a smaller residential street, less congested and dangerous than Woodley.

"That was pretty effective," Gail said. "Back there, the way you handled that kid."

Tyler grimaced at her in the gloom. "I'm tough, all right. Clubbing a junkie with the reaction time of a coma patient."

"A homicidal junkie."

"Murder seems to be the latest rage. Makes you wonder what was lying beneath the surface of our society a few weeks ago, doesn't it?"

"Could you have shot him if you had to?" she asked.

"Yes."

"Good. Maybe I won't worry so much then."

"What, about me? How about you? You up to it?"

"Absolutely. No psycho is going to keep me—us—from reaching Nikki. All the rules are different now."

It was dark by the time they reached Victory Boulevard, where Louise Avenue ended abruptly at a National Guard complex and a grassy park. Soldiers in fatigues milled about, illuminated by distant fires. Jeeps were parked in single file, but the number of weekend warriors gathered around was hopelessly inadequate to deal with the chaos sweeping the valley.

Tyler and Gail passed between the Guard building and the Valley Youth Center. They crossed railroad tracks, skirted a velodrome, and picked up Louise Avenue again.

Gail stumbled and fell. Tyler crouched beside her.

"You hurt?"

"No, just tired," she said wearily. She got to her feet. "This damn pack weighs a ton."

A nearby building was ablaze, limning the trees with rosy highlights. Flames speckled the Santa Monica Mountains, and the ragged, orange line of a brush fire moved slowly through the darkness.

"We've got a few miles to go yet. Want me to carry something, lighten your pack a bit?"

She managed a smile. "Thanks, no. I'll make it. You've got to be exhausted too."

They crossed the Ventura Freeway on the Louise Avenue overpass. A glinting sea of motionless cars stretched east and west in the uneven light, as still and inhospitable as a junkyard. The foliage on either side of the freeway had been torn up by cars that had gone over the embankment. Gunfire sounded, and sporadic flashes of flame were visible several blocks to the east.

They crossed Ventura Boulevard, where a third of the buildings had been gutted by fire or were still actively burning. They reached the foothills of the Santa Monica Mountains and began to climb. The streets meandered, following the contours of the hills. Tyler used a butane lighter to read street signs, checking their progress against the map.

It was five after eleven when they finally found the street Nan and Dan lived on, roughly equidistant from the El Caballero Country Club and the Encino Reservoir. From there, much of the San Fernando Valley was visible, silent now, the smoky pall above it pale orange in the light of ten thousand fires. A glassy building ten or twelve stories tall belched fire and smoke in the distance.

The power grid had failed. Viewed from afar, the valley possessed a certain murderous, primitive beauty—its great vista of darkness filled with flickering fires, the civilized rush of lights coagulated and dead in the city's arteries.

Nan's house stood before them, gloomy beneath ice-crusted trees. In the driveway was a pickup truck with wide tires, its bed piled high with supplies and covered with a canvas tarp, laced down securely with ropes.

CHAPTER 27 —————————

OVER A PERIOD of several days, the power distribution grid of the United States crumbled. Blackouts ravaged the country as switching stations dumped vast areas of electrical load. In Southern California, power lines that had never before experienced frost or ice loads came snaking down from their poles, and entire regions went suddenly and permanently dark.

As the nation's lights went out, furnaces grew cold, even in houses with diesel fuel or natural gas. Water pressure in municipal systems dropped and open faucets gave off empty, pneumatic hissing noises. Clocks stopped. Telephones were silenced. Television screens went blank.

Tyler's house grew colder. In darkness, Dr. Cooke found a can of olives in a cupboard, and a hand-operated can opener. Swathed in blankets, he ate the olives and drank the juice. Pressure remained in the water tank, and Dr. Cooke used the toilet twice, flushing it each time before it occurred to him that he might be wasting water he would need later if power wasn't restored soon and no one came out to rescue him.

The thought that he might be stuck here in the cold for days grew into a dark horror that squeezed itself into every portion of his mind. His thoughts began to jitter as panic set in. Only by an effort of will did he force himself to gather up half a dozen blankets and lie down in the bed Gail had used, after checking the telephone again for the hundredth time.

He was exhausted, mentally and physically, and he fell into a deep, nightmarish sleep almost immediately.

THE FINAL SOLAR READING in the United States was made by Dr. Avery Charles at 4:20 in the afternoon on Wednesday, the 24th of July. For a few hours the clouds parted, and Dr. Charles took photographs of a reddish, mottled sun. The spectrobolometer reading was 27 percent of normal, a fall in total solar flux of 25 percent in just twenty-four hours.

Although the observatory was on auxiliary generator power, the microwave link to Alamogordo was out, and Dr. Charles was unable to relay his information to the McMath Observatory in Michigan or to the special Washington number he'd been given. By seven o'clock, snow began to fall again.

All the others had left. The temperature stood at twelve degrees below zero, as registered by the indoor-outdoor thermometer. The Sacramento Peak Observatory had a modest store of emergency rations, and the refrigerator held a small amount of food, but Dr. Charles had no desire to remain at his post without communications, with dwindling reserves of diesel fuel for the generator, facing an uncertain future.

He loaded the old Chevy Blazer, locked the observatory, and climbed into the car. He turned the key in the ignition. The engine growled once, slowly, as if in pain, and then quit, utterly and forever.

Dr. Charles stared out the windshield at the dense, horizontal sheet of snow that was falling. Terror began to nibble at a box somewhere inside his brain, trying to escape so it could tear unhampered through his mind and send him screaming out into the cold and dark. Trembling, he got out of the car and hurried back into the mantled observatory as the sun, invisible behind clotted clouds, sank below the horizon and left New Mexico in darkness.

* * *

A CANDLE FLICKERED in a window of Nan's house. Gail rapped on the door, pushed it open, and called out: "Nikki!"

"Mommy!" A tearful, energetic bundle with dark hair came running out of the interior gloom and into Gail's arms. She scooped her up and held her and was suddenly crying, sobbing as she crushed Nikki to her, oblivious for the moment to anything around her.

"Thank God!" a woman said, appearing in the doorway. She held a candle that guttered in the wind and went out. In the brief moment before darkness, Tyler caught a glimpse of a dark-haired woman several years older than Gail. Her face appeared frightened but relieved, with features similar to Gail's, yet different. Her body was heavier, unsupple.

Nan, Gail's sister. Tyler felt light-headed with fatigue. The steady beam of a flashlight came bobbing into view.

Tyler ushered Gail and Nikki inside. Nan hugged Gail, and her husband, Dan, pumped Tyler's hand. The candles were relit, the flashlight turned off. Gail sat on a couch, holding Nikki. Two children hovered close to Nan with wide eyes—Lila and Little Dan—and a cocker spaniel named Charlie whined and moved nervously about underfoot, eyeing Tyler.

"My God," Nan said, "we thought you'd never get here!"

"Just about to move out," Dan said. He was a big man, but soft, with a beery, ice-cream-after-dinner look. Short blond hair, a reddish mustache, heavy shoulders and a thick waist, a broad, obdurate brow. His eyes had an outdoorsy, confident look, and he had a .45 automatic strapped to his belt.

"We were frantic," Nan continued. "You weren't here and we had to get going and we didn't know what to do about Nikki or if you were *ever* going to show up—"

"You can't get out by car," Gail interrupted.

Nan didn't hear her. "We're going up the coast to stay with Dan's aunt and uncle in Lompoc until this is over. We were going to leave this afternoon, but Nikki . . . oh, God, Gail, we didn't know *what* to do—"

"Highways are all blocked solid," Tyler said. "You can't get out that way."

Dan straightened, finding another inch of height. "We got the news on the radio. We're not taking the freeways. We've got a truck with four-wheel drive and we're going straight up into the mountains here. Jeep trails all over hell and gone. Don't figure to see a highway all the way to Oxnard."

In a clear, high voice, Nikki said, "Is that the stinker, Mommy?"

Gail laughed and stood with Nikki in her arms. The pack had long since slipped to the floor. "Yes, darling, he's the stinker. But he's nice, very nice." She looked deeply into her daughter's eyes. "In fact, he's your new daddy."

Nan made a choking sound. *"What!"*

Nikki looked confused. She gazed at Tyler, trying to determine how this could be.

"What on earth?" Nan said. "You . . . what—"

"We're married," Gail said in a husky voice. "All legal and proper. We stopped on the way through Las Vegas. It only took an hour." She smiled at Tyler.

"Hey, that's great. Congratulations, you two!" Dan pumped Tyler's hand again.

Nan stared at Gail in blank astonishment and then looked at Tyler and began to smile. "My God," she said.

Nikki squirmed in Gail's arms. "You're *married?*"

"Yes."

"To him?" She gave Tyler a shy, wondering look.

"To him."

Nikki continued to stare at him, and Gail passed her to Tyler. Tiny arms went around his neck and clung to him. For an instant he thought he would sink to the floor in exhaustion, but he managed to hold her and even to feel a new and wondrous sense of responsibility flood through him.

"It's so . . . well, sudden," Nan said. "I'm happy for both of you, of course." She gave Tyler an awkward hug and an even more awkward smile, and then clung briefly to Gail.

"Look, I'm real sorry, but we've got to get a move on," Dan said.

Still holding Nikki, Tyler said, "You'll never make it. We've seen what it's like out there. It's bad."

Dan shook his head. "I've got four-wheel drive, a chain hoist and a block and tackle in the truck, a heavy-duty winch in front. Snow tires, extra gas, food, water, a rifle behind the seat, and this—" He slapped the .45 on his hip. "Ain't nothing going to stop us."

"Tyler's right, Dan," Gail said. "It's impossible, terrible. People are dead all over." She gave Nan a quick look, and then gave her and Dan a brief description of what they'd seen, how the major routes had solidified into absolute impassability.

"We're not going down there," Dan said. "We're going up *there.*" He jerked a thumb at the hills.

"Won't make any difference," Tyler said.

Dan's eyes narrowed. "Look, I'm real happy Gail found herself someone. 'Bout time, I guess. You seem like a nice enough guy, and Nan said you were an astronomer or something, so I guess you're bright, too. But take a look around. The power's off and there's no water, no heat, not much food. We can't stay here, and that's a fact, so we're getting out. You want, you can come along. In fact, it'd be good to have you. The two of us'll bust a trail all the way through to Lompoc, what do you say?"

Tyler shook his head. "It can't be done."

Dan looked annoyed. "Truck's all loaded. We're leaving real soon." He shrugged. "You're welcome to come along, or stay here if you want."

"Thanks."

Nan clung to Gail's arm. "Come with us," she said in a high, frightened voice.

Gail shook her head. "No, Tyler's right." Tears suddenly filled her eyes. "God, Nan, I wish you weren't going. It's so awful out there."

An impasse had been reached. They all sensed the importance of the decisions being made, the impossibly bitter price that might be exacted by those who followed the wrong leader. The moment had a primitive, masculine flavor to it, like that of rams butting heads in high, windy places.

Suddenly Dan clapped Tyler on the shoulder. "Maybe when this is all over we can split a few beers," he said with hollow joviality. "You tell me all about the stars and I'll fill you in on the wholesale office furniture business."

"Sure." Tyler could think of nothing else to say.

Dan handed him the flashlight. "It's a spare. Maybe it'll help." He gave Tyler a strained grin. "Thermometer out back read seventeen degrees at four this afternoon. Really something, huh? Garden's dead, trees'll probably die too. Maybe next year we'll move the hell back to Massachusetts."

Ten minutes later they were gone, big and small Dans, Nan, Lila; the dog, Charlie. For several minutes Gail sat in the darkness with Nikki in her arms and wept. Feeling clumsy and inept, Tyler sat next to her, trying to comfort her.

Candlelight played on Nikki's face, danced in her eyes as she looked silently at Tyler, evaluating.

"What're we going to do?" Gail said finally.

He shrugged. "Right now, eat and then sleep. I'm starved, dead tired, and my brain feels like concrete. Anything we decide at this point would be suspect anyway, and we know what it's like out there. Let's plan our next move in the morning."

"Can we do that?" she asked in a weary voice. "Just go to sleep in the middle of all this?"

"I don't think we have much choice."

She hugged Nikki. "No, I suppose we don't."

CHAPTER 28 ─────────────

WHAT GOT Harry McGill out of bed and into his clothes without a sound in the dead of night was the thought of canisters of wheat. No doubt the cold was a factor too, and the panicky traffic that'd been pouring eastward out of Southern California on I-40 that Wednesday afternoon. Driving against that heavy, intense, *purposeful* flow had been unnerving; Harry had felt uneasy all the way from Williams to Needles.

He and Gordy had stopped at Needles. It was five in the afternoon. The day was dingy, the sky dark and clouded over, spitting snow. Nothing was on the car's radio but empty pops and hisses. Solar talk.

In Needles, the power was out. They bought overpriced cold-cut sandwiches at a crappy roadside inn and listened to a bunch of lurid talk about how Los Angeles was on fire, how the freeway system was hopelessly bottlenecked, and how people were dying out there by the thousands.

The talk made Harry jumpy. L.A. didn't sound good— not good at all. He decided to spend the night in Needles, assess the situation in the morning.

All the motels in town were full. At the last one, the Red River Lodge, Harry had talked the proprietor (a skeletal, half-bald, gloomy man with protruding eyes) into letting them crash the night in his personal motor home out back for $150, the deposit of their driver's licenses, and the keys to Harry's car. No telling what the old bastard was getting for his regular rooms, Harry thought, and without heat, too.

Late that night, Harry's eyes snapped open the instant he remembered those canisters of wheat in the doc's garage.

Harry had played the beam of a flashlight around the garage, looking for a motorcycle or other means of transportation while Gordy took care of the distributor rotor and cap. He hadn't given the wheat much thought. Now, back behind the Red River Lodge, a couple of things seemed to fall into place. The sun was screwing up somehow—looked like the doc was right about that. The weather was going all to hell, and people were running scared. And the doc, who'd somehow predicted all that, had canisters of wheat in his garage.

What it added up to was some sort of a survival shelter, or at least a big cache of food. Either way, it was certain that Harry would do a lot better out at the doc's place than at his crummy one-bedroom apartment in West Hollywood. And, to top it off, there was always the chance that the girl, Gail Dionne, would turn up again.

Not only was there cake, there was icing too.

So he got up in the bitter cold and put on his pants (which felt like skins of ice) and shirt and coat and, with three or four blankets in his arms, crept past the sleeping Gordon Tate and went out quietly into the night. The magnetic Hide-A-Key was right where he'd last seen it, three years ago, up under the left rear wheel well, clinging to the frame. He stood up and dusted oily asphalt grit from his knees, looking around at the frozen world.

Christ, it was cold! The Hide-A-Key hurt his fingers and the air seemed to sear his throat. When they'd fixed his car at the T&H Garage, Harry had given them the go-ahead on an oil change, tune-up, air filter, new antifreeze—so it wasn't too surprising when the engine caught after half a dozen agonizing seconds and shuddered to life on five cylinders. Half a minute later, they'd all caught, and the old mill was running as well as could be expected.

Harry put it in gear and rolled toward the interstate. *Luck, Gordy,* he thought, turning the heater on high. Gordy'd always been a heavy goddamned sleeper.

The time was 3:18, Thursday morning, and the temperature at the border between California and Arizona was fourteen degrees below zero.

A HUNDRED AND THIRTY-FIVE MILES east of Needles, twelve miles north of Seligman, in a dark, dank cave in the side of Trinity Mountain, a family of four slept soundly on beds of expensive air mattresses and thick down sleeping bags. A padded canvas flap covered the narrow entrance and kept out much of the cold of the night.

The temperature inside the cave was forty-eight degrees, cool but not uncomfortable, dark beyond imagining. The cave narrowed as it went into the mountain, almost a crack, reaching back fifty yards before it became too narrow to navigate. The channel gave the cave access to a huge quantity of low-grade heat contained within the mountain, and Jack Anderson, who knew a great deal about the principles of heat transfer, had been grateful for its existence the moment he saw it.

CHAPTER 29 ————————

Gail Dionne Tyler stared up at the ceiling. A dim glow filtered into the room through thick blue curtains. The clock on the nightstand was dark, useless now, and she didn't know what time it was, but she felt refreshed by the night's sleep. She stretched. Cool sheets lay at the foot of the bed, and a comfortable weight of blankets held her snugly in place. The air in the room was bitterly cold. She took a long look at Nikki, bundled safe and warm on a mattress beside the master bed, and then pressed herself against Tyler.

Not-quite-a-Morie.

Her husband.

A thrill of anticipation coursed through her, making the muscles in her belly tremble. She carefully stripped off her panties and then lay there for a moment with her pulse pounding, feeling strangely naughty, filled with a curious warmth and pressure that made it difficult to breathe. She smiled wanly at herself, at all these schoolgirl antics, and found to her surprise that it actually *hurt* to smile. Her hunger for him was simply too great.

Her hand found his thigh, covered with a small amount of curly masculine hair, and moved up over his hip to the flat hardness of his stomach—not quite as flat or as hard as her own, but almost, and so nice, so trembly, wrenchingly nice.

Ribs, a mat of hair on his chest over smooth, firm pads of muscle. Her hand moved lightly, exploring this sudden, unexpected love who had bought her a drink and ditched her in the smoky din of Red's Outpost. Why did that make him seem more precious to her? He slept with his mouth slightly open, just a quarter inch, and she could see a glint of teeth. He looked younger than he had last night. Sleep was repairing him. He had slain dragons for her, in a manner of speaking, and still the maiden was virginal, essentially untouched.

Her hand strayed lower, lambent on him, to a firmness beneath his undershorts. Her heart pounded. *Please, Tyler,* she thought. *Wake up.* Still, she was gentle, cupping softly, feeling wicked and damp and curiously voyeuristic as the firmness beneath her fingers responded, becoming a hardness. His eyes fluttered beneath closed lids. REM sleep. She smiled. What are you dreaming, my love? Somewhere in her fingertips she could feel the steady beating of his heart.

She rose up and kissed him. For a moment his lips were slack, and then came the slow, sweet response and his hands slid up and around her. "Watch out," he said in a thick, quiet voice.

"Whatever we do today will have to wait awhile," she said huskily.

His hands moved down, over her round, bare hips. "You're naked, lady," he whispered.

"You're always so inexpressibly perceptive in the mornings, sir."

"It's a family trait."

"A genetic thing."

"Right."

Deftly, carefully, she removed his one remaining article of clothing.

"What about Nikki?" he asked.

"We'll be quiet. This is our honeymoon, darling. So far it hasn't been all what I expected. I am unconsummated and, if you'll pardon the expression, horny, and more importantly, I absolutely ache for you, like I'm going out of my mind.''

He rolled her gently on her back and shrugged off half the blankets, supporting himself above her, lightly pressing himself against her. For a long while he kissed her, nudging her legs apart an inch at a time with his knees, and they stroked and nuzzled and explored in silence, looking into each other's eyes. Her eyes grew wide and her heart pounded thickly.

She let out a low, involuntary moan of pleasure and then they were together, joined in a slow and cautious rhythm, like the sigh of foaming surf running up on sand, gliding back out. The deliberateness of it was like the blade of a razor, drawn slowly and carefully across her belly.

She arched into him and the rhythm changed and became the slow, insistent gallop of horses on the surface of the moon, utterly silent, mystically beautiful, racing lazily toward a far, far horizon.

GAIL SAID, ''Yesterday I wasn't interested in how generals see things. Today I am. Nikki, *please* eat your breakfast.''

Nikki made a face. ''This milk tastes yucky.''

Gail sighed. Outside, three inches of snow had fallen. She'd gathered some into a pan, melted it above a ridiculous wad of smoky blazing newspapers in the fireplace, and mixed in some powdered milk she'd discovered way back in one of the kitchen cabinets. All three of them were seated at the dining table, eating bowls of Rice Krispies, and Nikki was right, of course, it *was* rather unpalatable—and, when you came right down to it, ''yucky'' was a far more interesting and descriptive word than ''unpalatable.''

Outside, snow continued to fall in a thin, slanting veil. The three of them were bundled in warm clothing; Nikki wearing a knit cap and her new ski suit, one size too large . . . a gaudy sugar-candy purple that delighted her.

Across the table, Tyler's face was bristly, disreputable, infinitely lovable. From time to time Nikki gave him a curious look, struggling in silence to incorporate this stranger, this new father, into the workings of her life.

"Yucky?" Tyler asked, leaning closer.

Nikki nodded shyly.

"Gruesome?" Tyler persisted.

"Yep." She smiled.

"Really, really *awful?*"

Nikki giggled. "Yep."

Gail stared at Tyler. "You're a big help, Professor."

Tyler ignored her. To Nikki he said, "What you do is take a big bite"—which he did—"and eat it, and say, 'That's the way the ball bounces.' Try it."

She did. "That's the way the ball bounces."

"Good." He took another bite. "That's the way the cookie crumbles."

She giggled again. "That's the way the cookie crumbles." She began eating with a certain wary enthusiasm.

Gail sighed. "That wouldn't work for me in a million years. You're new, vivid, charming, and, most of all, male. I can't compete with that."

"Thank God."

She gave him a risqué look. "Uh-huh."

"About generalship?"

Her voice grew serious. "What are we going to *do?*"

Tyler leaned forward. "What we're not going to do is bolt out of here without some sort of reasonable plan in mind. Your brother-in-law . . ." Tyler hesitated, glancing at Nikki.

"That's the way the cookie crumbles," she sang, and took another bite.

"We saw what it was like out there," Tyler went on. "It's a blind free-for-all . . . not one chance in a million of getting out by car. The odds of escaping on foot are probably better, but there's no place to go. People in outlying areas are very likely defending their homes and food supplies with guns, so it might be a virtual war zone out there.

"Everything's going to hell here, though. This isn't a society anymore. It's decay, rot. Looting, fires, gangs of crazed, murderous savages running around—"

"Is this helping?"

He shrugged. "I don't know. Maybe. We've got to face

reality, and that includes taking a long, careful look at what's going on.''

Her face was pale with fear. ''You're right, General. Continue.'' She gave Nikki a distracted smile.

''The crux of the problem is that everyone is reacting in the same few ways to the crisis. Hundreds of thousands of people, all doing the same things. We're no longer a functioning society, but an undifferentiated swarm.''

''There are millions of people here,'' Gail said. ''How can we come up with anything unique?''

''What we've got to decide first is . . . do we stay, or try to get out?''

''Stay here?'' She looked dismayed.

''Here or in the city somewhere. If we can't leave, we'll have no choice,'' he said reasonably. ''We'll need water, food, a way to keep warm.''

''For months, you said. In temperatures of a hundred below zero. People are already killing for food.''

''And for lesser reasons. If we're going to look for food and shelter, we've got to start soon . . . this morning.''

''It seems so . . . so futile,'' she said.

''Thousands of others will be doing the same thing,'' he said gently. ''Very few will succeed.''

Tears suddenly filled her eyes. ''Oh, God, Tyler. I'm so sorry. You've got that wonderful shelter back in—''

''Stop it!'' he said sharply.

Nikki looked at him with fearful eyes. ''I'm cold, Mommy,'' she said in a tiny voice. Gail put her in her lap and hugged her.

Tyler said, ''I love you, Gail, and I love you too, Nikki.'' He touched Nikki's cheek. ''If we . . . if it ends here, it ends, no regrets except that it wasn't nearly long enough.''

Tears coursed down Gail's cheeks. She brushed them away before Nikki could see them. ''I said I wouldn't do this again, didn't I?'' Her smile was unnatural, eyes luminous. ''People were getting out on motorcycles,'' she said. ''A few anyway.''

''Maybe we can do the same. Thousands of others will try the same thing, though. Gasoline would be a major stumbling block, and it might be difficult now to find a machine.''

"Trains?'' she said hopelessly.

"I doubt if they're still running. Probably not, but it's an idea.'' Suddenly he jumped up from his chair.

"What is it?'' Gail said anxiously.

Tyler paced. "My God . . .'' He picked up a phone book from a counter and began thumbing through the yellow pages.

"What *is* it?'' Gail asked again.

He looked at her with fevered eyes. "A balloon,'' he said in a thin voice. "Why didn't I think of it before?''

"A balloon?''

"Hot-air balloon.'' He set the book on the table. "Forget airplanes, helicopters—but a *balloon*. A balloon might have a chance, and the winds are out of the west . . .''

A dozen questions crowded into Gail's mind, all the words jumbled together. She sat mute and frozen, unable to sort the fragments of thought into coherent phrases.

Tyler quickly turned the pages. "Here!'' he exclaimed. "Balloons-Manned.'' He stared at the page. "Must be a couple dozen of them here.''

Gail's hand trembled. It sounded crazy and hopeless, and even in its hopelessness a thread of hope remained. She could see it blazing in Tyler's eyes.

"I-I saw a picture of you in your library,'' she said. "Do you . . . I mean, can you fly a balloon?'' Her voice was tremulous.

He looked up. In his eyes was a wild look. "I crewed for a fellow a few times, four or five years ago.''

"Crewed?''

"Crown line. Held the throat open during cold inflation. Ran the inflation fan. That kind of thing.''

She gave him a blank look.

He drew a deep breath. "I've helped inflate balloons. I went up once . . . not as a pilot, though. A professor at NAU, Jim LaCruze, was quite a balloonist. He'd say something about it every so often. It sounded fascinating, so I went and watched. I helped launch it a few times, from the north field up by the Natatorium, the pool.''

"I-I ran around that track," she said irrelevantly.

"I can't believe I didn't think of it last night," Tyler said.

"You were tired."

"Still—" His finger traced a path down the page and he eagerly read off a few names: "Freedom Flights. Magic Cloud. Magic Zephyr. Westwind Balloon Company."

"Is this our best chance, Tyler?"

He looked up, saw the serious look in her eyes. It seemed to draw him back from a great distance.

"I don't know," he said.

"Because if it isn't—if we go looking for a balloon instead of . . . well, it could be . . . a . . . a big mistake."

It could kill Nikki, kill you, kill this new and beautiful thing we have together, and do I have the right to hope for so much when so many are dying?—Oh, God!

"I don't know," he said again.

"It sounds wonderful, and it sounds crazy and hopeless and unreal too."

He smiled. "Balloons are like that."

"I mean it. Suppose we find a balloon and . . . and get it up. What then? How do you steer a balloon?"

"You don't."

She shuddered. "What good is it then?"

"It could carry us out of this death trap."

"And into another?"

"We don't have a lot of options right now."

"I know that. I just want us to pick the best one." She tried to smile. "At least yours is unusual."

"The wind is blowing in the right direction," Tyler said. "At a good velocity, too. Due to the crazy weather we're getting, most likely. It's conceivable we could get as far as Arizona, granting that we could find and launch a balloon, of course. And wind direction often changes with altitude. There is a way, if crude, to steer a balloon. You try various altitudes and watch what's called your ground track, sort of tack along. With luck . . . who knows? We might do all right."

"Luck," she said. Black clouds of doubt filled her mind. Her fingers felt numb.

He took her hand. Gently he said, "From now on, anything we do will depend heavily on luck."

"But a balloon," she said. "They seem so big and, well, frail and unmanageable. Are you sure about this?"

He stared down at the advertisements, at yellow pictures of balloons, names, addresses. "No," he said. He looked up at her. "But I can't think of anything with a better chance of getting us out of here, can you?"

She found she couldn't think at all.

CHAPTER 30 ——————————————————

HAROLD BRICE McGILL TURNED onto Tyler's road from the empty two-lane county road between Winona and Leupp. A hard, glassy snow was falling, piling up against fence posts and trees.

The gas gauge was on empty. The needle had given a final reluctant wiggle a few miles the other side of Flagstaff, but Harry had been certain he wouldn't find any gas at Flag, so he had gone straight on through without stopping, slowing only to maneuver around stranded cars that hadn't been towed off the interstate. A lone snowplow had been out, a couple of pickup trucks, but the place had a frightening look to it, frozen and dead. If he was wrong about Tyler's place—and he knew that was a very real possibility—he'd end up frozen and dead too.

Even though it was midmorning, the sky was dark, filled with clouds. Dark because the sun was going out. Going *out*. He gave a thin, fearful laugh. There wasn't much of anything more stable in the universe than stars, and this sonofabitching one was suddenly out of warranty.

He was three-quarters of a mile from Tyler's house when the engine started to miss. At the last moment he jerked the wheel to the right and took the car off into a thick stand of trees. Branches squealed against the windows, a hidden rock chunked against the undercarriage, and then there was a deep and eerie silence, broken only by the cold hiss of wind.

Even with blankets wrapped around him, the walk to Tyler's house was enough to stiffen his joints and make his nose burn and then go numb. His ears felt glassy. He carried his .45 in one hand, under the blankets.

The doc's house looked deserted. Harry couldn't waste time scouting the place, so he walked up the road in plain sight, dumped the blankets at the last moment, and kicked in the door for the second time. Pain shot up his frozen foot all the way to his hip. He leveled his gun at the room.

Nothing. Quiet as a tomb.

It was warmer in the house, but not much. Harry shut the door and stood in the hallway. He heard something from somewhere in the house—a man's voice. He held the gun ready and crept forward, eyes darting around. In a spare bedroom he found an old man, fat and bald, with flesh so sallow it looked cheesy. He was sitting on a bed piled high with blankets, wearing gray suit pants and a white shirt.

"Who're you?" Harry asked.

"Dr. Malcolm Cooke," the man replied.

"World's full of goddamn doctors. Anyone else around?"

"Might I ask who—"

Harry bounded across the room and jammed the muzzle of the gun against the bridge of Cooke's nose, right between his eyes. "Anyone else in the house?" he asked again.

Cooke's eyes bulged. "N-no."

"Okay, let's have a look." Harry dragged Dr. Cooke to his feet and pushed him ahead of him as they toured the house.

"Do you know who I am?" Dr. Cooke gasped.

"You're the old party who's gonna do just exactly as he's told or get hurt real bad. That answer your question?"

The house was indeed empty. Back in the bedroom, Cooke pulled on socks over feet that were veined and blue. He shoved his feet into brown wing tips suitable for boardroom meetings.

"Time for you to haul ass," Harry said, as Cooke shrugged into his suit coat.

"W-What do you mean?"

"Move out," Harry said, waving the gun. "Beat it, scram, get lost. Hit the road, Gramps."

"I . . . I don't know how to drive."

Harry laughed. "Great. There's nothing for you to drive anyway, so that'll work out fine."

Dr. Cooke gaped at him. "You can't be serious. I can't just . . . go out there."

"Up to you, old-timer. Bullet in the gut hurts pretty bad, though." Harry aimed the gun at Dr. Cooke's vast belly.

"Wait!" Cooke licked his lips. "This is murder," he said in a wheezy, disbelieving voice.

"Ain't it, though?" Harry gave him a fond, thoughtful look. "Course, you could think of it another way. You stay, you eat my food. That's kinda like murder too."

"Who *are* you?"

Harry tilted his head and smiled. "Harold McGill, private investigator. Here on official business. Gladt'meet-cha." He took Dr. Cooke by the arm and propelled him out of the room.

"Official business?"

Harry laughed. "I'm making sure Tyler doesn't go public with upsetting theories about the sun. Wouldn't want people getting nervous, now, would we?"

Dr. Cooke's eyes grew wide. "Oh dear Jesus . . ."

Harry pushed him out the front door. "Main road's that way, about five miles." He gathered up the blankets he had dropped outside before coming in the house. "All that blubber on you, you oughta be just fine."

Dr. Cooke trembled. "I can't—"

Harry thrust the gun up under Cooke's multiple chins. "Sure you can, Doc," he said. He spun Cooke around and kicked him in the rear. "You start feeling cold, just jog awhile."

HE FOUND two canisters of wheat in the garage and lugged them into the house, not sure what he was going to do with them. The red line of an alcohol thermometer on the wall outside the observatory registered twenty-four degrees below zero.

There was no shelter in the observatory that he could see, nothing out back. Draped in half a dozen blankets that kept sliding from his shoulders, breath misty, Harry began a search of the house. He thumped walls, checking to see that none of the rooms was smaller than it was supposed to be.

Later, because there wasn't anything else to do, he began tearing up carpet all over the house.

DR. MALCOLM COOKE'S LIPS WERE BLUE, as were his eyelids and his ears. He had trotted along in a swaying gallop for fifty yards or so, but his breath had come in tearing gasps and his heart had hammered painfully in his chest, so he'd given it up. Now he just stumbled along, feeling the deadly air steal heat from his body.

Harold McSomething, hired by someone with connections that ran untraceably back through Mr. Judd Ingram, former FBI deputy director, to one Dr. Malcolm Cooke, who'd started the ball rolling against Dr. Maurice Tyler. Good Heavens, the irony was murderous.

He wanted to cry; in fact, he *was* crying, sobbing even as he wheezed along, but no tears snaked down his cheeks. His legs felt leaden, the little-used muscles quivering with fatigue as his feet kicked up sprays of snow. He hugged himself, estimating that he'd come about a mile, possibly more, following the road because there was nothing else to do.

Four more miles to go.

The wind whipped snow into his face. Was it coming down harder? Did it matter, really? Did anything matter anymore?

Yes. Dr. Malcolm Cooke was dying. That mattered.

He stumbled and fell. The bones in his left wrist snapped with a dry sound, like thin glass rods breaking. A needle of pain shot up his arm, but not much pain, and it really didn't matter very much anyway. He got to his feet and staggered on, holding his wrist. Fifty yards, a hundred, two. He couldn't feel his feet, or the end of his nose or his ears.

He fell again, tried to get up, found he couldn't. He rolled over on his back. The position was restful and oddly comforting. His heart slowed. He gazed up at the sky.

Nothing mattered very much now. Nothing at all.

So he took a little nap.

CHAPTER 31 ─────────────

BEFORE LEAVING THE SAFETY of the Kinders' house, Tyler and Gail went through the yellow pages of the phone book, marking places on a street map of the Valley where balloon companies were listed. They found only four within a radius of twelve miles, and a single FAA-authorized balloon repair station.

"Ready?" Tyler asked.

"As much as I'll ever be." A dullness was in Gail's eyes. Her face had lost much of its color.

"It's going to be all right."

"I'm fine. Let's just go, Tyler, okay?"

Tyler carried Nikki on his back. Gail slipped her gun in a pocket of her parka, and at ten-fifteen they went outside. Even allowing for the heavy cloud cover, the day was unnaturally dark. Smoke billowed into the air from the valley floor, blotting out the hills to the north. Tyler and Gail began walking downhill.

The nearest balloon company, Pacific Wind, was on Ventura Boulevard in Tarzana, two miles from Nan's house. The tiny warehouse that housed it had been gutted by fire, so they went on to the next place on the map, moving warily through the smoky ruins like marines through a jungle. They avoided other people whenever possible, following streets that hadn't jammed solid with cars.

Snow had fallen in the night, cleansing the city, shrouding bodies that lay where they had fallen.

Lunatics were roaming about in even greater numbers than before. Many were dressed in an eclectic assortment of clothing, including one in a fur coat and a cowboy hat, wielding a rifle. They gave that one a wide berth. Around them, people hurried along in helter-skelter fashion, a few with children, frantic and desperate and therefore dangerous as well, moving with haste toward unknowable destinations.

The Vagabond Sky Balloon Company was at the private home of the Cordanos in Reseda, north of Vanowen Street. Like so many others, the house stood open and had been looted. Tyler and Gail went cautiously inside. Nothing remained of the Vagabond Sky but a couple of empty propane tanks in the garage and a beat-up canvas balloon bag filled with newspapers.

They continued on, headed for Ed Early's Balloon Repair four miles to the east in Van Nuys, moving through the sprawl of empty cars on Hart Street.

They scaled a fence to get across the south runway of the Van Nuys Airport. Half a mile away, the control tower was a blackened spire from which a thin trail of smoke wafted eastward. The wreckage of a dozen planes blocked the runway.

Further on, the fence bordering the San Diego Freeway had been flattened by cars that had crashed down the embankment. Tyler, Gail, and Nikki struggled up the slope and across the now-familiar morass of abandoned vehicles to the other side.

As they made their way across the city, Tyler told Gail everything he remembered about balloons: rip panels, propane, maneuvering vents, pilot lights, blast valves, inflation procedures. Gail tried to think, tried to remember what he told her, but found it almost impossible to concentrate.

Dozens of bodies lay in the streets; some snow-covered, others who had recently fallen victim to the horror that was sweeping the city—partly clothed, shot, beaten, frozen into terrible statuary that stared at them with sightless, accusing eyes. Gail kept one hand in a pocket, clinging to her gun.

Before crossing the cars blocking Sepulveda Boulevard, they came upon a boy huddled in the doorway of an insurance office, sobbing. He was about four years old, tugging at the head of a dead woman, crying, "Mommy, Mommy!" in a thin, wailing voice.

Gail's heart broke. She stopped. "Tyler—"

He looked at the boy, then back at her.

Tears glistened in Gail's eyes. "We can't just leave him."

Tyler nodded. "I know."

He passed Nikki to her. He knelt beside the child, who was wearing a thick blue coat. The woman was in her mid-twenties. Her blouse had been ripped open, exposing her breasts. A single bullet hole was in her chest, and her head was battered and bloody. The boy's hands were red, his coat and face streaked.

Tyler put his hands around the boy. Blind with terror and grief, the child clutched his mother and screamed, fingers gripping her hair.

Tyler pulled him gently but firmly away.

Gail took him. The boy clung to her, bellowing. She melted some snow and used it to wipe his face and hands. They took him away.

Later, when his tears had finally subsided, they learned his name: Joey.

"THIS CAN'T BE RIGHT," Gail said, staring at the sign on the gray cinder-block building:

EARLY'S HEATING AND SHEET METAL, INC.
14055 Millsetti Road

"It says Early's." Perplexed, Tyler gazed at the squat, functional structure with its dirty wire-meshed windows, the steel-plated front door that had thus far resisted assault by looters. In one of his pockets, a yellow page from the phone book read: Early's Balloon Repair; 14055 Millsetti Road, Van Nuys.

It was four-fifty in the afternoon. Flakes of snow tumbled out of a dead gray sky, and the temperature stood at seven degrees above zero. Tyler set Nikki down and massaged his aching arms.

Millsetti Road sat two blocks off Sherman Way, gloomy beneath oak trees with dead brown leaves. In the distance they heard shouts, a single booming gunshot. Gail sat on the bag she'd been carrying, still wearing her pack, hugging Nikki and Joey close to her. She looked up hopelessly at Tyler.

"Let's have a look around back," Tyler suggested.

A rutted access road ran between Early's place and what appeared to be a roofing contractor's supply yard. A chain-link fence topped with rusty strands of barbed wire enclosed its cluttered rear yard. Weeds, a scrap bin, plastic-covered sheets of metal in wooden racks, a scabrous air compressor. A large shed with double doors stood in back, painted a grisly shade of green. Beside the shed, an old balloon gondola lay on its side, a three-sided basket like the one Jim LaCruze had flown in Flagstaff years ago.

As he stared at it, Tyler's knees felt suddenly weak.

"Look!" he cried, pointing. He shrugged off his pack and circled the fenced-in yard, seeking a way in. He found a two-by-six lying in snow-crusted weeds by the fence, and he wedged it under the lower edge of the fence midway between two posts and heaved up on it, levering the stubborn wire upward. Its lower edge curled, protesting, leaving a foot-wide gap.

Gail lent a hand and they cranked it up a few more inches. She held it while Tyler squirmed under and into the yard. Nikki scooted under next, then Joey, the packs, and lastly Gail.

The gondola was made of wicker. Its bottom was torn out. Aged, yellow strands of broken wicker were like twisted teeth. No envelope was in sight, no propane tanks. The shed was padlocked. A smaller utility shed, also locked, stood nearby. Overhead, the branches of a huge oak heaved in the wind, shaking themselves free of snow.

A 1,620-gallon storage tank of propane sat on wooden blocks behind the shed, painted white. A dial mounted on top indicated it was a third full.

Gail found a length of discarded steel bar. Tyler jammed it under the hasp holding the doors to the main shed. They put their weight on it. Screws squealed; wood splintered as the hasp tore loose.

The windowless room was dim inside. Snow gusted through the open doors. A cluttered workbench stood against one wall, next to a smaller table that held an industrial sewing machine. Several empty propane tanks had been stacked near the door. A pair of wicker gondolas sat in the center of the room, scarred and beaten, but serviceable. Twin rows of overhead fluorescent fixtures hung uselessly from the rafters. Against a wall were three canvas bags, stacked one atop the other, each three or four feet across, two feet high.

"Eureka," Tyler breathed. "Maybe."

He pulled the top bag from the pile. Gail lifted the children to another table that sat in a corner of the shed and bundled them into one of the sleeping bags, after first removing Joey's blood-smeared coat.

Tyler examined the canvas bag. It was secured at the top with a drawstring laced through brass eyelets. A tag attached to the cord read:

Moulton, Brett. AX-7. 7/12
Replace Velcro/rip panel; pull test req'd.

Gail helped him lug the bag to one side, puffing under its weight.

Tyler grinned at her. "Heavy?"

"For a lighter-than-air balloon, yes."

"This is a fairly small one, maybe seven stories tall."

"Wonderful." She smiled at him. "Is this going to work?"

"Maybe. There's hope. Let's see what else we've got." He read the next tag:

Brannin, Tom. AX-8. 7/15
Annual insp.
250° telltale black; pull test req'd.

The final bag came with a more lengthy note on its tag, indicating that the envelope had been badly burned during an inflation attempt. Replacement of the lower portion of several gores was needed, followed by a full inspection of the envelope by a licensed FAA balloon inspector.

"Scratch that one," Tyler said. "Looks like our best bet is the AX-8 here." He nudged the second bag with his foot.

"What's a telltale?" Gail asked, reading the tag.

"An indicator sewn into the fabric near the top of the envelope where the air's the hottest. Every balloon has several. They go black if the temperature gets too high, which can weaken the fabric. Mr. Brannin might have tried to lift too heavy a load in warm weather."

She gave him a nervous look. "Is it safe? What about that first one there?"

He shook his head. "It's an AX-7."

"What's that mean?"

"It's sort of a model number, an indication of envelope size. The 'eight' is much larger, possibly twice the volume. In temperatures like this, it should be able to lift at least two thousand pounds, gross."

He made a quick mental calculation. They could carry as many as nine 20-gallon tanks, enough for a flight of sixteen to eighteen hours.

"Not much more than a hundred miles in this wind," Gail observed.

"At least it'd get us out of the city, beyond the mobs. We don't know what the winds aloft are like, either. At ten or twelve thousand feet, they'll be a lot faster than the surface winds we're getting here."

"Ten or twelve thousand—" She gave him a dismayed look. "That high?"

"We'll want to fly as high as we can. In air this cold, that means about as high as we can breathe."

They found a total of six tanks in the shed, all empty.

Another dozen in the smaller annex outside, along with nylon strap, propane hoses, and a miscellany of equipment, including an inflation fan—a five-horsepower gasoline engine that spun a three-foot wooden propellor, enclosed in a wire cage.

The legend *40 lbs empty/126 lbs full* was stenciled on each of the twenty-gallon flight tanks.

The blast of a handgun came nearby, on Millsetti Road. A woman screamed, another shot rang out, then silence.

Gail's face was white. "Can we fill them?" she asked in a low, strained voice.

"The storage tank out back has standard POL fittings. No problem, as long as we can get electricity to the pump."

Fear showed in her eyes. "The power's out."

"Maybe the sheet-metal shop's got a generator."

The door to the shop was locked, covered with heavy steel sheet. In a tool crib outside, Tyler found a five-pound sledgehammer. It took several minutes to pound a hole in the cinder blocks of the rear wall big enough to crawl through. He knocked a hole in the Sheetrock inside and squeezed in between wall studs, emerging in a small bathroom whose walls were plastered with dozens of pictures of naked women. Gail took one last look back at the shed and then followed.

In the murky shop area they found several treasures: a five-gallon portable propane bottle, bolt cutters, a handcart with a flat bed and big tires, rated at a thousand pounds.

No generator.

The bolt cutters would get them through the fence, however, and the cart would carry the gondola, envelope, and fuel to a launch site, if a suitable place could be found nearby.

Still, they had no way to fill the tanks.

They kept looking. In a corner, hanging on a wall, Tyler found a weed-burner torch tip with a fifteen-foot hose, used for heating large areas of sheet metal.

"We can use this to fill the tanks," he said.

"That? How?"

"Saturation pressure of a substance. Second-year physics. I'll show you."

Back in the shed, Tyler found wrenches that fit the brass fittings of the hoses. He and Gail hauled several tanks to the rear of the shed, and Brett Moulton's AX-7 envelope, which they arranged over the top of the storage tank as insulation.

Tyler attached the weed-burner to the five-gallon tank they'd found in the shop, and ignited the tip with a striker. He adjusted a valve until a foot-long bluish yellow flame came from the tip. He played the flame gently over the five-gallon tank, careful to keep it away from the line connections. In a short while, the flame grew stronger.

"As the tank temperature increases, its pressure goes up," he said. "The flame gets bigger, hotter."

She nodded her understanding.

Tyler began sweeping fire over the underside of the huge storage tank. He kept it moving, careful to avoid hot spots. It was a dangerous operation and he did it gingerly, checking the tank frequently with a bare hand.

Within the tank, convection currents quickly transferred heat from the steel shell to the propane. He gave the burner to Gail, telling her to continue.

He connected a refueling hose to a valve stem at the top of the big tank, and screwed the other end to a similar valve on an empty twenty-gallon flight tank. He opened both valves, then twisted the needle valve on the empty until a feeble hiss of vapor could be heard.

As the storage tank warmed, its rising internal pressure forced liquid propane from the large tank to the smaller at an ever-increasing rate. Slowly the needle on the flight tank inched off its peg.

Tyler pointed to the dial. "It's filling."

"Thank God," Gail said.

It took over twenty minutes to fill the first tank. The remaining tanks would take less time as the pressure in the storage tank continued to rise.

Tyler showed Gail how to disconnect one tank and hook up the next, explaining the mysteries of left-hand-threaded POL fittings and needle valves. The second tank began to take on propane. A gauge on the main tank showed 65 psi. Tyler told her to quit heating if it reached 120, even though the vessel was rated at 300 psi.

The yard behind the sheet metal shop was much too small an area from which to launch the balloon. The tree alone would make it impossible. Gail would have to continue filling the tanks while Tyler went out and scouted a suitable location. A suffocating fear came over her at the thought of her and Tyler splitting up, but it couldn't be helped. A launch site had to be found before dark, and the tanks had to be filled.

"Look in on the children before you go, please, Tyler," she said.

"Sure." He gave her a kiss and she clung to him tightly for a moment before letting go.

As he went around the shed, it seemed to him that the sky was getting darker. He glanced at his watch: 6:10. At most, two and a half hours of daylight remained, if the sun didn't just blow out like an incandescent bulb shot with a BB gun.

Nikki and Joey were on the table, buried in thick folds of shiny, down-filled nylon. Both were asleep, but Nikki came drowsily awake as he walked in.

"How's my girl?" he asked softly.

She gave him a small, uncertain smile. "Okay," she said, whispering.

"Hungry?"

She nodded.

"Let's see what we have." He rummaged in a pack and came up with a bagel. He broke it, gave her half.

"Can I have a drink?"

"Sure." He held a canteen for her as she drank thirstily.

"Are we gonna die?" she asked.

"No," he said. "We're going to fly away."

She smiled a big, disbelieving smile, and then began to munch her food.

CHAPTER 32 ────────────

IN TYLER'S HOUSE, Harry McGill lifted the piece of linoleum from the kitchen floor. The refrigerator had been shoved to one side.

Harry got on his knees in the failing light and examined the plywood underflooring. It took only seconds for him to discover the seam that ran around the edge, and the little turned-down place where a screwdriver or other instrument had been used to pry the wood out. With a cry of exultation he wedged a kitchen knife into the gap, and the square of laminated wood popped out into his hands.

He peered down into the gloom and plucked the steel cashbox from its niche. He opened it and began to laugh softly as he withdrew a wad of bills and fanned them. Fifteen hundred bucks. He'd found the doc's blood money—as useless now as tits on a pine tree. He threw the box across the room and flipped the money into the air, where it fluttered down around him.

"*Wheeeeeeee,*" he sang crazily.

THEY'D PICKED UP a bullet hole in the truck's windshield not two hours from home. Nan had been real quiet after that, scared. The kids had been quiet too. They hadn't seen the muzzle flash, hadn't even heard the report of the

259

gun. Just a sudden blast of glass that flew around the inside of the cab.

Dan had doused the lights, moved forward, and turned off the engine. They'd sat on the ridge overlooking the valley, where several thousand fires raged. Charlie whined uneasily. Half an hour later, clouds came and a freezing fog descended.

Dan started the truck again and inched forward, feeling his way along the ridge with visibility down to thirty or forty feet. On a steep uphill run they came across an old Cherokee crossways on the trail, burned-out but upright, with congealed black stumps where the tires had been. Dan couldn't go around and he didn't want to go back. He was afraid the winch would pull the damned thing down on top of them, so he got out in the cold and dark with Little Dan and they set up a block and tackle and spent several miserable hours dragging it off the road.

A horrid charred body lay slumped behind the wheel, a hairless thing of black ash. No telling how the man had died. A bullet in the head was as good a guess as any.

It wasn't until just before daybreak, Thursday morning, that they came bouncing out of the hills on Santa Maria Road, east of Topanga Canyon Boulevard. Dan was feeling better, now that they were on their way. Before they reached the winding thoroughfare, they encountered stalled, smoldering vehicles that had been coming in the other direction, headed into the hills. Dan felt a chill in the pit of his stomach. Vehicles grew more numerous, finally becoming an impenetrable snarl a few hundred yards from the two-lane road that snaked down the length of the wooded canyon.

Dan stopped the truck. Ahead, on Topanga, he could make out a twisty, unmoving line of cars that had made it only a short distance out of the San Fernando Valley. Several were on fire. The skin on the back of his neck began to crawl, the hair to rise. Shots rang out ahead and Dan saw the shapes of people darting about. He jammed the transmission into reverse and backed up hastily, past empty cars and trucks.

"Holy crow!" Little Dan exclaimed.

Nan stared with wide eyes. "Dan . . ." she said uncertainly.

The hillside was steep, forested with oak. Houses stood on either side of the road on one- and two-acre lots. Bodies lay on the ground in the dim, crepuscular light; others were slouched behind the ice-crusted windows of cars. Most of the cars were empty, doors flung wide.

"Dan . . ."

"Shut up!"

In the side mirror, Dan saw movement. A man. Two. Three. Behind the truck, all of them carrying guns. Dan stopped the truck. He jammed it into first just as a tall, thin man in a knee-length black coat raised a rifle at them.

The truck lunged forward. A fine spray of glass from the rear window exploded into the cab as Dan swerved through the gap between two ruined cars. Nan shrieked. Dan thumped the truck over a stiffened corpse and tore across a sloping field covered with dry grass and scattered trees. More shots rang out behind them. Slugs slapped into the truck's body.

"Faster, Dad," Little Dan shouted, panting.

Lila wailed, a tiny bird song of terror lost in the roar of the engine.

A whitewashed rail fence appeared ahead. Dan gunned the engine and crashed through it. A steeper slope was just beyond the fence, and they pounded down to a gravel drive and across a lawn. Dan was dimly aware of passing near the rear of a dark two-story house and smashing through a white gazebo like it wasn't there. At thirty miles an hour they went splintering through a solid fence of vertical planks, and suddenly, magically, they were airborne and the truck was in free-fall (its engine accelerating like an unleashed turbine), tilting, nosing in toward a pale blue concrete pad surrounding a pool fifteen feet below. They landed with a bone-jarring crash that snapped the front axle and dismounted the speeding engine. The engine seemed to blow up, throwing bits of metal up through the hood. The truck's frame cracked. It came to a halt amid lawn furniture and sat there, slumped and steaming.

The first bullet came from the house less than twenty

seconds later. It smacked into what was left of the wind-shield and tore Dan's jaw half off his face.

The next caught Lila in the back of the head. Nan cried out, turned toward her daughter, and a bullet caught her in the right elbow, spinning her halfway around. The next slug took her in the neck.

Little Dan sank to the floor and, in a kind of blind, unthinking daze, reached up and got his father's .45 from its holster. He knew how it worked. The fusillade of shots from the house ended and Little Dan waited in the freezing cold with blood dripping on the floor beside him. He didn't cry, didn't think. It took almost all his strength to pull back the slide of the .45. He aimed it just above the window frame of the passenger's door, sighting through one eye. The window was gone. When he saw a face, he pulled the trigger.

The bullet caught a Mr. Pierre Ives in the left nostril and blew out the back of his head.

CHAPTER 33 ———————————

TYLER WAS still gone, searching for a launch site. Gail had completed the task of filling the propane tanks and was keeping an eye on Nikki and Joey while familiarizing herself with the basket Tyler had said they would use. Nikki was quiet, watching her. She had thrown a protective arm over Joey, who was sound asleep with a thumb tucked in his mouth.

A stretch basket, Tyler had called the contraption before her. It was made mostly of wicker, with a wooden base covered in leather. Three and a half by four and a half feet inside. Gail wondered how they would all fit: her, Nikki, Joey, Tyler, all their supplies . . . and the torch she would use to play flames over the flight tanks to keep the propane warm enough to power the burners—*without* setting them all afire.

A nervous tremor passed through her, leaving her stomach knotted and queasy. All afternoon she'd battled her fears, and now her thoughts felt as if they'd been crowded into one exhausted, overworked portion of her mind.

Woven into the wicker of each of the longer sides of the basket was a window, six or seven inches wide. She ran a hand over the brown leather suede covering the basket's rim. Suede also wrapped the aluminum uprights that held the basket to the overhead assembly, where the dual burners and the balloon's huge envelope would attach.

Wooden handles extended from the basket's sides on short ropes. She grabbed one experimentally and lifted. The wicker gave a complaining creak but didn't budge. Empty, the basket seemed impossibly heavy, and they were planning on taking nine heavy tanks, and themselves.

She peered into the basket. A tank was strapped in place in the bottom. An empty tank.

She frowned. Why hadn't it been taken out? And filled. Had Tyler said anything to her about it? She couldn't remember.

Eight full tanks sat on the ground in front of the shed. Only eight.

Her heart began to pound.

Suddenly she remembered the five-gallon bottle she'd used to heat the storage tank. It was almost empty. Tyler had wanted it filled too. How could she have forgotten *that?*

Stupid. She sensed the impairment of her thoughts, fear and panic buffeting her brain. If she kept on this way, she was going to be all but useless to Tyler, and he thought they had a chance with this, so why didn't she?

Because.

Because she'd never flown in a balloon before, and the entire concept of propane, wicker cages, and nylon bags with the volume of four or five large houses still seemed unreal to her. Because propane and nylon seemed no more compatible a combination than gasoline and paper. Because it couldn't possibly work.

Because the city wouldn't let them.

That was it, wasn't it? The city was locked in a titanic death struggle, and theirs was just a tiny, insignificant part of that struggle. There could be no escape for the luckless, and luck had never been her style, not with Tony and not with John or Eric or—

Tyler. How does Tyler fit into this poor, unlucky life of mine?

Tyler, her husband, was magic.

Couldn't she believe in magic, just this once? Not even

magic, really, at least objectively—just filling a huge bag with hot air and hanging beneath it while swinging away into the clouds.

Put that way, it *sounded* like magic.

A new tremor of fear seized her. She shook it off, tried to concentrate on the task at hand.

She got into the basket and unstrapped the tank, hoisted it to the rim and balanced it as she climbed out.

"Oh, Mama, you lookin' fine!"

She whirled and saw a figure standing in the doorway, gun in hand. She scrabbled for her own weapon as the tank crashed back inside the basket.

"Hold it!" The voice was young, excited, dangerous. "Keep your hands out where I kin see 'em. Don't want me to shoot an' spoil the goods, do you?"

She froze. A despairing, icy feeling swept through her, weakening her limbs.

The figure stepped closer. Another appeared behind him in the misty light.

"Nice, huh, Cly?" the first man said. He was dirty with soot, slender, about twenty-five years old. He had a strange, girlish beauty, with a delicate face and large eyes that were cold and blue. A shiny revolver was in one hand.

"Lemme first this time, Hull," Cly said eagerly, wheedling in a childlike way. He was at least six four, 250 pounds, a few years older than Hull, unshaven, dull-eyed and gormless as an ox.

With his gun poked into her stomach, Hull reached into her pocket, grinning at her, and took out her .38.

"Everyone's got a gun," he said breathlessly, filled with an excitement that made his eyes shine. "Like the world ain't safe no more." He stepped back, still grinning, and set both guns on the nearby workbench without taking his eyes off her.

"Me first," Cly whined. "You said."

"What I said was maybe," Hull replied. "Gotta taste it first." He grabbed Gail's head and pulled her close. Nikki shrieked.

For an instant Gail yielded to him, then drove a knee into his crotch with all her strength, lifting him several inches off the ground. His eyes bulged and he made a damp gargling sound. She rammed a thumb into his left eye.

Hull screamed in agony.

He grabbed at her wrist and she shoved harder, her thumb rigid, lunging forward with all her strength as he threw his head back. Her thumb slipped further into the socket, into a stubborn, wet, gelatinous resistance. They toppled over and she landed on top of him.

"Hull!"

There was an explosion, distant in the high, singing sound that filled Gail's ears. Cly crashed on top of her, knocking the wind out of her. She still had her thumb buried in Hull's eye, still gouging. He struggled beneath her and suddenly Cly was gone and there was a fleshy thud that was repeated twice.

Arms grabbed her, lifted her, and she whirled with savage energy. Tyler was there, shouting her name. She hadn't heard him. She bounded to her feet. Hull writhed on the floor, clutching his face. Cly lay on his back. Blood spattered his forehead and a red stain spread across the front of his coat, down low at his right side, where Tyler had shot him with the .357 Magnum. The bullet had passed entirely through his body.

"I'm not going to cry," Gail said. "I'm all right, I'm not going to cry."

He held her. She breathed deeply, raggedly, and cried a little anyway. Nikki called to her. Gail moved out of Tyler's arms and retrieved her gun before going to her daughter. Joey was awake, wide-eyed and trembling.

Tyler chunked Hull on the head with the barrel of his gun. All things considered, it seemed the merciful thing to do, and the safest. As long as Hull was conscious, he was dangerous. Tyler rolled both men on their stomachs and tied their hands behind their backs with nylon cord, pulling the knots tight. He dragged them across the yard and into the shop.

"Are they alive?" Gail asked when he returned.

"Breathing."

"They're not really human, are they? I mean, they are,

but in a deeper sense, they really aren't.'' Her body shuddered.

"Try not to think about them,'' Tyler said. He held her, stroking her hair. "Anyway, I found us a place to launch the balloon.''

AN EARTHEN, snow-covered service road ran northward behind Early's shop. It intersected Alvin Street, a minor road too small to have filled solidly with cars. Tyler and Gail pulled the cart along, moving as quickly as they could, past people who gave them grim, questing looks, past others who saw right through them. Snow continued to fall, softening the lines of distant objects, muffling sound.

On the cart was the basket. The envelope was inside, packed in its canvas bag. Nikki and Joey rode on top of the packs and the cold weather gear, tucked in the sleeping bag. The last tank had been filled and put back in place, and two extras were beside the basket. A piece of the AX-7 envelope hid much of the cart's contents.

Although the cart rolled smoothly, it was heavy, weighed down with over eleven hundred pounds of equipment. At the far side of Alvin Street they stalled on an uphill grade that rose to the service road. Just as Gail thought they would have to remove part of the load to roll it up, a man with hollow, unshaven cheeks and distant gray eyes came along and, without a word to them, put his shoulder to the nylon-draped cargo from behind, shoved, and the cart groaned up the slope.

"Thank you,'' Tyler said, but the man was already moving away, a bulging knapsack bobbing on his back.

"It's not all bad,'' Gail said to herself. "There is reason and sanity and goodness left in the world.'' Suddenly she felt like crying.

On the far side of Alvin, the service road, lined with mature oaks, cut a straight course behind a block of houses on the right and an open field with soccer posts to the left. At the far end of the field, a concrete pad with basketball hoops ended at a junior high school gymnasium with a domed roof and the word WOLVERINES printed on its side in big block letters. Adjacent to the gym stood a dark row of classrooms.

Tyler clipped a hole in the fence behind the school with the bolt cutters while Gail stood guard. It took several minutes, and Gail had the sense that everything was happening too slowly. The light was failing. The wind was still right, and Tyler wanted to try to get away that evening, if possible, so they could land in daylight. He still had to go back and get the remaining tanks while she stood guard over the balloon and the children. She didn't want to split up again, but again it was unavoidable.

They peeled a section of fence back and wired it open, maneuvered the cart through the opening and hauled it across the field, leaving a scuffed track in the snow behind them.

Near the gymnasium, Tyler positioned the basket midway between two basketball posts and laid it on its side. The stanchions were twenty feet apart, standing back-to-back on separate courts.

Tyler pulled some of the envelope from the canvas bag. The lower portion came out first: a tangle of cables gathered together at one of two metal blocks, then yards of filmy maroon nylon. With cold hands, even though she wore gloves, Gail helped Tyler untwist the wires and attach the blocks to receptacles bolted to the framework above the basket. Steel pins held the burner assembly and the cable blocks to either side of the frame.

Tyler settled the children in a fold of the balloon, out of the wind. He lit the five-gallon propane torch so Gail could begin heating the flight tanks in the basket, telling her to stop when they were just warm to the touch.

He left, towing the cart. Gail kept her gun ready as she played flame over a tank, looking up frequently as a few shapeless forms trudged across the field between the balloon and the fence. She felt exposed and vulnerable, out in the open with Tyler gone.

The minutes passed slowly.

Devils, spawned in her imagination, began to plague her. Suppose Hull or Cly had gotten loose and overcome Tyler? What if someone took an interest in the cargo Tyler was moving? A bullet, intentional or otherwise, might have found him.

What made it worse was that these devils seemed so probable, that there were so many of them. How could one hope to slip past them all? How many people had already died in Los Angeles? A hundred thousand? A million? There was no way of knowing, but it was a huge, horrifying number. Too many. And as the days passed, countless others would be struck down, robbed of food and clothing until there was no one left and the cold finally claimed them all.

She sensed that most people still retained a civilized if wary attitude toward their fellows, but thousands were roaming the streets reveling in the chaos; demons like Hull and Cly, who stalked the city in wondering delight at the fragmenting world, freed by circumstance to satisfy their natural blood lust, driven by sick, sociopathic rage that was spinning ever further out of control.

If she could have rammed her thumb all the way through Hull's eye into his brain, the world would have been a better place. She felt no remorse for having tried to kill him; could not even remember what had been going through her mind at the time except a raw, thundering impulse for survival.

Her thoughts were dark and congested. She was tired and depressed, perhaps in a mild state of shock. She took a deep breath and tried to pull herself together.

The light was dying. The trees lining the road were dark and featureless, the shadows beneath them intense. Tyler would come from that direction, if at all.

She saw him then. A wave of relief swept through her. One tank was up to temperature, snuggled in an insulated jacket that'd come with the basket; the other wasn't yet warm enough. She played the small flame over its surface, glancing up occasionally to watch as Tyler hauled the cart across the snowy field toward her.

In addition to the tanks, he'd brought nylon straps, cord, and the inflation fan. He left the cart near the basket and plopped down next to her, breathing hard.

''You all right?'' she asked.

"Beat," he replied with a wilted smile.

"Maybe you ought to rest awhile."

"Can't. The light's going. How're you doing here?"

"Okay. The kids are being wonderful."

"How about the tanks?"

"One is ready. This one's getting there."

He smiled. "Keep at it."

He got up and began cutting lengths of nylon strap, using a sheath knife Gail remembered seeing in the shed, tying spare fuel tanks to the frame of the basket. He attached each tank with a strap longer than the one previous. It occurred to her that he was doing this to keep the tanks from banging into one another during the lift-off and flight, *if* they got that far.

No ifs, she told herself firmly. You will *not* give up on this!

After tying two lengths of nylon cord to the skirt of the envelope, Tyler walked the ends toward basketball hoops at either side. During inflation, they would be used to hold the mouth of the balloon open.

Tyler packed Nikki and Joey into the basket, which was still tipped on its side. He and Gail dragged the canvas bag out onto the field, freeing the envelope, letting the eighty feet of limp nylon trail out behind them, its far end attached to the basket by a web of wires. In the rapidly failing light, the nylon was dark, with just a hint of red in it. It riffled in the wind, making small fluttery sounds.

Tyler handed Gail the sheath knife; a four-inch gleaming steel blade with a bone handle, explaining that she would need it to cut lines during the launch. She fastened it to a belt she'd picked up at Nan's house.

Tyler indicated the cords he'd tied to the skirt. "Cut the lines as soon as the balloon begins to rise. Don't wait for me to ask. I'm going to be busy."

She nodded, her heart pounding. Her thoughts felt like sand, as if her brain were disintegrating. She hoped she could remember everything he was telling her.

He attached the fuel lines from the on-board tanks to the flight burners. The warmer of the two tanks was connected to the gimbal-mounted burner since it could be more accurately aimed to direct the flame into the envelope during inflation.

The darkness was deep enough now to hide their activity to some extent. The trees were a gloomy line on the shadowy edge of the world, backlit by a fire raging out of control half a mile to the east. The sky was a murky gray nothingness.

Tyler and Gail went to the crown of the balloon. Snow stung their eyes as Tyler checked the Velcro seal holding the rip panel in place. Gail held the flashlight that Dan Kinder had given them, staring at the nest of nylon straps that came together at the top of the balloon. They seemed hopelessly tangled, but Tyler ignored them as he worked at his task.

Back at the basket, Tyler located two thick lines coming from inside the balloon—one red, the other white—and tied them to the aluminum uprights.

"Time to inflate," he said. "You ready?"

Her throat was dry. "As I'll ever be."

She struggled to hold the mouth of the balloon open as Tyler took up the slack in the skirt lines and tied them to the basketball uprights.

Cold air gusted into the envelope, swelling the material, making it flutter. Tyler estimated the wind velocity at four or five miles an hour in the lee of the gym, still coming from the west. In the twilight, the fabric was a dark, billowing phantom, growing slowly in size as it filled with air.

Tyler rolled the cart on the lower edge of the envelope, pinning it in place. He gave Gail hurried instructions, and they went out on either side of the monstrous bag and began to tug the material sideways, aiding its inflation. It continued to grow, and soon Gail felt as if she were fighting a soft, surprisingly forceful will-o'-the-wisp the size of a gasoline truck. It swept above her, almost engulfing her at times, surging like some huge, indistinct beast, roiling, flapping, growing ever larger. She kept pulling on it, not sure what she was doing or how effective she was being. After a few minutes Tyler appeared at her side.

"Pretty soon now," he said. "Remember what I told you?" They hurried back to the basket.

"Yes." It was all she could do to keep her teeth from chattering.

"I hope so. We're only going to get one shot at this, at least tonight."

Her thoughts felt like confetti in the wind. She saw the balloon out of control, rolling across the field like a great tumbleweed, leaving them stranded and helpless; Nikki cold and dying, reaching out to her for help she could not give . . .

She shook her head savagely, angry at herself for allowing such wretched images a place in her mind.

You will not *give up!*

Tyler opened the valve on the fuel tank and checked the pressure gauge beneath the burner.

"A hundred and fifteen psi," he said. "Looking good."

He yanked on the rope that turned over the engine of the inflation fan. He'd tested it before bringing it along; even so, it took ten or twelve pulls before the engine caught and the fan, positioned beside the wicker basket, began to blast even more air into the mouth of the balloon.

The racket of the fan drowned out all other sound. Tyler showed her which lever to pull to turn it off, and for a few minutes they stood at the opening, watching the cavernous bag inflate, growing impossibly larger, blotting out half the sky. The wind took it, causing it to flutter and bow at the windward side, rolling, straining at its tethers.

"After you cut the lines, stay near the basket and get ready to climb in," he shouted. "Things will happen pretty fast."

She could barely see him. She sensed more than saw the huge balloon lying on its side before them, already thirty feet high, fifty feet wide. It writhed in the wind, the fabric whispering of the impossibility of what they were trying to do, chuckling to itself.

Tyler shined the flashlight into the basket behind him. Two wide pairs of eyes gleamed at him in the darkness.

"Tell Nikki to hold Joey tight," he said in Gail's ear.

She went to her daughter with assurances she did not

feel, hoping she sounded confident. She had to shout over the noise of the fan, and it gave her voice a frightened, almost hysterical quality.

Tyler opened valves to the gimbaled burner. The burner had a built-in pizoelectric striker. Tyler pushed the button firmly and a blue arc of electricity snapped across a quarter-inch gap between a steel post and the pilot light. A yellow flame with bluish highlights came on, casting a spectral glow amid the spidery lines that held the envelope to the basket. Tyler adjusted the flame.

He stood between the framework that passed between the overhead burners and the cage. He lifted the frame, tilting the basket up awkwardly. "Stop the fan and get ready to cut the lines," he shouted.

"Turn the fan off now?" she yelled back.

"Yes!"

She pulled the lever he'd shown her. Her heart hammered painfully in her chest.

Please don't let me let him down, she prayed.

The fan died. Sudden silence descended and she could hear the rustle of the envelope and see it, a blackness against the lesser blackness of the sky. A fine-grained snow swirled down around them.

Suddenly fifteen feet of raw flame burst into the night with a deep, bellowing roar. Nikki shrieked, and then Joey joined in. Gail had to clamp her own mouth shut to keep from screaming too. It took her a moment to realize that this terrifying great tongue of blue fire was what they wanted. She rushed to the basket and yelled down to Nikki that everything was fine, that they were safe, but her words were swallowed in the din. In the harsh glare, she saw the children's faces, their wide, fearful eyes. The flame's heat warmed her face, a welcome reprieve from the evening's bitter cold. She stared at it, fascinated and apprehensive by its terrible energy.

Abruptly the roar was gone. The pillar of fire sucked down into itself, and the night rushed back.

"Get ready," Tyler shouted. Then the flame was back, a deep bass rumble. Gail unzipped her ski suit to the waist and fumbled at her belt for the knife.

The envelope surged in the wind, larger now, bulged at the crown.

So vulnerable, she thought fearfully. So *ungovernable*.

Joey was crying, howling between terrified gasps, but Gail couldn't go to him, not yet. She stood to one side, able to look up at an angle into the vast interior of the envelope and see the delicate tracery of lines that ran up to the rip panel and the maneuvering vent, strung through interior loops.

The envelope twisted a little as it began to rise, bowed in at the windward side. Gail took hold of one of the lines that held the throat open; it hummed with tension. Blue fire blasted out at an angle, curling upward at its tip.

The balloon lifted free of the ground.

She cut the line. Still blasting flame up into the bag, Tyler hooked the handle of the cart with a foot and dragged it off the lower edge of the balloon. He released the blast valve, and abruptly the night grew dark and silent.

Half-blind, Gail staggered around the rear of the basket to reach the other line. The basket rocked up and the children tumbled to the bottom. Nikki shrieked again. Sitting on the rim as the basket was hauled upright, Tyler shot a huge gout of flame upward into the rising balloon.

Beneath the basket, the second line was out of reach. Gail ran to where it was tied and slashed at it. It parted, whipping away into the night. She looked up and saw the balloon's dark envelope rolling across the sky. Tons of heated air had been set in motion, pivoting around the weight of the basket, swinging into the wind now, falling. Tyler cut off the flame as the basket tipped and then crashed over backward. Without anyone holding the crown line to absorb energy as the balloon lifted, it was penduluming, out of control.

The balloon collapsed down around the skeletal basketball hoops and then slowly began to rise again. Tyler waited until it was most of the way up and the basket had been dragged upright again before hitting the blast valve. Gail clung to the basket, staring upward.

Tyler kept the flame roaring until the bag swung over too far, folding back on itself again. The basket tipped.

Still sitting on its rim, Tyler held it up at an angle. The envelope slowed, hung motionless, and began to climb back up, continuing its gigantic, ungainly oscillation.

After several more cycles, each weaker than the last, Tyler was able to stand in the basket and blast a continuous spire of flame into the balloon.

A glint of light caught Gail's eye, and she found she was still holding the knife in one hand. She slipped it back into the sheath at her waist. Overhead, steam poured off the envelope in a swirling white cloud.

"Get in!" Tyler yelled, still shooting a column of flame up into the balloon.

She kicked a foot over the lip of the basket and climbed in. Seconds later, the wind caught the envelope. The basket skidded uncertainly along the ground and then snagged on its fuel tanks, which were played out behind it like anchors.

The basket tilted. The envelope squashed inward, rolling sideways in a vast undulatory movement. It bulged outward again and Tyler jetted more flame into the bag. Ten seconds, twelve, fifteen. They lifted sluggishly. Fuel tanks came up one by one, and then the basket began to drift, twenty feet in the air, held down by the remaining two tanks as they dragged across the snow.

The wind carried the balloon toward the trees lining the service road, a hundred yards away. The envelope grew hotter, gained lift, and the remaining tanks came free of the ground, swinging beneath the basket, rocking it to and fro. Gail saw fires in the distance and realized suddenly that they were far enough above the ground to see at least a quarter mile. The swaying made her dizzy and she held tight to the basket's rim. Ahead, the black line of trees rose in their path. They swept toward them, rising, higher now than their wind-whipped tops, visible against the structural fire raging ahead.

Tyler kept blasting flame into the balloon. The envelope was a deep, gaudy maroon, encircled by three horizontal gold bands down low, near its throat. A gigantic eagle adorned one side, poised in flight.

Gail looked down. They were climbing rapidly now, passing twenty feet above the tops of the trees.

They had done it!

Suddenly the basket lurched sideways, tilted at almost a forty-five-degree angle. Gail was slammed against the rim, almost catapulted out into space. She shrieked involuntarily in terror.

"Cut the line!" Tyler bellowed.

Her thoughts streamed apart in rags. Wind tore past her face. The car rocked over further, yawning above a blackness of space. The envelope leaned far from vertical, pushed by a rush of air as the balloon lost its forward momentum.

"The line!" Tyler yelled.

What line? What—

In the glare of the flame she saw it, a taut, slender thread running from the basket into the uppermost limbs of a tree. A low-hanging fuel tank had snagged in its branches.

"Cut it!" Tyler yelled again. *"Cut it!"*

Snow swirled in her face. She groped for the knife, found it, pulled it free, almost dropped it into the bottom of the basket. The basket tilted a few more degrees. Furiously she hacked at the strap. All sense of reality began to slip away as blackness glazed her thoughts, filled her vision.

Please, please . . .

The strap gave way suddenly, without sound in the thunder of the flame, and the basket swung in a broad, sickening arc. Gail felt herself slipping over the edge. She clutched wildly at the frame. Shadows leapt over the ground below.

Joey and Nikki were howling. Gail got her feet under her. Behind them, trees were visible in the wavering light, higher now than the basket. The balloon was falling.

No!

A tank touched the ground and the balloon hovered, dragging the tank across the service road. Still the flame went on, and the trees fell away in the distance as the basket rocked, climbed, oscillating from the shocks it'd received. Gail gazed downward. With a sense of dislocation and wonder, she watched the soot-streaked chimney of a two-story house pass by to one side, not ten feet below the bottom of the basket, illuminated by the flame roaring steadily up into the balloon. Beneath the basket, fuel tanks swayed, gliding past the side of the house, missing it by mere feet. The lower tank drifted above snow-covered juniper bushes, then passed eerily through the crown of a lemon tree before swinging free.

The house and yard fell away in the gloom, and the world below was a swaying emptiness of darkness and distant fires. Silence descended as Tyler released the blast valve; the column of fire shrank to a glow just inches high. The children cried softly, whimpering.

The car continued to rock, settling down. Gail saw the city expand as they rose above it, moving upward quickly. She could see two miles, then three—to the edge of a filmy darkness in the falling snow. They passed over the fire that had once silhouetted the trees at the edge of the playground. In the airy silence, the muted pop of gunfire came from somewhere below. They drifted above a primitive, alien world, illuminated only by its own fiery death.

Tyler cracked the valve for another ten seconds. Gail looked down and saw the children staring up at the monstrous column of flame, still awed, its dancing blue light reflected in their eyes. Abruptly darkness and quiet descended again.

In the flickering glow of the pilot light, Tyler smiled at her, a gargoyle's shadowy grin.

"Well," he said, "it wasn't pretty, but we're on our way."

CHAPTER 34 ────────────

A BLACK VOID OPENED beneath the frail basket—a startling, airy emptiness of space, an abstract vista of smoke and fire. As they drifted over the doomed city, Gail felt weak-kneed and euphoric. They had done it! It *was* magic; if not of physics, then of the spirit, and if not of her spirit, then of Tyler's. He had kept them from sinking into despair. He had not lost faith.

Every thirty seconds or so, Tyler gave the balloon a ten-second burst of flame, causing them to gain altitude steadily. He explained the instrument panel to her: the altimeter, which gave their height above sea level, and the variometer, which measured their rate of ascent or descent. Already they were sixteen hundred feet above the world, rising at a rate of two hundred feet per minute. The pyrometer, which registered the temperature at the top of the balloon, hadn't been connected. The frigid air would give them more than enough lift without the possibility of overheating.

By Tyler's watch, the time was 9:20.

Gail crouched down and spoke to Joey and Nikki. Joey was quivering—huge eyes staring up at the frightful bursts of fire that came at intervals from above. Gail stroked the children's heads. She pointed to one of the small windows. Nikki looked out and said, "Oooooooh!" in a awed voice.

Tyler found a thermometer in a nylon utility pouch, tied to an eight-foot cord. He tied the free end of the cord to the basket's frame and lowered the thermometer over the side.

Below, the world began to grow indistinct, shrouded by a veil of the sheerest gauze.

"We're going into the clouds," Tyler announced.

The altimeter read twenty-four hundred feet; several minutes later they were surrounded by an impenetrable darkness.

"Better settle the kids in and get the next tank up to temperature," Tyler said. "We've got only thirty or forty minutes left on this one." He said nothing about the tank they'd lost during lift-off.

She arranged Nikki and Joey as far as possible from the spare tank, then tucked some flame-resistant nylon cloth from the sacrificed AX-7 envelope around the children and the tank.

She held the tip of the torch up near the pilot light and cracked the valve. The torch gave off a four-inch flame. She crouched down in the basket and began passing it over the surface of the tank, moving it constantly to avoid hot spots.

Tyler reached down and opened the valve that fed propane to the second flight burner. He indicated the pressure gauge on the overhead burner assembly. It read seventy-five psi.

"Stop when it reaches a hundred and fifteen."

She gave him a nod and a tired smile. Her spirits raised when he leaned down and they managed a clumsy, lingering kiss without setting themselves or the basket afire.

The pressure was up ten minutes before the blast flame from the first burner was only six feet long and sputtering. Tyler twisted valves and hit the pizoelectric starter on the second burner. The pilot light came on. He gave a trial blast on the valve and once again flame bellowed up into the envelope.

He disconnected the first tank, unstrapped it, and dumped it overboard. Forty pounds of dead weight sailed down into the empty night, dropped from seventy-five hundred feet. With Gail's help he hauled up the tank that hung from the longest strap, then wrestled it into position alone in the confined space, causing the basket to sway.

Soon after, they broke through the ragged top of a cloud. The full moon was just above the horizon. Gail gasped at the sight of the bloodred, malevolent eye among the stars. She couldn't determine which direction they were traveling. The balloon drifted with the clouds, and they seemed to be hanging almost motionless in the air. An awareness of the precariousness of their position returned. Images of the land below, so far and cold and black, made her feel faint. Six inches below their feet was nothing but empty air.

The ruddy moonlight illuminated the clouds in eldritch light, now several hundred feet below the basket; a mounded landscape of sullen red wisps and fetlocks and streamers; a sluggish, twilight sea of misty blood. The clouds slowly lifted and curled, fell back, churned and seethed, carrying them along on an unseen, almost imperceptible wind.

It became apparent after a while that they were moving somewhat faster than the clouds below.

"Look!" Gail cried.

In the distance, two black peaks loomed above the clouds. The higher mountain was north of the smaller.

"Better start heating the next tank," Tyler said.

Gail readied the tank and the five-gallon propane torch, lit the tip, and began the tiresome chore of heating the big stainless steel container. Dangling beneath the basket, it had lost all the heat it had gained during filling, hours ago. Tyler alternately sent roaring gouts of flame into the balloon and contemplated the map of California he'd carried with him ever since they'd left Las Vegas.

"We're going between them," he said finally, gazing at the mountains. "As near as I can tell, the big one to the north is Mt. San Antonio and the other is Cucamonga Peak, unless we went way off course somehow while passing through the clouds. Anyway, we're on an easterly track now, probably moving north of San Bernadino."

"Any idea how fast we're going?"

He glanced at his watch and then scaled mileage off the map. "We've been up about an hour and a half and we've gone forty miles, give or take."

She paused. "A little over twenty-five miles an hour."

"Maybe more, now that we're up higher."

She looked up at him. "I could be silly and ask if we're going to make it."

He smiled. "Keep praying. It looks like we're on a good track and we're moving along pretty fast. We'll see."

She played the flame over the tank, glancing up from time to time at the pressure gauge, watching the needle climb with painful slowness off its initial reading of just twenty psi.

A chill seeped through her ski suit and parka in spite of the flame billowing upward at evenly spaced intervals. Tyler lifted the thermometer and read it.

"Twenty below," he said. "We're at ten thousand six hundred feet. Cold up here." His eyes were lined with fatigue. He looked away, and all she could see was the bulky parka with its fur-lined hood, his hand reaching up for the blast valve.

Slowly the mountains fell away. Gail heated the tank to operating pressure in forty-five minutes, then stood up beside Tyler. She unzipped their coats and put her arms around him, holding him close. Flames rumbled overhead, died again. She pressed her face against his neck, sheltered in the hood, and closed her eyes.

"Magic man," she whispered, and felt him smile.

She fell asleep standing up, holding him while the bloody moon climbed higher in the sky and the land glided by silently beneath them, black and lost.

TYLER NEEDED SLEEP, but there could be no sleep, not even for a moment. Every thirty or forty seconds a five-second blast of flame had to be shot up into the envelope, keeping them suspended eleven thousand feet above sea level, some unknown distance above the invisible earth passing by below.

He held her, knowing she was asleep. Nikki and Joey were quiet, probably sleeping too. Though exhaustion clouded his mind, he felt surprisingly good, more married to Gail in just thirty-six hours than he'd ever been to Carol. His heart expanded until it ached with a fierce, protective love.

They were floating with an eerie sense of motionlessness in a wind of perhaps thirty knots, with only the subtle creak of wicker and a lambent breath of breeze, the ripple of fabric overhead as faint wind shears played with the envelope.

The cold was a medium, like air or water, that tried to work into their clothing, into their bones; he could feel it out there, stealing its quota of heat though the heavy coat he wore. The sun was wrapping itself in magnetic insulation, giving off less and less heat as it cycled into itself. In another week the temperature would be eighty or ninety below zero, possibly a hundred, and in the weeks that followed the Earth would grow colder still.

He struck the blast valve again, released it. They sailed in silence through the fevered dark of night. Several minutes later she stirred. Her arms tightened around him and she nuzzled him, kissed his neck.

"For thrills galore, honeymoon with Dr. Tyler," she murmured.

"What can I say? I'm a party kind of guy."

"Your takeoffs could use a little work, though."

"That was called a launch."

"Launch then."

"It's all part of the thrill of ballooning. With me, you pay your nickel and get your money's worth."

"What would I get for a dollar?" She nuzzled him again.

"You'll find out when it comes time to land this thing."

He tripped the blast valve and she looked into his face in the coarse blue light. When it was quiet again, she said, "Do you know where we are now?"

"It's iffy," he responded, pointing with a gloved finger in a direction opposite the moon. "You can still make out the higher of the two mountains we passed, but I lost the smaller one some time back. As near as I can tell, we're still on an easterly track, which is good. We'll probably reach Arizona, but how close to Flagstaff we'll get is any-body's guess. The winning numbers for this lottery haven't been posted yet.''

She pulled out the necklace Sam had given her. "For luck," she said. "How do you make it work?"

He smiled. "Pray that we reach *Doko'oosliid,* I sup-pose.''

"What's that? . . . *Doko'oosliid?''*

"One of the four sacred mountains of the Navajo. *Doko'oosliid* is the sacred mountain of the West. Hum-phrey's Peak to we interlopers, just north of Flagstaff on the Mogollon Rim.''

"Would you recognize it . . . from the air, I mean?''

"It's the highest point in Arizona, part of the San Fran-cisco Mountains. Angel Canyon is on its eastern slope. I'll know it if I see it."

They rode along in silence awhile, and then it was time to get the other burner in operation. He opened a valve and lit the pilot light. He blasted with the current tank until it could no longer support a usable flame, then dis-connected it from the hose and tossed it over the side. They hauled up the next tank for Gail to heat.

An hour and a half later, the next empty went over the side, and an hour and forty minutes after that, the next. As they used fuel and grew lighter, the temperature dif-ferential between the outside air and the heated air in the balloon was slowly reduced. Each tank that went over the side decreased the load on the balloon by 126 pounds. As the night wore on, the interval between blasts of flame grew longer.

The moon climbed high in the sky and then slowly be-gan to sink in the west.

CHAPTER 35 ─────────────────

AT THREE-TEN in the morning, just after they started drawing fuel from the fifth tank, the clouds began to break apart. Through the burgundy-tinted mist, a greater darkness appeared below—empty, endless, without distinguishing features. A short time after, the clouds vanished altogether.

After heating the sixth tank, Gail shared a can of applesauce with Tyler. Nikki and Joey were fast asleep, acclimated to the rhythmic din of the flight burner. The thermometer stood at minus thirty-one degrees, falling as they traveled inland from the coast.

Far below, a single lonely light crawled over the land. It could have been anywhere from Blythe to Death Valley.

Later, as they dumped the fifth tank over the side, Gail spotted several fires. They drew near, and Tyler saw a broad, meandering line below, darker than the land. Ruddy moonlight reflected from its surface; vapor boiled into the air and blew eastward.

"The Colorado!" he exclaimed, sending a thundery pillar of flame upward into the balloon.

"Are you sure?"

He checked the altimeter. "We're eleven thousand feet up. That's a big river down there. I don't see what else it could be."

As they watched,. a light crawled away from the fires that raged nearby, moving along the river—the intense white headlights of a vehicle of some kind.

Tyler pulled the map out again. "Riviera, Topock, Lake Havasu City, Parker, Ehrenberg. Could be any of those, maybe even something as far north as Hoover Dam."

Again they entered a wilderness without lights. And then, with little warning, the sun rose in the east. They stared at it, too awed to speak. In the layered atmosphere it was a huge, swollen, sickly crimson orb, flattened near the bottom, where it emerged from a muddy orange horizon.

Reluctantly it dragged itself free and began creeping upward in the sky, all the while retaining its bloody, ulcerous look. The land below turned shadowy red, limning a ridge that rose directly in their path. North of them sat a tall peak, the highest of a wandering chain of mountains.

"Is that it?" Gail cried. *"Doko'oosliid?"*

He stared at it. A panicky feeling of uncertainty swept through him. His head spun. If it was Humphreys Peak, they had to come down now or overshoot it by forty miles. But he wasn't *sure*.

Think! Decide . . . *now!*

He stared at the far, northern peak in a welter of indecision. No. It couldn't be *Doko'oosliid*.

The land was suddenly featureless, or so featured that it all looked the same. North-south chains of mountains, all of which looked identical; high peaks, too far away to even guess at their heights with any certainty. They passed over a ridge, above a panorama of valleys and mountains, darkly illuminated by a cancerous, mottled sun that gave off no discernible heat.

He had no map of Arizona. He felt certain they'd crossed the border . . .

No, not *certain*.

Yes, he was. It was impossible that the river they'd crossed could have been anything but the Colorado.

Still, he had doubts. They could be anywhere. At least they were moving eastward; the sun and the land told him that. If they'd crossed the Colorado, they were over Arizona now.

Gail was heating the next tank, their next to last. Mountains glided smoothly by beneath them. He had no way of telling exactly how fast the balloon was moving, but it was a good clip, maybe as much as thirty miles an hour.

A snow-covered road appeared, passing north and south through an empty valley. To the east lay yet another ridge.

With a sense of relief he realized there were no significant ridges immediately east of Humphreys Peak, east of *Doko'oosliid.* Beyond the Mogollon Rim, the land fell away to an undulating desert flatness that extended for miles—the reservations of the Navajo, the Zuni, and the Hopi. The Little Colorado River was also missing from the picture below.

He tried to determine which road they'd just passed over, but without a map of Arizona it was impossible. They were relying on his knowledge of the state's geography, knowledge that was beginning to show alarming gaps. He knew little of Arizona's secondary road system. From the air, he couldn't determine the size of the snow-covered road below, wasn't even certain it was paved. Given advance warning, he might have swooped down on it and, with luck, read a sign or mile-marker as they went over.

But no, that was just a desperate fantasy. He couldn't use their fuel in such a manner, or trust his flying prowess in maneuvers so close to the ground before they reached their destination . . . or ran out of propane.

On they went, over the next ridge and over canyons that worked up into the mountains beyond. Gail had the next tank up to operating temperature and was gazing out at the world, trying to spot something that would help him. Anything.

Five miles to the south, she spotted black streamers of smoke coming from a town of perhaps two thousand people. A few buildings were on fire. Tyler had no idea which town it might be. They passed behind a hill and the small settlement was gone. Another tank was jettisoned over the side, tumbling with reddish highlights to the ground below.

They floated above the broad slope of a mountain, passing south of its summit. As they crossed a ridge, Tyler saw a high, distant mountain, seventy or eighty miles away, across a gnarled expanse of hills and valleys. The highest peak stood at the north end of a range of mountains. Like *Doko'oosliid*. It lay northeast of them. Their current line of flight would take them perhaps forty miles south of it.

Gail was heating their last remaining tank. Tyler touched her shoulder and pointed. "There."

"Doko'oosliid?" she breathed in passable Navajo.

"I think so. See that high ridge ahead, stretching far to the south? I'm sure that's the Mogollon Rim."

Tears suddenly filled her eyes. "Do we have a chance, Tyler?"

"A chance. Maybe a good one."

"My God." The words caught in her throat as she stared at the distant mountain.

"Now we try to jockey for position," he told her. "See that valley ahead, running toward the north? If we drop in there, we might catch a current that'll take us closer."

For another twenty minutes he kept them at eleven thousand feet. Gail continued to heat their last tank. They flew over a small, sloped ridge into the valley, dropping at 250 feet per minute.

The valley was twenty miles across, sparsely populated with buildings. As they approached its western edge, Tyler took them to within a few hundred feet of the ground. They sailed northeast, under a dark blue sky and a tepid, crimson sun. A road came at them at an angle—a flat ribbon of snow paralleled by a run of power lines. A bend in the road took it away from them and they floated toward the hills.

Gail had their final tank up to 115 psi. She turned off the torch. The ridge drew near.

Tyler blasted heat into the bag.

They swept over a line of trees, just fifty feet above their tops, seeming to rush eastward at an exhilarating pace now that they were so low. Houses appeared, were swept behind them, and two miles to the north they saw another town. Tyler tried to think of which one it might be, could not, and turned his attention back to the terrain ahead.

They entered a narrow, twisty canyon. Power lines and a road snaked through the valley floor. The wind swept them southeast, through wooded mountains that rose higher than the balloon. Tyler fed more hot air into the envelope, and they climbed a few hundred feet, moving toward the eastern slope. Almost too late, he blasted more flame into the balloon; they cleared the ridge by less than thirty feet, riding the swell of the wind as it swept up the hills. They shot across the treetops at thirty miles an hour.

"My God, how will we land in this?" Gail cried.

"That's when you get your dollar's worth." He gave her a grimace, not a smile.

"I'll bet."

As they flew across the ridge, a narrow valley opened up before them, angling almost due north. Tyler dropped in as low as he dared. Twenty feet above the ground, the wind took them straight up the canyon, following a small, frozen river. A road had been cut into the side of the hill to their left.

"Power lines!" Gail yelped.

Ahead, black lines arced in silhouette across the sky. Tyler held the flight valve open in a long, thundering blast. The lines closed rapidly on them, like the blades of scythes. On and on the burner roared, and still they weren't lifting!

Yes, now, a little. Not enough!

Interia. Hysteresis. Give it time, Tyler thought madly, still holding the valve open. *Come on, come on!*

Suddenly their ascent rate was four hundred feet a minute. The power lines were gone and the valley dropped away below as the wind carried them toward the eastern ridge.

Tyler pulled the white cord, opening the maneuvering vent in the side of the balloon, dumping hot air through a twenty-foot slit in the fabric at the balloon's equator. He released the line when their rate of climb was zero. The self-sealing vent closed. And then they were coming down, falling rapidly toward the onrushing hillside.

He blasted more heat into the envelope, this time willing himself to quit before their descent had ended. The balloon began to rise, sailing up and over a slope of rock and trees, into a wide valley ending at a towering wall of rock that rose far above them, fifteen miles away. Due north, a high plateau was topped by a lofty mountain, thirty-five miles away.

"That's it!" Tyler called out.

"What's it?" Nikki said in a small but wide-awake voice.

Gail bent down and said something to her that Tyler was unable to hear. "She has to go to the bathroom," Gail said, standing again.

"Can she wait?"

"Apparently not."

Tyler gave her a smile and shrugged. "See what you can work out. I've got my hands full."

"Typical male cop-out. No points for originality."

He touched the blast valve, and the burner gave off only a dismal, sputtering flame. As Gail rummaged through the packs and bags, Tyler twisted the valve to their last tank and lit the pilot light. He closed valves to the other system, disconnected the tank, stripped off its insulating jacket, and lofted the tank over the side. Forty pounds lighter, the balloon rose slowly as it floated northeast over the valley.

Gail stood beside him. "She says she doesn't want you to look."

"Modest child, eh?"

"Very."

"Tell her I promise."

He concentrated on the task of flying the balloon while Gail and Nikki thrashed around at his feet. He flew close to the ground, watching the approach of the Mogollon Rim, trying to catch as much northward wind as possible. He hauled up the thermometer. Thirty-eight below zero. The splashing sound of water seemed to go on forever. Tyler smelled the pungent odor of urine. Voices drifted up to him—Nikki's and Joey's both. Then a slide of zippers, more rustling of fabric.

Gail appeared beside him. "I don't think she's ever been half so cold in her life."

"Gaining a new appreciation for indoor plumbing?"

"I imagine so." She grinned. "Or at least male plumbing. Were you aware that boys can use a canteen like a urinal?"

"Do tell."

"With all the snow down there, I figured we aren't going to die of thirst."

"Inventive lady."

"Desperate."

She ducked back down and found the children something to eat, now that they were awake.

They rode along in silence punctuated by lusty blasts of flame, approaching the towering ridge at an angle, a hundred feet from the ground. The land began to climb. A wide road came into view below and they sailed over a pickup truck that was working its way southward down the grade.

"Interstate Seventeen," Tyler announced. "Flagstaff to Phoenix. Flagstaff is twelve or fifteen miles north of us."

The wind carried them toward a tree-studded slope. Tyler sent more flame into the deep maroon envelope. Four hundred feet above the ground, they crested the ridge. South of them was Mormon Lake, and away to the north blazed the rosy crown of *Doko'oosliid.* Flagstaff was marked by a smoky pall, rising toward the east.

He pointed and she pressed herself close to him, watching. "It's burning," she said sadly.

"Parts of it, anyway. Like Los Angeles."

She groped for words. "I feel . . . humbled by all this . . . by how lucky we've been. More than just lucky."

"I know. Let's hope it keeps up. Setting this thing down will be more like planning a train wreck than a landing."

They glided across a shallow valley and up an even higher ridge. At the top, the world opened up and they could see for a hundred miles across to the Hopi Buttes, almost double that to the southeast along the Carrizo Wash, past Snowflake and Concho all the way to Quemado in New Mexico. The country was all ruddy grays and burnt plateaus; tips of mountains tinged with rose, as if by a glorious sunset; high, serrated clouds dyed in blood.

"It's breathtaking," Gail said. "Frightening."

"Make a hell of a postcard."

They descended the eastern slope, moving more east than north. Tyler gave Gail instructions concerning the landing they would soon be making, how best to protect the children and herself, telling her to stay with the basket.

"It's going to be rough," he said. "Very rough."

"A whole dollar's worth?"

He smiled grimly. "Maybe more."

She got Nikki and Joey ensconced in separate sleeping bags. After removing the torch tip, she threw the five-gallon propane tank over the side, then took off her coat and packed it into Joey's bag before working her way into the sleeping bag with Nikki.

Ten miles beyond the top of the ridge they floated at an angle over Interstate 40, two hundred feet in the air. The highway was white and empty, eerily desolate, littered with the snow-crusted, scattered remains of trucks and cars.

They sailed up and over a gentle rise. Tyler gave the blast valve short bursts as they crossed into the far, southwestern corner of the Navajo Indian Reservation, moving on a track that, if they stayed in the air, would take them just north of the town of Leupp. He let the balloon drop lower.

Soon they were skimming fifty feet off the ground, moving at twenty miles an hour. Tyler's heart hammered. Northwest of them he could see the steep walls of Angel Canyon. They hadn't yet reached the Leupp-Winona road. A tangent point was rapidly approaching at which he judged they would pass no closer to the house. Eight or ten miles.

Tselaa. Sanctuary.

Soon they would be down. Very soon.

Forty feet. Thirty.

The ground rushed by with deadly speed. The wind howled over the plain, fueled by forces impossible to calculate as weather patterns over the planet adjusted to new conditions of solar influx and energy distribution.

Twenty feet.

Tyler gave the burner a final three-second blast and then

turned off the valve to the tank. The flame died as he purged pressure from the line. Their descent slowed in response to the new heat, but didn't stop entirely.

Fifteen feet.

Tyler took hold of the red cord rising to the rip panel at the crown of the envelope.

Snow-covered sage and blackbrush whipped by, rising up to greet them. A stand of pinyon pines loomed ahead.

Twelve feet.

A blur of ground.

Ten.

Tyler yanked the rip cord with all his strength. He pulled again, drawing the line in, and again, opening a gaping hole in the top of the balloon. He dropped to the bottom of the basket, curling himself around the sleeping bag in which Joey had been bundled, trying to wedge himself into the basket with his legs and shoulders.

The basket clipped something soft, swayed—

Again, harder.

The bottom of the basket hammered into the ground and a thousand wicker voices squealed in pain. The basket spun, tilted, slammed into the ground again, and twisted on the end of its steel cables, sealing the throat of the balloon, preventing the hot air from rushing out quickly through the rip panel.

The envelope sagged, partly deflated, hanging in the air at a forty-five-degree angle as it dragged the basket kicking and spinning across the desert floor.

Snow and broken bits of sagebrush flew into the basket. Air pressure further collapsed the balloon, forcing hot air out the rip panel. They slowed as the balloon snagged on tough fingers of sage, pulled free, caught again, and then a final bone-jarring crash hammered the basket one last time and it lay unmoving on its side in a tearing wind, its support frame twisted by the impact with the trunk of a sturdy pinyon tree, burner coils battered to junk.

The canopy of the balloon fluttered in the wind, dying, settling. Wind hissed in the trees, sweeping savagely over the land.

CHAPTER 36 ────────────

JOEY WAS HOWLING. It took them a few minutes to quiet him down, and to ascertain that none of them—Joey included—had sustained anything worse than a little mild bruising.

The fierce cold became an even greater factor, now that they were no longer traveling with the wind, no longer warmed by the fiery blasts of the flight burners. Gail struggled out of the sleeping bag, in which she had protected Nikki, and put on her parka again.

"Get your money's worth?" Tyler asked.

"Uh-huh. Now I know why you're not a commercial pilot."

He gave her a wry smile. "On Tyler's Tours, it's generally considered enough not to have drunk from the stewardess's canteen."

"I see your point."

They settled the children into the basket, which lay on its side, and packed nylon sheeting around them to shield them from the wind. The thermometer had miraculously escaped annihilation during the landing. It read forty-one below zero. The air was a howling Siberian wraith with death in its heart.

Tyler and Gail donned ski masks for the first time since they'd purchased them in Las Vegas. Tyler struggled with the nylon canopy, holding it as she sliced it with the knife that had remained on her belt during the trip. They took out most of one gore, fighting the stubborn ripstop nylon every inch of the way.

They stowed the nylon sheet in the basket and dragged the rest of the canopy over itself and around the gondola, forming a nest protected from the wind. Tyler connected the torch tip to the final flight tank, which was still a quarter full. He lit the torch, turning it up to a hot blue flame. They huddled around the warmth while the arctic wind moaned across the frozen sage outside.

Gail opened cans of sardines and tuna, and doled out the remainder of the bagels. The pièce de résistance was a couple of well-mashed, nationally advertised pastries.

Tyler made a face at them.

"You bought them, sir," Gail reminded him. "I hope you have provisions with more substance than this in that shelter of yours."

"We'll see what you can whip up in a no-frills oven with grind-it-yourself wheat, yeast, salt, powdered milk and eggs, rice, that kind of stuff."

"Me?" Her eyes widened.

"Declarations of ignorance won't save you, dearest."

"I'll make you things you won't believe, Tyler, but first we have to get there. How far is it, anyway?"

His brow furrowed as he calculated. "About ten or twelve miles," he said finally.

They rested awhile. Tyler was beat, and they would have to carry the children somehow, through the snow and cold. The rest of the day was going to be anything but fun.

They'd come down at quarter to twelve. By one-fifteen they were ready to begin the last leg of their journey. Tyler had fashioned crude slings to carry the children, and Gail had created windbreakers for her and Tyler, using ten-foot circular sheets of nylon fabric with holes in the center for their heads, gathered loosely at their feet with circlets of cord. The windbreakers went over the children, who rode piggy-back-style in relative darkness, jostling against the backs of the adults, sheltered warmly in sleeping bags.

They set out, climbing a slope toward the northwest,

over rocky terrain covered with the ubiquitious sage. From time to time, Gail removed a glove and poked her hand up through the neckline of the makeshift poncho to adjust her hood. In spite of the ski mask, she walked with her head low, sheltering her face from the freezing wind, looking up every so often to keep track of Tyler and Nikki. The snow was only about six inches deep, though at the base of trees and brush it had formed into drifts a foot or more deep.

By the time they reached the Winona-Leupp road, she was already tired. Tyler turned left, estimating they were four miles from the turnoff to his ranch.

Four miles.

Five more after that.

Then they could quit. Then they would be safe.

Her shoulders began to ache. She stayed just a few feet behind Tyler, using him as a windbreak. She was uncomfortably warm where Joey pressed against her in the sleeping bag, cold almost everywhere else, particularly her feet and face. Her eyes watered. Her breath plumed in the frigid air, freezing into an amorphous icy mass on the fur of her hood.

She wore heavily insulated rubber boots. Her legs felt as if she were slogging through glue. Already Joey seemed to weigh a hundred pounds.

Clouds gathered in the west, perhaps the very ones they had flown over and outdistanced. The entire flight still seemed incredible to her. The sky was a deep, unnatural shade of blue, the sun a soft and sickly red, without heat. As time passed, the wind picked up and became a rushing, hissing gale that made walking even more difficult.

Nothing moved. No birds sailed on the wind. The Earth was white, stiff, sterile. Gail was alone with her thoughts, which drifted randomly through her mind as she struggled along behind Tyler. The flight from Los Angeles in the balloon was muddled with images of Tony and Eric and her mother; Tyler's gentle, easy lovemaking; Nikki's sweet face; Nan; the smells and sounds and frustrations of Red's Outpost; her thumb shoved deeply into Hull's eye; the psychotic grin of Harry McGill.

Two hours after beginning the trek down the Winona-Leupp road, they reached the turnoff to Tyler's ranch. Now the wind came at them from the side. The road was lumpy—treacherous compared to the snow-covered pavement they'd just left. In places, the snow had formed drifts up to eighteen inches deep, primarily in the protected bottoms of windswept washes. Gail trudged along behind Tyler, stepping where he stepped, using his trail to make her own passage easier. From time to time she looked up at the bulky lump that was her daughter, riding in warmth on her husband's back.

Her husband.

In spite of the searing pain in her shoulders, she managed a smile for the gods that had brought them this far, and given her a mate, a man of humor and strength and goodness. If the need arose, she would circle the globe for him with a piano on her back, or die trying.

She recognized the place where Harry and Gordy had stopped her, where she'd left her car. Gone now. They kept on, moving in a slow, steady shuffle that consumed both space and time.

With two miles to go, Tyler fell. He fell flat and hard in a bed of snow a foot deep, lay there while two heart-stopping seconds passed, and then pushed himself up and rolled to one side. Nikki whined uneasily.

Gail crouched beside him. "Can you go on?"

He tried to smile, but couldn't. "Sure. Just give me a moment. We've got to get there before it gets dark."

Nikki's weight rested on the snow as he closed his eyes and breathed deeply. After a minute he got slowly to his feet.

"Onward," he said in a weary voice.

Shortly after that it began to snow. Just a little at first, then harder, whipping blinding flakes of snow into the hoods of their parkas. Although it was not yet seven o'clock, the world grew twilight-dark, a ghastly shade of grayish rose. Visibility was less than two hundred yards, dropping at times to under a hundred feet.

They stepped around a lump in the road, walked a few yards farther, and then Tyler stopped.

"What is it?" Gail asked.

"I'm not sure."

He went back to the snowy lump, lifted the hem of the poncho, and brushed the snow away with a gloved hand. A man's suit appeared, stiff, frozen. Gail watched in horror as Tyler exhumed a pudgy, hardened face, the eyes wide and opaque, icy snow crusted between grimacing lips. She felt a queasy tremor in her stomach, grateful that the kids weren't able to witness this grisly apparition.

"Who is it?" she asked quietly.

"Dr. Malcolm Cooke," he said without emotion.

She stared. She'd seen Dr. Cooke on television any number of times in the past month or two, but this rigid, rimy corpse looked nothing like him, at least not to her.

"Wh-What is *he* doing here?" she wondered aloud.

"Your guess is as good as mine."

Almost without thought, her hand sought the hard, comforting lump of the .38 in her parka pocket.

Tyler drew her away and they went on. She felt the cold, unearthly presence of the dead man behind her, in recent times a household name, his eyes staring emptily up at the swirling gray sky.

Tyler fell again, then again; and then it was Gail's turn and they sat huddled in a snowbank just half a mile from their destination, gathering strength for the final push.

When they topped the final rise, the house was hidden by a blinding snowstorm. The world was a shadowy globe, extending no more than a hundred yards in any direction. With snow dragging sluggishly at her feet, Gail trudged down the slope behind Tyler. Her heart began to race.

Tselaa, their refuge . . . so close now. It seemed a miracle.

The fence in front of the house came into view as they plodded along, and then the evanescent, uncertain outline of the house itself, forty yards away, washed out to a colorless gray in the raging storm. They turned in to the drive, plowed through a drift nearly two feet deep that had piled up before the house.

Beneath the overhang of the porch, Tyler suddenly stood still. He pointed to the door, to the shattered jamb.

The house was dark, quiet. They lifted the ponchos over their heads, and let them fall to the ground. The bitter air pressed itself closer, smiling, nuzzling, burrowing, stealing. Gail found her gun, warmed by her body heat. Tyler had drawn his .357 and was holding it in an ungloved hand.

Tyler put his shoulder to the door and shoved, meeting a yielding resistance. It swung open and snow gusted down the foyer, spiraling in tiny devils. A chest of drawers had been pushed against the door.

Carpet had been torn up in the entrance hall. Tyler went in first and Gail followed. They pushed back their hoods and removed their ski masks, listening. They stood in the living room, guns drawn, taking in a scene of senseless devastation. Carpet had been pulled up and piled in one corner, furniture tumbled about, books scattered, paneling torn from the walls, exposing studs and wiring.

Suddenly Tyler slammed forward and sprawled to the floor. Nikki shrieked in terror. An arm snaked around Gail's neck and something cold and metallic was jammed against her temple, sending a searing bolt of agony through her skull.

"Drop the guns!" a voice yelled.

Harry! Recognition burrowed through her pain.

"Drop them!" he screamed. "You too, Doc, or the lady buys it right now!"

Tyler was on his side on the floor, still holding his gun. Nikki and Joey wailed. Tyler looked up. Harry stood behind Gail with an arm around her neck, the muzzle of his .45 shoved hard against her head. Tyler let his gun fall.

"You too," Harry said to Gail.

The pain in her head was excruciating. It took her a long moment to understand what he wanted her to do. She opened her fingers and let the gun drop.

He flung her to the floor. She landed on top of Joey and his howling grew louder. Gail struggled to a sitting position near the end of an overturned couch. Tyler sat to her left.

Harry McGill stood in the entrance. At the sight of him, Gail gasped involuntarily.

Harry was a mess. Matted hair, bloodshot eyes behind thick black rims. A greasy face with a crusted line of blood across his forehead.

He was dressed in layer upon layer of material, some of it wrapped around his thick waist and falling around his legs like a woman's skirts—others with holes cut in the middle and draped over his shoulders like the nylon ponchos Gail and Tyler had made for themselves.

Sheets and blankets and bedspreads, even large towels and curtains—everything suitable that Harry could find in the house had been pressed into service to keep him from freezing in the bitter cold. He was a mountain of multicolored fabric, a grim, psychotic bundle of cotton and wool and polyester, twill and corduroy; a discordant pastiche of paisley and plaid, checks and flowers, solids and stripes. Towels were flung over his head, tucked down under the poncho-shawls, giving him a dusky, Arabic look.

He grinned. A demonic light shone in his eyes.

He took several strangely silent steps toward them, and Gail noticed that he'd bound layers of cloth around his feet, swelling his calves and ankles to unwieldy elephantine stumps.

With effort he reached down and picked up their guns.

Nikki and Joey struggled to get their heads out of the sleeping bags. They stared at McGill with huge, frightened eyes. McGill ignored them.

"Thought you'd be back," he said in an unsteady, chuckling voice. "Thought you might've fixed up some kinda shelter somewhere around here. Just about gave up on you, though."

Tyler was silent.

"What's wrong?" McGill asked. "You ain't glad to see me?"

"Not very."

"Well, I'm glad to see you," McGill said with a black grin. "In particular, the lady. You see, her and me have got some unfinished business."

"You were hired to keep me quiet," Tyler said. "She's got nothing to do with that."

McGill smiled satanically. "Job's over, you oughta know that, Doc. This's personal now."

Tyler stared at McGill's gun. "We found a man in the snow on the way in," he said, stalling. "Dr. Cooke. Frozen."

With faint interest, McGill raised a bushy black eyebrow. "You found the old party, then?"

"You killed him?"

"Never laid a finger on him," Harry said, grinning. "In fact, last I saw, he was doing just fine."

Tyler's eyes narrowed. "He was here, wasn't he? You put him out in the cold, knowing he would die. That's murder."

Harry shrugged. "Surprise," he said softly. "By the way, I found your cashbox, under the refrigerator."

"It's all yours."

Harry gave a muddy chuckle. "Thanks. Where's the place, Doc?"

"Place? What place?"

"The reason you two came back. In all this weather, too. Some kind of shelter or something, maybe up in the hills."

Tyler gave him a perplexed look. "There isn't any shelter. Just the house here."

"Cut the crap, Doc," Harry said, frowning. "I found the canisters."

"Canisters?"

"The wheat. In the garage. Not your usual pantry item."

"I used to make my own bread. Healthier than store-bought. I gave it up, though. Too much work."

"Tell you what," Harry replied with a lazy smile, "after I get through with the lady here, we'll take up where we left off, you telling me about bread, me and the little girl I see peeking out of your pack there playing with knives. We'll see if you can't recall what those cans of wheat were for. Little girl like that has a way of making a man remember all kinds of interesting stuff."

Gail's blood froze. Her heart had been hammering, and now it seemed to be breaking apart in her chest. She felt faint with terror at the vision of this monster, this *horror*, carefully and methodically hacking Nikki to pieces with a dripping blade, grinning as he interrogated Tyler.

You will not faint, she screamed silently to herself.

"Strip," McGill said to Gail. "Dump the kid and then take it off, every scrap. It's your favorite party game, maybe you remember."

"McGill—" Tyler said.

Lazily, McGill swung the gun around. "Relax, Doc. Enjoy the show."

Moving slowly, mind racing, Gail shrugged off the sling that held Joey. McGill was crazy, homicidal. He meant to kill them all, she could see it in the deranged glimmer of his eyes. He'd fallen into some unimaginable abyss, into raging, implacable insanity. His eyes were pitiless, haunted, sunken, mad. Gail's mind spun, unable to settle into a groove that permitted coherent thought.

"Strip," McGill said again, this time with almost genial good humor.

"Let me," Tyler said. "Have me do it instead."

McGill grinned. "Wouldn't be the same, Doc, would it? How about you stay where you are, and leave the little girl where she is on your back. Wouldn't want you leaping up suddenlike, getting all heroic, would we?"

Gail looked at McGill. A thought came to her: *He couldn't possibly move quickly, weighed down as he is. Think.*

An insane idea occurred to her—that once she was dead, McGill might share the shelter with Tyler and Nikki and Joey; that her death might save the others. The idea flared hotly, faded, and suddenly a new and infinitely more terrifying one took its place: McGill and Nikki in the shelter alone—just the two of them.

Could he? . . . Might he? A wave of blackness filled her. She felt weak, nauseous. Some things were worse than death.

Thoughts fragmented, she removed her gloves and parka.

Better for Nikki to die than to go into the shelter with McGill. Much better.

He meant to kill them all. After McGill watched her die, he would kill the others.

But maybe not Nikki.

Weighed down . . .

She unzipped the front of her ski suit, felt the bitter cold slip inside.

If they were going to die anyhow, if McGill meant to kill them, or worse, what did she have to lose by fighting? If she could surprise him, knock him off his feet—

Weighed down. Slow.

Once she was out of her own bulky clothing, she would be able to move quickly, if she wasn't too cold to move at all.

The knife!

How could she have forgotten *that?*

She remembered it just in time to turn sideways to McGill, concealing the weapon from him as she tugged the ski suit off her shoulders and down to her hips. She bent down, unlaced her boots and pulled them off.

McGill's eyes gleamed in the dull gray light.

She pushed the ski suit over her hips, struggling, taking the knife from its sheath as she did so. She palmed it, holding it out of sight against her body, feeling the cool, smooth steel in her fingers.

I am a reporter. I work for Parsec *magazine. This can't be happening!*

But it is. McGill is real. *Real.*

Deal with it, girl.

The cold air tore heat from her. She stepped out of the ski suit, slipped the knife into a pocket of her jeans.

"Cold, ain't it?" McGill said in an eager voice. "Freeze a person's titties off."

Nikki whimpered.

Gail unstrapped the belt and unsnapped and unzipped her jeans, working quickly now, trying to conserve what heat she could by racing toward this terrible confrontation.

She palmed the knife again, shucked off the jeans, and then removed a plaid flannel shirt and the bottom half of her long johns, standing there in panties and the shirt top of her full-length insulated underwear. In the soft light, her strong, smooth legs gleamed, the muscles firm, taut.

"Nice," McGill commented. "You're doing real good so far, but I want the whole show."

"Please, Harry," she said, shivering. A ball of excitement flooded her stomach, making her arms and legs tremble.

"Everything," he said. "Every goddamn scrap."

She pulled the underwear over her head, and then the T-shirt that was underneath, revealing the silver and turquoise necklace she was wearing. She wore no bra. Still standing sideways to McGill, feeling the aching cold wash over her, she held the clothing in her left hand, the knife in her right.

McGill stared at her breasts. He smiled. "Nice. Maybe the best I've ever—"

She threw the clothing into his face and dove to the floor to his right, tumbling beneath the level of the gun.

McGill tried to whirl, staggered. His gun swept toward her, boomed, an ear-shattering blast in her face that stunned her. Something burned across her cheek, blurring her vision. Her ears rang.

She twisted on her back and kicked her feet into his legs as hard as she could, behind his knees, and there was another booming concussion as he toppled almost in place, falling half on top of her. He thrashed, driving an elbow into her ribs. For a dismal, terrifying moment, her vision went gray.

Her left arm and shoulder were pinned beneath him. Blankets and bedspreads flew in her face. She jerked free, trying to orient herself as McGill struggled to sit up, the gun rising in his hand, towels flapping, obscuring his vision.

Out of the corner of her eye, she saw Tyler staggering to his feet under Nikki's weight, McGill's gun coming up at them.

Harry wasn't worried about Gail; his thoughts were on Tyler. She lashed out at the gun and caught McGill on the wrist as bright yellow flame burst from the gun. With supple fury she scrambled off the floor and threw herself at him.

The .45 came sweeping down again. She pounded the barrel of the weapon down with a fist, holding the gleaming knife in an underhand grip, its tip pointed up at the ceiling.

The gun thundered again and McGill cried out.

A hand caught Gail in the side of the head and fingers

twisted into her hair. She heard his breath chuffing in and out of him, heard Nikki's terrified screams.

She crawled up on McGill, knees driving, fingers clawing at his great overpadded chest. He dragged her by the hair to one side with alarming strength, making her neck creak, her scalp sing, and in the confusion she saw the dark, gaping hole in the towels that hid his face. She plunged the knife point-first into the hole, putting all her wiry strength behind the thrust, pulling the knife slightly toward her until she felt his flesh at the hilt of the blade, along with a warm, sticky freshet of blood.

The world seemed to explode. His legs came up and a knee drove into the pit of her stomach. She rolled off him, fighting for air. Through a haze of pain she saw Tyler reach down and grab McGill's gun off the floor.

McGill kicked his legs, scrabbling with his hands at the hole formed by the towels around his head. A soft, gargling sound came from his throat.

Tyler aimed the gun and squeezed off three quick rounds into McGill's chest. Abruptly the blankets settled.

Tyler crouched next to Gail, helping her to sit up, trying to bundle clothing around her that she'd dropped to the floor. She sobbed, drawing in painful gasps of air, aware now of the numbing cold that was stealing over her. Tyler draped her ski suit over her legs and held her parka over her shoulders. As if from a great distance she heard Nikki crying, calling her.

Harry lay on the floor.

"Is he dead?" Gail asked when she could finally speak.

"Yes."

She lifted her head. Still drawing breath with effort, she gave him a pained smile. "I'm always saving your butt, Tyler. Next time it's your turn, okay?"

He helped her to her feet. "Don't nag."

CHAPTER 37 ─────────────

THE BLADE HAD NICKED Harry's carotid artery on the way in, then punched through his windpipe. He had three bullets in his chest, and one in his thigh where Gail had caused him to shoot himself. Tyler dragged him outside to the garage and left the cooling corpse wrapped in a dirty sheet of canvas.

The first bullet fired from McGill's gun had grazed Gail's cheek, an inch under her right eye. It bled determinedly as she got dressed, stopping only after Tyler made her lie down and applied direct pressure with a pad of gauze. It throbbed wickedly, a wound that would leave a scar that would last the rest of her life.

The kitchen floor was torn apart. McGill had ripped up carpet throughout the house, and much of the flooring. Money lay scattered about, torn and stepped on, ignored. The cashbox had done its work, however—the entrance to the shelter lay undiscovered.

Tyler unearthed a steel box he'd wrapped in plastic and buried over a year ago beneath a flagstone leading out to the observatory. The box held all the tools needed to remove the concrete slab and get into the shelter.

When he lifted the heavy block from its recess, Gail's eyes blurred with fresh tears.

They were safe, at least for the moment, but the world

was in peril. It came to her in that final moment that there
was no way to prepare for the extinction of nearly everything you have ever known—the death of a world, the end
of a thousand cultures, five billion people.

No way.

A deep sense of loss gripped her, then a feeling of eu-
phoria, followed by a numbing sense of guilt. Emotions
that would take weeks to sort out, possibly years.

And, assuming Tyler's cycle ran its course in as short a
time as Tyler had predicted, what would the world be like
when it ended?

A great sadness filled her.

Would there be animals, birds, insects? Trees? Grasses?
Would fish survive? What would remain after almost cryo-
genic temperatures raked the Earth?

Air, water, earth. Seeds. The heartiest of trees, the most
tenacious of shrubs. These, at least, would live again.

Certainly it would be a simpler world, freshly scoured,
purified by ice, requiring unknown skills and courage of
those who survived.

It was too much. She couldn't think about it now.

They stood before the entrance to *Tselaa,* each holding
a child. Outside, the wind rose to a howl.

She turned to him, shivered.

"I feel like saying a prayer," she said. "Before we go
in." With gratitude she touched the necklace Sam Hatathli
had given her—for luck. "Do you know anything in
Navajo? Somehow that seems appropriate."

He took her hand. *"Sa'á nagaí k'ad bik'eh hozhó."*

"Sounds nice. What does it mean?"

"Continuity, renewal, walking with long life on a path
of harmony and beauty. An understanding of the whole."

"We need all that. Please, say it again."

He did.

Softly she repeated, *"Sa' á nagaí k'ad bik'eh hozhó."*
They went down into *Tselaa.*

EPILOGUE ──────────

THE SOUND of Tyler's guitar filled the shelter, driving back the darkness, cheering their spirits. They sang the "Sneaky Mole Song," Tyler's creation and the children's favorite:

> "Sneaky brown moles, livin' in the ground,
> Sleep away the day and the clock all 'round.
> Can't go outside 'cause the sun's gone to bed;
> Can't holler loud enough to wake the sleepyhead.
>   Jo-ey Mole, never gonna get cold;
>   Nik-ki Mole, has a sneaky eyelash;
>   Mom-ma Mole, she say "Hey, old
>   Pa-pa Mole, why don'cha take out the trash?"
> Livin' way down in the ground (oh, yes);
> livin' way deep in the ground (oh, my!);
> livin' waaay . . . down deeeep . . . in the
>   grooooound."

Joey laughed and clapped his hands, sheltered in Gail's arms in the frugal light of a five-watt bulb. They sang other songs, dozens of them, but the one they sang about themselves was their favorite, its nonsense verses increasing in number at the rate of three or four a week, each new verse eagerly awaited. The music and singing drew them together, warmed them, gave them a deep, almost mystical sense of family.

Stories, too, filled the twilight gloom, told in Tyler's mellow voice or Gail's warm, feminine one: "Little Red Riding Hood," "Cinderella"—even rough-hewn versions of "Treasure Island" and "Moby Dick."

Thus occupied, the days crept slowly by.

ONE LATE AUGUST AFTERNOON it was Nikki's turn to go above ground. Only her eyes showed behind the ski mask; Gail had sewn a patch of cloth over the mouth and nose openings. Nikki had on her ski suit and was all but buried in her own coat and Gail's parka. ("Mole of a Thousand Skins," Tyler called her.) Her eyes shined with merriment as she waited eagerly to go outside.

Tyler pushed open the trapdoor and helped her up into the kitchen. Every surface was covered with gleaming crystals of ice. They went out the door into the backyard.

The sky was a deep, somber blue. Weighty . . . wondrous. Protected by a bubble of clear plastic, a hand-calibrated bimetallic thermometer read 112 degrees below zero. The fierce winds that had scoured the planet had died away. Once powered by the sun, the great thermal engine of the atmosphere was dormant now, biding its time, awaiting the sun's return. Several feet of snow lay on the ground, but none had fallen in recent weeks.

Though dressed as warmly as they were, they could remain outside in the bitter cold for only a few minutes, but even a brief respite from the shelter gave them a wonderful feeling of space and freedom.

Nikki pointed skyward. "Look!"

Tyler gazed up at the sun. Several luminous specks showed on its dull red surface, brilliant winks of yellow-white. For a long moment he stared at it, and then he smiled beneath his ski mask and offered a silent word of thanks. Sunspots in reverse! Light on dark. The sun had passed through its blackest hour and was beginning to emerge again.

It was going to be all right, just as Hal had predicted.

"Wait'll I tell Mommy!" Nikki said.

He hugged her. "In a few minutes, honey. Right now, why don't you run awhile?"

"Okay."

It was less run than struggle. Wrapped in the ridiculously baggy outfit, she galloped away down the snowy path Tyler had cleared weeks earlier behind the house, young, alive, and full of hope.

They survived Armageddon
to sail the oceans
of a ravaged nightmare world

OMEGA SUB   **76049-5/$2.95 US/$3.50 Can**
On top secret maneuvers beneath the polar ice cap, the awesome nuclear submarine U.S.S. *Liberator* surfaces to find the Earth in flames. Civilization is no more—once-great cities have been reduced to smoky piles of radioactive ash. As their last mission, the brave men of the *Liberator* must seek out survivors in the war-blackened land.

OMEGA SUB #2: COMMAND DECISION
           76206-4/$2.95 US/$3.50 Can
Beneath the still waters of the South Pacific, a high-tech Soviet submarine stalks the U.S.S. *Liberator*, intent on avenging the Motherland's destruction.

OMEGA SUB #3: CITY OF FEAR
           76050-9/$2.95 US/$3.50 Can
On a grim journey through the ruins of the Panama Canal, the U.S.S. *Liberator* discovers a nightmare city under siege, prowled by man-eating predators and radiation-crazed "whiteshirts."